APRIL HOPES

William Dean Howells

1st WORLD
LIBRARY
Literary Society

April Hopes

William Dean Howells

© 1st World Library, 2007
PO Box 2211
Fairfield, IA 52556
www.1stworldlibrary.com
First Edition

LCCN: 2007901842

Softcover ISBN: 978-1-4218-4313-1
Hardcover ISBN: 978-1-4218-4215-8
eBook ISBN: 978-1-4218-4411-4

Purchase *"April Hopes"*
as a traditional bound book at:
www.1stWorldLibrary.com/purchase.asp?ISBN=978-1-4218-4313-1

1st World Library is a literary, educational organization
dedicated to:

- Creating a free internet library of downloadable ebooks

- Hosting writing competitions and offering book
publishing scholarships.

Interested in more 1st World Library books?
contact: literacy@1stworldlibrary.com
Check us out at: www.1stworldlibrary.com

1ˢᵗ World Library Literary Society

Giving Back to the World

"If you want to work on the core problem, it's early school literacy."
- James Barksdale, former CEO of Netscape

"No skill is more crucial to the future of a child, or to a democratic and prosperous society, than literacy."

- Los Angeles Times

"Literacy... means far more than learning how to read and write... The aim is to transmit... knowledge and promote social participation."
- UNESCO

"Literacy is not a luxury, it is a right and a responsibility. If our world is to meet the challenges of the twenty-first century we must harness the energy and creativity of all our citizens."

- President Bill Clinton

"Parents should be encouraged to read to their children, and teachers should be equipped with all available techniques for teaching literacy, so the varying needs and capacities of individual kids can be taken into account."
- Hugh Mackay

I

From his place on the floor of the Hemenway Gymnasium Mr. Elbridge G. Mavering looked on at the Class Day gaiety with the advantage which his stature, gave him over most people there. Hundreds of these were pretty girls, in a great variety of charming costumes, such as the eclecticism of modern fashion permits, and all sorts of ingenious compromises between walking dress and ball dress. It struck him that the young men on whose arms they hung, in promenading around the long oval within the crowd of stationary spectators, were very much younger than students used to be, whether they wore the dress-coats of the Seniors or the cut-away of the Juniors and Sophomores; and the young girls themselves did not look so old as he remembered them in his day. There was a band playing somewhere, and the galleries were well filled with spectators seated at their ease, and intent on the party-coloured turmoil of the floor, where from time to time the younger promenaders broke away from the ranks into a waltz, and after some turns drifted back, smiling and controlling their quick breath, and resumed their promenade. The place was intensely light, in the candour of a summer day which had no reserves; and the brilliancy was not broken by the simple decorations. Ropes of wild laurel twisted up the pine posts of the aisles, and swung in festoons overhead; masses of tropical plants in pots were set along between the posts on one side of the room; and on the other were the lunch tables, where a great many people were standing about, eating chicken and salmon salads, or strawberries and ice-cream, and drinking claret-cup. From the whole rose that blended odour of viands, of flowers, of stuff's, of toilet perfumes, which is the characteristic expression of, all social festivities, and which exhilarates or depresses—according as one is new or old to it.

Elbridge Mavering kept looking at the faces of the young men as if he expected to see a certain one; then he turned his eyes patiently upon. the faces around him. He had been introduced to a good many persons, but he had come to that time of life when an introduction; unless charged with some special interest, only adds the pain of doubt to the wearisome encounter of unfamiliar people; and he had unconsciously put on the severity of a man who finds himself without acquaintance where others are meeting friends, when a small man, with a neatly trimmed reddish-grey beard and prominent eyes, stepped in front of him, and saluted him with the "Hello, Mavering!" of a contemporary.

His face, after a moment of question, relaxed into joyful recognition. "Why, John Munt! is that you?" he said, and he took into his large moist palm the dry little hand of his friend, while they both broke out into the incoherencies of people meeting after a long time. Mr. Mavering spoke in it voice soft yet firm, and with a certain thickness of tongue; which gave a boyish charm to his slow, utterance, and Mr. Munt used the sort of bronchial snuffle sometimes cultivated among us as a chest tone. But they were cut short in their intersecting questions and exclamations by the presence of the lady who detached herself from Mr. Munt's arm as if to leave him the freer for his hand-shaking.

"Oh!" he said, suddenly recurring to her; "let me introduce you to Mrs. Pasmer, Mr. Mavering," and the latter made a bow that creased his waistcoat at about the height of Mrs. Pasmer's pretty little nose.

His waistcoat had the curve which waistcoats often describe at his age; and his heavy shoulders were thrown well back to balance this curve. His coat hung carelessly open; the Panama hat in his hand suggested a certain habitual informality of

William Dean Howells

dress, but his smoothly shaven large handsome face, with its jaws slowly ruminant upon nothing, intimated the consequence of a man accustomed to supremacy in a subordinate place.

Mrs. Pasmer looked up to acknowledge the introduction with a sort of pseudo-respectfulness which it would be hard otherwise to describe. Whether she divined or not that she was in the presence of a magnate of some sort, she was rather superfluously demure in the first two or three things she said, and was all sympathy and interest in the meeting of these old friends. They declared that they had not seen each other for twenty years, or, at any rate, not since '59. She listened while they disputed about the exact date, and looked from time to time at Mr. Munt, as if for some explanation of Mr. Mavering; but Munt himself, when she saw him last, had only just begun to commend himself to society, which had since so fully accepted him, and she had so suddenly, the moment before, found her self hand in glove with him that she might well have appealed to a third person for some explanation of Munt. But she was not a woman to be troubled much by this momentary mystification, and she was not embarrassed at all when Munt said, as if it had all been pre-arranged, "Well, now, Mrs. Pasmer, if you'll let me leave you with Mr. Mavering a moment, I'll go off and bring that unnatural child to you; no use dragging you round through this crowd longer."

He made a gesture intended, in the American manner, to be at once polite and jocose, and was gone, leaving Mrs. Pasmer a little surprised, and Mr. Mavering in some misgiving, which he tried to overcome pressing his jaws together two or three times without speaking. She had no trouble in getting in the first remark. "Isn't all this charming, Mr. Mavering?" She spoke in a deep low voice, with a caressing manner, and stood looking up, at Mr. Mavering with one shoulder shrugged and the other drooped, and a tasteful composition of her fan and hands and handkerchief at her waist.

"Yes, ma'am, it is," said Mr. Mavering. He seemed to say

ma'am to her with a public or official accent, which sent Mrs. Primer's mind fluttering forth to poise briefly at such conjectures as, "Congressman from a country district? judge of the Common Pleas? bank president? railroad superintendent? leading physician in a large town?—no, Mr. Munt said Mister," and then to return to her pretty blue eyes, and to centre there in that pseudo-respectful attention under the arch of her neat brows and her soberly crinkled grey-threaded brown hair and her very appropriate bonnet. A bonnet, she said, was much more than half the battle after forty, and it was now quite after forty with Mrs. Pasmer; but she was very well dressed otherwise. Mr. Mavering went on to say, with a deliberation that seemed an element of his unknown dignity, whatever it might be, "A number of the young fellows together can give a much finer spread, and make more of the day, in a place like this, than we used to do in our rooms."

"Ah, then you're a Harvard man too!" said Mrs. Primer to herself, with surprise, which she kept to herself, and she said to Mavering: "Oh yes, indeed! It's altogether better. Aren't they nice looking fellows?" she said, putting up her glass to look at the promenaders.

"Yes," Mr. Mavering assented. "I suppose," he added, out of the consciousness of his own relation to the affair—"I suppose you've a son somewhere here?"

"Oh dear, no!" cried Mrs. Primer, with a mingling, super-human, but for her of ironical deprecation and derision. "Only a daughter, Mr. Mavering."

At this feat of Mrs. Pasmer's, Mr. Mavering looked at her with question as to her precise intention, and ended by repeating, hopelessly, "Only a daughter?"

"Yes," said Mrs. Pasmer, with a sigh of the same irony, "only a poor, despised young girl, Mr. Mavering."

"You speak," said Mr. Mavering, beginning to catch on a little,

William Dean Howells

"as if it were a misfortune," and his dignity broke up into a smile that had its queer fascination.

"Why, isn't it?" asked Mrs. Pasmer.

"Well, I shouldn't have thought so."

"Then you don't believe that all that old-fashioned chivalry and devotion have gone out? You don't think the young men are all spoiled nowadays, and expect the young ladies to offer them attentions?"

"No," said Mr. Mavering slowly, as if recovering from the shock of the novel ideas. "Do you?"

"Oh, I'm such a stranger in Boston—I've lived abroad so long—that I don't know. One hears all kinds of things. But I'm so glad you're not one of those—pessimists!"

"Well," said Mr. Mavering, still thoughtfully, "I don't know that I can speak by the card exactly. I can't say how it is now. I haven't been at a Class Day spread since my own Class Day; I haven't even been at Commencement more than once or twice. But in my time here we didn't expect the young ladies to show us attentions; at any rate, we didn't wait for them to do it. We were very glad, to be asked to meet them, and we thought it an honour if the young ladies would let us talk or dance with them, or take them to picnics. I don't think that any of them could complain of want of attention."

"Yes," said Mrs. Pasmer, "that's what I preached, that's what I prophesied, when I brought my daughter home from Europe. I told her that a girl's life in America was one long triumph; but they say now that girls have more attention in London even than in Cambridge. One hears such dreadful things!"

"Like what?" asked Mr. Mavering, with the unserious interest which Mrs. Primer made most people feel in her talk.

"Oh; it's too vast a subject. But they tell you about charming girls moping the whole evening through at Boston parties, with no young men to talk with, and sitting from the beginning to the end of an assembly and not going on the floor once. They say that unless a girl fairly throws herself at the young men's heads she isn't noticed. It's this terrible disproportion of the sexes that's at the root of it, I suppose; it reverses everything. There aren't enough young men to go half round, and they know it, and take advantage of it. I suppose it began in the war."

He laughed, and, "I should think," he said, laying hold of a single idea out of several which she had presented, "that there would always be enough young men in Cambridge to go round."

Mrs. Pasmer gave a little cry. "In Cambridge!"

"Yes; when I was in college our superiority was entirely numerical."

"But that's all passed long ago, from what I hear," retorted Mrs. Pasmer. "I know very well that it used to be thought a great advantage for a girl to be brought up in Cambridge, because it gave her independence and ease of manner to have so many young men attentive to her. But they say the students all go into Boston now, and if the Cambridge girls want to meet them, they have to go there too. Oh, I assure you that, from what I hear, they've changed all that since our time, Mr. Mavering."

Mrs. Pasmer was certainly letting herself go a little more than she would have approved of in another. The result was apparent in the jocosity of this heavy Mr. Mavering's reply.

"Well, then, I'm glad that I was of our time, and not of this wicked generation. But I presume that unnatural supremacy of the young men is brought low, so to speak, after marriage?"

Mrs. Primer let herself go a little further. "Oh, give us an equal chance," she laughed, "and we can always take care of ourselves, and something more. They say," she added, "that the young married women now have all the attention that girls could wish."

"H'm!" said Mr. Mavering, frowning. "I think I should be tempted to box my boy's ears if I saw him paying another man's wife attention."

"What a Roman father!" cried Mrs. Pasmer, greatly amused, and letting herself go a little further yet. She said to herself that she really must find out who this remarkable Mr. Mavering was, and she cast her eye over the hall for some glimpse of the absent Munt, whose arm she meant to take, and whose ear she meant to fill with questions. But she did not see him, and something else suggested itself. "He probably wouldn't let you see him, or if he did, you wouldn't know it."

"How not know it?"

Mrs. Primer did not answer. "One hears such dreadful things. What do you say—or you'll think I'm a terrible gossip—"

"Oh no;" said Mr. Mavering, impatient for the dreadful thing, whatever it was.

Mrs. Primer resumed: "—to the young married women meeting last winter just after a lot of pretty girls had came out, and magnanimously resolving to give the Buds a chance in society?"

"The Buds?"

"Yes, the Rose-buds—the debutantes; it's an odious little word, but everybody uses it. Don't you think that's a strange state of things for America? But I can't believe all those things," said Mrs. Pasmer, flinging off the shadow of this lurid social condition. "Isn't this a pretty scene?"

"Yes, it is," Mr. Mavering admitted, withdrawing his mind gradually from a consideration of Mrs. Pasmer's awful instances. "Yes!" he added, in final self-possession. "The young fellows certainly do things in a great deal better style nowadays than we used to."

"Oh yes, indeed! And all those pretty girls do seem to be having such a good time!"

"Yes; they don't have the despised and rejected appearance that you'd like to have one believe."

"Not in the least!" Mrs. Pasmer readily consented. "They look radiantly happy. It shows that you can't trust anything that people say to you." She abandoned the ground she had just been taking without apparent shame for her inconsistency. "I fancy it's pretty much as it's always been: if a girl is attractive, the young men find it out."

"Perhaps," said Mr. Mavering, unbending with dignity, "the young married women have held another meeting, and resolved to give the Buds one more chance."

"Oh, there are some pretty mature Roses here," said Mrs. Pasmer, laughing evasively. "But I suppose Class Day can never be taken from the young girls."

"I hope not," said Mr. Mavering. His wandering eye fell upon some young men bringing refreshments across the nave toward them, and he was reminded to ask Mrs. Pasmer, "Will you have something to eat?" He had himself had a good deal to eat, before he took up his position at the advantageous point where John Munt had found him.

"Why, yes, thank you," said Mrs. Pasmer. "I ought to say, 'An ice, please,' but I'm really hungry, and—"

"I'll get you some of the salad," said Mr. Mavering, with the increased liking a man feels for a woman when she owns to an appetite. "Sit down here," he added, and he caught a vacant chair toward her. When he turned about from doing so, he confronted a young gentleman coming up to Mrs. Pasmer with a young lady on his arm, and making a very low bow of relinquishment.

II

The men looked smilingly at each other without saying anything; and the younger took in due form the introduction which the young lady gave him.

"My mother, Mr. Mavering."

"Mr. Mavering!" cried Mrs. Pasmer, in a pure astonishment, before she had time to colour it with a polite variety of more conventional emotions. She glanced at the two men, and gave a little "Oh?" of inquiry and resignation, and then said, demurely, "Let me introduce you to Mr. Mavering, Alice," while the young fellow laughed nervously, and pulled out his handkerchief, partly to hide the play of his laughter, and partly to wipe away the perspiration which a great deal more laughing had already gathered on his forehead. He had a vein that showed prominently down its centre, and large, mobile, girlish blue eyes under good brows, an arched nose, and rather a long face and narrow chin. He had beautiful white teeth; as he laughed these were seen set in a jaw that contracted very much toward the front. He was tall and slim, and he wore with elegance the evening dress which Class Day custom prescribes for the Seniors; in his button-hole he had a club button.

"I shall not have to ask an introduction to Mr. Mavering; and you've robbed me of the pleasure of giving him one to you, Mrs. Pasmer," he said.

She heard the young man in the course of a swift review of

what she had said to his father, and with a formless resentment of the father's not having told her he had a son there; but she answered with the flattering sympathy she had the use of, "Oh, but you won't miss one pleasure out of so many to-day, Mr. Mavering; and think of the little dramatic surprise!"

"Oh, perfect," he said, with another laugh. "I told Miss Pasmer as we came up."

"Oh, then you were in the surprise, Alice!" said Mrs. Pasmer, searching her daughter's eyes for confession or denial of this little community of interest. The girl smiled slightly upon the young man, but not disapprovingly, and made no other answer to her mother, who went on: "Where in the world have you been? Did Mr. Munt find you? Who told you where I was? Did you see me? How did you know I was here? Was there ever anything so droll?" She did not mean her questions to be answered, or at least not then; for, while her daughter continued to smile rather more absently, and young Mavering broke out continuously in his nervous laugh, and his father stood regarding him with visible satisfaction, she hummed on, turning to the young man: "But I'm quite appalled at Alice's having monopolised even for a few minutes a whole Senior— and probably an official Senior at that," she said, with a glance at the pink and white club button in his coat lapel, "and I can't let you stay another instant, Mr. Mavering. I know very well how many demands you have upon you and you must go back directly to your sisters and your cousins and your aunts, and all the rest of them; you must indeed."

"Oh no! Don't drive me away, Mrs. Pasmer," pleaded the young man, laughing violently, and then wiping his face. "I assure you that I've no encumbrances of any kind here except my father, and he seems to have been taking very good care of himself." They all laughed at this, and the young fellow hurried on: "Don't be alarmed at my button; it only means a love of personal decoration, if that's where you got the notion of my being an official Senior. This isn't my spread; I shall hope to welcome you at Beck Hall after the Tree; and I wish you'd let me be of use to you. Wouldn't you like to go round to some of the smaller spreads? I think it would amuse you. And have you got tickets to the Tree, to see us make fools of ourselves? It's worth seeing, Mrs. Pasmer, I assure you."

He rattled on very rapidly but with such a frankness in his urgency, such amiable kindliness, that Mrs. Pasmer could not feel that it was pushing. She looked at her daughter, but she stood as passive in the transaction as the elder Mavering. She was taller than her mother, and as she waited, her supple figure described that fine lateral curve which one sees in some Louis Quinze portraits; this effect was enhanced by the fashion of her dress of pale sage green, with a wide stripe or sash of white dropping down the front, from her delicate waist. The same simple combination of colours was carried up into her hat, which surmounted darker hair than Mrs. Pasmer's, and a complexion of wholesome pallor; her eyes were grey and grave, with black brows, and her face, which was rather narrow, had a pleasing irregularity in the sharp jut of the nose; in profile the parting of the red lips showed well back into the cheek.

"I don't know," said Mrs. Pasmer, in her own behalf; and she added in his, "about letting you take so much trouble," so smoothly that it would have been quite impossible to detect the point of union in the two utterances.

"Well, don't call it names, anyway, Mrs. Pasmer," pleaded the young man. "I thought it was nothing but a pleasure and a privilege—"

"The fact is," she explained, neither consenting nor refusing, "that we were expecting to meet some friends who had tickets for us"—young Mavering's face fell—"and I can't imagine what's happened."

"Oh, let's hope something dreadful," he cried.

"Perhaps you know them," she delayed further. "Professor Saintsbury!"

"Well, rather! Why, they were here about an hour ago—both of them. They must have been looking for you."

"Yes; we were to meet them here. We waited to come out with other friends, and I was afraid we were late." Mrs. Pasmer's face expressed a tempered disappointment, and she looked at her daughter for indications of her wishes in the circumstances; seeing in her eye a willingness to accept young Mavering's invitation, she hesitated more decidedly than she had yet done, for she was, other things being equal, quite willing to accept it herself. But other things were not equal, and the whole situation was very odd. All that she knew of Mr. Mavering the elder was that he was the old friend of John Munt, and she knew far too little of John Munt, except that he seemed to go everywhere, and to be welcome, not to feel that his introduction was hardly a warrant for what looked like an impending intimacy. She did not dislike Mr. Mavering; he was evidently a country person of great self-respect, and no doubt of entire respectability. He seemed very intelligent, too. He was a Harvard man; he had rather a cultivated manner, or else naturally a clever way of saying things. But all that was really nothing, if she knew no more about him, and she certainly did not. If she could only have asked her daughter who it was that presented young Mavering to her, that might have formed some clew, but there was no earthly chance of asking this, and, besides, it was probably one of those haphazard introductions that people give on such occasions. Young Mavering's behaviour gave her still greater question: his self-possession, his entire absence of anxiety; or any expectation of rebuff or snub, might be the ease of unimpeachable social acceptance, or it might be merely adventurous effrontery; only something ingenuous and good in the young fellow's handsome face forbade this conclusion. That his face was so handsome was another of the complications. She recalled, in the dreamlike swiftness with which all these things passed through her mind, what her friends had said to Alice about her being sure to meet her fate on Class Day, and she looked at her again to see if she had met it.

"Well, mamma?" said the girl, smiling at her mother's look.

Mrs. Pasmer thought she must have been keeping young Mavering waiting a long time for his answer. "Why, of course, Alice. But I really don't know what to do about the Saintsburys." This was not in the least true, but it instantly seemed so to Mrs. Pasmer, as a plausible excuse will when we make it.

"Why, I'll tell you what, Mrs. Pasmer," said young Mavering, with a cordial unsuspicion that both won and reassured her, "we'll be sure to find them at some of the spreads. Let me be of that much use, anyway; you must."

"We really oughtn't to let you," said Mrs. Pasmer, making a last effort to cling to her reluctance, but feeling it fail, with a sensation that was not disagreeable. She could not help being pleased with the pleasure that she saw in her daughter's face.

Young Mavering's was radiant. "I'll be back in just half a minute," he said, and he took a gay leave of them in running to speak to another student at the opposite end of the hall.

III

"You must allow me to get you something to eat first, Mrs. Pasmer," said the elder Mavering.

"Oh no, thank you," Mrs. Pasmer began. But she changed her mind and said, "Or, yes; I will, Mr. Mavering: a very little salad, please." She had really forgotten her hunger, as a woman will in the presence of any social interest; but she suddenly thought his going would give her a chance for two words with her daughter, and so she sent him. As he creaked heavily across the smooth floor of the nave; "Alice," she whispered, "I don't know exactly what I've done: Who introduced this young Mr. Mavering to you?"

"Mr. Munt."

"Mr. Munt!"

"Yes; he came for me; he said you sent him. He introduced Mr. Mavering, and he was very polite. Mr. Mavering said we ought to go up into the gallery and see how it looked; and Mr. Munt said he'd been up, and Mr. Mavering promised to bring me back to him, but he was not there when we got back. Mr. Mavering got me some ice cream first, and then he found you for me."

"Really," said Mrs. Pasmer to herself, "the combat thickens!" To her daughter she said, "He's very handsome."

"He laughs too much," said the daughter. Her mother recognised her uncandour with a glance. "But he waltzes well," added the girl.

"Waltzes?" echoed the mother. "Did you waltz with him, Alice?"

"Everybody else was dancing. He asked me for a turn or two, and of course I did it. What difference?"

"Oh, none—none. Only—I didn't see you."

"Perhaps you weren't looking."

"Yes, I was looking all the time."

"What do you mean, mamma?"

"Well," said Mrs. Pasmer, in a final despair, "we don't know anything about them."

"We're the only people here who don't, then," said her daughter. "The ladies were bowing right left to him all the time, and he kept asking if I knew this one and that one, and all I could say was that some of them were distant cousins, but I wasn't acquainted with them. I would think he'd wonder who we were."

"Yes," said the mother thoughtfully.

"There! he's laughing with that other student. But don't look!"

Mrs. Pasmer saw well enough out of the corner of her eye the joking that went on between Mavering and his friend, and it did not displease her to think that it probably referred to Alice. While the young man came hurrying back to them she glanced at the girl standing near her with a keenly critical inspection, from which she was able to exclude all maternal partiality, and

William Dean Howells

justly decided that she was one of the most effective girls in the place. That costume of hers was perfect. Mrs. Pasmer wished now that she could have compared it more carefully with other costumes; she had noticed some very pretty cnes; and a feeling of vexation that Alice should have prevented this by being away so long just when the crowd was densest qualified her satisfaction. The people were going very fast now. The line of the oval in the nave was broken into groups of lingering talkers, who were conspicuous to each other, and Mrs. Pasmer felt that she and her daughter were conspicuous to all the rest where they stood apart, with the two Maverings converging upon them from different points, the son nodding and laughing to friends of both sexes as he came, the father wholly absorbed in not spilling the glass of claret punch which he carried in one hand, and not falling down on the slippery floor with the plate of salad which he bore in the other. She had thoughts of feigning unconsciousness; she would have had no scruple in practising this or any other social stratagem, for though she kept a conscience in regard to certain matters—what she considered essentials—she lived a thousand little lies every day, and taught her daughter by precept and example to do the same. You must seem to be looking one way when you were really looking another; you must say this when you meant that; you must act as if you were thinking one thing when you were thinking something quite different; and all to no end, for, as she constantly said, people always know perfectly well what you were about, whichever way you looked or whatever you said, or no matter how well you acted the part of thinking what you did not think. Now, although she seemed not to look, she saw all that has been described at a glance, and at another she saw young Mavering slide easily up to his father and relieve him of the plate and glass, with a laugh as pleasant and a show of teeth as dazzling as he bestowed upon any of the ladies he had passed. She owned to her recondite heart that she liked this in young Mavering, though at the same time she asked herself what motive he really had in being so polite to his father before people. But she had no time to decide; she had only time to pack the question hurriedly away for future consideration, when young Mavering arrived at her elbow, and she turned with a little "Oh!" of surprise so perfectly acted that it gave her the greatest pleasure.

IV

"I don't think my father would have got here alive with these things," said young Mavering. "Did you see how I came to his rescue?"

Mrs. Pasmer instantly threw away all pretext of not having seen. "Oh yes! my heart was in my mouth when you bore down upon him, Mr. Mavering. It was a beautiful instance of filial devotion."

"Well, do sit down now, Mrs. Pasmer, and take it comfortably," said the young fellow; and he got her one of the many empty chairs, and would not give her the things, which he put in another, till she sat down and let him spread a napkin over her lap.

"Really," she said, "I feel as if I were stopping all the wheels of Class Day. Am I keeping them from closing the Gymnasium, Mr. Mavering?"

"Not quite," said the young man, with one of his laughs. "I don't believe they will turn us out, and I'll see that they don't lock us in. Don't hurry, Mrs. Pasmer. I'm only sorry you hadn't something sooner."

"Oh, your father proposed getting me something a good while ago."

"Did he? Then I wonder you haven't had it. He's usually

on time."

"You're both very energetic, I think," said Mrs. Pasmer.

"He's the father of his son," said the young fellow, assuming the merit with a bow of burlesque modesty.

It went to Mrs. Pasmer's heart. "Let's hope he'll never forget that," she said, in an enjoyment of the excitement and the salad that was beginning to leave her question of these Maverings a light, diaphanous cloud on the verge of the horizon.

The elder Mavering had been trying, without success, to think of something to say to Miss Pasmer, he had twice cleared his throat for that purpose. But this comedy between his son and the young lady's mother seemed so much lighter and brighter than anything he could have said, that he said nothing, and looked on with his mouth set in its queer smile, while the girl listened with the gravity of a daughter who sees that her mother is losing her head. Mrs. Pasmer buzzed on in her badinage with the young man, and allowed him to go for a cup of coffee before she rose from her chair, and shook out her skirts with an air of pleasant expectation of whatever should come next.

He came back without it. "The coffee urn has dried up here, Mrs. Pasmer. But you can get some at the other spreads; they'd be inconsolable if you didn't take something everywhere."

They all started toward the door, but the elder Mavering said, holding back a little, "Dan, I think I'll go and see—"

"Oh no, you mustn't, father," cried the young man, laying his hand with caressing entreaty on his father's coat sleeve. "I don't want you to go anywhere till you've seen Professor Saintsbury. We shall be sure to meet him at some of the spreads. I want you to have that talk with him—" He corrected himself for the instant's deflection from the interests

William Dean Howells

of his guest, and added, "I want you to help me hunt him up for Mrs. Pasmer. Now, Mrs. Pasmer, you're not to think it's the least trouble, or anything but a boon, much less say it," he cried, turning to the deprecation in Mrs. Pasmer's face. He turned away from it to acknowledge the smiles and bows of people going out of the place, and he returned their salutations with charming heartiness.

In the vestibule they met the friends they were going in search of.

V

"With Mr. Mavering, of course!" exclaimed Mrs. Saintsbury: "I might have known it." Mrs. Pasmer would have given anything she could think of to be able to ask why her friend might have known it; but for the present they could only fall upon each other with flashes of self-accusal and explanation, and rejoicing for their deferred and now accomplished meeting. The Professor stood by with the satirical smile with which men witness the effusion of women. Young Mavering, after sharing the ladies' excitement fully with them, rewarded himself by an exclusive moment with Miss Pasmer.

"You must get Mrs. Pasmer to let me show you all of Class Day that a Senior can. I didn't know what a perfect serpent's tooth it was to be one before. Mrs. Saintsbury," he broke off, "have you got tickets for the Tree? Ah, she doesn't hear me!"

Mrs. Saintsbury was just then saying to the elder Mavering, "I'm so glad you decided to come today. It would have been a shame if none of you were here." She made a feint of dropping her voice, with a glance at Dan Mavering. "He's such a nice boy," which made him laugh, and cry out—

"Oh, now? Don't poison my father's mind, Mrs. Saintsbury."

"Oh, some one would be sure to tell him," retorted the Professor's wife, "and he'd better hear it from a friend."

The young fellow laughed again, and then he shook hands

William Dean Howells

with some ladies going out, and asked were they going so soon, from an abstract hospitality, apparently, for he was not one of the hosts; and so turned once more to Miss Pasmer. "We must get away from here, or the afternoon will get away from us, and leave us nothing to show for it. Suppose we make a start, Miss Pasmer?"

He led the way with her out of the vestibule, banked round with pots of palm and fern, and down the steps into the glare of the Cambridge sunshine, blown full, as is the case on Class Day, of fine Cambridge dust, which had drawn a delicate grey veil over the grass of the Gymnasium lawn, and mounted in light clouds from the wheels powdering it finer and finer in the street. Along the sidewalks dusty hacks and carriages were ranged, and others were driving up to let people dismount at the entrances to the college yard. Within the temporary picket-fences, secluding a part of the grounds for the students and their friends, were seen stretching from dormitory to dormitory long lines of Chinese lanterns, to be lit after nightfall, swung between the elms. Groups of ladies came and went, nearly always under the escort of some student; the caterers' carts, disburdened of their ice-creams and salads, were withdrawn under the shade in the street, and their drivers lounged or drowsed upon the seats; now and then a black waiter, brilliant as a bobolink in his white jacket and apron, appeared on some errand; the large, mild Cambridge police-men kept the entrances to the yard with a benevolent vigilance which was not harsh with the little Irish children coming up from the Marsh in their best to enjoy the sight of other people's pleasure.

"Isn't it a perfect Class Day?" cried young Mavering, as he crossed Kirkland Street with Miss Pasmer, and glanced down its vaulted perspective of elms, through which the sunlight broke, and lay in the road in pools and washes as far as the eye reached. "Did you ever see anything bluer than the sky to-day? I feel as if we'd ordered the weather, with the rest of the things, and I had some credit for it as host. Do make it a little compliment, Miss Pasmer; I assure you I ll be very modest about it."

"Ah, I think it's fully up to the occasion," said the girl, catching the spirit of his amiable satisfaction. "Is it the usual Class Day weather?"

"You spoil everything by asking that," cried the young man; "it obliges me to make a confession—it's always good weather on Class Day. There haven't been more than a dozen bad Class Days in the century. But you'll admit that there can't have been a better Class Day than this?"

"Oh yes; it's certainly the pleasantest Class Day I've seen;" said the girl; and now when Mavering laughed she laughed too.

"Thank you so much for saying that! I hope it will pass off in unclouded brilliancy; it will, if I can make it. Why, hallo! They're on the other side of the street yet, and looking about as if they were lost."

He pulled his handkerchief from his pocket, and waved it at the others of their party.

They caught sight of it, and came hurrying over through the dust.

Mrs. Saintsbury said, apparently as the sum of her consultations with Mrs. Pasmer: "The Tree is to be at half-past five; and after we've seen a few spreads, I'm going to take the ladies hone for a little rest."

"Oh no; don't do that," pleaded the young man. After making this protest he seemed not to have anything to say immediately in support of it. He merely added: "This is Miss Pasmer's first Class Day, and I want her to see it all."

"But you'll have to leave us very soon to get yourself ready for the Tree," suggested the Professor's lady, with a motherly prevision.

"I shall want just fifteen minutes for that."

"I know, better, Mr. Mavering," said Mrs. Saintsbury, with finality. "You will want a good three-quarters of an hour to make yourself as disreputable as you'll look at the Tree; and you'll have to take time for counsel and meditation. You may stay with us just half an hour, and then we shall part inexorably. I've seen a great many more Class Days than you have, and I know what they are in their demands upon the Seniors."

"Oh; well! Then we won't think about the time," said the young man, starting on with Miss Pasmer.

"Well, don't undertake too much," said the lady. She came last in the little procession, with the elder Mavering, and her husband and Mrs Pasmer preceded her.

"What?" young Mavering called back, with his smiling face over his shoulder.

"She says not to bite off more than you can chew," the professor answered for her.

Mavering broke into a conscious laugh, but full of delight, and with his handkerchief to his face had almost missed the greeting of some ladies who bowed to him. He had to turn round to acknowledge it, and he was saluting and returning salutations pretty well all along the line of their progress.

"I'm afraid you'll think I'm everybody's friend but my own, Miss Pasmer, but I assure you all this is purely accidental. I don't know so many people, after all; only all that I do know seem to be here this morning."

"I don't think it's a thing to be sorry for," said the girl. "I wish we knew more people. It's rather forlorn—"

"Oh, will you let me introduce some of the fellows to you?

They'll be so glad."

"If you'll tell them how forlorn I said I was," said the girl, with a smile.

"Oh, no, no, no! I understand that. And I assure you that I didn't suppose—But of course!" he arrested himself in the superfluous reassurance he was offering, "All that goes without saying. Only there are some of the fellows coming back to the law school, and if you'll allow me—"

"We shall be very happy indeed, Mr. Mavering," said Mrs. Pasmer, behind him.

"Oh, thank you ever so much, Mrs. Pasmer." This was occasion for another burst of laughter with him. He seemed filled with the intoxication of youth, whose spirit was in the bright air of the day and radiant in the young faces everywhere. The paths intersecting one another between the different dormitories under the drooping elms were thronged with people coming and going in pairs and groups; and the academic fete, the prettiest flower of our tough old Puritan stem, had that charm, at once sylvan and elegant, which enraptures in the pictured fables of the Renaissance. It falls at that moment of the year when the old university town, often so commonplace and sometimes so ugly, becomes briefly and almost pathetically beautiful under the leafage of her hovering elms and in, the perfume of her syringas, and bathed in this joyful tide of youth that overflows her heart. She seems fit then to be the home of the poets who have loved her and sung her, and the regret of any friend of the humanities who has left her.

"Alice," said Mrs. Pasmer, leaning forward a little to speak to her daughter, and ignoring a remark of the Professor's, "did you ever see so many pretty costumes?"

"Never," said the girl, with equal intensity.

"Well, it makes you feel that you have got a country, after all,"

William Dean Howells

sighed Mrs. Pasmer, in a sort of apostrophe to her European self. "You see splendid dressing abroad, but it's mostly upon old people who ought to be sick and ashamed of their pomps and vanities. But here it's the young girls who dress; and how lovely they are! I thought they were charming in the Gymnasium, but I see you must get them out-of-doors to have the full effect. Mr. Mavering, are they always so prettily dressed on Class Day?"

"Well, I'm beginning to feel as if it wouldn't be exactly modest for me to say so, whatever I think. You'd better ask Mrs. Saintsbury; she pretends to know all about it."

"No, I'm bound to say they're not," said the Professor's wife candidly. "Your daughter," she added, in a low tone for all to hear, "decides that question."

"I'm so glad you said that, Mrs. Saintsbury," said the young man. He looked at the girl; who blushed with a pleasure that seemed to thrill to the last fibre of her pretty costume.

She could not say anything, but her mother asked, with an effort at self-denial: "Do you think so really? It's one of those London things. They have so much taste there now," she added yielding to her own pride in the dress.

"Yes; I supposed it must be," said Mrs. Saintsbury, "We used to come in muslins and tremendous hoops—don't you remember?"

"Did you look like your photographs?" asked young Mavering, over his shoulder.

"Yes; but we didn't know it then," said the Professor's wife.

"Neither did we," said the Professor. "We supposed that there had never been anything equal to those hoops and white muslins."

"Thank you, my dear," said his wife, tapping him between the shoulders with her fan. "Now don't go any further."

"Do you mean about our first meeting here on Class Day?" asked her husband.

"They'll think so now," said Mrs. Saintsbury patiently, with a playful threat of consequences in her tone.

"When I first saw the present Mrs. Saintsbury," pursued the Professor—it was his joking way, of describing her, as if there had been several other Mrs. Saintsburys—"she was dancing on the green here."

"Ah, they don't dance on the green any more, I hear," sighed Mrs. Pasmer.

"No, they don't," said the other lady; "and I think it's just as well. It was always a ridiculous affectation of simplicity."

"It must have been rather public," said young Mavering, in a low voice, to Miss Pasmer.

"It doesn't seem as if it could ever have been in character quite," she answered.

"We're a thoroughly indoors people," said the Professor. "And it seems as if we hadn't really begun to get well as a race till we had come in out of the weather."

"How can you say that on a day like this?" cried Mrs. Pasmer. "I didn't suppose any one could be so unromantic."

"Don't flatter him," cried his wife.

"Does he consider that a compliment?"

"Not personally," he answered: "But it's the first duty of a Professor of Comparative Literature to be unromantic."

"I don't understand," faltered Mrs. Pasmer.

"He will be happy to explain, at the greatest possible length," said Mrs. Saintsbury. "But you shan't spoil our pleasure now, John."

They all laughed, and the Professor looked proud of the wit at his expense; the American husband is so, and the public attitude of the American husband and wife toward each other is apt to be amiably satirical; their relation seems never to have lost its novelty, or to lack droll and surprising contrasts for them.

Besides these passages with her husband, Mrs. Saintsbury kept up a full flow of talk with the elder Mavering, which Mrs. Pasmer did her best to overhear, for it related largely to his son, whom, it seemed, from the father's expressions, the Saintsburys had been especially kind to.

"No, I assure you," Mrs. Pasmer heard her protest, "Mr. Saintsbury has, been very much interested in him. I hope he has not put any troublesome ideas into his head. Of course he's very much interested in literature, from his point of view, and he's glad to find any of the young men interested in it, and that's apt to make him overdo matters a little."

"Dan wished me to talk with him, and I shall certainly be glad to do so," said the father, but in a tone which conveyed to Mrs. Pasmer the impression that though he was always open to conviction, his mind was made up on this point, whatever it was.

VI

The party went to half a dozen spreads, some of which were on a scale of public grandeur approaching that of the Gymnasium, and others of a subdued elegance befitting the more private hospitalities in the students' rooms. Mrs. Pasmer was very much interested in these rooms, whose luxurious appointments testified to the advance of riches and of the taste to apply them since she used to visit students' rooms in far-off Class Days. The deep window nooks and easy-chairs upholstered in the leather that seems sacred alike to the seats and the shelves of libraries; the aesthetic bookcases, low and topped with bric-a-brac; the etchings and prints on the walls, which the elder Mavering went up to look at with a mystifying air of understanding such things; the foils crossed over the chimney, and the mantel with its pipes, and its photographs of theatrical celebrities tilted about over it—spoke of conditions mostly foreign to Mrs. Pasmer's memories of Harvard. The photographed celebrities seemed to be chosen chiefly for their beauty, and for as much of their beauty as possible, Mrs. Pasmer perceived, with an obscure misgiving of the sort which an older generation always likes to feel concerning the younger, but with a tolerance, too, which was personal to herself; it was to be considered that the massive thought and honest amiability of Salvini's face, and the deep and spiritualized power of Booth's, varied the effect of these companies of posturing nymphs.

At many places she either met old friends with whom she clamoured over the wonder of their encounter there, or was

William Dean Howells

made acquainted with new people by the Saintsburys. She kept a mother's eye on her daughter, to whom young Mavering presented everybody within hail or reach, and whom she could see, whenever she looked at her, a radiant centre of admiration. She could hear her talk sometimes, and she said to herself that really Alice was coming out; she had never heard her say so many good things before; she did not know it was in her. She was very glad then that she had let her wear that dress; it was certainly distinguished, and the girl carried it off, to her mother's amusement, with the air of a superb lady of the period from which it dated. She thought what a simple child Alice really was, all the time those other children, the Seniors, were stealing their glances of bold or timid worship at her, and doubtless thinking her a brilliant woman of the world. But there could be no mistake that she was a success.

Part of her triumph was of course due to Mrs. Saintsbury; whose chaperonage; Mrs. Pasmer could see, was everywhere of effect. But it was also largely due to the vigilant politeness of young Mavering, who seemed bent on making her have good time, and who let no chance slip him. Mrs. Pasmer felt his kindness truly; and she did not feel it the less because she knew that there was but one thing that could, at his frankly selfish age, make a young fellow wish to make a girl have a good time; except for that reason he must be bending the whole soul of egotistic youth to making some other girl have a good time. But all the same, it gave her pause when some one to whom she was introduced spoke to her of her friends the Maverings, as if they were friends of the oldest standing instead of acquaintances of very recent accident. She did not think of disclaiming the intimacy, but "Really I shall die of these Maverings," she said to herself, "unless I find out something about them pretty soon."

"I'm not going to take you to the Omicron spread, Mrs. Pasmer," said young Mavering, coming up to her with such an effect of sympathetic devotion that she had to ask herself, "Are they my friends, the Maverings?" "The Saintsburys have been there already, and it is a little too common." The tone of superiority gave Mrs. Pasmer courage. "They're good fellows; and all that, but I want you to see the best. I suppose it will get back to giving the spreads all in the fellows' rooms again. It's a good deal pleasanter, don't you think?"

"Oh yes, indeed," assented Mrs. Pasmer, though she had really been thinking the private spreads were not nearly so amusing as the large spread she had seen at the Gymnasium. She had also wondered where all Mr. Mavering's relations and friends were, and the people who had social claims on him, that he could be giving up his Class Day in this reckless fashion to strangers. Alice would account for a good deal, but she would not account for everything. Mrs. Pasmer would have been willing to take him from others, but if he were so anomalous as to have no one to be taken from, of course it lessened his value as a trophy. These things went in and out of her mind, with a final resolution to get a full explanation from Mrs. Saintsbury, while she stood and smiled her winning assent up into the young man's handsome face.

Mrs. Saintsbury, caught sight of them, and as if suddenly reminded of a forgotten duty, rushed vividly upon him.

"Mr. Mavering, I shall not let you stay with us another minute. You must go to your room now and get ready. You ought to have a little rest."

He broke out in his laugh. "Do you think I want to go and lie down awhile, like a lady before a party?"

"I'm sure you'd be the stronger for it," said Mrs. Saintsbury. "But go, upon any theory. Don't you see there isn't a Senior left?"

He would not look round. "They've gone to other spreads," he said. "But now I'll tell you: it is pretty, near time, and if you'll take me to my room, I'll go."

"You're a spoiled boy," said Mrs. Saintsbury.

William Dean Howells

"But I want Mrs. Pasmer to see the room of a real student—a reading man, and all that—and we'll come, to humour you."

"Well, come upon any theory," said young Mavering.

His father, and Professor Saintsbury, who had been instructed by his wife not to lose sight of her, were at hand, and they crossed to that old hall which keeps its favour with the students in spite of the rivalry of the newer dormitories—it would be hard to say why.

Mrs. Pasmer willingly assented to its being much better, out of pure complaisance, though the ceilings were low and the windows small, and it did not seem to her that the Franklin stove and the aesthetic papering and painting of young Mavering's room brought it up to the level of those others that she had seen. But with her habit of saying some friendly lying thing, no matter what her impressions were, she exclaimed; "Oh, how cosy!" and glad of the word, she went about from one to another, asking, "Isn't this cosy?"

Mrs. Saintsbury said: "It's supposed to be the cell of a recluse; but it is cosy—yes."

"It looks as if some hermit had been using it as a store-room," said her husband; for there were odds and ends of furniture and clothes and boxes and handbags scattered about the floor.

"I forgot all about them when I asked you," cried Mavering, laughing out his delight. "They belong to some fellows that are giving spreads in their rooms, and I let them put them in here."

"Do you commonly let people put things in your room that they want to get rid off?" asked Mrs. Pasmer.

"Well, not when I'm expecting company."

"He couldn't refuse even then, if they pressed the matter," said

Mrs. Saintsbury, lecturing upon him to her friend.

"I'm afraid you're too amiable altogether, Mr. Mavering. I'm sure you let people impose upon you," said the other lady. "You have been letting us impose upon you."

"Ah! now that proves you're all wrong, Mrs. Pasmer."

"It proves that you know how to say things very prettily."

"Oh, thank you. I know when I'm having a good time, and I do my best to enjoy it." He ended with the nervous laugh which seemed habitual with him.

"He, does laugh a good deal;" thought Mrs. Pasmer, surveying him with smiling steadiness. "I suppose it tires Alice. Some of his teeth are filled at the sides. That vein in his forehead—they say that means genius." She said to him: "I hope you know when others are having a good time too, Mr. Mavering? You ought to have that reward."

They both looked at Alice. "Oh, I should be so happy to think you hadn't been bored with it all, Mrs. Pasmer," he returned;—with-deep feeling.

Alice was looking at one of the sketches which were pretty plentifully pinned about the wall, and apparently seeing it and apparently listening to what Professor Saintsbury was saying; but her mother believed from a tremor of the ribbons on her hat that she was conscious of nothing but young Mavering's gaze and the sound of his voice.

"We've been delighted, simply enchanted," said Mrs. Pasmer. And she thought; "Now if Alice were to turn round just as she stands, he could see all the best points of her face. I wonder what she really thinks of him? What is it you have there; Alice?" she asked aloud.

The girl turned her face over her shoulder so exactly in the way

William Dean Howells

her mother wished that Mrs. Pasmer could scarcely repress a cry of joy. "A sketch of Mr. Mavering's."

"Oh, how very interesting!" said Mrs. Pasmer. "Do you sketch, Mr. Mavering? But of course." She pressed forward, and studied the sketch inattentively. "How very, very good!" she buzzed deep in her throat, while, with a glance at her daughter, she thought, "How impassive Alice is! But she behaves with great dignity. Yes. Perhaps that's best. And are you going to be an artist?" she asked of Mavering.

"Not if it can be prevented," he answered, laughing again.

"But his laugh is very pleasant," reflected Mrs. Pasmer. "Does Alice dislike it so much?" She repeated aloud, "If it can be prevented?"

"They think I might spoil a great lawyer in the attempt."

"Oh, I see. And are you going to be a lawyer? But to be a great painter! And America has so few of them." She knew quite well that she was talking nonsense, but she was aware, through her own indifference to the topic that he was not minding what she said, but was trying to bring himself into talk with Alice again. The girl persistently listened to Professor Saintsbury.

"Is she punishing him for something?" her mother asked herself. "What can it be for. Does she think he's a little too pushing? Perhaps, he is a little pushing." She reflected, with an inward sigh, that she would know whether he was if she only knew more about him.

He did the honours of his room very simply and nicely, and he said it was pretty rough to think this was the last of it. After which he faltered, and something occurred to Mrs Saintsbury.

"Why, we're keeping you! It's time for you to dress for the Tree. John"—she reproached her husband—"how could you let us do it?"

"Far be it from me to hurry ladies out of other people's houses—especially ladies who have put themselves in charge of other people."

"No, don't hurry," pleaded Mavering; "there's plenty of time."

"How much time?" asked Mrs. Saintsbury.

He looked at his watch. "Well, a good quarter of an hour."

"And I was to have taken Mrs. Pasmer and Alice home for a little rest before the Tree!" cried Mrs Saintsbury. "And now we must go at once, or we shall get no sort of places."

In the civil and satirical parley which followed, no one answered another, but young Mavering bore as full a part as the elder ladies, and only his father and Alice were silent: his guests got themselves out of his room. They met at the threshold a young fellow, short and dark and stout, in an old tennis suit. He fell back at sight of them, and took off his hat to Mrs. Saintsbury.

"Why, Mr. Boardman!"

"Don't be bashful, Boardman?" young Mavering called out. "Come in and show them how I shall look in five minutes."

Mr. Boardman took his introductions with a sort of main-force self-possession, and then said, "You'll have to look it in less than five minutes now, Mavering. You're come for."

"What? Are they ready?"

"We must fly," panted Mrs. Saintsbury, without waiting for the answer, which was lost in the incoherencies of all sorts of au revoirs called after and called back.

VII

"That is one thing," said Mrs. Saintsbury, looking swiftly round to see that the elder Mavering was not within hearing, as she hurried ahead with Mrs. Pasmer, "that I can't stand in Dan Mavering. Why couldn't he have warned us that it was getting near the time? Why should he have gone on pretending that there was no hurry? It isn't insincerity exactly, but it isn't candour; no, it's uncandid. Oh, I suppose it's the artistic temperament—never coming straight to the point."

"What do you mean?" asked Mrs. Pasmer eagerly.

"I'll tell you sometime." She looked round and halted a little for Alice, who was walking detached and neglected by the preoccupation of the two elderly men. "I'm afraid you're tired," she said to the girl.

"Oh no."

"Of course not, on Class Day. But I hope we shall get seats. What weather!"

The sun had not been oppressive at any time during the day, though the crowded building had been close and warm, and now it lay like a painted light on the grass and paths over which they passed to the entrance of the grounds around the Tree. Holden Chapel, which enclosed the space on the right as they went in, shed back the sun from its brick-red flank, rising unrelieved in its venerable ugliness by any touch of the festive preparations; but to their left and diagonally across from them high stagings supported tiers of seats along the equally unlovely red bulks of Hollis and of Harvard. These seats, and the windows in the stories above them, were densely packed with people, mostly young girls dressed in a thousand enchanting shades and colours, and bonneted and hatted to the last effect of fashion. They were like vast terraces of flowers to the swift glance, and here and there some brilliant parasol, spread to catch the sun on the higher ranks, was like a flaunting poppy, rising to the light and lolling out above the blooms of lower stature. But the parasols were few, for the two halls flung wide curtains of shade over the greater part of the spectators, and across to the foot of the chapel, while a piece of the carpentry whose simplicity seems part of the Class Day tradition shut out the glare and the uninvited public, striving to penetrate the enclosure next the street. In front of this yellow pine wall; with its ranks of benches, stood the Class Day Tree, girded at ten or fifteen feet from the ground with a wide band of flowers.

Mrs. Pasmer and her friends found themselves so late that if some gentlemen who knew Professor Saintsbury had not given up their places they could have got no seats. But this happened, and the three ladies had harmoniously blended their hues with those of the others in that bank of bloom, and the gentlemen had somehow made away with their obstructiveness in different crouching and stooping postures at their feet, when the Junior Class filed into the green enclosure amidst the 'rahs of their friends; and sank in long ranks on the grass beside the chapel. Then the Sophomores appeared, and were received with cheers by the Juniors, with whom they joined, as soon as they were placed, in heaping ignominy upon the freshmen. The Seniors came last, grotesque in the variety of their old clothes, and a fierce uproar of 'rahs and yells met them from the students squatted upon the grass as they loosely grouped themselves in front of the Tree; the men of the younger classes formed in three rings, and began circling in different directions around them.

Mrs. Pasmer bent across Mrs. Saintsbury to her daughter:

William Dean Howells

"Can you make out Mr. Mavering among them, Alice?"

"No. Hush, mamma!" pleaded the girl.

With the subsidence of the tumult in the other classes, the Seniors had broken from the stoical silence they kept through it, and were now with an equally serious clamour applauding the first of a long list of personages, beginning with the President, and ranging through their favourites in the Faculty down to Billy the Postman. The leader who invited them to this expression of good feeling exacted the full tale of nine cheers for each person he named, and before he reached the last the 'rahs came in gasps from their dry throats.

In the midst of the tumult the marshal flung his hat at the elm; then the rush upon the tree took place, and the scramble for the flowers. The first who swarmed up the trunk were promptly plucked down by the legs and flung upon the ground, as if to form a base there for the operations of the rest; who surged and built themselves up around the elm in an irregular mass. From time to time some one appeared clambering over heads and shoulders to make a desperate lunge and snatch at the flowers, and then fall back into the fluctuant heap again. Yells, cries, and clappings of hands came from the other students, and the spectators in the seats, involuntarily dying away almost to silence as some stronger or wilfuler aspirant held his own on the heads and shoulders of the others, or was stayed there by his friends among them till he could make sure of a handful of the flowers. A rush was made upon him when he reached the ground; if he could keep his flowers from the hands that snatched at them, he staggered away with the fragments. The wreath began to show wide patches of the bark under it; the surging and struggling crowd below grew less dense; here and there one struggled out of it and walked slowly about, panting pitiably.

"Oh, I wonder they don't kill each other!" cried Mrs. Pasmer. "Isn't it terrible?" She would not have missed it on any account; but she liked to get all she could out of her emotions.

"They never get hurt," said Mrs. Saintsbury. "Oh, look! There's Dan Mavering!"

The crowd at the foot of the tree had closed densely, and a wilder roar went up from all the students. A tall, slim young fellow, lifted on the shoulders of the mass below, and staying himself with one hand against the tree, rapidly stripped away the remnants of the wreath, and flung them into the crowd under him. A single tuft remained; the crowd was melting away under him in a scramble for the fallen flowers; he made a crooked leap, caught the tuft, and tumbled with it headlong.

"Oh!" breathed the ladies on the Benches, with a general suspiration lost in the 'rahs and clappings, as Mavering reappeared with the bunch of flowers in his hand. He looked dizzily about, as if not sure, of his course; then his face, flushed and heated, with the hair pulled over the eyes, brightened with recognition, and he advanced upon Mrs. Saintsbury's party with rapid paces, each of which Mrs. Pasmer commentated with inward conjecture.

"Is he bringing the flowers to Alice? Isn't it altogether too conspicuous? Has he really the right to do it? What will people think? Will he give them to me for her, or will he hand them directly to her? Which should I prefer him to do? I wonder if I know?"

When she looked up with the air of surprise mixed with deprecation and ironical disclaimer which she had prepared while these things were passing through her mind, young Mavering had reached them, and had paused in a moment's hesitation before his father. With a bow of affectionate burlesque, from which he lifted his face to break into laughter at the look in all their eyes, he handed the tattered nosegay to his father.

"Oh, how delightful! how delicate! how perfect!" Mrs. Pasmer confided to herself.

William Dean Howells

"I think this must be for you, Mrs. Pasmer," said the elder Mavering, offering her the bouquet, with a grave smile at his son's whim.

"Oh no, indeed!" said Mrs. Pasmer. "For Mrs. Saintsbury, of course."

She gave it to her, and Mrs. Saintsbury at once transferred it to Miss Pasmer.

"They wished me to pass this to you, Alice;" and at this consummation Dan Mavering broke into another happy laugh.

"Mrs. Saintsbury, you always do the right thing at once," he cried.

"That's more than I can say of you, Mr. Mavering," she retorted.

"Oh, thank you, Mr. Mavering!" said the girl, receiving the flowers. It was as if she had been too intent upon them and him to have noticed the little comedy that had conveyed them to her.

VIII

As soon after Class Day as Mrs. Pasmer's complaisant sense of the decencies would let her, she went out from Boston to call on Mrs. Saintsbury in Cambridge, and thank her for her kindness to Alice and herself. "She will know well enough what I come for," she said to herself, and she felt it the more important to ignore Mrs. Saintsbury's penetration by every polite futility; this was due to them both: and she did not go till the second day after.

Mrs. Saintsbury came down into the darkened, syringa-scented library to find her, and give her a fan.

"You still live, Jenny," she said, kissing her gaily.

They called each other by their girl names, as is rather the custom in Boston with ladies who are in the same set, whether they are great friends or not. In the more changeful society of Cambridge, where so many new people are constantly coming and going in connection with the college, it is not so much the custom; but Mrs. Saintsbury was Boston born, as well as Mrs. Pasmer, and was Cantabrigian by marriage—though this is not saying that she was not also thoroughly so by convincement and usage she now rarely went into Boston society.

"Yes, Etta—just. But I wasn't sure of it," said Mrs. Pasmer, "when I woke yesterday. I was a mere aching jelly!"

"And Alice?"

William Dean Howells

"Oh; I don't think she had any physical consciousness. She was a mere rapturous memory!"

"She did have a good time, didn't she?" said Mrs. Saintsbury, in a generous retrospect. "I think she was on her feet every moment in the evening. It kept me from getting tired, to watch her."

"I was afraid you'd be quite worn out. I'd no idea it was so late. It must have been nearly half past seven before we got away from the Beck Hall spread, and then by the time we had walked round the college grounds—how extremely pretty the lanterns were, and how charming the whole effect was!—it must have been nine before the dancing began. Well, we owe it all to you, Etta."

"I don't know what you mean by owing. I'm always glad of an excuse for Class Day. And it was Dan Mavering who really managed the affair."

"He was very kind," said Mrs. Pasmer, with a feeling which was chiefly gratitude to her friend for bringing in his name so soon. Now that it had been spoken, she felt it decorous to throw aside the outer integument of pretense, which if it could have been entirely exfoliated would have caused Mrs. Pasmer morally to disappear, like an onion stripped of its successive laminae.

"What did you mean," she asked, leaning forward, with, her face averted, "about his having the artistic temperament? Is he going to be an artist? I should hope not." She remembered without shame that she had strongly urged him to consider how much better it would be to be a painter than a lawyer, in the dearth of great American painters.

"He could be a painter if he liked—up to a certain point," said Mrs. Saintsbury. "Or he could be any one of half-a-dozen other things—his last craze was journalism; but you know what I mean by the artistic temperament: it's that inability to be explicit; that habit of leaving things vague and undefined, and hoping they'll somehow come out as you want them of themselves; that way of taking the line of beauty to get at what you wish to do or say, and of being very finicking about little things and lag about essentials. That's what I mean by the artistic temperament."

"Yes; that's terrible," sighed Mrs. Pasmer, with the abstractly severe yet personally pitying perception of one whose every word and act was sincere and direct. "I know just what you mean. But how does it apply to Mr. Mavering?"

"It doesn't, exactly," returned her friend. "And I'm always ashamed when I say, or even think, anything against Dan Mavering. He's sweetness itself. We've known him ever since he came to Harvard, and I must say that a more constant and lovely follow I never saw. It wasn't merely when he was a Freshman, and he had that home feeling hanging about him still that makes all the Freshmen so appreciative of anything you do for them; but all through the Sophomore and Junior years, when they're so taken up with their athletics and their societies and their college life generally that they haven't a moment for people that have been kind to them, he was just as faithful as ever."

"How nice!" cried Mrs. Pasmer.

"Yes, indeed! And all the allurements of Boston society haven't taken him from us altogether. You can't imagine how much this means till you've been at home a while and seen how the students are petted and spoiled nowadays in the young society."

"Oh, I've heard of it," said Mrs. Pasmer. "And is it his versatility and brilliancy, or his amiability, that makes him such a universal favourite?"

"Universal favourite? I don't know that he's that."

"Well, popular, then."

"Oh, he's certainly very much liked. But, Jenny, there are no universal favourites in Harvard now, if there ever were: the classes are altogether too big. And it wouldn't be ability, and it wouldn't be amiability alone, that would give a man any sort of leadership."

"What in the world would it be?"

"That question, more than anything else, shows how long you've been away, Jenny. It would be family—family, with a judicious mixture of the others, and with money."

"Is it possible? But of course—I remember! Only at their age one thinks of students as being all hail-fellow-well-met with each other—"

"Yes; it's hard to realise how conventional they are—how very much worldlier than the world—till one sees it as one does in Cambridge. They pique themselves on it. And Mr. Saintsbury" —she was one of those women whom everything reminds of their husbands "says that it isn't a bad thing altogether. He says that Harvard is just like the world; and even if it's a little more so, these boys have got to live in the world, and they had better know what it is. You may not approve of the Harvard spirit, and Mr. Saintsbury doesn't sympathise with it; he only says it's the world's spirit. Harvard men—the swells—are far more exclusive than Oxford men. A student, 'comme il faut', wouldn't at all like to be supposed to know another student whom we valued for his brilliancy, unless he was popular and well known in college."

"Dear me!" cried Mrs. Pasmer. "But of course! It's perfectly natural, with young people. And it's well enough that they should begin to understand how things really are in the world early; it will save them from a great many disappointments."

"I assure you we have very little to teach Harvard men in those matters. They could give any of us points. Those who are of good family and station know how to protect themselves by reserves that the others wouldn't dare to transgress. But a merely rich man couldn't rise in their set any more than a merely gifted man. He could get on to a certain point by toadying, and some do; but he would never get to be popular, like Dan Mavering."

"And what makes him popular?—to go back to the point we started from," said Mrs. Pasmer.

"Ah, that's hard to say. It's—quality, I suppose. I don't mean social quality, exactly; but personal charm. He never had a mean thought; of course we're all full of mean thoughts, and Dan is too; but his first impulse is always generous and sweet, and at his age people act a great deal from impulse. I don't suppose he ever met a human being without wanting to make him like him, and trying to do it."

"Yes, he certainly makes you like him," sighed Mrs. Pasmer. "But I understand that he can't make people like him without family or money; and I don't understand that he's one of those 'nouveaux riches' who are giving Harvard such a reputation for extravagance nowadays."

There was an inquiring note in Mrs. Pasmer's voice; and in the syringa-scented obscurity, which protected the ladies from the expression of each other's faces, Mrs. Saintsbury gave a little laugh of intelligence, to which Mrs. Pasmer responded by a murmur of humorous enjoyment at being understood.

"Oh no! He isn't one of those. But the Maverings have plenty of money," said Mrs. Saintsbury, "and Dan's been very free with it, though not lavish. And he came here with a reputation for popularity from a very good school, and that always goes a very great way in college."

"Yes?" said Mrs. Pasmer, feeling herself getting hopelessly adrift in these unknown waters; but reposing a pious

William Dean Howells

confidence in her pilot.

"Yes; if a sufficient number of his class said he was the best fellow in the world, he would be pretty sure to be chosen one of the First Ten in the 'Dickey'."

"What mysteries!" gasped Mrs. Pasmer, disposed to make fun of them, but a little overawed all the same. "What in the world is the 'Dickey'?"

"It's the society that the Freshmen are the most eager to get into. They're chosen, ten at a time, by the old members, and to be one of the first ten—the only Freshmen chosen—is something quite ineffable."

"I see." Mrs. Pasmer fanned herself, after taking a long breath. "And when he had got into the—"

"Then it would depend upon himself, how he spent his money, and all that, and what sort of society success he was in Boston. That has a great deal to do with it from the first. Then another thing is caution—discreetness; not saying anything censorious or critical of other men, no matter what they do. And Dan Mavering is the perfection of prudence, because he's the perfection of good-nature."

Mrs. Pasmer had apparently got all of these facts that she could digest. "And who are the Maverings?"

"Why, it's an old Boston name—"

"It's too old, isn't it? Like Pasmer. There are no Maverings in Boston that I ever heard of."

"No; the name's quite died out just here, I believe: but it's old, and it bids fair to be replated at Ponkwasset Falls."

"At Ponk—"

"That's where they have their mills, or factories, or shops, or whatever institution they make wall-paper in."

"Wall-paper!" cried Mrs. Pasmer, austerely. After a moment she asked: "And is wall-paper the 'thing' now? I mean—" She tried to think of some way of modifying the commonness of her phrase, but did not. After all, it expressed her meaning.

"It isn't the extreme of fashion, of course. But it's manufacturing, and it isn't disgraceful. And the Mavering papers are very pretty, and you can live with them without becoming anaemic, or having your face twitch."

"Face twitch?" echoed Mrs. Pasmer.

"Yes; arsenical poisoning."

"Oh! Conscientious as well as aesthetic. I see. And does Mr. Mavering put his artistic temperament into them?"

"His father does. He's a very interesting man. He has the best taste in certain things—he knows more about etchings, I suppose, than any one else in Boston."

"Is it possible! And does he live at Ponkwasset Falls? It's in Rhode Island, isn't it?"

"New Hampshire. Yes; the whole family live there."

"The whole family? Are there many of them? I'd fancied, somehow, that Mr. Mavering was the only—Do tell me about them, Etta," said Mrs. Pasmer, leaning back in her chair, and fanning herself with an effect of impartial interest, to which the dim light of the room lent itself.

"He's the only son. But there are daughters, of course—very cultivated girls."

"And is he—is the elder Mr. Mavering a—I don't know what

made me think so—a widower?"

"Well, no—not exactly."

"Not exactly! He's not a grass-widower, I hope?"

"No, indeed. But his wife's a helpless invalid, and always has been. He's perfectly devoted to her; and he hurried home yesterday, though he wanted very much to stay for Commencement. He's never away from her longer than he can help. She's bedridden; and you can see from the moment you enter it that it's a man's house. Daughters can't change that, you know."

"Have you been there?" asked Mrs. Pasmer, surprised that she was getting so much information, but eager for more. "Why, how long have you known them, Etta?"

"Only since Dan came to Harvard. Mr. Saintsbury took a fancy to him from the start, and the boy was so fond of him that they were always insisting upon a visit; and last summer we stopped there on our way to the mountains."

"And the sisters—do they stay there the whole year round? Are they countrified?"

"One doesn't live in the country without being countrified," said Mrs. Saintsbury. "They're rather quiet girls, though they've been about a good deal—to Europe with friends, and to New York in the winter. They're older than Dan; they're more like their father. Are you afraid of that draught at the windows?"

"Oh no; it's delicious. And he's like the mother?"

"Yes."

"Then it's the father who has the artistic taste—he gets that from him; and the mother who has the—"

"Temperament—yes."

"How extremely interesting! And so he's going to be a lawyer. Why lawyer, if he's got the talent and the temperament of an artist? Does his father wish him to be a lawyer?"

"His father wishes him to be a wall-paper maker."

"And the young man compromises on the law. I see," said Mrs. Pasmer. "And you say he's been going into Boston a great deal? Where does he go?"

The ladies entered into this social inquiry with a zest which it would be hard to make the reader share, or perhaps to feel the importance of. It is enough that it ended in the social vindication of Dan Mavering. It would not have been enough for Mrs Pasmer that he was accepted in the best Cambridge houses; she knew of old how people were accepted in Cambridge for their intellectual brilliancy or solidity, their personal worth, and all sorts of things, without consideration of the mystical something which gives vogue in Boston.

"How superb Alice was!" Mrs. Saintsbury broke off abruptly. "She has such a beautiful manner. Such repose."

"Repose! Yes," said her mother, thoughtfully. "But she's very intense. And I don't see where she gets it. Her father has repose enough, but he has no intensity; and I'm all intensity, and no repose. But I'm no more like my mother than Alice is like me."

"I think she has the Hibbins face," said Mrs. Saintsbury.

"Oh! she's got the Hibbins face," said Mrs Pasmer, with a disdain of tone which she did not at all feel; the tone was mere absent-mindedness.

She was about to revert to the question of Mavering's family,

William Dean Howells

when the door-bell rang, and another visitor interrupted her talk with Mrs. Saintsbury.

IX

Mrs. Pasmer's husband looked a great deal older than herself, and, by operation of a well-known law of compensation, he was lean and silent, while she was plump and voluble. He had thick eyebrows, which remained black after his hair and beard had become white, and which gave him an aspect of fierceness, expressive of nothing in his character. It was from him that their daughter got her height, and, as Mrs. Pasmer freely owned, her distinction.

Soon after their marriage the Pasmers had gone to live in Paris, where they remained faithful to the fortunes of the Second Empire till its fall, with intervals of return to their own country of a year or two years at a time. After the fall of the Empire they made their sojourn in England, where they lived upon the edges and surfaces of things, as Americans must in Europe everywhere, but had more permanency of feeling than they had known in France, and something like a real social status. At one time it seemed as if they might end their days there; but that which makes Americans different from all other peoples, and which finally claims their allegiance for their own land, made them wish to come back to America, and to come back to Boston. After all, their place in England was strictly inferior, and must be. They knew titles, and consorted with them, but they had none themselves, and the English constancy which kept their friends faithful to them after they had become an old story, was correlated with the English honesty which never permitted them to mistake themselves for even the lowest of the nobility. They went out last, and they did not come in first, ever.

The invitations, upon these conditions, might have gone on indefinitely, but they did not imply a future for the young girl in whom the interests of her parents centred. After being so long a little girl, she had become a great girl, and then all at once she had become a young lady. They had to ask themselves, the mother definitely and the father formlessly, whether they wished their daughter to marry an Englishman, and their hearts answered them, like true Republican hearts, Not an untitled Englishman, while they saw no prospect of her getting any other. Mrs. Pasmer philosophised the case with a clearness and a courage which gave her husband a series of twinges analogous to the toothache, for a man naturally shrinks from such bold realisations. She said Alice had the beauty of a beauty, and she had the distinction of a beauty, but she had not the principles of a beauty; there was no use pretending that she had. For this reason the Prince of Wales's set, so accessible to American loveliness with the courage of its convictions, was beyond her; and the question was whether there was money enough for a younger son, or whether, if there was, a younger son was worth it.

However this might be, there was no question but there was now less money than there had been, and a great deal less. The investments had not turned out as they promised; not only had dividends been passed, but there had been permanent shrinkages. What was once an amiable competency from the pooling of their joint resources had dwindled to a sum that needed a careful eye both to the income and the outgo. Alice's becoming a young lady had increased their expenses by the suddenly mounting cost of her dresses, and of the dresses which her mother must now buy for the different role she had to sustain in society. They began to ask themselves what it was for, and to question whether, if she could not marry a noble Englishman, Alice had not better marry a good American.

Even with Mrs. Pasmer this question was tacit, and it need not be explained to any one who knows our life that in her most worldly dreams she intended at the bottom of her heart that her daughter should marry for love. It is the rule that Americans marry for love, and the very rare exception that they marry for anything else; and if our divorce courts are so busy in spite of this fact, it is perhaps because the Americans also unmarry for love, or perhaps because love is not so sufficient in matters of the heart as has been represented in the literature of people who have not been able to give it so fair a trial. But whether it is all in all in marriage, or only a very marked essential, it is certain that Mrs. Pasmer expected her daughter's marriage to involve it. She would have shrunk from intimating anything else to her as from a gross indecency; and she could not possibly, by any finest insinuation, have made her a partner in her design for her happiness. That, so far as Alice was concerned, was a thing which was to fall to her as from heaven; for this also is part of the American plan. We are the children of the poets, the devotees of the romancers, so far as that goes; and however material and practical we are in other things, in this we are a republic of shepherds and shepherdesses, and we live in a golden age; which if it sometimes seems an age of inconvertible paper, is certainly so through no want of faith in us.

Though the Pasmers said that they ought to go home for Alice's sake, they both understood that they were going home experimentally, and not with the intention of laying their bones in their native soil, unless they liked it, or found they could afford it. Mrs. Pasmer had no illusions in regard to it. She had learned from her former visits home that it was frightfully expensive; and, during the fifteen years which they had spent chiefly abroad, she had observed the decay of that distinction which formerly attended returning sojourners from Europe. She had seen them cease gradually from the romantic reverence which once clothed them, and decline through a gathering indifference into something like slight and compassion, as people who have not been able to make their place or hold their own at home; and she had taught herself so well how to pocket the superiority natural to the Europeanised American before arriving at consciousness of this disesteem,

William Dean Howells

that she paid a ready tribute to people who had always stayed at home.

In fact Mrs. Pasmer was a flatterer, and it cannot be claimed for her that she flattered adroitly always. But adroitness in flattery is not necessary for its successful use. There is no morsel of it too gross for the condor gullet and the ostrich stomach of human vanity; there is no society in which it does not give the utterer instant honour and acceptance in greater or less degree. Mrs. Pasmer, who was very good-natured, employed it because she liked it herself, and knowing how absolutely worthless it was from her own tongue, prized it from others. She could have rested perfectly safe without it in her social position, which she found unchanged by years of absence. She had not been a Hibbins for nothing, and she was not a Pasmer for nothing, though why she should have been either for something it would not be easy to say.

But while confessing the foibles of Mrs. Pasmer, it would not be fair to omit from the tale of her many virtues the final conscientiousness of her openly involuted character. Not to mention other things, she instituted and practised economies as alien to her nature as to her husband's, and in their narrowing affairs she kept him out of debt. She was prudent; she was alert; and while presenting to the world all the outward effect of a butterfly, she possessed some of the best qualities of the bee.

With his senatorial presence, his distinction of person and manner, Mr. Pasmer was inveterately selfish in that province of small personal things where his wife left him unmolested. In what related to his own comfort and convenience he was undisputed lord of himself. It was she who ordered their comings and goings, and decided in which hemisphere they should sojourn from time to time, and in what city, street, and house, but always with the understanding that the kitchen and all the domestic appointments were to her husband's mind. He was sensitive to degrees of heat and cold, and luxurious in the matter of lighting, and he had a fine nose for plumbing. If he had not occupied himself so much with these details, he was the sort of man to have thought Mrs. Pasmer, with her buzz of activities and pretences, rather a tedious little woman. He had some delicate tastes, if not refined interests, and was expensively fond of certain sorts of bric-a-brac: he spent a great deal of time in packing and unpacking it, and he had cases stored in Rome and London and Paris; it had been one of his motives in consenting to come home that he might get them out, and set up the various objects of bronze and porcelain in cabinets. He had no vices, unless absolute idleness ensuing uninterruptedly upon a remotely demonstrated unfitness for business can be called a vice. Like other people who have always been idle, he did not consider his idleness a vice. He rather plumed himself upon it, for the man who has done nothing all his life naturally looks down upon people who have done or are doing something. In Europe he had not all the advantage of this superiority which such a man has here; he was often thrown with other idle people, who had been useless for so many generations that they had almost ceased to have any consciousness of it. In their presence Pasmer felt that his uselessness had not that passive elegance which only ancestral uselessness can give; that it was positive, and to that degree vulgar.

A life like this was not one which would probably involve great passions or affections, and it would be hard to describe exactly the feeling with which he regarded his daughter. He liked her, of course, and he had naturally expected certain things of her, as a ladylike intelligence, behaviour, and appearance; but he had never shown any great tenderness for her, or even pride in her. She had never given him any displeasure, however, and he had not shared his wife's question of mind at a temporary phase of Alice's development when she showed a decided inclination for a religious life. He had apparently not observed that the girl had a pensive temperament in spite of the effect of worldly splendour which her mother contrived for her, and that this pensiveness occasionally deepened to gloom. He had certainly never seen that in a way of her own she was very romantic. Mrs. Pasmer had seen it, with amusement sometimes, and sometimes with anxiety, but always with the

　　　　William Dean Howells

courage to believe that she could cope with it when it was necessary.

Whenever it was necessary she had all the moral courage she wanted; it seemed as if she could have it or not as she liked; and in coming home she had taken a flat instead of a house, though she had not talked with her friends three minutes without perceiving that the moment when flats had promised to assert their social equality with houses in Boston was past for ever. There were, of course, cases in which there could be no question of them; but for the most part they were plainly regarded as makeshifts, the resorts of people of small means, or the defiances or errors of people who had lived too much abroad. They stamped their occupants as of transitory and fluctuant character; good people might live in them, and did, as good people sometimes boarded; but they could not be regarded as forming a social base, except in rare instances. They presented peculiar difficulties in calling, and for any sort of entertainment they were too—not public, perhaps, but— evident.

In spite of these objections Mrs. Pasmer took a flat in the Cavendish, and she took it furnished from people who were going abroad for a year.

X

Mrs. Pasmer stood at the drawing-room window of this apartment, the morning after her call upon Mrs. Saintsbury, looking out on the passage of an express-wagon load of trunks through Cavendish Square, and commenting the fact with the tacit reflection that it was quite time she should be getting away from Boston too, when her daughter, who was looking out of the other window, started significantly back.

"What is it, Alice?"

"Nothing! Mr. Mavering, I think, and that friend of his—"

"Which friend? But where? Don't look! They will think we were watching them. I can't see them at all. Which way were they going?" Mrs. Pasmer dramatised a careless unconsciousness to the square, while vividly betraying this anxiety to her daughter.

Alice walked away to the furthest part of the room. "They are coming this way," she said indifferently.

Before Mrs. Pasmer had time to prepare a conditional mood, adapted either to their coming that way or going some other, she heard the janitor below in colloquy with her maid in the kitchen, and then the maid came in to ask if she should say the ladies were at home. "Oh, certainly," said Mrs. Pasmer, with a caressing politeness that anticipated the tone she meant to use with Mavering and his friend. "Were you going, Alice? Better

William Dean Howells

stay. It would be awkward sending out for you. You look well enough."

"Well!"

The young men came in, Mavering with his nervous laugh first, and then Boardman with his twinkling black eyes, and his main-force self-possession.

"We couldn't go away as far as New London without coming to see whether you had really survived Class Day," said the former, addressing his solicitude to Mrs. Pasmer. "I tried to find out from, Mrs. Saintsbury, but she was very noncommittal." He laughed again, and shook hands with Alice, whom he now included in his inquiry.

"I'm glad she was," said Mrs. Pasmer—inwardly wondering what he meant by going to New London—"if it sent you to ask in person." She made them sit down; and she made as little as possible of the young ceremony they threw into the transaction. To be cosy, to be at ease instantly, was Mrs. Pasmer's way. "We've not only survived, we've taken a new lease of life from Class Day. I'd forgotten how charming it always was. Or perhaps it didn't use to be so charming? I don't believe they have anything like it in Europe. Is it always so brilliant?"

"I don't know," said Mavering. "I really believe it was rather a nice one."

"Oh, we were both enraptured," cried Mrs. Pasmer.

Alice added a quiet "Yes, indeed," and her mother went on—

"And we thought the Beck Hall spread was the crowning glory of the whole affair. We owe ever so much to your kindness."

"Oh, not at all," said Mavering.

"But we were talking afterward, Alice and I, about the sudden transformation of all that disheveled crew around the Tree into the imposing swells—may I say howling swells?—"

"Yes, do say 'howling,' Mrs. Pasmer!" implored the young man.

"—whom we met afterward at the spread," she concluded. "How did you manage it all? Mr. Irving in the 'Lyons Mail' was nothing to it. We thought we had walked directly over from the Tree; and there you were, all ready to receive us, in immaculate evening dress."

"It was pretty quick work," modestly admitted the young man. "Could you recognise any one in that hurly-burly round the Tree?"

"We didn't till you rose, like a statue of Victory, and began grabbing for the spoils from the heads and shoulders of your friends. Who was your pedestal?"

Mavering put his hand on his friend's broad shoulder, and gave him a playful push.

Boardman turned up his little black eyes at him, with a funny gleam in them.

"Poor Mr. Boardman!" said Mrs. Pasmer.

"It didn't hurt him a bit," said Mavering, pushing him. "He liked it."

"Of course he did," said Mrs. Pasmer, implying, in flattery of Mavering, that Boardman might be glad of the distinction; and now Boardman looked as if he were not. She began to get away in adding, "But I wonder you don't kill each other."

"Oh, we're not so easily killed," said Mavering.

"And what a fairy scene it was at the spread!" said Mrs. Pasmer, turning to Boardman. She had already talked its splendours over with Mavering the same evening. "I thought we should never get out of the Hall; but when we did get out of the window upon that tapestried platform, and down on the tennis-ground, with Turkey rugs to hide the bare spots in it—" She stopped as people do when it is better to leave the effect to the listener's imagination.

"Yes, I think it was rather nice," said Boardman.

"Nice?" repeated Mrs. Pasmer; and she looked at Mavering. "Is that the famous Harvard Indifferentism?"

"No, no, Mrs. Pasmer! It's just his personal envy. He wasn't in the spread, and of course he doesn't like to hear any one praise it. Go on!" They all laughed.

"Well, even Mr. Boardman will admit," said Mrs. Pasmer; "that nothing could have been prettier than that pavilion at the bottom of the lawn, and the little tables scattered about over it, and all those charming young creatures under that lovely evening sky."

"Ah! Even Boardman can't deny that. We did have the nicest crowd; didn't we?"

"Well," said Mrs. Pasmer, playfully checking herself in a ready adhesion, "that depends a good deal upon where Mr. Boardman's spread was."

"Thank you," said Boardman.

"He wasn't spreading anywhere," cried his friend. "Except himself—he was spreading himself everywhere."

"Then I think I should prefer to remain neutral," said Mrs. Pasmer, with a mock prudence which pleased the young men. In the midst of the pleasure the was giving and feeling she was all the time aware that her daughter had contributed but one remark to the conversation, and that she must be seeming very stiff and cold. She wondered what that meant, and whether she disliked this little Mr. Boardman, or whether she was again trying to punish Mr. Mavering for something, and, if so, what it was. Had he offended her in some way the other day? At any rate, she had no right to show it. She longed for some chance to scold the girl, and tell her that it would not do, and make her talk. Mr. Mavering was merely a friendly acquaintance, and there could be no question of anything personal. She forgot that between young people the social affair is always trembling to the personal affair.

In the little pause which these reflections gave her mother, the girl struck in, with the coolness that always astonished Mrs. Pasmer, and as if she had been merely waiting till some phase of the talk interested her.

"Are many of the students going to the race?" she asked Boardman.

"Yes; nearly everybody. That is—"

"The race?" queried Mrs. Pasmer.

"Yes, at New London," Mavering broke in. "Don't you know? The University race—Harvard and Yale."

"Oh—oh yes," cried Mrs. Pasmer, wondering how her daughter should know about the race, and she not. "Had they talked it over together on Class Day?" she asked herself. She felt herself, in spite of her efforts to keep even with them; left behind and left out, as later age must be distanced and excluded by youth. "Are you gentlemen going to row?" she asked Mavering.

"No; they've ruled the tubs out this time; and we should send anything else to the bottom."

Mrs. Pasmer perceived that he was joking, but also that they were not of the crew; and she said that if that was the case the should not go.

"Oh, don't let that keep you away! Aren't you going? I hoped you were going," continued the young man, speaking with his eyes on Mrs. Pasmer, but with his mind, as she could see by his eyes, on her daughter.

"No, no."

"Oh, do go, Mrs. Pasmer!" he urged: "I wish you'd go along to chaperon us."

Mrs. Pasmer accepted the notion with amusement. "I should think you might look after each other. At any rate, I think I must trust you to Mr. Boardman this time."

"Yes; but he's going on business," persisted Mavering, as if for the pleasure he found in fencing with the air, "and he can't look after me."

"On business?" said Mrs. Pasmer, dropping her outspread fan on her lap, incredulously.

"Yes; he's going into journalism—he's gone into it," laughed Mavering; "and he's going down to report the race for the 'Events'."

"Really!" asked Mrs. Pasmer, with a glance at Boardman, whose droll embarrassment did not contradict his friend's words. "How splendid!" she cried. "I had, heard that a great many Harvard men were taking up journalism. I'm so glad of it! It will do everything to elevate its tone."

Boardman seemed to suffer under these expectations a little, and he stole a glance of comical menace at his friend.

"Yes," said Mavering; "you'll see a very different tone about the fires, and the fights, and the distressing accidents, in the 'Events' after this."

"What does he mean?" she asked Boardman, giving him unavoidably the advantage of the caressing manner which was in her mind for Mavering.

"Well, you see," said Boardman, "we have to begin pretty low down."

"Oh, but all departments of our press need reforming, don't they?" she inquired consolingly. "One hears such shocking things about our papers abroad. I'm sure that the more Harvard men go into them the better. And how splendid it is to have them going into politics the way they are! They're going into politics too, aren't they?" She looked from one young man to the other with an idea that she was perhaps shooting rather wild, and an amiable willingness to be laughed at if she were. "Why don't you go into politics, Mr. Mavering?"

"Well, the fact is—"

"So many of the young University men do in England," said Mrs. Pasmer, fortifying her position.

"Well, you see, they haven't got such a complete machine in England—"

"Oh yes, that dreadful machine!" sighed Mrs. Pasmer, who had heard of it, but did not know in the least what it was.

"Do you think the Harvard crew will beat this time?" Alice asked of Boardman.

"Well, to tell you the truth—"

"Oh, but you must never believe him when he begins that way!" cried Mavering. "To be sure they will beat. And you

William Dean Howells

ought to be there to see it. Now, why won't you come, Mrs. Pasmer?" he pleaded, turning to her mother.

"Oh, I'm afraid we must be getting away from Boston by that time. It's very tiresome, but there seems to be nobody left; and one can't stay quite alone, even if you're sick of moving about. Have you ever been—we think of going there—to Campobello?"

"No; but I hear that it's charming, there. I had a friend who was there last year, and he said it was charming. The only trouble is it's so far. You're pretty well on the way to Europe when you get there. You know it's all hotel life?"

"Yes. It's quite a new place, isn't it?"

"Well, it's been opened up several years. And they say it isn't like the hotel life anywhere else; it's charming. And there's the very nicest class of people."

"Very nice Philadelphia people, I hear," said Mrs. Pasmer; "and Baltimore. Don't you think it's well;" she asked deferentially, and under correction, if she were hazarding too much, "to see somebody besides Boston people sometimes—if they're nice? That seems to be one of the great advantages of living abroad."

"Oh, I think there are nice people everywhere," said the young man, with the bold expansion of youth.

"Yes," sighed Mrs. Pasmer. "We saw two such delightful young people coming in and out of the hotel in Rome. We were sure they were English. And they were from Chicago! But there are not many Western people at Campobello, are there?"

"I really don't know," said Mavering. "How is it, Boardman? Do many of your people go there?"

"You know you do make it so frightfully expensive with your

money," said Mrs. Pasmer, explaining with a prompt effect of having known all along that Boardman was from the West, "You drive us poor people all away."

"I don't think my money would do it," said Boardman quietly.

"Oh, you wait till you're a Syndicate Correspondent," said, Mavering, putting his hand on his friend's shoulder, and rising by aid of it. He left Mrs. Pasmer to fill the chasm that had so suddenly yawned between her and Boardman; and while she tumbled into every sort of flowery friendliness and compliment, telling him she should look out for his account of the race with the greatest interest, and expressing the hope that he would get as far as Campobello during the summer, Mavering found some minutes for talk with Alice. He was graver with her—far graver than with her mother—not only because she was a more serious nature, but because they were both young, and youth is not free with youth except by slow and cautious degrees. In that little space of time they talked of pictures, 'a propos' of some on the wall, and of books, because of those on the table.

"Oh yes," said Mrs. Pasmer when they paused, and she felt that her piece of difficult engineering had been quite successful, "Mrs. Saintsbury was telling me what a wonderful connoisseur of etchings your father is."

"I believe he does know something about them," said the young man modestly.

"And he's gone back already?"

"Oh yes. He never stays long away from my mother. I shall be going home myself as soon as I get back from the race."

"And shall you spend the summer there?"

"Part of it. I always like to do that."

William Dean Howells

"Perhaps when you get away you'll come as far as Campobello—with Mr. Boardman," she added.

"Has Boardman promised to go?" laughed Mavering. "He will promise anything. Well, I'll come to Campobello if you'll come to New London. Do come, Mrs. Pasmer!"

The mother stood watching the two young men from the window as they made their way across the square together. She had now, for some reason; no apparent scruple in being seen to do so.

"How ridiculous that stout little Mr. Boardman is with him!" said Mrs. Pasmer. "He hardly comes up to his shoulder. Why in the world should he have brought him?"

"I thought he was very pleasant," said the girl.

"Yes, yes, of course. And I suppose he'd have felt that it was rather pointed coming alone."

"Pointed?"

"Young men are so queer! Did you like that kind of collar he had on?"

"I didn't notice it."

"So very, very high."

"I suppose he has rather a long neck."

"Well, what did you think of his urging us to go to the race? Do you think he meant it? Do you think he intended it for an invitation?"

"I don't think he meant anything; or, if he did, I think he didn't know what."

"Yes," said Mrs. Pasmer vaguely; "that must be what Mrs. Saintsbury meant by the artistic temperament."

"I like people to be sincere, and not to say things they don't mean, or don't know whether they mean or not," said Alice.

"Yes, of course, that's the best way," admitted Mrs. Pasmer. "It's the only way," she added, as if it were her own invariable practice. Then she added further, "I wonder what he did mean?"

She began to yawn, for after her simulation of vivid interest in them the visit of the young men had fatigued her. In the midst of her yawn her daughter went out of the room, with an impatient gesture, and she suspended the yawn long enough to smile, and then finished it.

William Dean Howells

XI

After first going to the Owen, at Campobello, the Pasmers took rooms at the Ty'n-y-Coed, which is so much gayer, even if it is not so characteristic of the old Welsh Admiral's baronial possession of the island. It is characteristic enough, and perched on its bluff overlooking the bay, or whatever the body of water is, it sees a score of pretty isles and long reaches of mainland coast, with a white marble effect of white-painted wooden Eastport, nestled in the wide lap of the shore, in apparent luxury and apparent innocence of smuggling and the manufacture of herring sardines. The waters that wrap the island in morning and evening fog temper the air of the latitude to a Newport softness in summer, with a sort of inner coolness that is peculiarly delicious, lulling the day with long calms and light breezes, and after nightfall commonly sending a stiff gale to try the stops of the hotel's gables and casements, and to make the cheerful blaze on its public hearths acceptable. Once or twice a day the Eastport ferry-boat arrives, with passengers from the southward, at a floating wharf that sinks or swims half a hundred feet on the mighty tides of the Northeast; but all night long the island is shut up to its own memories and devices. The pretty romance of the old sailor who left England to become a sort of feudal seigneur here, with a holding of the entire island, and its fisher-folk for his villeins, forms a picturesque background for the aesthetic leisure and society in the three hotels remembering him and his language in their names, and housing with a few cottages all the sojourners on the island. By day the broad hotel piazzas shelter such of the guests as prefer to let others make their excursions into the heart of the island, and around its rocky, sea-beaten borders; and at night, when the falling mists have brought the early dark, and from lighthouse to lighthouse the fog-horns moan and low to one another, the piazzas cede to the corridors and the parlours and smoking-rooms. The life does not greatly differ from other seaside hotel life on the surface, and if one were to make distinctions one would perhaps begin by saying that hotel society there has much of the tone of cottage society elsewhere, with a little more accessibility. As the reader doubtless knows, the great mass of Boston society, thoughtful of its own weight and bulk, transports itself down the North Shore scarcely further than Manchester at the furthest; but there are more courageous or more detachable spirits who venture into more distant regions. These contribute somewhat toward peopling Bar Harbour in the summer, but they scarcely characterise it in any degree; while at Campobello they settle in little daring colonies, whose self-reliance will enlist the admiration of the sympathetic observer. They do not refuse the knowledge of other colonies of other stirps and origins, and they even combine in temporary alliance with them. But, after all, Boston speaks one language, and New York another, and Washington a third, and though the several dialects have only slight differences of inflection, their moral accents render each a little difficult for the others. In fact every society is repellant of strangers in the degree that it is sufficient to itself, and is incurious concerning the rest of the world. If it has not the elements of self-satisfaction in it, if it is uninformed and new and restless, it is more hospitable than an older society which has a sense of merit founded upon historical documents, and need no longer go out of itself for comparisons of any sort, knowing that if it seeks anything better it will probably be disappointed. The natural man, the savage, is as indifferent to others as the exclusive, and those who accuse the coldness of the Bostonians, and their reluctant or repellant behaviour toward unknown people, accuse not only civilisation, but nature itself.

That love of independence which is notable in us even in our most acquiescent phases at home is perhaps what brings these

　　　　　William Dean Howells

cultivated and agreeable people so far away, where they can achieve a sort of sylvan urbanity without responsibility, and without that measuring of purses which attends the summer display elsewhere. At Campobello one might be poor with almost as little shame as in Cambridge if one were cultivated. Mrs. Pasmer, who seldom failed of doing just the right thing for herself, had promptly divined the advantages of Campobello for her family. She knew, by dint of a little inquiry, and from the volunteer information of enthusiasts who had been there the summer before, just who was likely to be there during the summer with which she now found herself confronted. Campobello being yet a new thing, it was not open to the objection that you were sure to meet such and such people, more or less common or disagreeable, there; whatever happened, it could be lightly handled in the retrospect as the adventure of a partial and fragmentary summer when really she hardly cared where they went.

They did not get away from Boston before the middle of July, and after the solitude they left behind them there, the Owen at first seemed very gay. But when they had once or twice compared it with the Ty'n-y-Coed, riding to and fro in the barge which formed the connecting link with the Saturday evening hops of the latter hotel, Mrs. Pasmer decided that, from Alice's point of view, they had made a mistake, and she repaired it without delay. The young people were, in fact, all at the Ty'n-y-Coed, and though she found the Owen perfectly satisfying for herself and Mr. Pasmer, she was willing to make the sacrifice of going to a new place: it was not a great sacrifice for one who had dwelt so long in tents.

There were scarcely any young girls at the Owen, and no young men, of course. Even at the Ty'n-y-Coed, where young girls abounded, it would not be right to pretend that there were young men enough. Nowhere, perhaps, except at Bar Harbour, is the long-lost balance of the sexes trimmed in New England; and even there the observer, abstractly delighting in the young girls and their dresses at that grand love-exchange of Rodick's, must question whether the adjustment is perfectly accurate.

At Campobello there were not more than half enough young men, and there was not enough flirtation to affect the prevailing social mood of the place: an unfevered, expectationless tranquillity, in which to-day is like yesterday, and to-morrow cannot be different. It is a quiet of light reading, and slowly, brokenly murmured, contented gossip for the ladies, of old newspapers and old stories and luxuriously meditated cigars for the men, with occasional combinations for a steam-launch cruise among the eddies and islands of the nearer waters, or a voyage further off in the Bay of Fundy to the Grand Menan, and a return for the late dinner which marks the high civilisation of Campobello, and then an evening of more reading and gossip and cigars, while the night wind whistles outside, and the brawl and crash of the balls among the tenpins comes softened from the distant alleys. There are pleasant walks, which people seldom take, in many directions, and there are drives and bridle-paths all through the dense, sad, Northern woods which still savagely clothe the greater part of the island to its further shores, where there are shelves and plateaus of rock incomparable for picnicking.

One need ask nothing better, in fact, than to stroll down the sylvan road that leads to the Owen, past the little fishing-village with its sheds for curing herring; and the pale blue smoke and appetising savour escaping from them; and past the little chapel with which the old Admiral attested his love of the Established rite. On this road you may sometimes meet a little English bishop from the Provinces, in his apron and knee-breeches; and there is a certain bridge over a narrow estuary, where in the shallow land-locked pools of the deeply ebbing tide you may throw stones at sculpin, and witness the admirable indifference of those fish to human cruelty and folly. In the middle distance you will see a group of herring weirs, which with their coronals of tufted saplings form the very most picturesque aspect of any fishing industry. You may, now and then find an artist at this point, who, crouched over his easel, or hers, seems to agree with you about the village and the weirs.

But Alice Pasmer cared little more for such things than her mother did, and Mrs. Pasmer regarded Nature in all her aspects simply as an adjunct of society, or an occasional feature of the entourage. The girl had no such worldly feeling about it, but she found slight sympathy in the moods of earth and sky with her peculiar temperament. This temperament, whose recondite origin had almost wholly broken up Mrs. Pasmer's faith in heredity, was like other temperaments, not always in evidence, and Alice was variously regarded as cold, of shy, or proud, or insipid, by the various other temperaments brought in contact with her own. She was apt to be liked because she was as careful of others as she was of herself, and she never was childishly greedy about such admiration as she won, as girls often are, perhaps because she did not care for it. Up to this time it is doubtful if her heart had been touched even by the fancies that shake the surface of the soul of youth, and perhaps it was for this reason that her seriousness at first fretted Mrs. Pasmer with a vague anxiety for her future.

Mrs. Pasmer herself remained inalienably Unitarian, but she was aware of the prodigious-growth which the Church had been making in society, and when Alice showed her inclination for it, she felt that it was not at all as if she had developed a taste for orthodoxy; when finally it did not seem likely to go too far, it amused Mrs. Pasmer that her daughter should have taken so intensely to the Anglican rite.

In the hotel it attached to her by a common interest several of the ladies who had seen her earnestly responsive at the little Owen chapel—ladies left to that affectional solitude which awaits long widowhood through the death or marriage of children; and other ladies, younger, but yet beginning to grow old with touching courage. Alice was especially a favourite with the three or four who represented their class and condition at the Ty'n-y Coed, and who read the best books read there, and had the gentlest manners. There was a tacit agreement among these ladies, who could not help seeing the difference in the temperaments of the mother and daughter, that Mrs. Pasmer did not understand Alice; but probably there were very few people except herself whom Mrs. Pasmer did not understand quite well. She understood these ladies and their compassion for Alice, and she did not in the least resent it. She was willing that people should like Alice for any reason they chose, if they did not go too far. With her little flutter of futile deceits, her irreverence for every form of human worth and her trust in a providence which had seldom failed her, she smiled at the cult of Alice's friends, as she did at the girl's seriousness, which also she felt herself able to keep from going too far.

While she did not object to the sympathy of these ladies, whatever inspired it, she encouraged another intimacy which grew up contemporaneously with theirs, and which was frankly secular and practical, though the girl who attached herself to Alice with one of those instant passions of girlhood was also in every exterior observance a strict and diligent Churchwoman. The difference was through the difference of Boston and New York in everything: the difference between idealising and the realising tendency. The elderly and middle-aged Boston women who liked Alice had been touched by something high yet sad in the beauty of her face at church; the New York girl promptly owned that she had liked her effect the first Sunday she saw her there, and she knew in a minute she never got those things on this side; her obeisances and genuflections throughout the service, much more profound and punctilious than those of any one else there, had apparently not prevented her from making a thorough study of Alice's costume and a correct conjecture as to its authorship.

Miss Anderson, who claimed a collateral Dutch ancestry by the Van Hook, tucked in between her non-committal family name and the Julia given her in christening, was of the ordinary slender make of American girlhood, with dull blond hair, and a dull blond complexion, which would have left her face uninteresting if it had not been for the caprice of her nose in suddenly changing from the ordinary American regularity,

William Dean Howells

after getting over its bridge, and turning out distinctly 'retrousse'. This gave her profile animation and character; you could not expect a girl with that nose to be either irresolute or commonplace, and for good or for ill Miss Anderson was decided and original. She carried her figure, which was no great things of a figure as to height, with vigorous erectness; she walked with long strides, knocking her skirts into fine eddies and tangles as she went; and she spoke in a bold, deep voice, with tones like a man in it, all the more amusing and fascinating because of the perfectly feminine eyes with which she looked at you, and the nervous, feminine gestures which she used while she spoke.

She took Mrs. Pasmer into her confidence with regard to Alice at an early stage of their acquaintance, which from the first had a patronising or rather protecting quality in it; if she owned herself less fine, she knew herself shrewder, and more capable of coping with actualities.

"I think she's moybid, Alice is," she said. "She isn't moybid in the usual sense of the word, but she expects more of herself and of the woyld generally than anybody's going to get out of it. She thinks she's going to get as much as she gives, and that's a great mistake, Mrs. Pasmer," she said, with that peculiar liquefaction of the canine letter which the New-Yorkers alone have the trick of, and which it would be tiresome and futile to try to represent throughout her talk.

"Oh yes, I quite agree with you," said Mrs. Pasmer, deep in her throat, and reserving deeper still her enjoyment of this early wisdom of Miss Anderson's.

"Now, even at church—she carries the same spirit into the church. She doesn't make allowance for human nature, and the church does."

"Oh, certainly!" Mrs. Pasmer agreed.

"She isn't like a person that's been brought up in the church.

It's more like the old Puritan spirit.—Excuse me, Mrs. Pasmer!"

"Yes, indeed! Say anything you like about the Puritans!" said Mrs. Pasmer, delighted that, as a Bostonian, she should be thought to care for them.

"I always forget that you're a Bostonian," Miss Anderson apologized.

"Oh, thank you!" cried Mrs. Pasmer.

"I'm going to try to make her like other girls," continued Miss Anderson.

"Do," said Alice's mother, with the effect of wishing her joy of the undertaking.

"If there were a few young men about, a little over seventeen and a little under fifty, it would be easier," said Miss Anderson thoughtfully. "But how are you going to make a girl like other girls when there are no young men?"

"That's very true," said Mrs. Pasmer, with an interest which she of course did her best to make impersonal. "Do you think there will be more, later on?"

"They will have to Huey up if they are comin'," said Miss Anderson. "It's the middle of August now, and the hotel closes the second week in September."

"Yes," said Mrs. Pasmer, vaguely looking at Alice. She had just appeared over the brow of the precipice, along whose face the arrivals and departures by the ferry-boat at Campobello obliquely ascend and descend.

She came walking swiftly toward the hotel, and, for her, so excitedly that Mrs. Pasmer involuntarily rose and went to meet her at the top of the broad hotel steps.

"What is it, Alice?"

"Oh, nothing! I thought I saw Mr. Munt coming off the boat."

"Mr. Munt?"

"Yes." She would not stay for further question.

Her mother looked after her with the edge of her fan over her mouth till she disappeared in the depths of the hotel corridor; then she sat down near the steps, and chatted with some half-grown boys lounging on the balustrade, and waited for Munt to come up over the brink of the precipice. Dan Mavering came with him, running forward with a polite eagerness at sight of Mrs. Pasmer. She distributed a skillful astonishment equally between the two men she had equally expected to see, and was extremely cordial with them, not only because she was pleased with them, but because she was still more pleased with her daughter's being, after all, like other girls, when it came to essentials.

XII

Alice came down to lunch in a dress which reconciled the seaside and the drawing-room in an effect entirely satisfactory to her mother, and gave her hand to both the gentlemen without the affectation of surprise at seeing either.

"I saw Mr. Munt coning up from the boat," she said in answer to Mavering's demand for some sort of astonishment from her. "I wasn't certain that it was you."

Mrs. Pasmer, whose pretences had been all given away by this simple confession, did not resent it, she was so much pleased with her daughter's evident excitement at the young man's having come. Without being conscious of it, perhaps, Alice prettily assumed the part of hostess from the moment of their meeting, and did the honours of the hotel with a tacit implication of knowing that he had come to see her there. They had only met twice, but now, the third time, meeting after a little separation, their manner toward each other was as if their acquaintance had been making progress in the interval. She took him about quite as if he had joined their family party, and introduced him to Miss Anderson and to all her particular friends, for each of whom, within five minutes after his presentation, he contrived to do some winning service. She introduced him to her father, whom he treated with deep respect and said "Sir" to. She showed him the bowling alley, and began to play tennis with him.

Her mother, sitting with John Munt on the piazza, followed

William Dean Howells

these polite attentions to Mavering with humorous satis-faction, which was qualified as they went on.

"Alice," she said to her, at a chance which offered itself during the evening, and then she hesitated for the right word.

"Well; mamma?" said the girl impatiently, stopping on her way to walk up and down the piazza with Mavering; she had run in to get a wrap and a Tam-o'-Shanter cap.

"Don't—overdo—the honours."

"What do you mean, mamma?" asked the girl; dropping her arms before her, and letting the shawl trail on the floor.

"Don't you think he was very kind to us on Class Day?"

Her mother laughed. "But every one mayn't know it's gratitude."

Alice went out, but she came back in a little while, and went up to her room without speaking to any one.

The fits of elation and depression with which this first day passed for her succeeded one another during Mavering's stay. He did not need Alice's chaperonage long. By the next morning he seemed to know and to like everybody in the hotel, where he enjoyed a general favour which at that moment had no exceptions. In the afternoon he began to organise excursions and amusements with the help of Miss Anderson.

The plans all referred to Alice, who accepted and approved with an authority which every one tacitly admitted, just as every one recognised that Mavering had come to Campobello because she was there. Such a phase is perhaps the prettiest in the history of a love affair. All is yet in solution; nothing has been precipitated in word or fact. The parties to it even reserve a final construction of what they themselves say or do; they will not own to their hearts that they mean exactly this or that.

It is this phase which in its perfect freedom is the most American of all; under other conditions it is an instant, perceptible or imperceptible; under ours it is a distinct stage, unhurried by any outside influences.

The nearest approach to a definition of the situation was in a walk between Mavering and Mrs. Pasmer, and this talk, too, light and brief, might have had no such intention as her fancy assigned his part of it.

She recurred to something that had been said on Class Day about his taking up the law immediately, or going abroad first for a year.

"Oh, I've abandoned Europe altogether for the present," he said laughing. "And I don't know but I may go back on the law too."

"Indeed! Then you are going to be an artist?"

"Oh no; not so bad as that. It isn't settled yet, and I'm off here to think it over a while before the law school opens in September. My father wants me to go into his business and turn my powers to account in designing wall-papers."

"Oh, how very interesting!" At the same time Mrs. Pasmer ran over the whole field of her acquaintance without finding another wall-paper maker in it. But she remembered what Mrs. Saintsbury had said: it was manufacturing. This reminded her to ask if he had seen the Saintsburys lately, and he said, No; he believed they were still in Cambridge, though.

"And we shall actually see a young man," she said finally, "in the act of deciding his own destiny!"

He laughed for pleasure in her persiflage. "Yes; only don't give me away. Nobody else knows it."

"Oh no, indeed. Too much flattered, Mr. Mavering. Shall you

William Dean Howells

let me know when you've decided? I shall be dying to know, and I shall be too high-minded to ask."

It was not then too late to adapt 'Pinafore' to any exigency of life, and Mavering said, "You will learn from the expression of my eyes."

XIII

The witnesses of Mavering's successful efforts to make everybody like him were interested in his differentiation of the attentions he offered every age and sex from those he paid Alice. But while they all agreed that there never was a sweeter fellow, they would have been puzzled to say in just what this difference consisted, and much as they liked him, the ladies of her cult were not quite satisfied with him till they decided that it was marked by an anxiety, a timidity, which was perfectly fascinating in a man so far from bashfulness as he. That is, he did nice things for others without asking; but with her there was always an explicit pause, and an implicit prayer and permission, first. Upon this condition they consented to the glamour which he had for her, and which was evident to every one probably but him.

Once agreeing that no one was good enough for Alice Pasmer, whose qualities they felt that only women could really appreciate, they were interested to see how near Mavering could come to being good enough; and as the drama played itself before their eyes, they pleased themselves in analysing its hero.

"He is not bashful, certainly," said one of a little group who sat midway of the piazza while Alice and Mavering walked up and down together. "But don't you think he's modest? There's that difference, you know."

The lady addressed waited so long before answering that the

William Dean Howells

young couple came abreast of the group, and then she had to wait till they were out of hearing. "Yes," she said then, with a tender, sighing thoughtfulness, "I've felt that in him. And really think he is a very loveable nature. The only question would be whether he wasn't too loveable."

"Yes," said the first lady, with the same kind of suspiration, "I know what you mean. And I suppose they ought to be something more alike in disposition."

"Or sympathies?" suggested the other.

"Yes, or sympathies."

A third lady laughed a little. "Mr. Mavering has so many sympathies that he ought to be like her in some of them."

"Do you mean that he's too sympathetic—that he isn't sincere?" asked the first—a single lady of forty-nine, a Miss Cotton, who had a little knot of conscience between her pretty eyebrows, tied there by the unremitting effort of half a century to do and say exactly the truth, and to find it out.

Mrs. Brinkley, whom she addressed, was of that obesity which seems often to incline people to sarcasm. "No, I don't think he's insincere. I think he always means what he says and does—Well, do you think a little more concentration of good-will would hurt him for Miss Pasmer's purpose—if she has it?"

"Yes, I see," said Miss Cotton. She waited, with her kind eyes fixed wistfully upon Alice, for the young people to approach and get by. "I wonder what the men think of him?"

"You might ask Miss Anderson," said Mrs. Brinkley.

"Oh, do you think they tell her?"

"Not that exactly," said Mrs. Brinkley, shaking with good-humoured pleasure in her joke.

"Her voice—oh yes. She and Alice are great friends, of course."

"I should think," said Mrs. Stamwell, the second speaker, "that Mr. Mavering would be jealous sometimes—till he looked twice."

"Yes," said Miss Cotton, obliged to admit the force of the remark, but feeling that Mr. Mavering had been carried out of the field of her vision by the turn of the talk. "I suppose," she continued, "that he wouldn't be so well liked by other young men as she is by other girls, do you think?"

"I don't think, as a rule," said Mrs. Brinkley, "that men are half so appreciative of one another as women are. It's most amusing to see the open scorn with which two young fellows treat each other if a pretty girl introduces them."

All the ladies joined in the laugh with which Mrs. Brinkley herself led off. But Miss Cotton stopped laughing first.

"Do you mean,", she asked, "that if a gentleman were generally popular with gentlemen it would be—"

"Because he wasn't generally so with women? Something like that—if you'll leave Mr. Mavering out of the question. Oh, how very good of them!" she broke off, and all the ladies glanced at Mavering and Alice where they had stopped at the further end of the piazza, and were looking off. "Now I can probably finish before they get back here again. What I do mean, Miss Cotton, is that neither sex willingly accepts the favourites of the other."

"Yes," said Miss Cotton admissively.

"And all that saves Miss Pasmer is that she has not only the qualities that women like in women, but some of the qualities that men, like in them. She's thoroughly human."

A little sensation, almost a murmur, not wholly of assent, went round that circle which had so nearly voted Alice a saint.

"In the first place, she likes to please men."

"Oh!" came from the group.

"And that makes them like her—if it doesn't go too far, as her mother says."

The ladies all laughed, recognising a common turn of phrase in Mrs. Pasmer.

"I should think," said Mrs. Stamwell, "that she would believe a little in heredity if she noticed that in her daughter;" and the ladies laughed again.

"Then," Mrs. Brinkley resumed concerning Alice, "she has a very pretty face—an extremely pretty face: she has a tender voice, and she's very, very graceful—in rather an odd way; perhaps it's only a fascinating awkwardness. Then she dresses—or her mother dresses her—exquisitely." The ladies, with another sensation, admitted the perfect accuracy with which these points had been touched.

"That's what men like, what they fall in love with, what Mr. Mavering's in love with this instant. It's no use women's flattering themselves that they don't, for they do. The rest of the virtues and graces and charms are for women. If that serious girl could only know the silly things that that amiable simpleton is taken with in her, she'd—"

"Never speak to him again?" suggested Miss Cotton.

"No, I don't say that. But she would think twice before marrying him."

"And then do it," said Mrs. Stamwell pensively, with eyes that seemed looking far into the past.

"Yes, and quite right to do it," said Mrs. Brinkley. "I don't know that we should be very proud ourselves if we confessed just what caught our fancy in our husbands. For my part I shouldn't like to say how much a light hat that Mr. Brinkley happened to be wearing had to do with the matter."

The ladies broke into another laugh, and then checked themselves, so that Mrs. Pasmer, coming out of the corridor upon them, naturally thought they were laughing at her. She reflected that if she had been in their place she would have shown greater tact by not stopping just at that instant.

But she did not mind. She knew that they talked her over, but having a very good conscience, she simply talked them over in return. "Have you seen my daughter within a few minutes?" she asked.

"She was with Mr. Mavering at the end of the piazza a moment ago," said Mrs. Brinkley. "They must leave just gone round the corner of the building."

"Oh," said Mrs. Pasmer. She had a novel, with her finger between its leaves, pressed against her heart, after the manner of ladies coming out on hotel piazzas. She sat down and rested it on her knee, with her hand over the top.

Miss Cotton bent forward, and Mrs. Pasmer lifted her fingers to let her see the name of the book.

"Oh yes," said Miss Cotton. "But he's so terribly pessimistic, don't you think?"

"What is it?" asked Mrs. Brinkley.

"Fumée," said Mrs. Pasmer, laying the book title upward on her lap for every one to see.

"Oh yes," said Mrs. Brinkley, fanning herself. "Tourguenief. That man gave me the worst quarter of an hour with his 'Lisa' that I ever had."

"That's the same as the 'Nichee des Gentilshommes', isn't it?" asked Mrs. Pasmer, with the involuntary superiority of a woman who reads her Tourguenief in French.

"I don't know. I had it in English. I don't build my ships to cross the sea in, as Emerson says; I take those I find built."

"Ah! I was already on the other side," said Mrs. Pasmer softly. She added: "I must get Lisa. I like a good heart-break; don't you? If that's what gave you the bad moment."

"Heart-break? Heart-crush! Where Lavretsky comes back old to the scene of his love for Lisa, and strikes that chord on the piano—well, I simply wonder that I'm alive to recommend the book to you.

"Do you know," said Miss Cotton, very deferentially, "that your daughter always made me think of Lisa?"

"Indeed!" cried Mrs. Pasmer, not wholly pleased, but gratified that she was able to hide her displeasure. "You make me very curious."

"Oh, I doubt if you'll see more than a mere likeness of temperament," Mrs. Brinkley interfered bluntly. "All the conditions are so different. There couldn't be an American Lisa. That's the charm of these Russian tragedies. You feel that they're so perfectly true there, and so perfectly impossible here. Lavretsky would simply have got himself divorced from Varvara Pavlovna, and no clergyman could have objected to marrying him to Lisa."

"That's what I mean by his pessimism," said Miss Cotton. "He leaves you no hope. And I think that despair should never be used in a novel except for some good purpose; don't you, Mrs. Brinkley?"

"Well," said Mrs. Brinkley, "I was trying to think what good purpose despair could be put to, in a book or out of it."

"I don't think," said Mrs. Pasmer, referring to the book in her lap, "that he leaves you altogether in despair here, unless you'd rather he'd run off with Irene than married Tatiana."

"Oh, I certainly didn't wish that;" said Miss Cotton, in self-defence, as if the shot had been aimed at her.

"The book ends with a marriage; there's no denying that," said Mrs. Brinkley, with a reserve in her tone which caused Mrs. Pasmer to continue for her—

"And marriage means happiness—in a book."

"I'm not sure that it does in this case. The time would come, after Litvinof had told Tatiana everything, when she would have to ask herself, and not once only, what sort of man it really was who was willing to break his engagement and run off with another man's wife, and whether he could ever repent enough for it. She could make excuses for him, and would, but at the bottom of her heart—No, it seems to me that there, almost for the only time, Tourguenief permitted himself an amiable weakness. All that part of the book has the air of begging the question."

"But don't you see," said Miss Cotton, leaning forward in the way she had when very earnest, "that he means to show that her love is strong enough for all that?"

"But he doesn't, because it isn't. Love isn't strong enough to save people from unhappiness through each other's faults. Do you suppose that so many married people are unhappy in each other because they don't love each other? No; it's because they do love each other that their faults are such a mutual torment. If they were indifferent, they wouldn't mind each other's faults. Perhaps that's the reason why there are so many American divorces; if they didn't care, like Europeans, who

William Dean Howells

don't marry for love, they could stand it."

"Then the moral is," said Mrs. Pasmer, at her lightest through the surrounding gravity, "that as all Americans marry for love, only Americans who have been very good ought to get married."

"I'm not sure that the have-been goodness is enough either," said Mrs. Brinkley, willing to push it to the absurd. "You marry a man's future as well as his past."

"Dear me! You are terribly exigeante, Mrs. Brinkley," said Mrs. Pasmer.

"One can afford to be so—in the abstract," answered Mrs. Brinkley.

They all stopped talking and looked at John Munt, who was coming toward them, and each felt a longing to lay the matter before him.

There was probably not a woman among them but had felt more, read more, and thought more than John Munt, but he was a man, and the mind of a man is the court of final appeal for the wisest women. Till some man has pronounced upon their wisdom, they do not know whether it is wisdom or not.

Munt drew up his chair, and addressed himself to the whole group through Mrs. Pasmer: "We are thinking of getting up a little picnic to-morrow."

XIV

The day of the picnic struggled till ten o'clock to peer through the fog that wrapt it with that remote damp and coolness and that nearer drouth and warmth which some fogs have. The low pine groves hung full of it, and it gave a silvery definition to the gossamer threads running from one grass spear to another in spacious networks over the open levels of the old fields that stretch back from the bluff to the woods. At last it grew thinner, somewhere over the bay; then you could see the smooth water through it; then it drifted off in ragged fringes before a light breeze: when you looked landward again it was all gone there, and seaward it had gathered itself in a low, dun bank along the horizon. It was the kind of fog that people interested in Campobello admitted as apt to be common there, but claimed as a kind of local virtue when it began to break away. They said that it was a very dry fog, not like Newport, and asked you to notice that it did not wet you at all.

Four or five carriages, driven by the gentlemen of the party, held the picnic, which was destined for that beautiful cove on the Bay of Fundy where the red granite ledges, smooth-washed by ages of storm and sun, lend themselves to such festivities as if they had been artificially fashioned into shelves and tables. The whole place is yet so new to men that this haunt has not acquired that air of repulsive custom which the egg shells and broken bottles and sardine boxes of many seasons give. Or perhaps the winter tempests heap the tides of the bay over the ledge, and wash it clean of these vulgar traces of human resort, and enable it to offer as fresh a welcome to the picnics of each

William Dean Howells

successive summer as if there had never been a picnic in that place before.

This was the sense that Mavering professed to have received from it, when he jumped out of the beach wagon in which he had preceded the other carriages through the weird forest lying between the fringe of farm fields and fishing-villages on the western shore of the island and these lonely coasts of the bay. As far as the signs of settled human habitation last, the road is the good hard country road of New England, climbing steep little hills, and presently leading through long tracts of woodland. But at a certain point beyond the furthest cottage you leave it, and plunge deep into the heart of the forest, vaguely traversed by the wheel-path carried through since the island was opened to summer sojourn. Road you can hardly call it, remembering its curious pauses and hesitations when confronted with stretches of marshy ground, and its staggering progress over the thick stubble of saplings through which it is cut. The progress of teams over it is slow, but there is such joy of wildness in the solitudes it penetrates that; if the horses had any gait slower than a walk, one might still wish to stay them. It is a Northern forest, with the air of having sprang quickly up in the fierce heat and haste of the Northern summers. The small firs are set almost as dense as rye in a field, and in their struggle to the light they have choked one another so that there is a strange blight of death and defeat on all that vigour of life. Few of the trees have won any lofty growth; they seem to have died and fallen when they were about to outstrip the others in size, and from their decay a new sylvan generation riots rankly upward. The surface of the ground is thinly clothed with a deciduous undergrowth, above which are the bare, spare stems of the evergreens, and then their limbs thrusting into one another in a sombre tangle, with locks of long yellowish-white moss, like the grey pendants of the Southern pines, dripping from them and draining their brief life.

In such a place you must surrender yourself to its influences, profoundly yet vaguely melancholy, or you must resist them with whatever gaiety is in you, or may be conjured out of others. It was conceded that Mavering was the life of the party, as the phrase goes. His light-heartedness, as kindly and sympathetic as it was inexhaustible, served to carry them over the worst places in the road of itself. He jumped down and ran back, when he had passed a bad bit, to see if the others were getting through safely; the least interesting of the party had some proof of his impartial friendliness; he promised an early and triumphant emergence from all difficulties; he started singing, and sacrificed himself in several tunes, for he could not sing well; his laugh seemed to be always coming back to Alice, where she rode late in the little procession; several times, with the deference which he delicately qualified for her, he came himself to see if he could not do something for her.

"Miss Pasmer," croaked her friend Miss Anderson, who always began in that ceremonious way with her, and got to calling her Alice further along in the conversation, "if you don't drop something for that poor fellow to run back two or three miles and get, pretty soon, I'll do it myself. It's peyfectly disheaytening to see his disappointment when you tell him theye's nothing to be done."

"He seems to get over it," said Alice evasively. She smiled with pleasure in Miss Anderson's impeachment, however.

"Oh, he keeps coming, if that's what you mean. But do drop an umbrella, or a rubber, or something, next time, just to show a proper appreciation."

But Mavering did not come any more. Just before they got to the cove, Miss Anderson leaned over again to whisper in Alice's ear, "I told you he was huyt. Now you must be very good to him the rest of the time."

Upon theory a girl of Alice Pasmer's reserve ought to have resented this intervention, but it is not probable she did. She flushed a little, but not with offence, apparently; and she was kinder to Mavering, and let him do everything for her that he could invent in transferring the things from the wagons to

William Dean Howells

the rocks.

The party gave a gaiety to the wild place which accented its proper charm, as they scattered themselves over the ledges on the bright shawls spread upon the level spaces. On either hand craggy bluffs hemmed the cove in, but below the ledge it had a pebbly beach strewn with drift-wood, and the Bay of Fundy gloomed before it with small fishing craft tipping and tilting on the swell in the foreground, and dim sail melting into the dun fog bank at the horizon's edge.

The elder ladies of the party stood up, or stretched themselves on the shawls, as they found this or that posture more restful after their long drive; one, who was skilled in making coffee, had taken possession of the pot, and was demanding fire and water for it. The men scattered themselves over the beach, and brought her drift enough to roast an ox; two of them fetched water from the spring at the back of the ledge, whither they then carried the bottles of ale to cool in its thrilling pool. Each after his or her fashion symbolised a return to nature by some act or word of self-abandon.

"You ought to have brought heavier shoes," said Mrs. Pasmer, with a serious glance at her daughter's feet. "Well, never mind," she added. "It doesn't matter if you do spoil them."

"Really," cried Mrs Brinkley, casting her sandals from her, "I will not be enslaved to rubbers in such a sylvan scene as this, at any rate."

"Look at Mrs. Stamwell!" said Miss Cotton. "She's actually taken her hat off."

Mrs. Stamwell had not only gone to this extreme, but had tied a lightly fluttering handkerchief round her hair. She said she should certainly not put on that heavy thing again till she got in sight of civilisation.

At these words Miss Cotton boldly drew off her gloves, and

put them in her pocket.

The young girls, slim in their blues flannel skirts and their broad white canvas belts, went and came over the rocks. There were some children in the party, who were allowed to scream uninterruptedly in the games which they began to play as soon as they found their feet after getting out of the wagons.

Some of the gentlemen drove a stake into the beach, and threw stones at it, to see which could knock off the pebble balanced on its top. Several of the ladies joined them in the sport, and shrieked and laughed when they made wild shots with the missiles the men politely gathered for them.

Alice had remained with Mavering to help the hostess of the picnic lay the tables, but her mother had followed those who went down to the beach. At first Mrs. Pasmer looked on at the practice of the stone-throwers with disapproval; but suddenly she let herself go in this, as she did in other matters that her judgment condemned, and began to throw stones herself; she became excited, and made the wildest shots of any, accepting missiles right and left, and making herself dangerous to everybody within a wide circle. A gentleman who had fallen a victim to her skill said, "Just wait, Mrs. Pasmer, till I get in front of the stake."

The men became seriously interested, and worked themselves red and hot; the ladies soon gave it up, and sat down on the sand and began to talk. They all owned themselves hungry, and from time to time they looked up anxiously at the preparations for lunch on the ledge, where white napkins were spread, with bottles at the four corners to keep them from blowing away. This use of the bottles was considered very amusing; the ladies tried to make jokes about it, and the desire to be funny spread to certain of the men who had quietly left off throwing at the stake because they had wrenched their shoulders; they succeeded in being merry. They said they thought that coffee took a long time to boil.

A lull of expectation fell upon all; even Mavering sat down on the rocks near the fire, and was at rest a few minutes, by order of Miss Anderson, who said that the sight of his activity tired her to death.

"I wonder why always boiled ham at a picnic!" said the lady who took a final plate of it from a basket. "Under the ordinary conditions, few of us can be persuaded to touch it."

"It seems to be dear to nature, and to nature's children," said Mrs. Brinkley. "Perhaps because their digestions are strong."

"Don't you wish that something could be substituted for it?" asked Miss. Cotton.

"There have been efforts to replace it with chicken and tongue in sandwiches;" said Mrs. Brinkley; "but I think they've only measurably succeeded—about as temperance drinks have in place of the real strong waters."

"On the boat coming up," said Mavering, "we had a troupe of genuine darky minstrels. One of them sang a song about ham that rather took me—

"'Ham, good old ham! Ham is de best ob meat; It's always good and sweet; You can bake it, you can boil it, You can fry it, you can broil it—Ham, good old ham!'"

"Oh, how good!" sighed Mrs. Brinkley. "How sincere! How native! Go on, Mr. Mavering, for ever."

"I haven't the materials," said Mavering, with his laugh. "The rest was da capo. But there was another song, about a coloured lady—"

"'Six foot high and eight foot round, Holler ob her foot made a hole in de ground.'"

"Ah, that's an old friend," said Mrs. Brinkley. "I remember

hearing of that coloured lady when I was a girl. But it's a fine flight of the imagination. What else did they sing?"

"I can't remember. But there was something they danced—to show how a rheumatic old coloured uncle dances."

He jumped nimbly up, and sketched the stiff and limping figure he had seen. It was over in a flash. He dropped down again, laughing.

"Oh, how wonderfully good!" cried Mrs. Brinkley, with frank joy. "Do it again."

"Encore! Oh, encore!" came from the people on the beach.

Mavering jumped to his feet, and burlesqued the profuse bows of an actor who refuses to repeat; he was about to drop down again amidst their wails of protest.

"No, don't sit down, Mr. Mavering," said the lady who had introduced the subject of ham. "Get some of the young ladies, and go and gather some blueberries for the dessert. There are all the necessaries of life here, but none of the luxuries."

"I'm at the service of the young ladies as an escort," said Mavering gallantly, with an infusion of joke. "Will you come and pick blueberries under my watchful eyes, Miss Pasmer?"

"They've gone to pick blueberries," called the lady through her tubed hand to the people on the beach, and the younger among them scrambled up the rocks for cups and bowls to follow them.

Mrs. Pasmer had an impulse to call her daughter back, and to make some excuse to keep her from going. She was in an access of decorum, naturally following upon her late outbreak, and it seemed a very pronounced thing for Alice to be going off into the woods with the young man; but it would have been a pronounced thing to prevent her, and so Mrs. Pasmer submitted.

"Isn't it delightful," asked Mrs. Brinkley, following them with her eyes, "to see the charm that gay young fellow has for that serious girl? She looked at him while he was dancing as if she couldn't take her eyes off him, and she followed him as if he drew her by an invisible spell. Not that spells are ever visible," she added, saving herself. "Though this one seems to be," she added further, again saving herself.

"Do you really think so?" pleaded Miss Cotton.

"Well, I say so, whatever I think. And I'm not going to be caught up on the tenter-hooks of conscience as to all my meanings, Miss Cotton. I don't know them all. But I'm not one of the Aliceolaters, you know."

"No; of course not. But shouldn't you—Don't you think it would be a great pity—She's so superior, so very uncommon in every way, that it hardly seems—Ah, I should so like to see some one really fine—not a coarse fibre in him, don't you know. Not that Mr. Mavering's coarse. But beside her he does seem so light!"

"Perhaps that's the reason she likes him."

"No, no! I can't believe that. She must see more in him than we can."

"I dare say she thinks she does. At any rate, it's a perfectly evident case on both sides; and the frank way he's followed her up here, and devoted himself to her, as if—well, not as if she were the only girl in the world, but incomparably the best—is certainly not common."

"No," sighed Miss Cotton, glad to admit it; "that's beautiful."

XV

In the edge of the woods and the open spaces among the trees the blueberries grew larger and sweeter in the late Northern summer than a more southern sun seems to make them. They hung dense upon the low bushes, and gave them their tint through the soft grey bloom that veiled their blue. Sweet-fern in patches broke their mass here and there, and exhaled its wild perfume to the foot or skirt brushing through it.

"I don't think there's anything much prettier than these clusters; do you, Miss Pasmer?" asked Mavering, as he lifted a bunch pendent from the little tree before he stripped it into the bowl he carried. "And see! it spoils the bloom to gather them." He held out a handful, and then tossed them away. "It ought to be managed more aesthetically for an occasion like this. I'll tell you what, Miss Pasmer: are you used to blueberrying?"

"No," she said; "I don't know that I ever went blueberrying before. Why?" she asked.

"Because, if you haven't, you wouldn't be very efficient perhaps, and so you might resign yourself to sitting on that log and holding the berries in your lap, while I pick them."

"But what about the bowls, then?"

"Oh, never mind them. I've got an idea. See here!" He clipped off a bunch with his knife, and held it up before her, tilting it

　　　　　William Dean Howells

this way and that. "Could anything be more graceful! My idea is to serve the blueberry on its native stem at this picnic. What do you think? Sugar would profane it, and of course they've only got milk enough for the coffee."

"Delightful!" Alice arranged herself on the log, and made a lap for the bunch. He would not allow that the arrangement was perfect till he had cushioned the seat and carpeted the ground for her feet with sweet-fern.

"Now you're something like a wood-nymph," he laughed. "Only, wouldn't a real wood-nymph have an apron?" he asked, looking down at her dress.

"Oh, it won't hurt the dress. You must begin now, or they'll be calling us."

He was standing and gazing at her with a distracted enjoyment of her pose. "Oh yes, yes," he answered, coming to himself, and he set about his work.

He might have got on faster if he had not come to her with nearly every bunch he cut at first, and when he began to deny himself this pleasure he stopped to admire an idea of hers.

"Well, that's charming—making them into bouquets."

"Yes, isn't it?" she cried delightedly, holding a bunch of the berries up at arm's-length to get the effect.

"Ah, but you must have some of this fern and this tall grass to go with it. Why, it's sweet-grass—the sweet-grass of the Indian baskets!"

"Is it?" She looked up at him. "And do you think that the mixture would be better than the modest simplicity of the berries, with a few leaves of the same?"

"No; you're right; it wouldn't," he said, throwing away his

ferns. "But you'll want something to tie the stems with; you must use the grass." He left that with her, and went back to his bushes. He added, from beyond a little thicket, as if what he said were part of the subject, "I was afraid you wouldn't like my skipping about there on the rocks, doing the coloured uncle."

"Like it?"

"I mean—I—you thought it undignified—trivial—"

She said, after a moment: "It was very funny; and people do all sorts of things at picnics. That's the pleasure of it, isn't it?"

"Yes, it is; but I know you don't always like that kind of thing."

"Do I seem so very severe?" she asked.

"Oh no, not severe. I should be afraid of you if you were. I shouldn't have dared to come to Campobello."

He looked at her across the blueberry bushes. His gay speech meant everything or nothing. She could parry it with a jest, and then it would mean nothing. She let her head droop over her work, and made no answer.

"I wish you could have seen those fellows on the boat," said Mavering.

"Hello, Mavering!" called the voice of John Munt, from another part of the woods.

"Alice!—Miss Pasmer!" came that of Miss Anderson.

He was going to answer, when he looked at Alice. "We'll let them see if they can find us," he said, and smiled.

Alice said nothing at first; she smiled too. "You know more

William Dean Howells

about the woods than I do. I suppose if they keep looking—"

"Oh yes." He came toward her with a mass of clusters which he had clipped. "How fast you do them!" he said, standing and looking down at her. "I wish you'd let me come and make up the withes for you when you need them."

"No, I couldn't allow that on any account," she answered, twisting some stems of the grass together.

"Well, will you let me hold the bunches while you tie them; or tie them when you hold them?"

"No."

"This once, then?"

"This once, perhaps."

"How little you let me do for you!" he sighed.

"That gives you a chance to do more for other people," she answered; and then she dropped her eyes, as if she had been surprised into that answer. She made haste to add: "That's what makes you so popular with—everybody!"

"Ah, but I'd rather be popular with somebody!"

He laughed, and then they both laughed together consciously; and still nothing or everything had been said. A little silly silence followed, and he said, for escape from it, "I never saw such berries before, even in September, on the top of Ponkwasset."

"Why, is it a mountain?" she asked. 'I thought it was a—falls."

"It's both," he said.

"I suppose it's very beautiful, isn't it! All America seems so lovely, so large."

"It's pretty in the summer. I don't know that I shall like it there in the winter if I conclude to—Did your—did Mrs. Pasmer tell you what my father wants me to do?"

"About going there to—manufacture?"

Mavering nodded. "He's given me three weeks to decide whether I would like to do that or go in for law. That's what I came up here for."

There was a little pause. She bent her head down over the clusters she was grouping. "Is the light of Campobello particularly good on such questions?" she asked.

"I don't mean that exactly, but I wish you could help me to some conclusion."

"Yes; why not?"

"It's the first time I've ever had a business question referred to me."

"Well, then, you can bring a perfectly fresh mind to it."

"Let me see," she said, affecting to consider. "It's really a very important matter?"

"It is to me."

After a moment she looked up at him. "I should think that you wouldn't mind living there if your business was there. I suppose it's being idle in places that makes them dull. I thought it was dull in London. One ought to be glad—oughtn't he?—to live in any place where there's something to do."

"Well, that isn't the way people usually feel," said Mavering.

"That's the kind of a place most of them fight shy of."

Alice laughed with an undercurrent of protest, perhaps because she had seen her parents' whole life, so far as she knew it, passed in this sort of struggle. "I mean that I hate my own life because there seems nothing for me to do with it. I like to have people do something."

"Do you really?" asked Mavering soberly, as if struck by the novelty of the idea.

"Yes!" she said, with exaltation. "If I were a man—"

He burst into a ringing laugh. "Oh no; don't!"

"Why?" she demanded, with provisional indignation.

"Because then there wouldn't be any Miss Pasmer."

It seemed to Alice that this joking was rather an unwarranted liberty. Again she could not help joining in his light-heartedness; but she checked herself so abruptly, and put on a look so austere, that he was quelled by it.

"I mean," he began—"that is to say—I mean that I don't understand why ladies are always saying that. I am sure they can do what they like, as it is."

"Do you mean that everything is open to them now?" she asked, disentangling a cluster of the berries from those in her lap, and beginning a fresh bunch.

"Yes," said Mavering. "Something like that—yes. They can do anything they like. Lots of them do."

"Oh yes, I know," said the girl. "But people don't like them to."

"Why, what would you like to be?" he asked.

She did not answer, but sorted over the clusters in her lap. "We've got enough now, haven't we?" she said.

"Oh, not half," he said. "But if you're tired you must let me make up some of the bunches."

"No, no! I want to do them all myself," she said, gesturing his offered hands away, with a little nether appeal in her laughing refusal.

"So as to feel that you've been of some use in the world?" he said, dropping contentedly on the ground near her, and watching her industry.

"Do you think that would be very wrong?" she asked. "What made that friend of yours—Mr. Boardman—go into journalism?"

"Oh, virtuous poverty. You're not thinking of becoming a newspaper woman, Miss Pasmer!"

"Why not?" She put the final cluster into the bunch in hand, and began to wind a withe of sweet-grass around the stems. He dropped forward on his knees to help her, and together they managed the knot. They were both flushed a little when it was tied, and were serious.

"Why shouldn't one be a newspaper woman, if Harvard graduates are to be journalists?"

"Well, you know, only a certain kind are."

"What kind?"

"Well, not exactly what you'd call the gentlemanly sort."

"I thought Mr. Boardman was a great friend of yours?"

"He is. He is one of the best fellows in the world. But you

William Dean Howells

must have seen that he wasn't a swell.'

"I should think he'd be glad he was doing something at once. If I were a—" She stopped, and they laughed together. "I mean that I should hate to be so long getting ready to do something as men are."

"Then you'd rather begin making wall-paper at once than studying law?"

"Oh, I don't say that. I'm not competent to advise. But I should like to feel that I was doing something. I suppose it's hereditary." Mavering stared a little. "One of my father's sisters has gone into a sisterhood. She's in England."

"Is she a—Catholic?" asked Mavering.

"She isn't a Roman Catholic."

"Oh yes!" He dropped forward on his knees again to help her tie the bunch she had finished. It was not so easy as the first.

"Oh, thank you!" she said, with unnecessary fervour.

"But you shouldn't like to go into a sisterhood, I suppose?" said Mavering, ready to laugh.

"Oh, I don't know. Why not?" She looked at him with a flying glance, and dropped her eyes.

"Oh, no reason, if you have a fancy for that kind of thing."

"That kind of thing?" repeated Alice severely.

"Oh, I don't mean anything disrespectful to it," said Mavering, throwing his anxiety off in the laugh he had been holding back. "And I beg your pardon. But I don't suppose you're in earnest."

"Oh no, I'm not in earnest," said the girl, letting her wrists fall upon her knees, and the clusters drop from her hands. "I'm not in earnest about anything; that's the truth—that's the shame. Wouldn't you like," she broke off, "to be a priest, and go round among these people up here on their frozen islands in the winter?"

"No," shouted Mavering, "I certainly shouldn't. I don't see how anybody stands it. Ponkwasset Falls is bad enough in the winter, and compared to this region Ponkwasset Falls is a metropolis. I believe in getting all the good you can out of the world you were born in—of course without hurting anybody else." He stretched his legs out on the bed of sweet-fern, where he had thrown himself, and rested his head on his hand lifted on his elbow. "I think this is what this place is fit for—a picnic; and I wish every one well out of it for nine months of the year."

"I don't," said the girl, with a passionate regret in her voice. "It would be heavenly here with—But you—no, you're different. You always want to share your happiness."

"I shouldn't call that happiness. But don't you?" asked Mavering.

"No. I'm selfish."

"You don't expect me to be believe that, I suppose."

"Yes," she went on, "it must be selfishness. You don't believe I'm so, because you can't imagine it. But it's true. If I were to be happy, I should be very greedy about it; I couldn't endure to let any one else have a part in it. So it's best for me to be wretched, don't you see—to give myself up entirely to doing for others, and not expect any one to do anything for me; then I can be of some use in the world. That's why I should like to go into a sisterhood."

Mavering treated it as the best kind of joke, and he was

confirmed in this view of it by her laughing with him, after a first glance of what he thought mock piteousness.

XVI

The clouds sailed across the irregular space of pale blue Northern sky which the break in the woods opened for them overhead. It was so still that they heard, and smiled to hear, the broken voices of the others, who had gone to get berries in another direction—Miss Anderson's hoarse murmur and Munt's artificial bass. Some words came from the party on the rocks.

"Isn't it perfect?" cried the young fellow in utter content.

"Yes, too perfect," answered the girl, rousing herself from the reverie in which they had both lost themselves, she did not know how long. "Shall you gather any more?"

"No; I guess there's enough. Let's count them." He stooped over on his hand's and knees, and made as much of counting the bunches as he could. "There's about one bunch and a half a piece. How shall we carry them? We ought to come into camp as impressively as possible."

"Yes," said Alice, looking into his face with dreamy absence. It was going through her mind, from some romance she had read, What if he were some sylvan creature, with that gaiety, that natural gladness and sweetness of his, so far from any happiness that was possible to her? Ought not she to be afraid of him? She was thinking she was not afraid.

"I'll tell you," he said. "Tie the stems of all the bunches

William Dean Howells

together, and swing them over a pole, like grapes of Eshcol. Don't you know the picture?"

"Oh yes."

"Hold on! I'll get the pole." He cut a white birch sapling, and swept off its twigs and leaves, then he tied the bunches together, and slung them over the middle of the pole.

"Well?" she asked.

"Now we must rest the ends on our shoulders."

"Do you think so?" she asked, with the reluctance that complies.

"Yes, but not right away. I'll carry them out of the woods, and we'll form the procession just before we come in sight."

Every one on the ledge recognised the tableau when it appeared, and saluted it with cheers and hand-clapping. Mrs. Pasmer bent a look on her daughter which she faced impenetrably.

"Where have you been?" "We thought you were lost!" "We were just organising a search expedition!" different ones shouted at them.

The lady with the coffee-pot was kneeling over it with her hand on it. "Have some coffee, you poor things! You must be almost starved."

"We looked about for you everywhere," said Munt, "and shouted ourselves dumb."

Miss Anderson passed near Alice. "I knew where you were all the time!"

Then the whole party fell to praising the novel conception of the bouquets of blueberries, and the talk began to flow away from Alice and Mavering in various channels.

All that had happened a few minutes ago in the blueberry patch seemed a far-off dream; the reality had died out of the looks and words.

He ran about from one to another, serving every one; in a little while the whole affair was in his hospitable hands, and his laugh interspersed and brightened the talk.

She got a little back of the others, and sat looking wistfully out over the bay, with her hands in her lap.

"Hold on just half a minute, Miss Pasmer! don't move!" exclaimed the amateur photographer, who is now of all excursions; he jumped to his feet, and ran for his apparatus. She sat still, to please him; but when he had developed his picture, in a dark corner of the rocks, roofed with a water-proof, he accused her of having changed her position. "But it's going to be splendid," he said, with another look at it.

He took several pictures of the whole party, for which they fell into various attitudes of consciousness. Then he shouted to a boat-load of sailors who had beached their craft while they gathered some drift for their galley fire. They had flung their arm-loads into the boat, and had bent themselves to shove it into the water.

"Keep still! don't move!" he yelled at them, with the imperiousness of the amateur photographer, and they obeyed with the helplessness of his victims. But they looked round.

"Oh, idiots!" groaned the artist.

"I always wonder what that kind of people think of us kind of people," said Mrs. Brinkley, with her eye on the photographer's subjects.

William Dean Howells

"Yes, I wonder what they do?" said Miss Cotton, pleased with the speculative turn which the talk might take from this. "I suppose they envy us?" she suggested.

"Well, not all of them; and those that do. not respectfully. They view, us as the possessors of ill-gotten gains, who would be in a very different place if we had our deserts."

"Do you really think so?"

"Yes, I think so; but I don't know that I really think so. That's another matter," said Mrs. Brinkley, with the whimsical resentment which Miss Cotton's conscientious pursuit seemed always to rouse in her.

"I supposed," continued Miss Cotton, "that it was only among the poor in the cities, who have begin misled by agitators, that the-well-to-do classes were regarded with suspicion."

"It seems to have begun a great while ago," said Mrs. Brinkley, "and not exactly with agitators. It was considered very difficult for us to get into the kingdom of heaven, you know."

"Yes, I know," assented Miss Cotton.

"And there certainly are some things against us. Even when the chance was given us to sell all we had and give it to the poor, we couldn't bring our minds to it, and went away exceeding sorrowful."

"I wonder," said Miss Cotton, "whether those things were ever intended to be taken literally?"

"Let's hope not," said John Munt, seeing his chance to make a laugh.

Mrs. Stamwell said, "Well, I shall take another cup of coffee, at any rate," and her hardihood raised another laugh.

"That always seems to me the most pitiful thing in the whole Bible," said Alice, from her place. "To see the right so clearly, and not to be strong enough to do it."

"My dear, it happens every day," said Mrs. Brinkley.

"I always felt sorry for that poor fellow, too," said Mavering. "He seemed to be a good fellow, and it was pretty hard lines for him."

Alice looked round at him with deepening gravity.

"Confound those fellows!" said the photographer, glancing at his hastily developed plate. "They moved."

XVII

The picnic party gathered itself up after the lunch, and while some of the men, emulous of Mavering's public spirit, helped some of the ladies to pack the dishes and baskets away under the wagon seats, others threw a corked bottle into the water, and threw stones at it. A few of the ladies joined them, but nobody hit the bottle, which was finally left bobbing about on the tide.

Mrs. Brinkley addressed the defeated group, of whom her husband was one, as they came up the beach toward the wagons. "Do you think that display was calculated to inspire the lower middle classes with respectful envy?"

Her husband made himself spokesman for the rest: "No; but you can't tell how they'd have felt if we'd hit it."

They all now climbed to a higher level, grassy and smooth, on the bluff, from which there was a particular view; and Mavering came, carrying the wraps of Mrs. Pasmer and Alice, with which he associated his overcoat. A book fell out of one of the pockets when he threw it down.

Miss Anderson picked the volume up. "Browning! He reads Browning! Superior young man!"

"Oh, don't say that!" pleaded Mavering.

"Oh, read something aloud!" cried another of the young ladies.

"Isn't Browning rather serious for a picnic?" he asked, with a glance at Alice; he still had a doubt of the effect of the rheumatic uncle's dance upon her, and would have been glad to give her some other aesthetic impression of him.

"Oh no!" said Mrs. Brinkley, "nothing is more appropriate to a picnic than conundrums; they always have them. Choose a good tough one."

"I don't know anything tougher than the 'Legend of Pernik'— or lovelier," he said, and he began to read, simply, and with a passionate pleasure in the subtle study, feeling its control over his hearers.

The gentlemen lay smoking about at their ease; at the end a deep sigh went up from the ladies, cut short by the question which they immediately fell into.

They could not agree, but they said, one after another: "But you read beautifully, Mr. Mavering!" "Beautifully!" "Yes, indeed!"

"Well, I'm glad there is one point clear," he said, putting the book away, and "I'm afraid you'll think I'm rather sentimental," he added, in a low voice to Alice, "carrying poetry around with me."

"Oh no!" she replied intensely; "I thank you."

"I thank you," he retorted, and their eyes met in a deep look.

One of the outer circle of smokers came up with his watch in his hand, and addressed the company, "Do you know what time it's got to be? It's four o'clock."

They all sprang up with a clamour of surprise.

Mrs. Pasmer, under cover of the noise, said, in a low tone, to her daughter, "Alice, I think you'd better keep a little more with me now."

"Yes," said the girl, in a sympathy with her mother in which she did not always find herself.

But when Mavering, whom their tacit treaty concerned, turned toward them, and put himself in charge of Alice, Mrs. Pasmer found herself dispossessed by the charm of his confidence, and relinquished her to him. They were going to walk to the Castle Rocks by the path that now loses and now finds itself among the fastnesses of the forest, stretching to the loftiest outlook on the bay. The savage woodland is penetrated only by this forgetful path, that passes now and then aver the bridge of a ravine, and offers to the eye on either hand the mystery deepening into wilder and weirder tracts of solitude. The party resolved itself into twos and threes, and these straggled far apart, out of conversational reach of one another. Mrs. Pasmer found herself walking and talking with John Munt.

"Mr. Pasmer hasn't much interest in these excursions," he suggested.

"No; he never goes," she answered, and, by one of the agile intellectual processes natural to women, she arrived at the question, "You and the Maverings are old friends, Mr. Munt?"

"I can't say about the son, but I'm his father's friend, and I suppose that I'm his friend too. Everybody seems to be so," suggested Munt.

"Oh Yes," Mrs. Pasmer assented; "he appears to be a universal favourite."

"We used to expect great things of Elbridge Mavering in college. We were rather more romantic than the Harvard men are nowadays, and we believed in one another more than they do. Perhaps we idealised one another. But anyway, our class thought Mavering could do anything. You know about his taste for etchings?"

"Yes," said Mrs. Pasmer, with a sigh of deep appreciation. "What gifted people!"

"I understand that the son inherits all his father's talent."

"He sketches delightfully."

"And Mavering wrote. Why, he was our class poet!" cried Munt, remembering the fact with surprise and gratification to himself. "He was a tremendous satirist."

"Really? And he seems so amiable now."

"Oh, it was only on paper."

"Perhaps he still keeps it up—on wall-paper?" suggested Mrs. Pasmer.

Munt laughed at the little joke with a good-will that flattered the veteran flatterer. "I should like to ask him that some time. Will you lend it to me?"

"Yes, if such a sayer of good things will deign to borrow—"

"Oh, Mrs. Pasmer!" cried Munt, otherwise speechless.

"And the mother? Do you know Mrs. Mavering?"

"Mrs. Mavering I've never seen."

"Oh!" said Mrs. Pasmer, with a disappointment for which Munt tried to console her.

"I've never even been at their place. He asked me once a great while ago; but you know how those things are. I've heard that she used to be very pretty and very gay. They went about a great deal, to Saratoga and Cape May and such places—rather out of our beat."

"And now?"

"And now she's been an invalid for a great many years. Bedridden, I believe. Paralysis, I think."

"Yes; Mrs. Saintsbury said something of the kind."

"Well," said Munt, anxious to add to the store of knowledge which this remark let him understand he had not materially increased, "I think Mrs. Mavering was the origin of the wallpaper—or her money. Mavering was poor; her father had started it, and Mavering turned in his talent."

"How very interesting! And is that the reason—its being ancestral—that Mr. Mavering wishes his son to go into it?"

"Is he going into it?" asked Munt.

"He's come up here to think about it."

"I should suppose it would be a very good thing," said Munt.

"What a very remarkable forest!" said Mrs. Pasmer, examining it on either side, and turning quite round. This gave her, from her place in the van of the straggling procession, a glimpse of Alice and Dan Mavering far in the rear.

"Don't you know," he was saying to the girl at the same moment, "it's like some of those Doré illustrations to the Inferno, or the Wandering Jew."

"Oh yes. I was trying to think what it was made me think I had seen it before," she answered. "It must be that. But how strange it is!" she exclaimed, "that sensation of having been there before—in some place before where you can't possibly have been."

"And do you feel it here?" he asked, as vividly interested as if they two had been the first to notice the phenomenon which has been a psychical consolation to so many young observers.

"Yes," she cried.

"I hope I was with you," he said, with a sudden turn of levity, which did not displease her, for there seemed to be a tender earnestness lurking in it. "I couldn't bear to think of your being alone in such a howling wilderness."

"Oh, I was with a large picnic," she retorted gaily. "You might have been among the rest. I didn't notice."

"Well, the next time, I wish you'd look closer. I don't like being left out." They were so far behind the rest that he devoted himself entirely to her, and they had grown more and more confidential.

They came to a narrow foot-bridge over a deep gorge. The hand-rail had fallen away. He sprang forward and gave her his hand for the passage. "Who helped you over here?" he demanded. "Don't say I didn't."

"Perhaps it was you," she murmured, letting him keep the fingers to which he clung a moment after they had crossed the bridge. Then she took them away, and said: "But I can't be sure. There were so many others."

"Other fellows?" he demanded, placing himself before her on the narrow path, so that she could not get by. "Try to remember, Miss Pasmer. This is very important. It would break my heart if it was really some one else." She stole a glance at his face, but it was smiling, though his voice was so earnest. "I want to help you over all the bad places, and I don't want any one else to have a hand in it."

The voice and the face still belied each other, and between them the girl chose to feel herself trifled with by the artistic temperament. "If you'll please step out of the way, Mr. Mavering," she said severely, "I shall not need anybody's help just here."

He instantly moved aside, and they were both silent, till she said, as she quickened her pace to overtake the others in front, "I don't see how you can help liking nature in such a place as this."

"I can't—human nature," he said. It was mere folly; and an abstract folly at that; but the face that she held down and away from him flushed with sweet consciousness as she laughed.

On the cliff beetling above the bay, where she sat to look out over the sad northern sea, lit with the fishing sail they had seen before, and the surge washed into the rocky coves far beneath them, he threw himself at her feet, and made her alone in the company that came and went and tried this view and that from the different points where the picnic hostess insisted they should enjoy it. She left the young couple to themselves, and Mrs. Pasmer seemed to have forgotten that she had bidden Alice to be a little more with her.

Alice had forgotten it too. She sat listening to Mavering's talk with a certain fascination, but not so much apparently because the meaning of the words pleased her as the sound of his voice, the motion of his lips in speaking, charmed her. At first he was serious, and even melancholy, as if he were afraid he had offended her; but apparently he soon believed that he had been forgiven, and began to burlesque his own mood, but still with a deference and a watchful observance of her changes of feeling which was delicately flattering in its way. Now and then when she answered something it was not always to the purpose; he accused her of not hearing what he said, but she would have it that she did, and then he tried to test her by proofs and questions. It did not matter for anything that was spoken or done; speech and action of whatever sort were mere masks of their young joy in each other, so that when he said, after he had quoted some lines befitting the scene they looked out on; "Now was that from Tennyson or from Tupper?" and she answered, "Neither; it was from Shakespeare," they joined, in the same happy laugh, and they laughed now and then without saying anything. Neither this nor that made them more glad or less; they were in a trance, vulnerable to nothing but the summons which must come to leave their dream behind, and issue into the waking world.

In hope or in experience such a moment has come to all, and it is so pretty to those who recognise it from the outside that no one has the heart to hurry it away while it can be helped. The affair between Alice and Mavering had evidently her mother's sanction, and all the rest were eager to help it on. When the party had started to return, they called to them, and let them come behind together. At the carriages they had what Miss Anderson called a new deal, and Alice and Mavering found themselves together in the rear seat of the last.

The fog began to come in from the sea, and followed them through the woods. When they emerged upon the highway it wrapped them densely round, and formed a little world, cosy, intimate, where they two dwelt alone with these friends of theirs, each of whom they praised for delightful qualities. The horses beat along through the mist, in which there seemed no progress, and they lived in a blissful arrest of time. Miss Anderson called back from the front seat, "My ear buyns; you're talkin' about me."

"Which ear?" cried Mavering.

"Oh, the left, of couyse."

"Then it's merely habit, Julie. You ought to have heard the nice things we were saying about you," Alice called.

"I'd like to hear all the nice things you've been saying."

This seemed the last effect of subtle wit. Mavering broke out in his laugh, and Alice's laugh rang above it.

Mrs. Pasmer looked involuntarily round from the carriage ahead.

"They seem to be having a good time," said Mrs. Brinkley at her side.

"Yes; I hope Alice isn't overdoing."

"I'm afraid you're dreadfully tired," said Mavering to the girl, in a low voice, as he lifted her from her place when they reached the hotel through the provisional darkness, and found that after all it was only dinner-time.

"Oh no. I feel as if the picnic were just beginning."

"Then you will come to-night?"

"I will see what mamma says."

"Shall I ask her?"

"Oh, perhaps not," said the girl, repressing his ardour, but not severely.

XVIII

They were going to have some theatricals at one of the cottages, and the lady at whose house they were to be given made haste to invite all the picnic party before it dispersed. Mrs. Pasmer accepted with a mental reservation, meaning to send an excuse later if she chose; and before she decided the point she kept her husband from going after dinner into the reading-room, where he spent nearly all his time over a paper and a cigar, or in sitting absolutely silent and unoccupied, and made him go to their own room with her.

"There is something that I must speak to you about," she said, closing the door, "and you must decide for yourself whether you wish to let it go any further."

"What go any further?" asked Mr. Pasmer, sitting down and putting his hand to the pocket that held his cigar-case with the same series of motions.

"No, don't smoke," she said, staying his hand impatiently. "I want you to think."

"How can I think if I don't smoke?"

"Very well; smoke, then. Do you want this affair with young Mavering to go any farther?"

"Oh!" said Pasmer, "I thought you had been looking after that." He had in fact relegated that to the company of the great

William Dean Howells

questions exterior to his personal comfort which she always decided.

"I have been looking after it, but now the time has come when you must, as a father, take some interest in it."

Pasmer's noble mask of a face, from the point of his full white beard to his fine forehead, crossed by his impressive black eyebrows, expressed all the dignified concern which a father ought to feel in such an affair; but what he was really feeling was a grave reluctance to have to intervene in any way. "What do you want me to say to him?" he asked.

"Why, I don't know that he's going to ask you anything. I don't know whether he's said anything to Alice yet," said Mrs. Pasmer, with some exasperation.

Her husband was silent, but his silence insinuated a degree of wonder that she should approach him prematurely on such a point.

"They have been thrown together all day, and there is no use to conceal from ourselves that they are very much taken with each other?"

"I thought," Pasmer said, "that you said that from the beginning. Didn't you want them to be taken with each other?"

"That is what you are to decide."

Pasmer silently refused to assume the responsibility.

"Well?" demanded his wife, after waiting for him to speak.

"Well what?"

"What do you decide?"

"What is the use of deciding a thing when it is all over?"

"It isn't over at all. It can be broken off at any moment."

"Well, break it off, then, if you like."

Mrs. Pasmer resumed the responsibility with a sigh. She felt the burden, the penalty, of power, after having so long enjoyed its sweets, and she would willingly have abdicated the sovereignty which she had spent her whole married life in establishing. But there was no one to take it up. "No, I shall not break it off," she said resentfully; "I shall let it go on." Then seeing that her husband was not shaken by her threat from his long-confirmed subjection, she added: "It isn't an ideal affair, but I think it will be a very good thing for Alice. He is not what I expected, but he is thoroughly nice, and I should think his family was nice. I've been talking with Mr. Munt about them to-day, and he confirms all that Etta Saintsbury said. I don't think there can be any doubt of his intentions in coming here. He isn't a particularly artless young man, but he's been sufficiently frank about Alice since he's been here." Her husband smoked on. "His father seems to have taken up the business from the artistic side, and Mr. Mavering won't be expected to enter into the commercial part at once. If it wasn't for Alice, I don't believe he would think of the business for a moment; he would study law. Of course it's a little embarrassing to have her engaged at once before she's seen anything of society here, but perhaps it's all for the best, after all: the main thing is that she should be satisfied, and I can see that she's only too much so. Yes, she's very much taken with him; and I don't wonder. He is charming."

It was not the first time that Mrs. Pasmer had reasoned in this round; but the utterance of her thoughts seemed to throw a new light on them, and she took a courage from them that they did not always impart. She arrived at the final opinion expressed, with a throb of tenderness for the young fellow whom she believed eager to take her daughter from her, and now for the first time she experienced a desolation in the prospect, as if it were an accomplished fact. She was morally a bundle of finesses, but at the bottom of her heart her daughter was all the world to her. She had made the girl her idol, and if, like some other heathen, she had not always used her idol with the greatest deference, if she had often expected the impossible from it, and made it pay for her disappointment, still she had never swerved from her worship of it. She suddenly asked herself, What if this young fellow, so charming and so good, should so wholly monopolise her child that she should no longer have any share in her? What if Alice, who had so long formed her first care and chief object in life, should contentedly lose herself in the love and care of another, and both should ignore her right to her? She answered herself with a pang that this might happen with any one Alice married, and that it would be no worse, at the worst, with Dan Mavering than with another, while her husband remained impartially silent. Always keeping within the lines to which his wife's supremacy had driven him, he felt safe there, and was not to be easily coaxed out of them.

Mrs. Pasmer rose and left him, with his perfect acquiescence, and went into her daughter's room. She found Alice there, with a pretty evening dress laid out on her bed. Mrs. Pasmer was very fond of that dress, and at the thought of Alice in it her spirits rose again.

"Oh, are you going, Alice?"

"Why, yes," answered the girl. "Didn't you accept?"

"Why, yes," Mrs. Pasmer admitted. "But aren't you tired?"

"Oh, not in the least. I feel as fresh as I did this morning. Don't you want me to go?"

"Oh yes, certainly, I want you to go—if you think you'll enjoy it."

"Enjoy it? Why, why shouldn't I enjoy it, mamma!"

"What are you thinking about? It's going to be the greatest kind of fun."

"But do you think you ought to look at everything simply as fun?" asked the mother, with unwonted didacticism.

"How everything? What are you thinking about, mamma?"

"Oh, nothing! I'm so glad you're going to wear that dress."

"Why, of course! It's my best. But what are you driving at, mamma?"

Mrs. Pasmer was really seeking in her daughter that comfort of a distinct volition which she had failed to find in her husband, and she wished to assure herself of it more and more, that she might share with some one the responsibility which he had refused any part in.

"Nothing. But I'm glad you wish so much to go." The girl dropped her hands and stared. "You must have enjoyed yourself to-day," she added, as if that were an explanation.

"Of course I enjoyed myself! But what has that to do with my wanting to go to-night?"

"Oh, nothing. But I hope, Alice, that there is one thing you have looked fully in the face."

"What thing?" faltered the girl, and now showed herself unable to confront it by dropping her eyes.

"Well, whatever you may have heard or seen, nobody else is in doubt about it. What do you suppose has brought Mr. Mavering here!"

"I don't know." The denial not only confessed that she did know, but it informed her mother that all was as yet tacit between the young people.

"Very well, then, I know," said Mrs. Pasmer; "and there is one thing that you must know before long, Alice."

"What?" she asked faintly.

"Your own mind," said her mother. "I don't ask you what it is, and I shall wait till you tell me. Of course I shouldn't have let him stay here if I had objected—"

"O mamma!" murmured the girl, dyed with shame to have the facts so boldly touched, but not, probably, too deeply displeased.

"Yes. And I know that he would never have thought of going into that business if he had not expected—hoped—"

"Mamma!"

"And you ought to consider—"

"Oh, don't! don't! don't!" implored the girl.

"That's all," said her mother, turning from Alice, who had hidden her face in her hands, to inspect the costume on the bed. She lifted one piece of it after another, turned it over, looked at it, and laid it down. "You can never get such a dress in this country."

She went out of the room, as the girl dropped her face in the pillow. An hour later they met equipped for the evening's pleasure. To the keen glance that her mother gave her, the daughter's eyes had the brightness of eyes that have been weeping, but they were also bright with that knowledge of her own mind which Mrs. Pasmer had desired for her. She met her mother's glance fearlessly, even proudly, and she carried her stylish costume with a splendour to which only occasions could stimulate her. They dramatised a perfect unconsciousness to each other, but Mrs. Pasmer was by no means satisfied with the decision which she had read in her daughter's looks. Somehow it did not relieve her of the responsibility, and it did not change the nature of the case. It was gratifying, of course, to see Alice the object of a passion so sincere and so ardent; so far the triumph was complete, and there was really nothing objectionable in the young man and his circumstances, though there was nothing very distinguished. But the affair was altogether different from anything that Mrs. Pasmer had imagined. She had supposed and intended that Alice should meet some one in Boston, and go through a course of society before reaching any decisive step. There was to be a whole season in which to look the ground carefully over, and the ground was to be all within certain well-ascertained and guarded precincts. But this that had happened was outside of these precincts, of at least on their mere outskirts. Class Day, of course, was all right; and she could not say that the summer colony at Campobello was not thoroughly and essentially Boston; and yet she felt that certain influences, certain sanctions, were absent. To tell the truth, she would not have cared for the feelings of Mavering's family in regard to the matter, except as they might afterward concern Alice, and the time had not come when she could recognise their existence in regard to the affair; and yet she could have wished that even as it was his family could have seen and approved it from the start. It would have been more regular.

With Alice it was a simpler matter, and of course deeper. For her it was only a question of himself and herself; no one else existed to the sublime egotism of her love. She did not call it by that name; she did not permit it to assert itself by any name; it was a mere formless joy in her soul, a trustful and blissful expectance, which she now no more believed he could disappoint than that she could die within that hour. All the rebellion that she had sometimes felt at the anomalous attitude exacted of her sex in regard to such matters was gone. She no longer thought it strange that a girl should be expected to ignore the admiration of a young man till he explicitly declared it, and should then be fully possessed of all the materials of a decision on the most momentous question in life; for she knew that this state of ignorance could never really exist; she had known from the first moment that he had thought her beautiful. To-night she was radiant for him. Her eyes shone with the look in which they should meet and give themselves to each other before they spoke—the look in which they had met already, in which they had lived that whole day.

XIX

The evening's entertainment was something that must fail before an audience which was not very kind. They were to present a burlesque of classic fable, and the parts, with their general intention, had been distributed to the different actors; but nothing had been written down, and, beyond the situations and a few points of dialogue, all had to be improvised. The costumes and properties had been invented from such things as came to hand. Sheets sculpturesquely draped the deities who took part; a fox-pelt from the hearth did duty as the leopard skin of Bacchus; a feather duster served Neptune for a trident; the lyre of Apollo was a dust-pan; a gull's breast furnished Jove with his grey beard.

The fable was adapted to modern life, and the scene had been laid in Campobello, the peculiarities of which were to be satirised throughout. The principal situation was to be a passage between Jupiter, represented by Mavering, and Juno, whom Miss Anderson personated; it was to be a scene of conjugal reproaches and reprisals, and to end in reconciliation, in which the father of the gods sacrificed himself on the altar of domestic peace by promising to bring his family to Campobello every year.

This was to be followed by a sketch of the Judgment of Paris, in which Juno and Pallas were to be personated by two young men, and Miss Anderson took the part of Venus.

The pretty drawing-room of the Trevors—young people from

Albany, and cousins of Miss Anderson—was curtained off at one end for a stage, and beyond the sliding doors which divided it in half were set chairs for the spectators. People had come in whatever dress they liked; the men were mostly in morning coats; the ladies had generally made some attempt at evening toilet, but they joined in admiring Alice Pasmer's costume, and one of them said that they would let it represent them all, and express what each might have done if she would. There was not much time for their tributes; all the lamps were presently taken away and set along the floor in front of the curtain as foot-lights, leaving the company in a darkness which Mrs. Brinkley pronounced sepulchral. She made her reproaches to the master of the house, who had effected this transposition of the lamps. "I was just thinking some very pretty and valuable things about your charming cottage, Mr. Trevor: a rug on a bare floor, a trim of varnished pine, a wall with half a dozen simple etchings on it, an open fire, and a mantelpiece without bric-a-brac, how entirely satisfying it all is! And how it upbraids us for heaping up upholstery as we do in town!"

"Go on," said the host. "Those are beautiful thoughts."

"But I can't go on in the dark," retorted Mrs. Brinkley. "You can't think in the dark, much less talk. Can you, Mrs. Pasmer?" Mrs. Pasmer, with Alice next to her, sat just in front of Mrs. Brinkley.

"No," she assented; "but if I could—YOU can thick anywhere, Mrs. Brinkley—Mrs. Trevor's lovely house would inspire me to it."

"Two birds with one stone—thank you, Mrs. Pasmer, for my part of the compliment. Pick yourself up, Mr. Trevor."

"Oh, thank you, I'm all right," said Trevor, panting after the ladies' meanings, as a man must. "I suppose thinking and talking in the dark is a good deal like smoking in the dark."

"No; thinking and talking are not at all like smoking under any conditions. Why in the world should they be?"

"Oh, I can't get any fun out of a cigar unless I can see the smoke," the host explained.

"Do you follow him, Mrs. Pasmer?"

"Yes, perfectly."

"Thank you, Mrs. Pasmer," said Trevor.

"I'll get you to tell me how you did it some time," said Mrs. Brinkley. "But your house is a gem, Mr. Trevor."

"Isn't it?" cried Trevor. "I want my wife to live here the year round." It was the Trevors' first summer in their cottage, and the experienced reader will easily recognise his mood. "But she's such a worldly spirit, she won't."

"Oh, I don't know about the year round. Do you, Mrs. Pasmer?"

"I should," said Alice, with the suddenness of youth, breaking into the talk which she had not been supposed to take any interest in.

"Is it proper to kiss a young lady's hand?" said Trevor gratefully, appealing to Mrs. Brinkley.

"It isn't very customary in the nineteenth century," said Mrs. Brinkley. "But you might kiss her fan. He might kiss her fan, mightn't he, Mrs. Pasmer?"

"Certainly. Alice, hold out your fan instantly."

The girl humoured the joke, laughing.

Trevor pressed his lips to the perfumed sticks. "I will tell Mrs.

Trevor," he said, "and that will decide her."

"It will decide her not to come here at all next year if you tell her all."

"He never tells me all," said Mrs. Trevor, catching so much of the talk as she came in from some hospitable cares in the dining-room. "They're incapable of it. What has he been doing now?"

"Nothing. Or I will tell you when we are alone, Mrs. Trevor," said Mrs. Brinkley, with burlesque sympathy. "We oughtn't to have a scene on both sides of the foot-lights."

A boyish face, all excitement, was thrust out between the curtains forming the proscenium of the little theatre. "All ready, Mrs. Trevor?"

"Yes, all ready, Jim."

He dashed the curtains apart, and marred the effect of his own disappearance from the scene by tripping over the long legs of Jove, stretched out to the front, where he sat on Mrs. Trevor's richest rug, propped with sofa cushions on either hand.

"So perish all the impious race of titans, enemies of the gods!" said Mavering solemnly, as the boy fell sprawling. "Pick the earth-born giant up, Vulcan, my son."

The boy was very small for his age; every one saw that the accident had not been premeditated, and when Vulcan appeared, with an exaggerated limp, and carried the boy off, a burst of laughter went up from the company.

It did not matter what the play was to have been after that; it all turned upon the accident. Juno came on, and began to reproach Jupiter for his carelessness. "I've sent Mercury upstairs for the aynica; but he says it s no use: that boy won't be able to pass ball for a week. How often have I told you not to sit with your feet out that way! I knew you'd hurt somebody."

"I didn't have my feet out," retorted Jupiter. "Besides," he added, with dignity, and a burlesque of marital special pleading which every wife and husband recognised, "I always sit with my feet out so, and I always will, so long as I've the spirit of a god."

"Isn't he delicious?" buzzed Mrs. Pasmer, leaning backward to whisper to Mrs. Brinkley; it was not that she thought what Dan had just said was so very fanny, but people are immoderately applausive of amateur dramatics, and she was feeling very fond of the young fellow.

The improvisation went wildly and adventurously on, and the curtains dropped together amidst the facile acclaim of the audience:

"It's very well for Jupiter that he happened to think of the curtain," said Mrs. Brinkley. "They couldn't have kept it up at that level much longer."

"Oh, do you think so?" softly murmured Mrs. Pasmer. "It seemed as if they could have kept it up all night if they liked."

"I doubt it. Mr. Trevor," said Mrs. Brinkley to the host, who had come up for her congratulations, "do you always have such brilliant performances?"

"Well, we have so far," he answered modestly; and Mrs. Brinkley laughed with him. This was the first entertainment at Trevor cottage.

"'Sh!" went up all round them, and Mrs. Trevor called across the room, in a reproachful whisper loud enough for every one to hear, "My dear!—enjoying yourself!" while Mavering stood between the parted curtains waiting for the attention of the company.

"On account of an accident to the call-boy and the mental exhaustion of some of the deities, the next piece will be omitted, and the performance will begin with the one after. While the audience is waiting, Mercury will go round and take up a collection for the victim of the recent accident, who will probably be indisposed for life. The collector will be accompanied by a policeman, and may be safely trusted."

He disappeared behind the curtain with a pas and r swirl of his draperies like the Lord Chancellor in Iolanthe, and the audience again abandoned itself to applause.

"How very witty he is!" said Miss Cotton, who sat near John Munt. "Don't you think he's really witty?"

"Yes," Munt assented critically. "But you should have known his father."

"Oh, do you know his father?"

"I was in college with him."

"Oh, do tell me about him, and all Mr. Mavering's family. We're so interested, you know, on account of—Isn't it pretty to have that little love idyl going on here? I wonder—I've been wondering all the time—what she thinks of all this. Do you suppose she quite likes it? His costume is so very remarkable!" Miss Cotton, in the absence of any lady of her intimate circle, was appealing confidentially to John Munt.

"Why, do you think there's anything serious between them?" he asked, dropping his head forward as people do in church when they wish to whisper to some one in the same pew.

"Why, yes, it seems so," murmured Miss Cotton. "His admiration is quite undisguised, isn't it?"

"A man never can tell," said Munt. "We have to leave those things to you ladies."

"Oh, every one's talking of it, I assure you. And you know his family?"

"I knew his father once rather better than anybody else."

"Indeed!"

"Yes." Munt sketched rather a flattered portrait of the elder Mavering, his ability, his goodness, his shyness, which he had always had to make such a hard fight with. Munt was sensible of an access of popularity in knowing Dan Mavering's people, and he did not spare his colours.

"Then it isn't from his father that he gets everything. He isn't in the least shy," said Miss Cotton.

"That must be the mother."

"And the mother?"

"The mother I don't know."

Miss Cotton sighed. "Sometimes I wish that he did show a little more trepidation. It would seem as if he were more alive to the great difference that there is between Alice Pasmer and other girls."

Munt laughed a man's laugh. "I guess he's pretty well alive to that, if he's in love with her."

"Oh, in a certain way, of course, but not in the highest way. Now, for instance, if he felt all her fineness as—as we do, I don't believe he'd be willing to appear before her just like that." The father of the gods wore a damask tablecloth of a pale golden hue and a classic pattern; his arms were bare, and rather absurdly white; on his feet a pair of lawn-tennis shoes had a very striking effect of sandals.

"It seems to me," Miss Cotton pursued; "that if he really

appreciated her in the highest way, he would wish never to do an undignified or trivial thing in her presence."

"Oh, perhaps it's that that pleases her in him. They say we're always taken with opposites."

"Yes—do you think so?" asked Miss Cotton.

The curtains were flung apart, and the Judgment of Paris followed rather tamely upon what had gone before, though the two young fellows who did Juno and Minerva were very amusing, and the dialogue was full of hits. Some of the audience, an appreciative minority, were of opinion that Mavering and Miss Anderson surpassed themselves in it; she promised him the most beautiful and cultured wife in Greece. "That settles it," he answered. They came out arm in arm, and Paris, having put on a striped tennis coat over his short-sleeved Greek tunic, moved round among the company for their congratulations, Venus ostentatiously showing the apple she had won.

"I can haydly keep from eating it," she explained to Alice; before whom she dropped Mavering's arm. "I'm awfully hungry. It's hayd woyk."

Alice stood with her head drawn back, looking at the excited girl with a smile, in which seemed to hover somewhere a latent bitterness.

Mavering, with a flushed face and a flying tongue, was exchanging sallies with her mother, who smothered him in flatteries.

Mrs. Trevor came toward the group, and announced supper. "Mr. Paris, will you take Miss Aphrodite out?"

Miss Anderson swept a low bow of renunciation, and tacitly relinquished Mavering to Alice.

"Oh, no, no!" said Alice, shrinking back from him, with an intensification of her uncertain smile. "A mere mortal?"

"Oh, how very good!" said Mrs. Trevor.

There began to be, without any one's intending it, that sort of tacit misunderstanding which is all the worse because it can only follow upon a tacit understanding like that which had established itself between Alice and Mavering. They laughed and joked together gaily about all that went on; they were perfectly good friends; he saw that she and her mother were promptly served; he brought them salad and ice-cream and coffee himself, only waiting officially upon Miss Anderson first, and Alice thanked him, with the politest deprecation of his devotion; but if their eyes met, it was defensively, and the security between them was gone. Mavering vaguely felt the loss, without knowing how to retrieve it, and it made him go on more desperately with Miss Anderson. He laughed and joked recklessly, and Alice began to mark a more explicit displeasure with her. She made her mother go rather early.

On her part, Miss Anderson seemed to find reason for resentment in Alice's bearing toward her. As if she had said to herself that her frank loyalty had been thrown away upon a cold and unresponsive nature, and that her harmless follies in the play had been met with unjust suspicions, she began to make reprisals, she began in dead earnest to flirt with Mavering. Before the evening passed she had made him seem taken with her; but how justly she had done this, and with how much fault of his, no one could have said. There were some who did not notice it at all, but these were not people who knew Mavering, or knew Alice very well.

William Dean Howells

XX

The next morning Alice was walking slowly along the road toward the fishing village, when she heard rapid, plunging strides down the wooded hillside on her right. She knew them for Mavering's, and she did not affect surprise when he made a final leap into the road, and shortened his pace beside her.

"May I join you, Miss Pasmer?"

"I am only going down to the herring-houses," she began.

"And you'll let me go with you?" said the young fellow. "The fact is—you're always so frank that you make everything else seem silly—I've been waiting up there in the woods for you to come by. Mrs. Pasmer told me you had started this way, and I cut across lots to overtake you, and then, when you came in sight, I had to let you pass before I could screw my courage up to the point of running after you. How is that for open-mindedness?"

"It's a very good beginning, I should think."

"Well, don't you think you ought to say now that you're sorry you were so formidable?"

"Am I so formidable?" she asked, and then recognised that she had been trapped into a leading question.

"You are to me. Because I would like always to be sure that I had pleased you, and for the last twelve hours I've only been able to make sure that I hadn't. That's the consolation I'm going away with. I thought I'd get you to confirm my impression explicitly. That's why I wished to join you."

"Are you—were you going away?"

"I'm going by the next boat. What's the use of staying? I should only make bad worse. Yesterday I hoped But last night spoiled everything. 'Miss Pasmer,'" he broke out, with a rush of feeling, "you must know why I came up here to Campobello."

His steps took him a little ahead of her, and he could look back into her face as he spoke. But apparently he saw nothing in it to give him courage to go on, for he stopped, and then continued, lightly: "And I'm going away because I feel that I've made a failure of the expedition. I knew that you were supremely disgusted with me last night; but it will be a sort of comfort if you'll tell me so."

"Oh," said Alice, "everybody thought it was very brilliant, I'm sure."

"And you thought it was a piece of buffoonery. Well, it was. I wish you'd say so, Miss Pasmer; though I didn't mean the playing entirely. It would be something to start from, and I want to make a beginning—turn over a new leaf. Can't you help me to inscribe a good resolution of the most iron-clad description on the stainless page? I've lain awake all night composing one. Wouldn't you like to hear it?"

"I can't see what good that would do," she said, with some relenting toward a smile, in which he instantly prepared himself to bask.

"But you will when I've done it. Now listen!"

"Please don't go on." She cut him short with a return to her severity, which he would not recognise.

"Well, perhaps I'd better not," he consented. "It's rather a long resolution, and I don't know that I've committed it perfectly yet. But I do assure you that if you were disgusted last night, you were not the only one. I was immensely disgusted myself; and why I wanted you to tell me so, was because when I have a strong pressure brought to bear I can brace up, and do almost anything," he said, dropping into earnest. Then he rose lightly again, and added, "You have no idea how unpleasant it is to lie awake all night throwing dust in the eyes of an accusing conscience."

"It must have been, if you didn't succeed," said Alice drily.

"Yes, that's it—that's just the point. If I'd succeeded, I should be all right, don't you see. But it was a difficult case." She turned her face away, but he saw the smile on her cheek, and he laughed as if this were what he had been trying to make her do. "I got beaten. I had to give up, and own it. I had to say that I had thrown my chance away, and I had better take myself off." He looked at her with a real anxiety in his gay eyes.

"The boat goes just after lunch, I believe," she said indifferently.

"Oh yes, I shall have time to get lunch before I go," he said, with bitterness. "But lunch isn't the only thing; it isn't even the main thing, Miss Pasmer."

"No?" She hardened her heart.

He waited for her to say something more, and then he went on. "The question is whether there's time to undo last night, abolish it, erase it from the calendar of recorded time—sponge it out, in short—and get back to yesterday afternoon." She made no reply to this. "Don't you think it was a very pleasant picnic, Miss Pasmer?" he asked, with pensive respectfulness.

"Very," she answered drily.

He cast a glance at the woods that bordered the road on either side. "That weird forest—I shall never forget it."

"No; it was something to remember," she said.

"And the blueberry patch? We mustn't forget the blueberry patch."

"There were a great many blueberries."

She walked on, and he said, "And that bridge—you don't have that feeling of having been here before?"

"No."

"Am I walking too fast for you, Miss Pasmer?"

"No; I like to walk fast."

"But wouldn't you like to sit down? On this wayside log, for example?" He pointed it out with his stick. "It seems to invite repose, and I know you must be tired."

"I'm not tired."

"Ah, that shows that you didn't lie awake grieving over your follies all night. I hope you rested well, Miss Pasmer." She said nothing. "If I thought—if I could hope that you hadn't, it would be a bond of sympathy, and I would give almost anything for a bond of sympathy just now, Miss Pasmer. Alice!" he said, with sudden seriousness. "I know that I'm not worthy even to think of you, and that you're whole worlds above me in every way. It's that that takes all heart out of me, and leaves me without a word to say when I'd like to say so much. I would like to speak—tell you—"

She interrupted him. "I wish to speak to you, Mr. Mavering,

William Dean Howells

and tell you that—I'm very tired, and I'm going back to the hotel. I must ask you to let me go back alone."

"Alice, I love you."

"I'm sorry you said it—sorry, sorry."

"Why?" he asked, with hopeless futility.

"Because there can be no love between us—not friendship even—not acquaintance."

"I shouldn't have asked for your acquaintance, your friendship, if—" His words conveyed a delicate reproach, and they stung her, because they put her in the wrong.

"No matter," she began wildly. "I didn't mean to wound you. But we must part, and we must never see each other again:"

He stood confused, as if he could not make it out or believe it. "But yesterday—"

"It's to-day now."

"Ah, no! It's last night. And I can explain."

"No!" she cried. "You shall not make me out so mean and vindictive. I don't care for last night, nor for anything that happened." This was not true, but it seemed so to her at the moment; she thought that she really no longer resented his association with Miss Anderson and his separation from herself in all that had taken place.

"Then what is it?"

"I can't tell you. But everything is over between us—that's all."

"But yesterday—and all these days past—you seemed—"

"It's unfair of you to insist—it's ungenerous, ungentlemanly."

That word, which from a woman's tongue always strikes a man like a blow in the face, silenced Mavering. He set his lips and bowed, and they parted. She turned upon her way, and he kept the path which she had been going.

It was not the hour when the piazzas were very full, and she slipped into the dim hotel corridor undetected, or at least undetained. She flung into her room, and confronted her mother.

Mrs. Pasmer was there looking into a trunk that had overflowed from her own chamber. "What is the matter?" she said to her daughter's excited face.

"Mr. Mavering—"

"Well?"

"And I refused him."

Mrs. Pasmer was one of those ladies who in any finality have a keen retrovision of all the advantages of a different conclusion. She had been thinking, since she told Dan Mavering which way Alice had gone to walk, that if he were to speak to her now, and she were to accept him, it would involve a great many embarrassing consequences; but she had consoled herself with the probability that he would not speak so soon after the effects of last night, but would only try at the furthest to make his peace with Alice. Since he had spoken, though, and she had refused him, Mrs. Pasmer instantly saw all the pleasant things that would have followed in another event. "Refused him?" she repeated provisionally, while she gathered herself for a full exploration of all the facts.

"Yes, mamma; and I can't talk about it. I wish never to hear his name again, or to see him, or to speak to him."

William Dean Howells

"Why, of course not," said Mrs. Pasmer, with a fine smile, from the vantage-ground of her superior years, "if you've refused him." She left the trunk which she had been standing over, and sat down, while Alice swept to and fro before her excitedly. "But why did you refuse him, my dear?"

"Why? Because he's detestable—perfectly ignoble."

Her mother probably knew how to translate these exalted expressions into the more accurate language of maturer life. "Do you mean last night?"

"Last night?" cried Alice tragically. "No. Why should I care for last night?"

"Then I don't understand what you mean," retorted Mrs. Pasmer. "What did he say?" she demanded, with authority.

"Mamma, I can't talk about it—I won't."

"But you must, Alice. It's your duty. Of course I must know about it. What did he say?"

Alice walked up and down the room with her lips firmly closed—like Mavering's lips, it occurred to her; and then she opened them, but without speaking.

"What did he say?" persisted her mother, and her persistence had its effect.

"Say?" exclaimed the girl indignantly. "He tried to make me say."

"I see," said Mrs. Pasmer. "Well?"

"But I forced him to speak, and then—I rejected him. That's all."

"Poor fellow!" said Mrs. Pasmer. "He was afraid of you."

"And that's what made it the more odious. Do you think I wished him to be afraid of me? Would that be any pleasure? I should hate myself if I had to quell anybody into being unlike themselves." She sat down for a moment, and then jumped up again, and went to the window, for no reason, and came back.

"Yes," said her mother impartially, "he's light, and he's round-about. He couldn't come straight at anything."

"And would you have me accept such a—being?"

Mrs. Pasmer smiled a little at the literary word, and continued: "But he's very sweet, and he's as good as the day's long, and he's very fond of you, and—I thought you liked him."

The girl threw up her arms across her eyes. "Oh, how can you say such a thing, mamma?"

She dropped into a chair at the bedside, and let her face fall into her hands, and cried.

Her mother waited for the gust of tears to pass before she said, "But if you feel so about it—"

"Mamma!" Alice sprang to her feet.

"It needn't come from you. I could make some excuse to see him—write him a little note—"

"Never!" exclaimed Alice grandly. "What I've done I've done from my reason, and my feelings have nothing to do with it."

"Oh, very well," said her mother, going out of the room, not wholly disappointed with what she viewed as a respite, and amused by her daughter's tragics. "But if you think that the feelings have nothing to do with such a matter, you're very much mistaken." If she believed that her daughter did not know her real motives in rejecting Dan Mavering, or had not been able to give them, she did not say so.

William Dean Howells

The little group of Aliceolaters on the piazza, who began to canvass the causes of Mavering's going before the top of his hat disappeared below the bank on the path leading to the ferry-boat, were of two minds. One faction held that he was going because Alice had refused him, and that his gaiety up to the last moment was only a mask to hide his despair. The other side contended that, if he and Alice were not actually engaged, they understood each other, and he was going away because he wanted to tell his family, or something of that kind. Between the two opinions Miss Cotton wavered with a sentimental attraction to either. "What do you really think?" she asked Mrs. Brinkley, arriving from lunch at the corner of the piazza where the group was seated.

"Oh, what does it matter, at their age?" she demanded.

"But they're just of the age when it does happen to matter," suggested Mrs. Stamwell.

"Yes," said Mrs. Brinkley, "and that's what makes the whole thing so perfectly ridiculous. Just think of two children, one of twenty and the other of twenty-three, proposing to decide their lifelong destiny in such a vital matter! Should we trust their judgment in regard to the smallest business affair? Of course not. They're babes in arms, morally and mentally speaking. People haven't the data for being wisely in love till they've reached the age when they haven't the least wish to be so. Oh, I suppose I thought that I was a grown woman too when I was twenty; I can look back and see that I did; and, what's more preposterous still, I thought Mr. Brinkley was a man at twenty-four. But we were no more fit to accept or reject each other at that infantile period—"

"Do you really think so?" asked Miss Cotton, only partially credulous of Mrs. Brinkley's irony.

"Yes, it does seem out of all reason," admitted Mrs. Stamwell.

"Of course it is," said Mrs. Brinkley. "If she has rejected him, she's done a very safe thing. Nobody should be allowed to marry before fifty. Then, if people married, it would be because they knew that they loved each other."

Miss Cotton reflected a moment. "It is strange that such an important question should have to be decided at an age when the judgment is so far from mature. I never happened to look at it in that light before."

"Yes," said Mrs. Brinkley—and she made herself comfortable in an arm chair commanding a stretch of the bay over which the ferry-boat must pass—"but it's only part and parcel of the whole affair. I'm sure that no grown person can see the ridiculous young things—inexperienced, ignorant, feather-brained—that nature intrusts with children, their immortal little souls and their extremely perishable little bodies, without rebelling at the whole system. When you see what most young mothers are, how perfectly unfit and incapable, you wonder that the whole race doesn't teeth and die. Yes, there's one thing I feel pretty sure of—that, as matters are arranged now, there oughtn't to be mothers at all, there ought to be only grandmothers."

The group all laughed, even Miss Cotton, but she was the first to become grave. At the bottom of her heart there was a doubt whether so light a way of treating serious things was not a little wicked.

"Perhaps," she said, "we shall have to go back to the idea that engagements and marriages are not intended to be regulated by the judgment, but by the affections."

"I don't know what's intended," said Mrs. Brinkley, "but I know what is. In ninety-nine cases out of a hundred the affections have it their own way, and I must say I don't think the judgment could make a greater mess of it. In fact," she continued, perhaps provoked to the excess by the deprecation she saw in Miss Cotton's eye, "I consider every broken engagement nowadays a blessing in disguise."

William Dean Howells

Miss Cotton said nothing. The other ladies said, "Why, Mrs. Brinkley!"

"Yes. The thing has gone altogether too far. The pendulum has swung in that direction out of all measure. We are married too much. And as a natural consequence we are divorced too much. The whole case is in a nutshell: if there were no marriages, there would be no divorces, and that great abuse would be corrected, at any rate."

All the ladies laughed, Miss Cotton more and more sorrowfully. She liked to have people talk as they do in genteel novels. Mrs. Brinkley's bold expressions were a series of violent shocks to her nature, and imparted a terrible vibration to the fabric of her whole little rose-coloured ideal world; if they had not been the expressions of a person whom a great many unquestionable persons accepted, who had such an undoubted standing, she would have thought them very coarse. As it was, they had a great fascination for her. "But in a case like that of"—she looked round and lowered her voice—"our young friends, I'm sure you couldn't rejoice if the engagement were broken off."

"Well, I'm not going to be 'a mush of concession,' as Emerson says, Miss Cotton. And, in the first place, how do you know they're engaged?"

"Ah, I don't; I didn't mean that they were. But wouldn't it be a little pathetic if, after all that we've seen going on, his coming here expressly on her account, and his perfect devotion to her for the past two weeks, it should end in nothing?"

"Two weeks isn't a very long time to settle the business of a lifetime."

"No."

"Perhaps she's proposed delay; a little further acquaintance."

"Oh, of course that would be perfectly right. Do you think she did?"

"Not if she's as wise as the rest of us would have been at her age. But I think she ought."

"Yes?" said Miss Cotton semi-interrogatively.

"Do you think his behaviour last night would naturally impress her with his wisdom and constancy?"

"No, I can't say that it would, but—"

"And this Alice of yours is rather a severe young person. She has her ideas, and I'm afraid they're rather heroic. She'd be just with him, of course. But there's nothing a man dreads so much as justice—some men."

"Yes," pursued Miss Cotton, "but that very disparity—I know they're very unlike—don't you think—"

"Oh yes, I know the theory about that. But if they were exactly alike in temperament, they'd be sufficiently unlike for the purposes of counterparts. That was arranged once for all when 'male and female created He them.' I've no doubt their fancy was caught by all the kinds of difference they find in each other; that's just as natural as it's silly. But the misunderstanding, the trouble, the quarrelling, the wear and tear of spirit, that they'd have to go through before they assimilated—it makes me tired, as the boys say. No: I hope, for the young man's own sake, he's got his conge."

"But he's so kind, so good—"

"My dear, the world is surfeited with kind, good men. There are half a dozen of them at the other end of the piazza smoking; and there comes another to join them," she added, as a large figure, semicircular in profile, advanced itself from a doorway toward a vacant chair among the smokers. "The very soul of kindness and goodness." She beckoned toward her husband, who caught sight of her gesture. "Now I can tell you all his mental processes. First, surprise at seeing some one beckoning; then astonishment that it's I, though who else should beckon him?—then wonder what I can want; then conjecture that I may want him to come here; then pride in his conjecture; rebellion; compliance."

The ladies were in a scream of laughter as Mr. Brinkley lumbered heavily to their group.

"What is it?" he asked.

"Do you believe in broken engagements? Now quick—off-hand!"

"Who's engaged?"

"No matter."

"Well, you know Punch's advice to those about to marry?"

"I know—chestnuts," said his wife scornfully. They dismissed each other with tender bluntness, and he went in to get a match.

"Ah, Mrs. Brinkley," said one of the ladies, "it would be of no use for you to preach broken engagements to any one who saw you and Mr. Brinkley together." They fell upon her, one after another, and mocked her with the difference between her doctrine and practice; and they were all the more against her because they had been perhaps a little put down by her whimsical sayings.

"Yes," she admitted. "But we've been thirty years coming to the understanding that you all admire so much; and do you think it was worth the time?"

XXI

Mavering kept up until he took leave of the party of young people who had come over on the ferry-boat to Eastport for the frolic of seeing him off. It was a tremendous tour de force to accept their company as if he were glad of it, and to respond to all their gay nothings gaily; to maintain a sunny surface on his turbid misery. They had tried to make Alice come with them, but her mother pleaded a bad headache for her; and he had to parry a hundred sallies about her, and from his sick heart humour the popular insinuation that there was an understanding between them, and that they had agreed together she should not come. He had to stand about on the steamboat wharf and listen to amiable innuendoes for nearly an hour before the steamer came in from St. John. The fond adieux of his friends, their offers to take any message back, lasted during the interminable fifteen minutes that she lay at her moorings, and then he showed himself at the stern of the boat, and waved his handkerchief in acknowledgment of the last parting salutations on shore.

When it was all over, he went down into his state-room, and shut himself in, and let his misery rollover him. He felt as if there were a flood of it, and it washed him to and fro, one gall of shame, of self-accusal, of bitterness, from head to foot. But in it all he felt no resentment toward Alice, no wish to wreak any smallest part of his suffering upon her. Even while he had hoped for her love, it seemed to him that he had not seen her in all that perfection which she now had in irreparable loss. His soul bowed itself fondly over the thought of her; and,

William Dean Howells

stung as he was by that last cruel word of hers, he could not upbraid her. That humility which is love casting out selfishness, the most egotistic of the passions triumphing over itself—Mavering experienced it to the full. He took all the blame. He could not see that she had ever encouraged him to hope for her love, which now appeared a treasure heaven—far beyond his scope; he could only call himself fool, and fool, and fool, and wonder that he could have met her in the remoteness of that morning with the belief that but for the follies of last night she might have answered him differently. He believed now that, whatever had gone before, she must still have rejected him. She had treated his presumption very leniently; she had really spared him.

It went on, over and over. Sometimes it varied a little, as when he thought of how, when she should tell her mother, Mrs. Pasmer must laugh. He pictured them both laughing at him; and then Mr. Pasmer—he had scarcely passed a dozen words with him-coming in and asking what they were laughing at, and their saying, and his laughing too.

At other times he figured them as incensed at his temerity, which must seem to them greater and greater, as now it seemed to him. He had never thought meanly of himself, and the world so far had seemed to think well of him; but because Alice Pasmer was impossible to him, he felt that it was an unpardonable boldness in him to have dreamed of her. What must they be saying of his having passed from the ground of society compliments and light flirtation to actually telling Alice that he loved her?

He wondered what Mrs. Pasmer had thought of his telling her that he had come to Campobello to consider the question whether he should study law or go into business, and what motive she had supposed he had in telling her that. He asked himself what motive he had, and tried to pretend that he had none. He dramatised conversations with Mrs. Pasmer in which he laughed it off.

He tried to remember all that had passed the day before at the picnic, and whether Alice had done or said anything to encourage him, and he could not find that she had. All her trust and freedom was because she felt perfectly safe with him from any such disgusting absurdity as he had been guilty of. The ride home through the mist, with its sweet intimacy, that parting which had seemed so full of tender intelligence, were parts of the same illusion. There had been nothing of it on her side from the beginning but a kindliness which he had now flung away for ever.

He went back to the beginning, and tried to remember the point where he had started in this fatal labyrinth of error. She had never misled him, but he had misled himself from the first glimpse of her.

Whatever was best in his light nature, whatever was generous and self-denying, came out in this humiliation. From the vision of her derision he passed to a picture of her suffering from pity for him, and wrung with a sense of the pain she had given him. He promised himself to write to her, and beg her not to care for him, because he was not worthy of that. He framed a letter in his mind, in which he posed in some noble attitudes, and brought tears into his eyes by his magnanimous appeal to her not to suffer for the sake of one so unworthy of her serious thought. He pictured her greatly moved by some of the phrases, and he composed for her a reply, which led to another letter from him, and so to a correspondence and a long and tender friendship. In the end he died suddenly, and then she discovered that she had always loved him. He discovered that he was playing the fool again, and he rose from the berth where he had tumbled himself. The state-room had that smell of parboiled paint which state-rooms have, and reminded him of the steamer in which he had gone to Europe when a boy, with the family, just after his mother's health began to fail.

He went down on the deck near the ladies' saloon, where the second-class passengers were gathered listening to the same band of plantation negroes who had amused him so much on the eastward trip. The passengers were mostly pock marked Provincials, and many of them were women; they lounged on the barrels of apples neatly piled up, and listened to the music without smiling. One of the negroes was singing to the banjo, and another began to do the rheumatic uncle's breakdown. Mavering said to himself: "I can't stand that. Oh, what a fool I am! Alice, I love you. O merciful heavens! O infernal jackass! Ow! Gaw!"

At the bow of the boat he found a gang of Italian labourers returning to the States after some job in the Provinces. They smoked their pipes and whined their Neapolitan dialect together. It made Mavering think of Dante, of the Inferno, to which he passed naturally from his self-denunciation for having been an infernal jackass. The inscription on the gate of hell ran through his mind. He thought he would make his life—his desolate, broken life—a perpetual exile, like Dante's. At the same time he ground his teeth, and muttered: "Oh, what a fool I am! Oh, idiot! beast! Oh! oh!" The pipes reminded him to smoke, and he took out his cigarette case. The Italians looked at him; he gave all the cigarettes among them, without keeping any for himself. He determined to spend the miserable remnant of his life in going about doing good and bestowing alms.

He groaned aloud, so that the Italians noticed it, and doubtless spoke of it among themselves. He could not understand their dialect, but he feigned them saying respectfully compassionate things. Then he gnashed his teeth again, and cursed his folly. When the bell rang for supper he found himself very hungry, and ate heavily. After that he went out in front of the cabin, and walked up and down, thinking, and trying not to think. The turmoil in his mind tired him like a prodigious physical exertion.

Toward ten o'clock the night grew rougher. The sea was so phosphorescent that it broke in sheets and flakes of pale bluish flame from the bows and wheel-houses, and out in the dark the waves revealed themselves in flashes and long gleams of fire. One of the officers of the boat came and hung with Mavering over the guard. The weird light from the water was reflected on their faces, and showed them to each other.

"Well, I never saw anything like this before. Looks like hell; don't it?" said the officer.

"Yes," said Mavering. "Is it uncommon?"

"Well, I should say so. I guess we're going to have a picnic."

Mavering thought of blueberries, but he did not say anything.

"I guess it's going to be a regular circus."

Mavering did not care. He asked incuriously, "How do you find your course in such weather?"

"Well, we guess where we are, and then give her so many turns of the wheel." The officer laughed, and Mavering laughed too. He was struck by the hollow note in his laugh; it seemed to him pathetic; he wondered if he should now always laugh so, and if people would remark it. He tried another laugh; it sounded mechanical.

He went to bed, and was so worn out that he fell asleep and began to dream. A face came up out of the sea, and brooded over the waters, as in that picture of Vedder's which he calls "Memory," but the hair was not blond; it was the colour of those phosphorescent flames, and the eyes were like it. "Horrible! horrible!" he tried to shriek, but he cried, "Alice, I love you." There was a burglar in the room, and he was running after Miss Pasmer. Mavering caught him, and tried to beat him; his fists fell like bolls of cotton; the burglar drew his breath in with a long, washing sound like water.

Mavering woke deathly sick, and heard the sweep of the waves. The boat was pitching frightfully. He struggled out into the saloon, and saw that it was five o'clock. In five hours more it would be a day since he told Alice that he loved her; it now seemed very improbable. There were a good many half-dressed people in the saloon, and a woman came running out of her state-room straight to Mavering. She was in her stocking feet, and her hair hung down her back.

"Oh! are we going down?" she implored him. "Have we struck? Oughtn't we to pray—somebody? Shall I wake the children?"

"Mavering reassured her, and told her there was no danger.

"Well, then," she said, "I'll go back for my shoes."

"Yes, better get your shoes."

The saloon rose round him and sank. He controlled his sickness by planting a chair in the centre and sitting in it with his eyes shut. As he grew more comfortable he reflected how he had calmed that woman, and he resolved again to spend his life in doing good. "Yes, that's the only ticket," he said to himself, with involuntary frivolity. He thought of what the officer had said, and he helplessly added, "Circus ticket—reserved seat." Then he began again, and loaded himself with execration.

The boat got into Portland at nine o'clock, and Mavering left her, taking his hand-bag with him, and letting his trunk go on to Boston.

The officer who received his ticket at the gangplank noticed the destination on it, and said, "Got enough?"

"Yes, for one while." Mavering recognised his acquaintance of the night before.

"Don't like picnics very much."

"No," said Mavering, with abysmal gloom. "They don't agree with me. Never did." He was aware of trying to make his laugh bitter. The officer did not notice.

Mavering was surprised, after the chill of the storm at sea, to find it rather a warm, close morning in Portland. The restaurant to which the hackman took him as the best in town was full of flies; they bit him awake out of the dreary reveries he fell into while waiting for his breakfast. In a mirror opposite he saw his face. It did not look haggard; it looked very much as it always did. He fancied playing a part through life—hiding a broken heart under a smile. "O you incorrigible ass!" he said to himself, and was afraid he had said it to the young lady who brought him his breakfast, and looked haughtily at him from under her bang. She was very thin, and wore a black jersey.

He tried to find out whether he had spoken aloud by addressing her pleasantly. "It's pretty cold this morning."

"What say?"

"Pretty cool."

"Oh yes. But it's pretty clo-ose," she replied, in her Yankee cantillation. She went away and left him to the bacon and eggs he had ordered at random. There was a fly under one of the slices of bacon, and Mavering confined himself to the coffee.

A man came up in a white cap and jacket from a basement in the front of the restaurant, where confectionery was sold, and threw down a mass of malleable candy on a marble slab, and began to work it. Mavering watched him, thinking fuzzily all the time of Alice, and holding long, fatiguing dialogues with the people at the Ty'n-y-Coed, whose several voices he heard.

He said to himself that it was worse than yesterday. He wondered if it would go on getting worse every day.

He saw a man pass the door of the restaurant who looked exactly like Boardman as he glanced in. The resemblance was explained by the man's coming back, and proving to be really Boardman.

XXII

Mavering sprang at him with a demand for the reason of his being there.

"I thought it was you as I passed," said Boardman, "but I couldn't make sure—so dark back here."

"And I thought it was you, but I couldn't believe it," said Mavering, with equal force, cutting short an interior conversation with Mr. Pasmer, which had begun to hold itself since his first glimpse of Boardman.

"I came down here to do a sort of one-horse yacht race to-day," Boardman explained.

"Going to be a yacht race? Better have some breakfast. Or better not—here. Flies under your bacon."

"Rough on the flies," said Boardman, snapping the bell which summoned the spectre in the black jersey, and he sat down. "What are you doing in Portland?"

Mavering told him, and then Boardman asked him how he had left the Pasmers. Mavering needed no other hint to speak, and he spoke fully, while Boardman listened with an agreeable silence, letting the hero of the tale break into self-scornful groans and doleful laughs, and ease his heart with grotesque, inarticulate noises, and made little or no comments.

William Dean Howells

By the time his breakfast came, Boardman was ready to say, "I didn't suppose it was so much of a mash."

"I didn't either," said Mavering, "when I left Boston. Of course I knew I was going down there to see her, but when I got there it kept going on, just like anything else, up to the last moment. I didn't realise till it came to the worst that I had become a mere pulp."

"Well, you won't stay so," said Boardman, making the first vain attempt at consolation. He lifted the steak he had ordered, and peered beneath it. "All right this time, any way."

"I don't know what you mean by staying so," replied Mavering, with gloomy rejection of the comfort offered.

"You'll see that it's all for the best; that you're well out of it. If she could throw you over, after leading you on—"

"But she didn't lead me on!" exclaimed Mavering. "Don't you understand that it was all my mistake from the first? If I hadn't been perfectly besotted I should have seen that she was only tolerating me. Don't you see? Why, hang it, Boardman, I must have had a kind of consciousness of it under my thick-skinned conceit, after all, for when I came to the point—when I did come to the point—I hadn't the sand to stick to it like a man, and I tried to get her to help me. Yes, I can see that I did now. I kept fooling about, and fooling about, and it was because I had that sort of prescience—of whatever you call it—that I was mistaken about it from the very beginning."

He wished to tell Boardman about the events of the night before; but he could not. He said to himself that he did not care about their being hardly to his credit; but he did not choose to let Alice seem to have resented anything in them; it belittled her, and claimed too much for him. So Boardman had to proceed upon a partial knowledge of the facts.

"I don't suppose that boomerang way of yours, if that's what you mean, was of much use," he said.

"Use? It ruined me! But what are you going to do? How are you going to presuppose that a girl like Miss Pasmer is interested in an idiot like you? I mean me, of course." Mavering broke off with a dolorous laugh. "And if you can't presuppose it, what are you going to do when it comes to the point? You've got to shillyshally, and then you've got to go it blind. I tell you it's a leap in the dark."

"Well, then, if you've got yourself to blame—"

"How am I to blame, I should like to know?" retorted Mavering, rejecting the first offer from another of the censure which he had been heaping upon himself: the irritation of his nerves spoke. "I did speak out at last—when it was too late. Well, let it all go," he groaned aimlessly. "I don't care. But she isn't to blame. I don't think I could admire anybody very much who admired me. No, sir. She did just right. I was a fool, and she couldn't have treated me differently."

"Oh, I guess it'll come out all right," said Boardman, abandoning himself to mere optimism.

"How come all right?" demanded Mavering, flattered by the hope he refused. "It's come right now. I've got my deserts; that's all."

"Oh no, you haven't. What harm have you done? It's all right for you to think small beer of yourself, and I don't see how you could think anything else just at present. But you wait awhile. When did it happen?"

Mavering took out his watch. "One day, one hour, twenty minutes, and fifteen seconds ago."

"Sure about the seconds? I suppose you didn't hang round a great while afterward?"

"Well, people don't, generally," said Mavering, with scorn.

"Never tried it," said Boardman, looking critically at his fried potatoes before venturing upon them. "If you had stayed, perhaps she might have changed her mind," he added, as if encouraged to this hopeful view by the result of his scrutiny.

"Where did you get your fraudulent reputation for common-sense, Boardman?" retorted Mavering, who had followed his examination of the potatoes with involuntary interest. "She won't change her mind; she isn't one of that kind. But she's the one woman in this world who could have made a man of me, Boardman."

"Is that so?" asked Boardman lightly. "Well, she is a good-looking girl."

"She's divine!"

"What a dress that was she had on Class Day!"

"I never think what she has on. She makes everything perfect, and then makes you forget it."

"She's got style; there's no mistake about that."

"Style!" sighed Mavering; but he attempted no exemplification.

"She's awfully graceful. What a walk she's got!"

"Oh, don't, don't, Boardman! All that's true, and all that's nothing—nothing to her goodness. She's so good, Boardman! Well, I give it up! She's religious. You wouldn't think that, may be; you can't imagine a pretty girl religious. And she's all the more intoxicating when she's serious; and when she's forgotten your whole worthless existence she's ten thousand times more fascinating than and other girl when she's going right for you. There's a kind of look comes into her eyes—kind of absence, rapture, don't you know—when she's serious, that brings your heart right into your mouth. She makes you think of some of those pictures—I want to tell you what she said the other day at a picnic when we were off getting blueberries, and you'll understand that she isn't like other girls—that she has a soul fall of—of—you know what, Boardman. She has high thoughts about everything. I don't believe she's ever had a mean or ignoble impulse—she couldn't have." In the business of imparting his ideas confidentially, Mavering had drawn himself across the table toward Boardman, without heed to what was on it.

"Look out! You'll be into my steak first thing you know."

"Oh, confound your steak?" cried Mavering, pushing the dish away. "What difference does it make? I've lost her, anyway."

"I don't believe you've lost her," said Boardman.

"What's the reason you don't?" retorted Mavering, with contempt.

"Because, if she's the serious kind of a girl you say she is, she wouldn't let you come up there and dangle round a whole fortnight without letting you know she didn't like it, unless she did like it. Now you just go a little into detail."

Mavering was quite willing. He went so much into detail that he left nothing to Boardman's imagination. He lost the sense of its calamitous close in recounting the facts of his story at Campobello; he smiled and blushed and laughed in telling certain things; he described Miss Anderson and imitated her voice; he drew heads of some of the ladies on the margin of a newspaper, and the tears came into his eyes when he repeated the cruel words which Alice had used at their last meeting.

"Oh, well, you must brace up," said Boardman. "I've got to go now. She didn't mean it, of course."

"Mean what?"

William Dean Howells

"That you were ungentlemanly. Women don't know half the time how hard they're hitting."

"I guess she meant that she didn't want me, anyway," said Mavering gloomily.

"Ah, I don't know about that. You'd better ask her the next time you see her. Good-bye." He had risen, and he offered his hand to Mavering, who was still seated.

"Why, I've half a mind to go with you."

"All right, come along. But I thought you might be going right on to Boston."

"No; I'll wait and go on with you. How, do you go to the race?"

"In the press boat."

"Any women?"

"No; we don't send them on this sort of duty."

"That settles it. I have got all I want of that particular sex for the time being." Mavering wore a very bitter air as he said this; it seemed to him that he would always be cynical; he rose, and arranged to leave his bag with the restaurateur, who put it under the counter, and then he went out with his friend.

The sun had come out, and the fog was burning away; there was life and lift in the air, which the rejected lover could not refuse to feel, and he said, looking round, and up and down the animated street. "I guess you're going to have a good day for it."

The pavement was pretty well filled with women who had begun shopping. Carriages were standing beside the pavement; a lady crossed the pavement from a shop door toward a coupe just in front of them, with her hand full of light packages; she dropped one of them, and Mavering sprang forward instinctively and picked it up for her.

"Oh, thank you!" she said, with the deep gratitude which society cultivates for the smallest services. Then she lifted her drooped eyelashes, and, with a flash of surprise, exclaimed, "Mr. Mavering!" and dropped all her packages that she might shake hands with him.

Boardman sauntered slowly on, but saw with a backward glance Mavering carrying the lady's packages to the coupe for her; saw him lift his hat there, and shake hands with somebody in the coupe, and then stand talking beside it. He waited at the corner of the block for Mavering to come up, affecting an interest in the neck-wear of a furnisher's window.

In about five minutes Mavering joined him.

"Look here, Boardman! Those ladies have snagged onto me."

"Are there two of them?"

"Yes, one inside. And they want me to go with then to see the race. Their father's got a little steam-yacht. They want you to go too."

Boardman shook his head.

"Well, that's what I told them—told them that you had to go on the press boat. They said they wished they were going on the press boat too. But I don't see how I can refuse. They're ladies that I met Class Day, and I ought to have shown them a little more attention then; but I got so taken up with—"

"I see," said Boardman, showing his teeth, fine and even as grains of pop-corn, in a slight sarcastic smile. "Sort of poetical justice," he suggested.

"Well, it is—sort of," said Mavering, with a shamefaced consciousness. "What train are you going back on?"

"Seven o'clock."

"I'll be there."

He hurried back to rejoin the ladies, and Boardman saw him, after some parley and laughter, get into the coupe, from which he inferred that they had turned down the little seat in front, and made him take it; and he inferred that they must be very jolly, sociable girls.

He did not see Mavering again till the train was on its way, when he came in, looking distraughtly about for his friend. He was again very melancholy, and said dejectedly that they had made him stay to dinner, and had then driven him down to the station, bag and all. "The old gentleman came too. I was in hopes I'd find you hanging round somewhere, so that I could introduce you. They're awfully nice. None of that infernal Boston stiffness. The one you saw me talking with is married, though."

Boardman was writing out his report from a little book with shorthand notes in it. There were half a dozen other reporters in the car busy with their work. A man who seemed to be in authority said to one of them, "Try to throw in a little humour."

Mavering pulled his hat over his eyes, and leaned his head on the back of his seat, and tried to sleep.

XXIII

At his father's agency in Boston he found, the next morning, a letter from him saying that he expected to be down that day, and asking Dan to meet him at the Parker House for dinner. The letter intimated the elder Mavering's expectation that his son had reached some conclusion in the matter they had talked of before he left for Campobello.

It gave Dan a shiver of self-disgust and a sick feeling of hopelessness. He was quite willing now to do whatever his father wished, but he did not see haw he could face him and own his defeat.

When they met, his father did not seem to notice his despondency, and he asked him nothing about the Pasmers, of course. That would not have been the American way. Nothing had been said between the father and son as to the special advantages of Campobello for the decision of the question pending when they saw each other last; but the son knew that the father guessed why he chose that island for the purpose; and now the elder knew that if the younger had anything to tell him he would tell it, and if he had not he would keep it. It was tacitly understood that there was no objection on the father's part to Miss Pasmer; in fact, there had been a glimmer of humorous intelligence in his eye when the son said he thought he should run down to Bar Harbour, and perhaps to Campobello, but he had said nothing to betray his consciousness.

William Dean Howells

They met in the reading-room at Parker's, and Dan said, "Hello, father," and his father answered, "Well, Dan;" and they shyly touched the hands dropped at their sides as they pressed together in the crowd. The father gave his boy a keen glance, and then took the lead into the dining-room, where he chose a corner table, and they disposed of their hats on the window-seat.

"All well at home?" asked the young fellow, as he took up the bill of fare to order the dinner. His father hated that, and always made him do it.

"Yes, yes; as usual, I believe. Minnie is off for a week at the mountains; Eunice is at home."

"Oh! How would you like some green goose, with apple-sauce, sweet-potatoes, and succotash?"

"It seems to me that was pretty good, the last time. All right, if you like it."

"I don't know that I care for anything much. I'm a little off my feed. No soup," he said, looking up at the waiter bending over him; and then he gave the order. "I think you may bring me half a dozen Blue Points, if they're good," he called after him.

"Didn't Bar Harbour agree with you—or Campobello?" asked Mr. Mavering, taking the opening offered him.

"No, not very well," said Dan; and he said no more about it, leaving his father to make his own inferences as to the kind or degree of the disagreement.

"Well, have you made up your mind?" asked the father, resting his elbows on either side of his plate, and putting his hands together softly, while he looked across them with a cheery kindness at his boy.

"Yes, I have," said Dan slowly.

"Well?"

"I don't believe I care to go into the law."

"Sure?"

"Yes."

"Well, that's all right, then. I wished you to choose freely, and I suppose you've done so."

"Oh Yes."

"I think you've chosen wisely, and I'm very glad. It's a weight off my mind. I think you'll be happier in the business than you would in the law; I think you'll enjoy it. You needn't look forward to a great deal of Ponkwasset Falls, unless you like."

"I shouldn't mind going there," said Dan listlessly.

"It won't be necessary—at first. In fact, it won't be desirable. I want you to look up the business at this end a little."

Dan gave a start. "In Boston?"

"Yes. It isn't in the shape I want to have it. I propose to open a place of our own, and to put you in charge." Something in the young man's face expressed reluctance, and his father asked kindly, "Would that be distasteful to you?"

"Oh no. It isn't the thing I object to, but I don't know that I care to be in Boston." He lifted his face and looked his father full in the eyes, but with a gaze that refused to convey anything definite. Then the father knew that the boy's love affair had gone seriously wrong.

The waiter came with the dinner, and made an interruption in which they could be naturally silent. When he had put the dinner before them, and cumbered them with superfluous service, after the fashion of his kind, he withdrew a little way, and left them to resume their talk.

"Well," said the elder lightly, as if Dan's not caring to be in Boston had no particular significance for him, "I don't know that I care to have you settle down to it immediately. I rather think I'd like to have you look about first a little. Go to New York, go to Philadelphia, and see their processes there. We can't afford to get old-fashioned in our ways. I've always been more interested by the aesthetic side of the business, but you ought to have a taste for the mechanism, from your grandfather; your mother has it."

"Oh yes, sir. I think all that's very interesting," said Dan.

"Well, go to France, and see how those fellows do it. Go to London, and look up William Morris."

"Yes, that would be very nice," admitted the young fellow, beginning to catch on. "But I didn't suppose—I didn't expect to begin life with a picnic." He entered upon his sentence with a jocular buoyancy, but at the last word, which he fatally drifted upon, his voice fell. He said to himself that he was greatly changed; that, he should never be gay and bright again; there would always be this undercurrent of sadness; he had noticed the undercurrent yesterday when he was laughing and joking with those girls at Portland.

"Oh, I don't want you to buckle down at once," said his father, smiling. "If you'd decided upon the law, I should have felt that you'd better not lose time. But as you're going into the business, I don't mind your taking a year off. It won't be lost time if you keep your eyes open. I think you'd better go down into Italy and Spain. Look up the old tapestries and stamped leathers. You may get some ideas. How would you like it?"

"First-rate. I should like it," said Dan, rising on the waft of his father's suggestion, but gloomily lapsing again. Still, it was pleasing to picture himself going about through Europe with a broken heart, and he did not deny himself the consolation of the vision.

"Well, there's nobody to dislike it," said his father cheerily. He was sure now that Dan had been jilted; otherwise he would have put forth some objection to a scheme which must interrupt his lovemaking. "There's no reason why, with our resources, we shouldn't take the lead in this business."

He went on to speak more fully of his plans, and Dan listened with a nether reference of it all to Alice, but still with a surface intelligence on which nothing was lost.

"Are you going home with me to-morrow?" asked his father as they rose from the table.

"Well, perhaps not to-morrow. I've got some of my things to put together in Cambridge yet, and perhaps I'd better look after them. But I've a notion I'd better spend the winter at home, and get an idea of the manufacture before I go abroad. I might sail in January; they say it's a good month."

"Yes, there's sense in that," said his father.

"And perhaps I won't break up in Cambridge till I've been to New York and Philadelphia. What do you think? It's easier striking them from here."

"I don't know but you're right," said his father easily.

They had come out of the dining-room, and Dan stopped to get some cigarettes in the office. He looked mechanically at the theatre bills over the cigar case. "I see Irving's at the 'Boston.'"

"Oh, you don't say!" said his father. "Let's go and see him."

"If you wish it, sir," said Dan, with pensive acquiescence. All the Maverings were fond of the theatre, and made any mood

William Dean Howells

the occasion or the pretext of going to the play. If they were sad, they went; if they were gay, they went. As long as Dan's mother could get out-of-doors she used to have herself carried to a box in the theatre whenever she was in town; now that she no longer left her room, she had a dominant passion for hearing about actors and acting; it was almost a work of piety in her husband and children to see them and report to her.

His father left him the next afternoon, and Dan, who had spent the day with him looking into business for the first time, with a running accompaniment of Alice in all the details, remained to uninterrupted misery. He spent the evening in his room, too wretched even for the theatre. It is true that he tried to find Boardman, but Boardman was again off on some newspaper duty; and after trying at several houses in the hope, which he knew was vain, of finding any one in town yet, he shut himself up with his thoughts. They did not differ from the thoughts of the night before, and the night before that, but they were calmer, and they portended more distinctly a life of self-abnegation and solitude from that time forth. He tested his feelings, and found that it was not hurt vanity that he was suffering from: it was really wounded affection. He did not resent Alice's cruelty; he wished that she might be happy; he could endure to see her happy.

He wrote a letter to the married one of the two ladies he had spent the day with in Portland, and thanked them for making pass pleasantly a day which he would not otherwise have known how to get through. He let a soft, mysterious melancholy pervade his letter; he hinted darkly at trouble and sorrow of which he could not definitely speak. He had the good sense to tear his letter up when he had finished it, and to send a short, sprightly note instead, saying that if Mrs. Frobisher and her sister came to Boston at the end of the month, as they had spoken of doing, they must be sure to let him know. Upon the impulse given him by this letter he went more cheerfully to bed, and fell instantly asleep.

During the next three weeks he bent himself faithfully to the schemes of work his father had outlined for him. He visited New York and Philadelphia, and looked into the business and the processes there; and he returned to Ponkwasset Falls to report and compare his facts intelligently with those which he now examined in his father's manufactory for the first time. He began to understand how his father, who was a man of intellectual and artistic interests, should be fond of the work.

He spent a good deal of time with his mother, and read to her, and got upon better terms with her than they usually were. They were very much alike, and she objected to him that he was too light and frivolous. He sat with his sisters, and took an interest in their pursuits. He drove them about with his father's sorrels, and resumed something of the old relations with them which the selfish years of his college life had broken off. As yet he could not speak of Campobello or of what had happened there; and his mother and sisters, whatever they thought, made no more allusion to it than his father had done.

They mercifully took it for granted that matters must have gone wrong there, or else he would speak about them, for there had been some gay banter among them concerning the objects of his expedition before he left home. They had heard of the heroine of his Class Day, and they had their doubts of her, such as girls have of their brothers' heroines. They were not inconsolably sorry to have her prove unkind; and their mother found in the probable event another proof of their father's total want of discernment where women were concerned, for the elder Mavering had come home from Class Day about as much smitten with this mysterious Miss Pasmer as Dan was. She talked it over indignantly with her daughters; they were glad of Dan's escape, but they were incensed with the girl who could let him escape, and they inculpated her in a high degree of heartless flirtation. They knew how sweet Dan was, and they believed him most sincere and good. He had been brilliantly popular in college, and he was as bright as he could be. What was it she chose not to like in him? They vexed themselves with asking how or in what way she thought herself better. They would not have had her love Dan, but they were hot against her for not loving him.

They did not question him, but they tried in every way to find out how much he was hurt, and they watched him in every word and look for signs of change to better or worse, with a growing belief that he was not very much hurt.

It could not be said that in three weeks he forgot Alice, or had begun to forget her; but he had begun to reconcile himself to his fate, as people do in their bereavements by death. His consciousness habituated itself to the facts as something irretrievable. He no longer framed in his mind situations in which the past was restored. He knew that he should never love again, but he had moments, and more and more of them, in which he experienced that life had objects besides love. There were times when he tingled with all the anguish of the first moment of his rejection, when he stopped in whatever he was doing, or stood stock-still, as a man does when arrested by a physical pang, breathless, waiting. There were other times when he went about steeped in gloom so black that all the world darkened with it, and some mornings when he woke he wished that the night had lasted for ever, and felt as if the daylight had uncovered his misery and his shame to every one. He never knew when he should have these moods, and he thought he should have them as long as he lived. He thought this would be something rather fine. He had still other moods, in which he saw an old man with a grey moustache, like Colonel Newcome, meeting a beautiful white-haired lady; the man had never married, and he had not seen this lady for fifty years. He bent over, and kissed her hand.

"You idiot!" said Mavering to himself. Throughout he kept a good appetite. In fact, after that first morning in Portland, he had been hungry three times a day with perfect regularity. He lost the idea of being sick; he had not even a furred tongue. He fell asleep pretty early, and he slept through the night without a break. He had to laugh a great deal with his mother and sisters, since he could not very well mope without expecting them to ask why, and he did not wish to say why. But there were some laughs which he really enjoyed with the Yankee foreman of the works, who was a droll, after a common American pattern, and said things that were killingly funny, especially about women, of whom his opinions were sarcastic.

Dan Mavering suffered, but not solidly. His suffering was short, and crossed with many gleams of respite and even joy. His disappointment made him really unhappy, but not wholly so; it was a genuine sorrow, but a sorrow to which he began to resign himself even in the monotony of Ponkwasset Falls, and which admitted the thought of Mrs. Frobisher's sister by the time business called him to Boston.

William Dean Howells

XXIV

Before the end of the first week after Dan came back to town, that which was likely to happen whenever chance brought him and Alice together had taken place.

It was one of the soft days that fall in late October, when the impending winter seems stayed, and the warm breath of the land draws seaward and over a thousand miles of Indian summer. The bloom came and went in quick pulses over the girl's temples as she sat with her head thrown back in the corner of the car, and from moment to moment she stirred slightly as if some stress of rapture made it hard for her to get her breath; a little gleam of light fell from under her fallen eyelids into the eyes of the young man beside her, who leaned forward slightly and slanted his face upward to meet her glances. They said some words, now and then, indistinguishable to the others; in speaking they smiled slightly. Sometimes her hand wavered across her lap; in both their faces there was something beyond happiness—a transport, a passion, the brief splendour of a supreme moment.

They left the car at the Arlington Street corner of the Public Garden, and followed the winding paths diagonally to the further corner on Charles Street.

"How stupid we were to get into that ridiculous horse-car!" she said. "What in the world possessed us to do it?"

"I can't imagine," he answered. "What a waste of time it was!

If we had walked, we might have been twice as long coming. And now you're going to send me off so soon!"

"I don't send you," she murmured.

"But you want me to go."

"Oh no! But you'd better."

"I can't do anything against your wish."

"I wish it—for your own good."

"Ah, do let me go home with you, Alice?"

"Don't ask it, or I must say yes."

"Part of the way, then?"

"No; not a step! You must take the first car for Cambridge. What time is it now?"

"You can see by the clock on the Providence Depot."

"But I wish you to go by your watch, now. Look!"

"Alice!" he cried, in pure rapture.

"Look!"

"It's a quarter of one."

"And we've been three hours together already! Now you must simply fly. If you came home with me I should be sure to let you come in, and if I don't see mamma alone first, I shall die. Can't you understand?"

"No; but I can do the next best thing: I can misunderstand. You want to be rid of me."

"Shall you be rid of me when we've parted?" she asked, with an inner thrill of earnestness in her gay tone.

"Alice!"

"You know I didn't mean it, Dan."

"Say it again."

"What?"

"Dan."

"Dan, love! Dan, dearest!"

"Will that car of yours never come? I've promised myself not to leave you till it does, and if I stay here any longer I shall go wild. I can't believe it's happened. Say it again!"

"Say what?"

"That—"

"That I love you? That we're engaged?"

"I don't believe it. I can't." She looked impatiently up the street. "Oh, there comes your car! Run! Stop it!"

"I don't run to stop cars." He made a sign, which the conductor obeyed, and the car halted at the further crossing.

She seemed to have forgotten it, and made no movement to dismiss him. "Oh, doesn't it seem too good to be standing here talking in this way, and people think it's about the weather, or society?" She set her head a little on one side, and twirled the open parasol on her shoulder.

"Yes, it does. Tell me it's true, love!"

"It's true. How splendid you are!" She said it with an effect for the world outside of saying it was a lovely day.

He retorted, with the same apparent nonchalance, "How beautiful you are! How good! How divine!"

The conductor, seeing himself apparently forgotten, gave his bell a vicious snap, and his car jolted away.

She started nervously. "There! you've lost your car, Dan."

"Have I?" asked Mavering, without troubling himself to look after it.

She laughed now, with a faint suggestion of unwillingness in her laugh. "What are you going to do?"

"Walk home with you."

"No, indeed; you know I can't let you."

"And are you going to leave me here alone on the street corner, to be run over by the first bicycle that comes along?"

"You can sit down in the Garden, and wait for the next car."

"No; I would rather go back to the Art Museum, and make a fresh start."

"To the Art Museum?" she murmured, tenderly.

"Yes. Wouldn't you like to see it again?"

"Again? I should like to pass my whole life in it!"

"Well, walk back with me a little way. There's no hurry about the car."

"Dan!" she said, in a helpless compliance, and they paced very,

very slowly along the Beacon Street path in the Garden. "This is ridiculous."

"Yes, but it's delightful."

"Yes, that's what I meant. Do you suppose any one ever—ever—"

"Made love there before?"

"How can you say such things? Yes. I always supposed it would be—somewhere else."

"It was somewhere else—once."

"Oh, I meant—the second time."

"Then you did think there was going to be a second time?"

"How do I know? I wished it. Do you like me to say that?"

"I wish you would never say anything else."

"Yes; there can't be any harm in it now. I thought that if you had ever—liked me, you would still—"

"So did I; but I couldn't believe that you—"

"Oh, I could."

"Alice!"

"Don't you like my confessing it! You asked me to."

"Like it!"

"How silly we are!"

"Not half so silly as we've been for the last two months. I think we've just come to our senses. At least I have."

"Two months!" she sighed. "Has it really been so long as that?"

"Two years! Two centuries! It was back in the Dark Ages when you refused me."

"Dark Ages! I should think so! But don't say refused. It wasn't refusing, exactly."

"What was it, then?"

"Oh, I don't know. Don't speak of it now."

"But, Alice, why did you refuse me?"

"Oh, I don't know. You mustn't ask me now. I'll tell you some time."

"Well, come to think of it," said Mavering, laughing it all lightly away, "there's no hurry. Tell me why you accepted me to-day."

"I—I couldn't help it. When I saw you I wanted to fall at your feet."

"What an idea! I didn't want to fall at yours. I was awfully mad. I shouldn't have spoken to you if you hadn't stopped me and held out your hand."

"Really? Did you really hate me, Dan?"

"Well, I haven't exactly doted on you since we last met."

She did not seem offended at this. "Yes, I suppose so. And I've gone on being fonder and fonder of you every minute since that day. I wanted to call you back when you had got half-way to Eastport."

"I wouldn't have come. It's bad luck to turn back."

She laughed at his drolling. "How funny you are! Now I'm of rather a gloomy temperament. Did, you know it?"

"You don't look it."

"Oh, but I am. Just now I'm rather excited and—happy."

"So glad!"

"Go on! go on! I like you to make fun of me."

The benches on either side were filled with nursemaids in charge of baby-carriages, and of young children who were digging in the sand with their little beach shovels, and playing their games back and forth across the walk unrebuked by the indulgent policemen. A number of them had enclosed a square in the middle of the path with four of the benches, which they made believe was a fort. The lovers had to walk round it; and the children, chasing one another, dashed into them headlong, or, backing off from pursuit, bumped up against them. They did not seem to know it, but walked slowly on without noticing: they were not aware of an occasional benchful of rather shabby young fellows who stared hard at the stylish girl and well-dressed young man talking together in such intense low tones, with rapid interchange of radiant glances.

"Oh, as to making fun of you, I was going to say—" Mavering began, and after a pause he broke off with a laugh. "I forget what I was going to say."

"Try to remember."

"I can't."

"How strange that we should have both happened to go to the Museum this morning!" she sighed. Then, "Dan," she broke in, "do you suppose that heaven is any different from this?"

"I hope not—if I'm to go there."

"Hush, dear; you mustn't talk so."

"Why, you provoked me to it."

"Did I? Did I really? Do you think I tempted you to do it? Then I must be wicked, whether I knew I was doing it or not. Yes."

The break in her voice made him look more keenly at her, and he saw the tears glimmer in her eyes. "Alice!"

"No; I'm not good enough for you. I always said that."

"Then don't say it any more. That's the only thing I won't let you say."

"Do you forbid it, really? Won't you let me even think it?"

"No, not even think it."

"How lovely you are! Oh! I like to be commanded by you."

"Do you? You'll have lots of fun, then. I'm an awfully commanding spirit."

"I didn't suppose you were so humorous—always. I'm afraid you won't like me. I've no sense of fun."

"And I'm a little too funny sometimes, I'm afraid."

"No, you never are. When?"

"That night at the Trevors'. You didn't like it."

"I thought Miss Anderson was rather ridiculous," said Alice. "I don't like buffoonery in women."

"Nor I in men," said Mavering, smiling. "I've dropped it."

"Well, now we must part. I must go home at once," said Alice. "It's perfectly insane."

"Oh no, not yet; not till we've said something else; not till we've changed the subject."

"What subject?"

"Miss Anderson."

Alice laughed and blushed, but she was not vexed. She liked to have him understand her. "Well, now," she said, as if that were the next thing, "I'm going to cross here at once and walk up the other pavement, and you must go back through the Garden; or else I shall never get away from you."

"May I look over at you?"

"You may glance, but you needn't expect me to return your glance."

"Oh no."

"And I want you to take the very first Cambridge car that comes along. I command you to."

"I thought you wanted me to do the commanding."

"So I do—in essentials. If you command me not to cry when I get home, I won't."

She looked at him with an ecstasy of self-sacrifice in her eyes.

"Ah, I sha'n't do that. I can't tell what would open. But— Alice!"

"Well, what?" She drifted closely to him, and looked fondly up into his face. In walking they had insensibly drawn nearer together, and she had been obliged constantly to put space between them. Now, standing at the corner of Arlington Street, and looking tentatively across Beacon, she abandoned all precautions.

"What! I forget. Oh yes! I love you!"

"But you said that before, dearest!"

"Yes; but just now it struck me as a very novel idea. What if your mother shouldn't like the idea?"

"Nonsense! you know she perfectly idolises you. She did from the first. And doesn't she know how I've begin behaving about you ever since I—lost you?"

"How have you behaved? Do tell me, Alice?"

"Some time; not now," she said; and with something that was like a gasp, and threatened to be a sob, she suddenly whipped across the road. He walked back to Charles Street by the Garden path, keeping abreast of her, and not losing sight of her for a moment, except when the bulk of a string team watering at the trough beside the pavement intervened. He hurried by, and when he had passed it he found himself exactly abreast of her again. Her face was turned toward him; they exchanged a smile, lost in space. At the corner of Charles Street he deliberately crossed over to her.

"O dearest love! why did you come?" she implored.

"Because you signed to me."

"I hoped you wouldn't see it. If we're both to be so weak as this, what are we going to do?"

"But I'm glad you came. Yes: I was frightened. They must have overheard us there when we were talking."

William Dean Howells

"Well, I didn't say anything I'm ashamed of. Besides, I shouldn't care much for the opinion of those nurses and babies."

"Of course not. But people must have seen us. Don't stand here talking, Dan! Do come on!" She hurried him across the street, and walked him swiftly up the incline of Beacon Street. There, in her new fall suit, with him, glossy-hatted, faultlessly gloved, at a fit distance from her side, she felt more in keeping with the social frame of things than in the Garden path, which was really only a shade better than the Beacon Street Mall of the Common. "Do you suppose anybody saw us that knew us?"

"I hope so! Don't you want people to know it?"

"Yes, of course. They will have to know it—in the right way. Can you believe that it's only half a year since we met? It won't be a year till Class Day."

"I don't believe it, Alice. I can't recollect anything before I knew you."

"Well, now, as time is so confused, we must try to live for eternity. We must try to help each other to be good. Oh, when I think what a happy girl I am, I feel that I should be the most ungrateful person under the sun not to be good. Let's try to make our lives perfect—perfect! They can be. And we mustn't live for each other alone. We must try to do good as well as be good. We must be kind and forbearing with every one."

He answered, with tender seriousness, "My life's in your hands, Alice. It shall be whatever you wish."

They were both silent in their deep belief of this. When they spoke again, she began gaily: "I shall never get over the wonder of it. How strange that we should meet at the Museum!" They had both said this already, but that did not matter; they had said nearly everything two or three times. "How did you happen to be there?" she asked, and the question was so novel that she added, "I haven't asked you before."

He stopped, with a look of dismay that broke up in a hopeless laugh. "Why, I went there to meet some people—some ladies. And when I saw you I forgot all about them."

Alice laughed to; this was a part of their joy, their triumph.

"Who are they?" she asked indifferently, and only to heighten the absurdity by realising the persons.

"You don't know them," he said. "Mrs. Frobisher and her sister, of Portland. I promised to meet them there and go out to Cambridge with them."

"What will they think?" asked Alice. "It's too amusing."

"They'll think I didn't come," said Mavering, with the easy conscience of youth and love; and again they laughed at the ridiculous position together. "I remember now I was to be at the door, and they were to take me up in their carriage. I wonder how long they waited? You put everything else out of my head."

"Do you think I'll keep it out?" she asked archly.

"Oh yes; there is nothing else but you now."

The eyes that she dropped, after a glance at him, glistened with tears.

A lump came into his throat. "Do you suppose," he asked huskily, "that we can ever misunderstand each other again?"

"Never. I see everything clearly now. We shall trust each other implicitly, and at the least thing that isn't clear we can speak. Promise me that you'll speak."

"I will, Alice. But after this all will be clear. We shall deal with each other as we do with ourselves."

"Yes; that will be the way."

"And we mustn't wait for question from each other. We shall know—we shall feel—when there's any misgiving, and then the one that's caused it will speak."

"Yes," she sighed emphatically. "How perfectly you say it? But that's because you feel it, because you are good."

They walked on, treading the air in a transport of fondness for each other. Suddenly he stopped.

"Miss Pasmer, I feel it my duty to warn you that you're letting me go home with you."

"Am I? How noble of you to tell me, Dan; for I know you don't want to tell. Well, I might as well. But I sha'n't let you come in. You won't try, will you? Promise me you won't try."

"I shall only want to come in the first door."

"What for?"

"What for? Oh, for half a second."

She turned away her face.

He went on. "This engagement has been such a very public affair, so far, that I think I'd like to see my fiancee alone for a moment."

"I don't know what in the world you can have to say more."

He went into the first door with her, and then he went with her upstairs to the door of Mrs. Pasmer's apartment. The passages of the Cavendish were not well lighted; the little lane or alley that led down to this door from the stairs landing was very dim.

"So dark here!" murmured Alice, in a low voice, somewhat tremulous.

"But not too dark."

XXV

She burst into the room where her mother sat looking over some housekeeping accounts. His kiss and his name were upon her lips; her soul was full of him.

"Mamma!" she panted.

Her mother did not look round. She could have had no premonition of the vital news that her daughter was bringing, and she went on comparing the first autumn month's provision bill with that of the last spring month, and trying to account for the difference.

The silence, broken by the rattling of the two bills in her mother's hands as she glanced from one to the other through her glasses, seemed suddenly impenetrable, and the prismatic world of the girl's rapture burst like a bubble against it. There is no explanation of the effect outside of temperament and overwrought sensibilities. She stared across the room at her mother, who had not heard her, and then she broke into a storm of tears.

"Alice!" cried her mother, with that sanative anger which comes to rescue women from the terror of any sudden shock. "What is the matter with you?—what do you mean?" She dropped both of the provision bills to the floor, and started toward her daughter.

"Nothing—nothing! Let me go. I want to go to my room."

She tried to reach the door beyond her mother.

"Indeed you shall not!" cried Mrs. Pasmer. "I will not have you behaving so! What has happened to you? Tell me. You have frightened me half out of my senses."

The girl gave up her efforts to escape, and flung herself on the sofa, with her face in the pillow, where she continued to sob. Her mother began to relent at the sight of her passion. As a woman and as a mother she knew her daughter, and she knew that this passion, whatever it was, must have vent before there could be anything intelligible between them. She did not press her with further question, but set about making her a little more comfortable on the sofa; she pulled the pillow straight, and dropped a light shawl over the girl's shoulders, so that she should not take cold.

Then Mrs. Pasmer had made up her mind that Alice had met Mavering somewhere, and that this outburst was the retarded effect of seeing him. During the last six weeks she had assisted at many phases of feeling in regard to him, and knew more clearly than Alice herself the meaning of them all. She had been patient and kind, with the resources that every woman finds in herself when it is the question of a daughter's ordeal in an affair of the heart which she has favoured.

The storm passed as quickly as it came, and Alice sat upright casting off the wraps. But once checked with the fact on her tongue, she found it hard to utter it.

"What is it, Alice?—what is it?" urged her mother.

"Nothing. I—Mr. Mavering—we met—I met him at the Museum, and—we're engaged! It's really so. It seems like raving, but it's true. He came with me to the door; I wouldn't let him come in. Don't you believe it? Oh, we are! indeed we are! Are you glad, mamma? You know I couldn't have lived without him."

She trembled on the verge of another outbreak.

Mrs. Pasmer sacrificed her astonishment in the interest of sanity, and returned quietly: "Glad, Alice! You know that I think he's the sweetest and best fellow in the world."

"O mamma!"

"But are you sure—"

"Yes, Yes. I'm not crazy; it isn't a dream he was there—and I met him—I couldn't run away—I put out my hand; I couldn't help it—I thought I should give way; and he took it; and then—then we were engaged. I don't know what we said: I went in to look at the 'Joan of Arc' again, and there was no one else there. He seemed to feel just as I did. I don't know whether either of us spoke. But we knew we were engaged, and we began to talk."

Mrs. Pasmer began to laugh. To her irreverent soul only the droll side of the statement appeared.

"Don't, mamma!" pleaded Alice piteously.

"No, no; I won't. But I hope Dan Mavering will be a little more definite about it when I'm allowed to see him. Why couldn't he have come in with you?"

"It would have killed me. I couldn't let him see me cry, and I knew I should break down."

"He'll have to see you cry a great many times, Alice," said her mother, with almost unexampled seriousness.

"Yes, but not yet—not so soon. He must think I'm very gloomy, and I want to be always bright and cheerful with him. He knows why I wouldn't let him come in; he knew I was going to have a cry."

Mrs. Pasmer continued to laugh.

"Don't, mamma!" pleaded Alice.

"No, I won't," replied her mother, as before. "I suppose he was mystified. But now, if it's really settled between you, he'll be coming here soon to see your papa and me."

"Yes—to-night."

"Well, it's very sudden," said Mrs. Pasmer. "Though I suppose these things always seem so."

"Is it too sudden?" asked Alice, with misgiving. "It seemed so to me when it was going on, but I couldn't stop it."

Her mother laughed at her simplicity. "No, when it begins once, nothing can stop it. But you've really known each other a good while, and for the last six weeks at least you've known you own mind about him pretty clearly. It's a pity you couldn't have known it before."

"Yes, that's what he says. He says it was such a waste of time. Oh, everything he says is perfectly fascinating!"

Her mother laughed and laughed again.

"What is it, mamma? Are you laughing at me?"

"Oh no. What an idea!"

"He couldn't seem to understand why I didn't say Yes the first time, if I meant it." She looked down dreamily at her hands in her lap, and then she said, with a blush and a start, "They're very queer, don't you think?"

"Who?"

"Young men."

"Oh, very."

"Yes," Alice went on musingly. "Their minds are so different. Everything they say and do is so unexpected, and yet it seems to be just right."

Mrs. Pasmer asked herself if this single-mindedness was to go on for ever, but she had not the heart to treat it with her natural levity. Probably it was what charmed Mavering with the child. Mrs. Pasmer had the firm belief that Mavering was not single-minded, and she respected him for it. She would not spoil her daughter's perfect trust and hope by any of the cynical suggestions of her own dark wisdom, but entered into her mood, as such women are able to do, and flattered out of her every detail of the morning's history. This was a feat which Mrs. Pasmer enjoyed for its own sake, and it fully satisfied the curiosity which she naturally felt to know all. She did not comment upon many of the particulars; she opened her eyes a little at the notion of her daughter sitting for two or three hours and talking with a young man in the galleries of the Museum, and she asked if anybody they knew had come in. When she heard that there were only strangers, and very few of them, she said nothing; and she had the same consolation in regard to the walking back and forth in the Garden. She was so full of potential escapades herself, so apt to let herself go at times, that the fact of Alice's innocent self-forgetfulness rather satisfied a need of her mother's nature; she exulted in it when she learned that there were only nurses and children in the Garden.

"And so you think you won't take up art this winter?" she said, when, in the process of her cross-examination, Alice had left the sofa and got as far as the door, with her hat in her hand and her sacque on her arm.

"No."

"And the Sisters of St. James—you won't join them either?"

The girl escaped from the room.

"Alice! Alice!" her mother called after her; she came back. "You haven't told me how he happened to be there."

"Oh, that was the most amusing part of it. He had gone there to keep an appointment with two ladies from Portland. They were to take him up in their carriage and drive out to Cambridge, and when he saw me he forgot all about them."

"And what became of them?"

"We don't know. Isn't it ridiculous?"

If it appeared other or more than this to Mrs. Pasmer, she did not say. She merely said, after a moment, "Well, it was certainly devoted, Alice," and let her go.

XXVI

Mavering came in the evening, rather excessively well dressed, and with a hot face and cold hands. While he waited, nominally alone, in the little drawing room for Mr. Pasmer, Alice flew in upon him for a swift embrace, which prolonged itself till the father's step was heard outside the door, and then she still had time to vanish by another: the affair was so nicely adjusted that if Mavering had been in his usual mind he might have fancied the connivance of Mrs. Pasmer.

He did not say what he had meant to say to Alice's father, but it seemed to serve the purpose, for he emerged presently from the sound of his own voice, unnaturally clamorous, and found Mr. Pasmer saying some very civil things to him about his character and disposition, so far as they had been able to observe it, and their belief and trust in him. There seemed to be something provisional or probational intended, but Dan could not make out what it was, and finally it proved of no practical effect. He merely inferred that the approval of his family was respectfully expected, and he hastened to say, "Oh, that's all right, sir." Mr. Pasmer went on with more civilities, and lost himself in dumb conjecture as to whether Mavering's father had been in the class before him or the class after him in Harvard. He used his black eyebrows a good deal during the interview, and Mavering conceived an awe of him greater than he had felt at Campobello, yet not unmixed with the affection in which the newly accepted lover embraces even the relations of his betrothed. From time to time Mr. Pasmer looked about with the vague glance of a man unused to being so long left to his own guidance; and one of these appeals seemed at last to bring Mrs. Pasmer through the door, to the relief of both the men, for they had improvidently despatched their business, and were getting out of talk. Mr. Pasmer had, in fact, already asked Dan about the weather outside when his wife appeared.

Dan did not know whether he ought to kiss her or not, but Mrs. Pasmer did not in the abstract seem like a very kissing kind of person, and he let himself be guided by this impression, in the absence of any fixed principle applying to the case. She made some neat remark concerning the probable settlement of the affair with her husband, and began to laugh and joke about it in a manner that was very welcome to Dan; it did not seem to him that it ought to be treated so solemnly.

But though Mrs. Pasmer laughed and joked; he was aware of her meaning business—business in the nicest sort of a way, but business after all, and he liked her for it. He was glad to be explicit about his hopes and plans, and told what his circumstances were so fully that Mrs. Pasmer, whom his frankness gratified and amused, felt obliged to say that she had not meant to ask so much about his affairs, and he must excuse her if she had seemed to do so. She had her own belief that Mavering would understand, but she did not mind that. She said that, of course, till his own family had been consulted, it must not be considered seriously—that Mr. Pasmer insisted upon that point; and when Dan vehemently asserted the acquiescence of his family beforehand, and urged his father's admiration for Alice in proof, she reminded him that his mother was to be considered, and put Mr. Pasmer's scruples forward as her own reason for obduracy. In her husband's presence she attributed to him, with his silent assent, all sorts of reluctances and delicate compunctions; she gave him the importance which would have been naturally a husband's due in such an affair, and ingratiated herself more and more with the young man. She ignored Mr. Pasmer's withdrawal when it took place, after a certain lapse of time, and as the moment had come for that, she began to let herself go. She especially approved of the idea of going abroad and confessed her disappointment with her present experiment of America, where it appeared there was no leisure class of men sufficiently large to satisfy the social needs of Mr. Pasmer's nature, and she told Dan that he might expect them in Europe before long. Perhaps they might all three meet him there. At this he betrayed so clearly that he now intended his going to Europe merely as a sequel to his marrying Alice, while he affected to fall in with all Mrs. Pasmer said, that she grew fonder than ever of him for his ardour and his futile duplicity. If it had been in Dan's mind to take part in the rite, Mrs. Pasmer was quite ready at this point to embrace him with motherly tenderness. Her tough little heart was really in her throat with sympathy when she made an errand for the photograph of an English vicarage, which they had hired the summer of the year before, and she sent Alice back with it alone.

It seemed so long since they had met that the change in Alice did not strike him as strange or as too rapidly operated. They met with the fervour natural after such a separation, and she did not so much assume as resume possession of him. It was charming to have her do it, to have her act as if they had always been engaged, to have her try to press down the cowlick that started capriciously across his crown, and to straighten his necktie, and then to drop beside him on the sofa; it thrilled and awed him; and he silently worshipped the superior composure which her sex has in such matters. Whatever was the provisional interpretation which her father and mother pretended to put upon the affair, she apparently had no reservations, and they talked of their future as a thing assured. The Dark Ages, as they agreed to call the period of despair for ever closed that morning, had matured their love till now it was a rapture of pure trust. They talked as if nothing could prevent its fulfilment, and they did not even affect to consider the question of his family's liking it or not liking it. She said that she thought his father was delightful, and he told her that his father had taken the greatest fancy to her at the beginning, and knew that Dan was in love with her. She asked him about his mother, and she said just what he could have wished her to say about his mother's sufferings, and the way she bore them.

They talked about Alice's going to see her.

"Of course your father will bring your sisters to see me first."

"Is that the way?" he asked: "You may depend upon his doing the right thing, whatever it is."

"Well, that's the right thing," she said. "I've thought it out; and that reminds me of a duty of ours, Dan!"

"A duty?" he repeated, with a note of reluctance for its untimeliness.

"Yes. Can't you think what?"

"No; I didn't know there was a duty left in the world."

"It's full of them."

"Oh, don't say that, Alice!" He did not like this mood so well as that of the morning, but his dislike was only a vague discomfort—nothing formulated or distinct.

"Yes," she persisted; "and we must do them. You must go to those ladies you disappointed so this morning, and apologise— explain."

Dan laughed. "Why, it wasn't such a very ironclad engagement as all that, Alice. They said they were going to drive out to Cambridge over the Milldam, and I said I was going out there to get some of my traps together, and they could pick me up at the Art Museum if they liked. Besides, how could I explain?"

She laughed consciously with him. "Of course. But," she added ruefully, "I wish you hadn't disappointed them."

"Oh, they'll get over it. If I hadn't disappointed them, I shouldn't be here, and I shouldn't like that. Should you?"

"No; but I wish it hadn't happened. It's a blot, and I didn't want a blot on this day."

"Oh, well, it isn't very much of a blot, and I can easily wipe it off. I'll tell you what, Alice! I can write to Mrs. Frobisher, when our engagement comes out, and tell her how it was. She'll enjoy the joke, and so will Miss Wrayne. They're jolly and easygoing; they won't mind."

"How long have you known them?"

"I met them on Class Day, and then I saw them—the day after I left Campobello." Dan laughed a little.

"How, saw them?"

"Well, I went to a yacht race with them. I happened to meet them in the street, and they wanted me to go; and I was all broken up, and—I Went."

"Oh!" said Alice. "The day after I—you left Campobello?"

"Well—yes."

"And I was thinking of you all that day as—And I couldn't bear to look at anybody that day, or speak!"

"Well, the fact is, I—I was distracted, and I didn't know what I was doing. I was desperate; I didn't care."

"How did you find out about the yacht race?"

"Boardman told me. Boardman was there."

"Did he know the ladies? Did he go too?"

"No. He was there to report the race for the Events. He went on the press boat."

"Oh!" said Alice. "Was there a large party?"

"No, no. Not very. Just ourselves, in fact. They were awfully kind. And they made me go home to dinner with them."

"They must have been rather peculiar people," said Alice. "And I don't see how—so soon—" She could not realise that Mavering was then a rejected man, on whom she had voluntarily renounced all claim. A retroactive resentment which she could not control possessed her with the wish to punish those bold women for being agreeable to one who had since become everything to her, though then he was ostensibly nothing.

In a vague way, Dan felt her displeasure with that passage of his history, but no man could have fully imagined it.

"I couldn't tell half the time what I was saying or eating. I talked at random and ate at random. I guess they thought something was wrong; they asked me who was at Campobello."

"Indeed!"

"But you may be sure I didn't give myself away. I was awfully broken up," he concluded inconsequently.

She liked his being broken up, but she did not like the rest. She would not press the question further now. She only said rather gravely, "If it's such a short acquaintance, can you write to them in that familiar way?"

"Oh yes! Mrs. Frobisher is one of that kind."

Alice was silent a moment before she said, "I think you'd better not write. Let it go," she sighed.

"Yes, that's what I think," said Dan. "Better let it go. I guess it will explain itself in the course of time. But I don't want any blots around." He leaned over and looked her smilingly in the face.

"Oh no," she murmured; and then suddenly she caught him round the neck, crying and sobbing. "It's only—because I wanted it to be—perfect. Oh, I wonder if I've done right? Perhaps I oughtn't to have taken you, after all; but I do love you—dearly, dearly! And I was so unhappy when I'd lost you. And now I'm afraid I shall be a trial to you—nothing but a trial."

The first tears that a young man sees a woman shed for love of him are inexpressibly sweeter than her smiles. Dan choked with tender pride and pity. When he found his voice, he raved out with incoherent endearments that she only made him more and more happy by her wish to have the affair perfect, and that he wished her always to be exacting with him, for that would give him a chance to do something for her, and all that he desired, as long as he lived, was to do just what she wished.

At the end of his vows and entreaties, she lifted her face radiantly, and bent a smile upon him as sunny as that with which the sky after a summer storm denies that there has ever been rain in the world.

"Ah! you—" He could say no more. He could not be more enraptured than he was. He could only pass from surprise to surprise, from delight to delight. It was her love of him which wrought these miracles. It was all a miracle, and no part more wonderful than another. That she, who had seemed as distant as a star, and divinely sacred from human touch, should be there in his arms, with her head on his shoulder, where his kiss could reach her lips, not only unforbidden, but eagerly welcome, was impossible, and yet it was true.. But it was no more impossible and no truer, than that a being so poised, so perfectly self-centred as she, should already be so helplessly dependent upon him for her happiness. In the depths of his soul he invoked awful penalties upon himself if ever he should betray her trust, if ever he should grieve that tender heart in the slightest thing, if from that moment he did not make his whole life a sacrifice and an expiation.

He uttered some of these exalted thoughts, and they did not seem to appear crazy to her. She said yes, they must make their separate lives offerings to each other, and their joint lives an offering to God. The tears came into his eyes at these words of hers: they were so beautiful and holy and wise. He agreed that one ought always to go to church, and that now he should never miss a service. He owned that he had been culpable in the past. He drew her closer to him—if that were possible—and sealed his words with a kiss.

But he could not realise his happiness then, or afterward, when he walked the streets under the thinly misted moon of that Indian summer night.

He went down to the Events office when he left Alice, and found Boardman, and told him that he was engaged, and tried to work Boardman up to some sense of the greatness of the fact. Boardman shoved his fine white teeth under his spare moustache, and made acceptable jokes, but he did not ask indiscreet questions, and Dan's statement of the fact did not seem to give it any more verity than it had before. He tried to get Boardman to come and walk with him and talk it over; but Boardman said he had just been detailed to go and work up the case of a Chinaman who had suicided a little earlier in the evening.

"Very well, then; I'll go with you," said Mavering. "How can you live in such a den as this?" he asked, looking about the little room before Boardman turned down his incandescent electric. "There isn't anything big enough to hold me but all outdoors."

In the street he linked his arm through his friend's, and said he felt that he had a right to know all about the happy ending of the affair, since he had been told of that miserable phase of it at Portland. But when he came to the facts he found himself unable to give them with the fulness he had promised. He only imparted a succinct statement as to the where and when of the whole matter, leaving the how of it untold.

The sketch was apparently enough for Boardman. For all comment, he reminded Mavering that he had told him at Portland it would come out all right.

"Yes, you did, Boardman; that's a fact," said Dan; and he conceived a higher respect for the penetration of Boardman than he had before.

They stopped at a door in a poor court which they had somehow reached without Mavering's privity. "Will you come in?" asked Boardman.

"What for?"

"Chinaman."

"Chinaman?" Then Mavering remembered. "Good heavens! no. What have I got to do with him?"

"Both mortal," suggested the reporter.

The absurdity of this idea, though a little grisly, struck Dan as a good joke. He hit the companionable Boardman on the shoulder, and then gave him a little hug, and remounted his path of air, and walked off in it.

XXVII

Mavering first woke in the morning with the mechanical recurrence of that shame and grief which each day had brought him since Alice refused him. Then with a leap of the heart came the recollection of all that had happened yesterday. Yet lurking within his rapture was a mystery of regret: a reasonless sense of loss, as if the old feeling had been something he would have kept. Then this faded, and he had only the longing to see her, to realise in her presence and with her help the fact that she was his. An unspeakable pride filled him, and a joy in her love. He tried to see some outward vision of his bliss in the glass; but, like the mirror which had refused to interpret his tragedy in the Portland restaurant, it gave back no image of his transport: his face looked as it always did, and he and the refection laughed at each other:

He asked himself how soon he could go and see her. It was now seven o'clock: eight would be too early, of course—it would be ridiculous; and nine—he wondered if he might go to see her at nine. Would they have done breakfast? Had he any right to call before ten? He was miserable at the thought of waiting till ten: it would be three hours. He thought of pretexts—of inviting her to go somewhere, but that was absurd, for he could see her at home all day if he liked; of carrying her a book, but there could be no such haste about a book; of going to ask if he had left his cane, but why should he be in such a hurry for his cane? All at once he thought he could take her some flowers—a bouquet to lay beside her plate at breakfast. He dramatised himself charging the servant who

William Dean Howells

should take it from him at the door not to say who left it; but Alice would know, of course, and they would all know; it would be very pretty. He made Mrs. Pasmer say some flattering things of him; and he made Alice blush deliciously to hear them. He could not manage Mr. Pasmer very well, and he left him out of the scene: he imagined him shaving in another room; then he remembered his wearing a full beard.

He dressed himself as quickly as he could, and went down into the hotel vestibule, where he had noticed people selling flowers the evening before, but there was no one there with them now, and none of the florists' shops on the street were open yet. He could not find anything till he went to the Providence Depot, and the man there had to take some of his yesterday's flowers out of the refrigerator where he kept them; he was not sure they would be very fresh; but the heavy rosebuds had fallen open, and they were superb. Dan took all there were, and when they had been sprinkled with water, and wrapped in cotton batting, and tied round with paper, it was still only quarter of eight, and he left them with the man till he could get his breakfast at the Depot restaurant. There it had a consoling effect of not being so early; many people were already breakfasting, and when Dan said, with his order, "Hurry it up, please," he knew that he was taken for a passenger just arrived or departing. By a fantastic impulse he ordered eggs and bacon again; he felt, it a fine derision of the past and a seal of triumph upon the present to have the same breakfast after his acceptance as he had ordered after his rejection; he would tell Alice about it, and it would amuse her. He imagined how he would say it, and she would laugh; but she would be full of a ravishing compassion for his past suffering. They were long bringing the breakfast; when it came he despatched it so quickly that it was only half after eight when he paid his check at the counter. He tried to be five minutes more getting his flowers, but the man had them all ready for him, and it did not take him ten seconds. He had said he would carry them at half-past nine; but thinking it over on a bench in the Garden, he decided that he had better go sooner; they might breakfast earlier, and there would be no fun if Alice did not find the roses beside her plate: that was the whole idea. It was not till he stood at the door of the Pasmer apartment that he reflected that he was not accomplishing his wish to see Alice by leaving her those flowers; he was a fool, for now he would have to postpone coming a little, because he had already come.

The girl who answered the bell did not understand the charge he gave her about the roses, and he repeated his words. Some one passing through the room beyond seemed to hesitate and pause at the sound of his voice. Could it be Alice? Then he should see her, after all! The girl looked over her shoulder, and said, "Mrs. Pasmer."

Mrs. Pasmer came forward, and he fell into a complicated explanation and apology. At the end she said, "You had better give them yourself. She will be here directly." They were in the room now, and Mrs. Pasmer made the time pass in rapid talk; but Dan felt that he ought to apologise from time to time. "No!" she said, letting herself go. "Stay and breakfast with us, Mr. Mavering. We shall be so glad to have you."

At last Alice came in, and they decorously shook hands. Mrs. Pasmer turned away a smile at their decorum. "I will see that there's a place for you," she said, leaving them.

They were instantly in each other's arms. It seemed to him that all this had happened because he had so strongly wished it.

"What is it, Dan? What did you come for?" she asked.

"To see if it was really true, Alice. I couldn't believe it."

"Well—let me go—you mustn't—it's too silly. Of course it's true." She pulled herself free. "Is my hair tumbled? You oughtn't to have come; it's ridiculous; but I'm glad you came. I've been thinking it all over, and I've got a great many things to say to you. But come to breakfast now."

She had a business-like way of treating the situation that was more intoxicating than sentiment would have been, and gave it more actuality.

Mrs. Pasmer was alone at the table, and explained that Alice's father never breakfasted with them, or very seldom. "Where are your flowers?" she asked Alice.

"Flowers? What flowers?"

"That Mr. Mavering brought."

They all looked at one another. Dan ran out and brought in his roses.

"They were trying to get away in the excitement, I guess, Mrs. Pasmer; I found them behind the door." He had flung them there, without knowing it, when Mrs. Pasmer left him with Alice.

He expected her to join him and her mother in being amused at this, but he was as well pleased to have her touched at his having brought them, and to turn their gaiety off in praise of the roses. She got a vase for them, and set it on the table. He noticed for the first time the pretty house-dress she had on, with its barred corsage and under-skirt, and the heavy silken rope knotted round it at the waist, and dropping in heavy tufts or balls in front.

The breakfast was Continental in its simplicity, and Mrs. Pasmer said that they had always kept up their Paris habit of a light breakfast, even in London, where it was not so easy to follow foreign customs as it was in America. She was afraid he might find it too light. Then he told all about his morning's adventure, ending with his breakfast at the Providence Depot. Mrs. Pasmer entered into the fun of it, but she said it was for only once in a way, and he must not expect to be let in if he came at that hour another morning. He said no; he understood what an extraordinary piece of luck it was for him to be there;

and he was there to be bidden to do whatever they wished. He said so much in recognition of their goodness, that he became abashed by it. Mrs. Pasmer sat at the head of the table, and Alice across it from him, so far off that she seemed parted from him by an insuperable moral distance. A warm flush seemed to rise from his heart into his throat and stifle him. He wished to shed tears. His eyes were wet with grateful happiness in answering Mrs. Pasmer that he would not have any more coffee. "Then," she said, "we will go into the drawing-room;" but she allowed him and Alice to go alone.

He was still in that illusion of awe and of distance, and he submitted to the interposition of another table between their chairs.

"I wish to talk with you," she said, so seriously that he was frightened, and said to himself: "Now she is going to break it off. She has thought it over, and she finds she can't endure me."

"Well?" he said huskily.

"You oughtn't to have come here, you know, this morning."

"I know it," he vaguely conceded. "But I didn't expect to get in."

"Well, now you're here, we may as well talk. You must tell your family at once."

"Yes; I'm going to write to them as soon as I get back to my room. I couldn't last night."

"But you mustn't write; you must go—and prepare their minds."

"Go?" he echoed. "Oh, that isn't necessary! My father knew about it from the beginning, and I guess they've all talked it over. Their minds are prepared." The sense of his immeasurable superiority to any one's opposition began to dissipate Dan's unnatural awe; at the pleading face which Alice put on, resting one cheek against the back of one of her clasped hands, and leaning on the table with her elbows, he began to be teased by that silken rope round her waist.

"But you don't understand, dear," she said; and she said "dear" as if they were old married people. "You must go to see them, and tell them; and then some of them must come to see me—your father and sisters."

"Why, of course." His eye now became fastened to one of the fluffy silken balls.

"And then mamma and I must go to see your mother, mustn't we?"

"It'll be very nice of you—yes. You know she can't come to you."

"Yes, that's what I thought, and—What are you looking at?" she drew herself back from the table and followed the direction of his eye with a woman's instinctive apprehension of disarray.

He was ashamed to tell. "Oh, nothing. I was just thinking."

"What?"

"Well, I don't know. That it seems so strange any one else should have any to do with it—my family and yours. But I suppose they must. Yes, it's all right."

"Why, of course. If your family didn t like it—"

"It wouldn't make any difference to me," said Dan resolutely.

"It would to me," she retorted, with tender reproach. "Do you suppose it would be pleasant to go into a family that didn't like you? Suppose papa and mamma didn't like you?"

"But I thought they did," said Mavering, with his mind still partly on the rope and the fluffy ball, but keeping his eyes away.

"Yes, they do," said Alice. "But your family don't know me at all; and your father's only seen me once. Can't you understand? I'm afraid we don't look at it seriously enough— earnestly—and oh, I do wish to have everything done as it should be! Sometimes, when I think of it, it makes me tremble. I've been thinking about it all the morning, and—and— praying."

Dan wanted to fall on his knees to her. The idea of Alice in prayer was fascinating.

"I wish our life to begin with others, and not with ourselves. If we're intrusted with so much happiness, doesn't it mean that we're to do good with it—to give it to others as if it were money?"

The nobleness of this thought stirred Dan greatly; his eyes wandered back to the silken rope; but now it seemed to him an emblem of voluntary suffering and self-sacrifice, like a devotee's hempen girdle. He perceived that the love of this angelic girl would elevate him and hallow his whole life if he would let it. He answered her, fervently, that he would be guided by her in this as in everything; that he knew he was selfish, and he was afraid he was not very good; but it was not because he had not wished to be so; it was because he had not had any incentive. He thought how much nobler and better this was than the talk he had usually had with girls. He said that of course he would go home and tell his people; he saw now that it would make them happier if they could hear it directly from him. He had only thought of writing because he could not bear to think of letting a day pass without seeing her; but if he took the early morning train he could get back the same night, and still have three hours at Ponkwasset Falls, and he would go the next day, if she said so.

William Dean Howells

"Go to-day, Dan," she said, and she stretched out her hand impressively across the table toward him. He seized it with a gush of tenderness, and they drew together in their resolution to live for others. He said he would go at once. But the next train did not leave till two o'clock, and there was plenty of time. In the meanwhile it was in the accomplishment of their high aims that they sat down on the sofa together and talked of their future; Alice conditioned it wholly upon his people's approval of her, which seemed wildly unnecessary to Mavering, and amused him immensely.

"Yes," she said, "I know you will think me strange in a great many things; but I shall never keep anything from you, and I'm going to tell you that I went to matins this morning."

"To matins?" echoed Dan. He would not quite have liked her a Catholic; he remembered with relief that she had said she was not a Roman Catholic; though when he came to think, he would not have cared a great deal. Nothing could have changed her from being Alice.

"Yes, I wished to consecrate the first morning of our engagement; and I'm always going. I determined that I would go before breakfast—that was what made breakfast so late. Don't you like it?" she asked timidly.

"Like it!" he said. "I'm going with you."

"Oh no!" she turned upon him. "That wouldn't do." She became grave again. "I'm glad you approve of it, for I should feel that there was something wanting to our happiness. If marriage is a sacrament, why shouldn't an engagement be?"

"It is," said Dan, and he felt that it was holy; till then he had never realised that marriage was a sacrament, though he had often heard the phrase.

At the end of an hour they took a tender leave of each other, hastened by the sound of Mrs. Pasmer's voice without. Alice escaped from one door before her mother entered by the other. Dan remained, trying to look unconcerned, but he was sensible of succeeding so poorly that he thought he had better offer his hand to Mrs. Pasmer at once. He told her that he was going up to Ponkwasset Falls at two o'clock, and asked her to please remember him to Mr. Pasmer.

She said she would, and asked him if he were to be gone long.

"Oh no; just overnight—till I can tell them what's happened." He felt it a comfort to be trivial with Mrs. Pasmer, after bracing up to Alice's ideals. "I suppose they'll have to know."

"What an exemplary son!" said Mrs. Pasmer. "Yes, I suppose they will."

"I supposed it would be enough if I wrote, but Alice thinks I'd better report in person."

"I think you had, indeed! And it will be a good thing for you both to have the time for clarifying your ideas. Did she tell you she had been at matins this morning?" A light of laughter trembled in Mrs. Pasmer's eyes, and Mavering could not keep a responsive gleam out of his own. In an instant the dedication of his engagement by morning prayer ceased to be a high and solemn thought, and became deliciously amusing; and this laughing Alice over with her mother did more to realise the fact that she was his than anything else had yet done.

In that dark passage outside he felt two arms go tenderly round his neck; and a soft shape strain itself to his heart. "I know you have been laughing about me. But you may. I'm yours now, even to laugh at, if you want."

"You are mine to fall down and worship," he vowed, with an instant revulsion of feeling.

Alice didn't say anything; he felt her hand fumbling about his coat lapel. "Where is your breast pocket?" she asked; and he took hold of her hand, which left a carte-de-visite-shaped something in his.

"It isn't very good," she murmured, as well as she could, with her lips against his cheek, "but I thought you'd like to show them some proof of my existence. I shall have none of yours while you're gone."

"O Alice! you think of everything!"

His heart was pierced by the soft reproach implied in her words; he had not thought to ask her for her photograph, but she had thought to give it; she must have felt it strange that he had not asked for it, and she had meant to slip it in his pocket and let him find it there. But even his pang of self-upbraiding was a part of his transport. He seemed to float down the stairs; his mind was in a delirious whirl. "I shall go mad," he said to himself in the excess of his joy—"I shall die!'

XXVIII

The parting scene with Alice persisted in Mavering's thought far on the way to Ponkwasset Falls. He now succeeded in saying everything to her: how deeply he felt her giving him her photograph to cheer him in his separation from her; how much he appreciated her forethought in providing him with some answer when his mother and sisters should ask him about her looks. He took out the picture, and pretended to the other passengers to be looking very closely at it, and so managed to kiss it. He told her that now he understood what love really was; how powerful; how it did conquer everything; that it had changed him and made him already a better man. He made her refuse all merit in the work.

When he began to formulate the facts for communication to his family, love did not seem so potent; he found himself ashamed of his passion, or at least unwilling to let it be its own excuse even; he had a wish to give it almost any other appearance. Until he came in sight of the station and the Works, it had not seemed possible for any one to object to Alice. He had been going home as a matter of form to receive the adhesion of his family. But now he was forced to see that she might be considered critically, even reluctantly. This would only be because his family did not understand how perfect Alice was; but they might not understand.

With his father there would be no difficulty. His father had seen Alice and admired her; he would be all right. Dan found himself hoping this rather anxiously, as if from the instinctive

William Dean Howells

need of his father's support with his mother and sisters. He stopped at the Works when he left the train, and found his father in his private office beyond the book-keeper's picket-fence, which he penetrated, with a nod to the accountant.

"Hello, Dan!" said his father, looking up; and "Hello, father!" said Dan. Being alone, the father and son not only shook hands, but kissed each other, as they used to do in meeting after an absence when Dan was younger.

He had closed his father's door with his left hand in giving his right, and now he said at once, "Father, I've come home to tell you that I'm engaged to be married."

Dan had prearranged his father's behaviour at this announcement, but he now perceived that he would have to modify the scene if it were to represent the facts. His father did not brighten all over and demand, "Miss Pasmer, of course?" he contrived to hide whatever start the news had given him, and was some time in asking, with his soft lisp, "Isn't that rather sudden, Dan?"

"Well, not for me," said Dan, laughing uneasily. "It's—you know her, father—Miss Pasmer."

"Oh yes," said his father, certainly not with displeasure, and yet not with enthusiasm.

"I've had ever since Class Day to think it over, and it—came to a climax yesterday."

"And then you stopped thinking," said his father—to gain time, it appeared to Dan.

"Yes, sir," said Dan. "I haven't thought since."

"Well," said his father, with an amusement which was not unfriendly. He added, after a moment, "But I thought that had been broken off," and Dan's instinct penetrated to the lurking fact that his father must have talked the rupture over with his mother, and not wholly regretted it.

"There was a kind of—hitch at one time," he admitted; "but it's all right now."

"Well, well," said his father, "this is great news—great news," and he seemed to be shaping himself to the new posture of affairs, while giving it a conditional recognition. "She's a beautiful creature."

"Isn't she?" cried Dan, with a little break in his voice, for he had found his father's manner rather trying. "And she's good too. I assure you that she is—she is simply perfect every way."

"Well," said the elder Mavering, rising and pulling down the rolling top of his desk, "I'm glad to hear it, for your sake, Dan. Have you been up at the house yet?"

"No; I'm just off the train."

"How is her mother—how is Mrs. Pasmer? All well?"

"Yes, sir," said Dan; "they're all very well. You don't know Mr. Pasmer, I believe, sir, do you?"

"Not since college. What sort of person is he?"

"He's very refined and quiet. Very handsome. Very courteous. Very nice indeed."

"Ah! that's good," said Elbridge Mavering, with the effect of not having been very attentive to his son's answer.

They walked up the long slope of the hillside on which the house stood, overlooking the valley where the Works were, and fronting the plateau across the river where the village of operatives' houses was scattered. The paling light of what had been a very red sunset flushed them, and brought out the picturesqueness which the architect, who designed them for a particular effect in the view from the owner's mansion, had intended.

A good carriage road followed the easiest line of ascent towards this edifice, and reached a gateway. Within it began to describe a curve bordered with asphalted footways to the broad verandah of the house, and then descended again to the gate. The grounds enclosed were planted with deciduous shrubs, which had now mostly dropped their leaves, and clumps of firs darkening in the evening light with the gleam of some garden statues shivering about the lawn next the house. The breeze grew colder and stiffer as the father and son mounted toward the mansion which Dan used to believe was like a chateau, with its Mansard-roof and dormer windows and chimneys. It now blocked its space sharply out of the thin pink of the western sky, and its lights sparkled with a wintry keenness which had often thrilled Dan when he climbed the hill from the station in former homecomings. Their brilliancy gave him a strange sinking of the heart for no reason. He and his father had kept up a sort of desultory talk about Alice, and he could not have said that his father had seemed indifferent; he had touched the affair only too acquiescently; it was painfully like everything else. When they came in full sight of the house, Dan left the subject, as he realised presently, from a reasonless fear of being overheard.

"It seems much later here, sir, than it does in Boston," he said, glancing round at the maples, which stood ragged, with half their leaves blown from them.

"Yes; we're in the hills, and we're further north," answered his father. "There's Minnie."

Dan had seen his sister on the verandah, pausing at sight of him, and puzzled to make out who was with her father. He had an impulse to hail her with a shout, but he could not. In his last walk with her he had told her that he should never marry, and they had planned to live together. It was a joke; but now he felt as if he had come to rob her of something, and he walked soberly on with his father.

"Why, Dan, you good-for-nothing fellow!" she called out when he came near enough to be unmistakable, and ran down the steps to kiss him. "What in the world are you doing here? When did you come? Why didn't you hollo, instead of letting me stand here guessing? You're not sick, are you?"

The father got himself indoors unnoticed in the excitement of the brother's arrival. This would have been the best moment for Dan to tell his sister of his engagement; he knew it, but he parried her curiosity about his coming; and then his sister Eunice came out, and he could not speak. They all went together into the house flaming with naphtha gas, and with the steam heat already on, and Dan said he would take his bag to his room, and then come down again. He knew that he had left them to think that there was something very mysterious in his coming, and while he washed away the grime of his journey he was planning how to appear perfectly natural when he should get back to his sisters. He recollected that he had not asked either them or his father how his mother was, but it was certainly not because his mind was not full of her. Alice now seemed very remote from him, further even than his gun, or his boyish collection of moths and butterflies, on which his eye fell in roving about his room. For a bitter instant it seemed to him as if they were all alike toys, and in a sudden despair he asked himself what had become of his happiness. It was scarcely half a day since he had parted in transport from Alice.

He made pretexts to keep from returning at once to his sisters, and it was nearly half an hour before he went down to them. By that time his father was with them in the library, and they were waiting tea for him.

XXIX

A family of rich people in the country, apart from intellectual interests, is apt to gormandise; and the Maverings always sat down to a luxurious table, which was most abundant and tempting at the meal they called tea, when the invention of the Portuguese man-cook was taxed to supply the demands of appetites at once eager and fastidious. They prolonged the meal as much as possible in winter, and Dan used to like to get home just in time for tea when he came up from Harvard; it was always very jolly, and he brought a boy's hunger to its abundance. The dining-room, full of shining light, and treated from the low-down grate, was a pleasant place. But now his spirits failed to rise with the physical cheer; he was almost bashfully silent; he sat cowed in the presence of his sisters, and careworn in the place where he used to be so gay and bold. They were waiting to have him begin about himself, as he always did when he had been away, and were ready to sympathise with his egotism, whatever new turn it took. He mystified them by asking about them and their affairs, and by dealing in futile generalities, instead of launching out with any business that he happened at the time to be full of. But he did not attend to their answers to his questions; he was absent-minded, and only knew that his face was flushed, and that he was obviously ill at ease.

His younger sister turned from him impatiently at last. "Father, what is the matter with Dan?"

Her bold recognition of their common constraint broke it

down. Dan looked at his father with helpless consent, and his father said quietly, "He tells me he's engaged."

"What nonsense!" said his sister Eunice.

"Why, Dan!" cried Minnie; and he felt a reproach in her words which the words did not express. A silence followed, in which the father along went on with his supper. The girls sat staring at Dan with incredulous eyes. He became suddenly angry.

"I don't know what's so very extraordinary about it, or why there should be such a pother," he began; and he knew that he was insolently ignoring abundant reasons for pother, if there had been any pother. "Yes, I'm engaged."

He expected now that they would believe him, and ask whom he was engaged to; but apparently they were still unable to realise it. He was obliged to go on. "I'm engaged to Miss Pasmer."

"To Miss Pasmer!" repeated Eunice.

"But I thought——" Minnie began, and then stopped.

Dan commanded his temper by a strong effort, and condescended to explain. "There was a misunderstanding, but it's all right now; I only met her yesterday, and—it's all right." He had to keep on ignoring what had passed between him and his sisters during the month he spent at home after his return from Campobello. He did not wish to do so; he would have been glad to laugh over that epoch of ill-concealed heart-break with them; but the way they had taken the fact of his engagement made it impossible. He was forced to keep them at a distance; they forced him. "I'm glad," he added bitterly, "that the news seems to be so agreeable to my family. Thank you for your cordial congratulations." He swallowed a large cup of tea, and kept looking down.

"How silly!" said Eunice, who was much the oldest of the

William Dean Howells

three. "Did you expect us to fall upon your neck before we could believe it wasn't a hoax of father's?"

"A hoax!" Dan burst out.

"I suppose," said Minnie, with mock meekness, "that if we're to be devoured, it's no use saying we didn't roil the brook. I'm sure I congratulate you, Dan, with all my heart," she added, with a trembling voice.

"I congratulate Miss Pasmer," said Eunice, "on securing such a very reasonable husband."

When Eunice first became a young lady she was so much older than Dan that in his mother's absence she sometimes authorised herself to box his ears, till she was finally over-thrown in battle by the growing boy. She still felt herself so much his tutelary genius that she could not let the idea of his engagement awe her, or keep her from giving him a needed lesson. Dan jumped to his feet, and passionately threw his napkin on his chair.

"There, that will do, Eunice!" interposed the father. "Sit down, Dan, and don't be an ass, if you are engaged. Do you expect to come up here with a bombshell in your pocket, and explode it among us without causing any commotion? We all desire your happiness, and we are glad if you think you've found it, but we want to have time to realise it. We had only adjusted our minds to the apparent fact that you hadn't found it when you were here before." His father began very severely, but when he ended with this recognition of what they had all blinked till then, they laughed together.

"My pillow isn't dry yet, with the tears I shed for you, Dan," said Minnie demurely.

"I shall have to countermand my mourning," said Eunice, "and wear louder colours than ever. Unless," she added, "Miss Pasmer changes her mind again."

This divination of the past gave them all a chance for another laugh, and Dan's sisters began to reconcile themselves to the fact of his engagement, if not to Miss Pasmer. In what was abstractly so disagreeable there was the comfort that they could joke about his happiness; they had not felt free to make light of his misery when he was at home before. They began to ask all the questions they could think of as to how and when, and they assimilated the fact more and more in acquiring these particulars and making a mock of them and him.

"Of course you haven't got her photograph," suggested Eunice. "You know we've never had the pleasure of meeting the young lady yet."

"Yes," Dan owned, blushing, "I have. She thought I might like to show it to mother: But it isn't—"

"A very good one—they never are," said Minnie.

"And it was taken several years ago—they always are," said Eunice.

"And she doesn't photograph well, anyway."

"And this one was just after a long fit of sickness."

Dan drew it out of his pocket, after some fumbling for it, while he tolerated their gibes.

Eunice put her nose to it. "I hope it's your cigarettes it smells of," she said.

"Yes; she doesn't use the weed," answered Dan.

"Oh, I didn't mean that, exactly," returned his sister, holding the picture off at arm's length, and viewing it critically with contracted eyes.

Dan could not help laughing. "I don't think it's been near any other cigar-case," he answered tranquilly.

Minnie looked at it very near to, covering all but the face with her hand. "Dan, she's lovely!" she cried, and Dan's heart leaped into his throat As he gratefully met his sister's eyes.

"You'll like her, Min."

Eunice took the photograph from her for a second scrutiny. "She's certainly very stylish. Rather a beak of a nose, and a little too bird—like on the whole. But she isn't so bad. Is it like her?" she asked with a glance at her father.

"I might say—after looking," he replied.

"True! I didn't know but Dan had shown it to you as soon as you met. He seemed to be in such a hurry to let us all know."

The father said, "I don't think it flatters her," and he looked at it more carefully. "Not much of her mother there?" he suggested to Dan.

"No, sir; she's more like her father."

"Well, after all this excitement, I believe I'll have another cup of tea, and take something to eat, if Miss Pasmer's photograph doesn't object," said Eunice, and she replenished her cup and plate.

"What coloured hair and eyes has she, Dan?' asked Minnie.

He had to think so as to be exact. "Well, you might say they were black, her eyebrows are so dark. But I believe they're a sort of greyish-blue."

"Not an uncommon colour for eyes," said Eunice, "but rather peculiar for hair."

They got to making fun of the picture, and Dan told them

about Alice and her family; the father left them at the table, and then came back with word from Dan's mother that she was ready to see him.

William Dean Howells

XXX

By eight o'clock in the evening the pain with which every day
began for Mrs. Mavering was lulled, and her jarred nerves were
stayed by the opiates till she fell asleep about midnight. In this
interval the family gathered into her room, and brought her
their news and the cheer of their health. The girls chattered on
one side of her bed, and their father sat with his newspaper on
the other, and read aloud the passages which he thought would
interest her, while she lay propped among her pillows,
brilliantly eager for the world opening this glimpse of itself to
her shining eyes. That was on her good nights, when the drugs
did their work, but there were times when they failed, and the
day's agony prolonged itself through the evening, and the sleep
won at last was a heavy stupor. Then the sufferer's temper gave
way under the stress; she became the torment she suffered, and
tore the hearts she loved. Most of all, she afflicted the man
who had been so faithful to her misery, and maddened him to
reprisals, of which he afterward abjectly repented. Her tongue
was sharpened by pain, and pitilessly skilled to inculpate and
to punish; it pierced and burned like fire but when a good day
came again she made it up to the victims by the angelic
sweetness and sanity which they felt was her real self; the
cruelty was only the mask of her suffering.

When she was better they brought to her room anybody who
was staying with them, and she liked them to be jolly in the
spacious chamber. The pleasantest things of the house were
assembled, and all its comforts concentrated, in the place
which she and they knew she should quit but once. It was

made gay with flowers and pictures; it was the salon for those fortunate hours when she became the lightest and blithest of the company in it, and made the youngest guest forget that there was sickness or pain in the world by the spirit with which she ignored her own. Her laugh became young again; she joked; she entered into what they were doing and reading and thinking, and sent them away full of the sympathy which in this mood of hers she had for every mood in others. Girls sighed out their wonder and envy to her daughters when they left her; the young men whom she captivated with her divination of their passions or ambitions went away celebrating her supernatural knowledge of human nature. The next evening after some night of rare and happy excitement, the family saw her nurse carrying the pictures and flowers and vases out of her room, in sign of her renunciation of them all, and assembled silently, shrinkingly, in her chamber, to take each their portion of her anguish, of the blame and the penalty. The household adjusted itself to her humours, for she was supreme in it.

When Dan used to come home from Harvard she put on a pretty cap for him, and distinguished him as company by certain laces hiding her wasted frame, and giving their pathetic coquetry to her transparent wrists. He was her favourite, and the girls acknowledged him so, and made their fun of her for spoiling him. He found out as he grew up that her broken health dated from his birth, and at first this deeply affected him; but his young life soon lost the keenness of the impression, and he loved his mother because she loved him, and not because she had been dying for him so many years.

As he now came into her room, and the waiting-woman went out of it with her usual, "Well, Mr. Dan!" the tenderness which filled him at sight of his mother was mixed with that sense of guilt which had tormented him at times ever since he met his sisters. He was going to take himself from her; he realised that.

"Well, Dan!" she called, so gaily that he said to himself, "No, father hasn't told her anything about it," and was instantly able to answer her as cheerfully, "Well, mother!"

He bent over her to kiss her, and the odour of the clean linen mingling with that of the opium, and the cologne with which she had tried to banish its scent, opened to him one of those vast reaches of associations which perfumes can unlock, and he saw her lying there through those years of pain, as many as half his life, and suddenly the tears gushed into his eyes, and he fell on his knees, and hid his face in the bed-clothes and sobbed.

She kept smoothing his head, which shook under her thin hand, and saying, "Poor Dan! poor Dan!" but did not question him. He knew that she knew what he had come to tell her, and that his tears, which had not been meant for that, had made interest with her for him and his cause, and that she was already on his side.

He tried boyishly to dignify the situation when he lifted his face, and he said, "I didn't mean to come boohooing to you in this way, and I'm ashamed of myself."

"I know, Dan; but you've been wrought up, and I don't wonder. You mustn't mind your father and your sisters. Of course, they're rather surprised, and they don't like your taking yourself from them—we, none of us do."

At these honest words Dan tried to become honest too. At least he dropped his pretence of dignity, and became as a little child in his simple greed for sympathy. "But it isn't necessarily that; is it, mother?"

"Yes, it's all that, Dan; and it's all right, because it's that. We don't like it, but our not liking it has nothing to do with its being right or wrong."

"I supposed that father would have been pleased, anyway; for he has seen her, and—and. Of course the girls haven't, but I think they might have trusted my judgment a little. I'm not quite a fool."

His mother smiled. "Oh, it isn't a question of the wisdom of your choice; it's the unexpectedness. We all saw that you were very unhappy when you were here before, and we supposed it had gone wrong."

"It had, mother," said Dan. "She refused me at Campobello. But it was a misunderstanding, and as soon as we met—"

"I knew you had met again, and what you had come home for, and I told your father so, when he came to say you were here."

"Did you, mother?" he asked, charmed at her having guessed that.

"Yes. She must be a good girl to send you straight home to tell us."

"You knew I wouldn't have thought of that myself," said Dan joyously. "I wanted to write; I thought that would do just as well. I hated to leave her, but she made me come. She is the best, and the wisest, and the most unselfish—O mother, I can't tell you about her! You must see her. You can't realise her till you see her, mother. You'll like each other, I'm sure of that. You're just alike." It seemed to Dan that they were exactly alike.

"Then perhaps we sha'n't," suggested his mother. "Let me see her picture."

"How did you know I had it? If it hadn't been for her, I shouldn't have brought any. She put it into my pocket just as I was leaving. She said you would all want to see what she looked like."

He had taken it out of his pocket, and he held it, smiling fondly upon it. Alice seemed to smile back at him. He had lost her in the reluctance of his father and sisters; and now his mother—it was his mother who had given her to him again. He thought how tenderly he loved his mother.

When he could yield her the photograph, she looked long and silently at it. "She has a great deal of character, Dan."

"There you've hit it, mother! I'd rather you would have said that than anything else. But don't you think she's beautiful? She's the gentlest creature, when you come to know her! I was awfully afraid of her at first. I thought she was very haughty. But she isn't at all. She's really very self-depreciatory; she thinks she isn't good enough for me. You ought to hear her talk, mother, as I have. She's full of the noblest ideals—of being of some use in the world, of being self-devoted, and—all that kind of thing. And you can see that she's capable of it. Her aunt's in a Protestant sisterhood," he said, with a solemnity which did not seem to communicate itself to his mother, for Mrs. Mavering smiled. Dan smiled too, and said: "But I can't tell you about Alice, mother. She's perfect." His heart overflowed with proud delight in her, and he was fool enough to add, "She's so affectionate!"

His mother kept herself from laughing. "I dare say she is, Dan—with you." Then she hid all but her eyes with the photograph, and gave way.

"What a donkey!" said Dan, meaning himself. "If I go on, I shall disgust you with her. What I mean is that she isn't at all proud, as I used to think she was."

"No girl is, under the circumstances. She has all she can do to be proud of you."

"Do you think so, mother?" he said, enraptured with the notion. "I've done my best—or my worst—not to give her any reason to be so."

"She doesn't 'want any—the less the better. You silly boy! Don't you suppose she wants to make you out of whole cloth just as you do with her? She doesn't want any facts to start with; they'd be in the way. Well, now, I can make out, with your help, what the young lady is; but what are the father and mother? They're rather important in these cases."

"Oh, they're the nicest kind of people," said Dan, in optimistic generalisation. "You'd like Mrs. Pasmer. She's awfully nice."

"Do you say that because you think I wouldn't?" asked his mother. "Isn't she rather sly and hum-bugging?"

"Well, yes, she is, to a certain extent," Dan admitted, with a laugh. "But she doesn't mean any harm by it. She's extremely kind-hearted."

"To you? I dare say. And Mr. Pasmer is rather under her thumb?"

"Well, yes, you might say thumb," Dan consented, feeling it useless to defend the Pasmers against this analysis.

"We won't say heel," returned his mother; "we're too polite. And your father says he had the reputation in college of being one of the most selfish fellows in the world. He's never done anything since but lose most of his money. He's been absolutely idle and useless all his days." She turned her vivid blue eyes suddenly upon her son's.

Dan winced. "You know how hard father is upon people who haven't done anything. It's a mania of his. Of course Mr. Pasmer doesn't show to advantage where there's no—no leisure class."

"Poor man!"

Dan was going to say, "He's very amiable, though," but he was afraid of his mother's retorting, "To you?" and he held his peace, looking chapfallen.

William Dean Howells

Whether his mother took pity on him or not, her next sally was consoling. "But your Alice may not take after either of them. Her father is the worst of his breed, it seems; the rest are useful people, from what your father knows, and there's a great deal to be hoped for collaterally. She had an uncle in college at the same time who was everything that her father was not."

"One of her aunts is in one of those Protestant religious houses in England," repeated Dan.

"Oh!" said his mother shortly, "I don't know that I like that particularly. But probably she isn't useless there. Is Alice very religious?"

"Well, I suppose," said Dan, with a smile for the devotions that came into his thought, "she's what would be called 'Piscopal pious."

Mrs. Mavering referred to the photograph, which she still held in her hand. "Well, she's pure and good, at any rate. I suppose you look forward to a long engagement?"

Dan was somewhat taken aback at a supposition so very contrary to what was in his mind. "Well, I don't know. Why?"

"It might be said that you are very young. How old is Agnes—Alice, I mean?"

"Twenty-one. But now, look here, mother! It's no use considering such a thing in the abstract, is it?"

"No," said his mother, with a smile for what might be coming.

"This is the way I've been viewing it; I may say it's the way Alice has been viewing it—or Mrs. Pasmer, rather."

"Decidedly Mrs. Pasmer, rather. Better be honest, Dan."

"I'll do my best. I was thinking, hoping, that is, that as I'm going right into the business—have gone into it already, in fact—and could begin life at once, that perhaps there wouldn't be much sense in waiting a great while."

"Yes?"

"That's all. That is, if you and father are agreed." He reflected upon this provision, and added, with a laugh of confusion and pleasure: "It seems to be so very much more of a family affair than I used to think it was."

"You thought it concerned just you and her?" said his mother, with arch sympathy.

"Well, yes."

"Poor fellow! She knew better than that, you may be sure. At any rate, her mother did."

"What Mrs. Pasmer doesn't know isn't probably worth knowing," said Dan, with an amused sense of her omniscience.

"I thought so," sighed his mother, smiling too. "And now you begin to find out that it concerns the families in all their branches on both sides."

"Oh, if it stopped at the families and their ramifications! But it seems to take in society and the general public."

"So it does—more than you can realise. You can't get married to yourself alone, as young people think; and if you don't marry happily, you sin against the peace and comfort of the whole community."

"Yes, that's what I'm chiefly looking out for now. I don't want any of those people in Central Africa to suffer. That's the reason I want to marry Alice at the earliest opportunity. But I suppose there'll have to be a Mavering embassy to the high contracting powers of the other part now?"

"Your father and one of the girls had better go down."

"Yes?"

"And invite Mr. and Mrs. Pasmer and their daughter to come up here."

"All on probation?"

"Oh no. If you're pleased, Dan—"

"I am, mother—measurably." They both laughed at this mild way of putting it.

"Why, then it's to be supposed that we're all pleased. You needn't bring the whole Pasmer family home to live with you, if you do marry them all."

"No," said Dan, and suddenly he became very distraught. It flashed through him that his mother was expecting him to come home with Alice to live, and that she would not be at all pleased with his scheme of a European sojourn, which Mrs. Pasmer had so cordially adopted. He was amazed that he had not thought of that, but he refused to see any difficulty which his happiness could not cope with.

"No, there's that view of it," he said jollily; and he buried his momentary anxiety out of sight, and, as it were, danced upon its grave. Nevertheless, he had a desire to get quickly away from the spot. "I hope the Mavering embassy won't be a great while getting ready to go," he said. "Of course it's all right; but I shouldn't want an appearance of reluctance exactly, you know, mother; and if there should be much of an interval between my getting back and their coming on, don't you know, why, the cat might let herself out of the bag."

"What cat?" asked his mother demurely.

"Well, you know, you haven't received my engagement with

unmingled enthusiasm, and—and I suppose they would find it out from me—from my manner; and—and I wish they'd come along pretty soon, mother."

"Poor boy! I'm afraid the cat got out of the bag when Mrs. Pasmer came to the years of discretion. But you sha'n't be left a prey to her. They shall go back with you. Ring the bell, and let's talk it over with them now."

Dan joyfully obeyed. He could see that his mother was all on fire with interest in his affair, and that the idea of somehow circumventing Mrs. Pasmer by prompt action was fascinating her.

His sisters came up at once, and his father followed a moment later. They all took their cue from the mother's gaiety, and began talking and laughing, except the father, who sat looking on with a smile at their lively spirits and the jokes of which Dan became the victim. Each family has its own fantastic medium, in which it gets affairs to relieve them of their concrete seriousness, and the Maverings now did this with Dan's engagement, and played with it as an airy abstraction. They debated the character of the embassy which was to be sent down to Boston on their behalf, and it was decided that Eunice had better go with her father, as representing more fully the age and respectability of the family: at first glance the Pasmers would take her for Dan's mother, and this would be a tremendous advantage.

"And if I like the ridiculous little chit," said Eunice, "I think I shall let Dan marry her at once. I see no reason why he shouldn't and I couldn't stand a long engagement; I should break it off."

"I guess there are others who will have something to say about that," retorted the younger sister. "I've always wanted a long engagement in this family, and as there seems to be no chance for it with the ladies, I wish to make the most of Dan's. I always like it where the hero gets sick and the heroine nurses

William Dean Howells

him. I want Dan to get sick, and have Alice come here and take care of him."

"No; this marriage must take place at once. What do you say, father?" asked Eunice.

Her father sat, enjoying the talk, at the foot of the bed, with a tendency to doze. "You might ask Dan," he said, with a lazy cast of his eye toward his son.

"Dan has nothing to do with it."

"Dan shall not be consulted."

The two girls stormed upon their father with their different reasons.

"Now I will tell you Girls, be still!' their mother broke in. "Listen to me: I have an idea."

"Listen to her: she has an idea!" echoed Eunice, in recitative.

"Will you be quiet?" demanded the mother.

"We will be du-u-mb!"

When they became so, at the verge of their mother's patience, of which they knew the limits, she went on. "I think Dan had better get married at once."

"There, Minnie!"

"But what does Dan say?"

"I will—make the sacrifice," said Dan meekly.

"Noble boy! That's exactly what Washington said to his mother when she asked him not to go to sea," said Minnie.

"And then he went into the militia, and made it all right with himself that way," said Eunice. "Dan can't play his filial piety on this family. Go on, mother."

"I want him to bring his wife home, and live with us," continued his mother.

"In the L part!" cried Minnie, clasping her hands in rapture. "I've always said what a perfect little apartment it was by itself."

"Well, don't say it again, then," returned her sister. "Always is often enough. Well, in the L part Go on, mother! Don't ask where you were, when it's so exciting."

"I don't care whether it's in the L part or not. There's plenty of room in the great barn of a place everywhere."

"But what about his taking care of the business in Boston?" suggested Eunice, looking at her father.

"There's no hurry about that."

"And about the excursion to aesthetic centres abroad?" Minnie added.

"That could be managed," said her father, with the same ironical smile.

The mother and the girls went on wildly planning Dan's future for him. It was all in a strain of extravagant burlesque. But he could not take his part in it with his usual zest. He laughed and joked too, but at the bottom of his heart was an uneasy remembrance of the different future he had talked over with Mrs. Pasmer so confidently. But he said to himself buoyantly at last that it would come out all right. His mother would give in, or else Alice could reconcile her mother to whatever seemed really best.

He parted from his mother with fond gaiety. His sisters came out of the room with him.

"I'm perfectly sore with laughing," said Minnie. "It seems like old times—doesn't it, Dan?—such a gale with mother."

XXXI

An engagement must always be a little incredible at first to the families of the betrothed, and especially to the family of the young man; in the girl's, the mother, at least, will have a more realising sense of the situation. If there are elder sisters who have been accustomed to regard their brother as very young, he will seem all the younger because in such a matter he has treated himself as if he were a man; and Eunice Mavering said, after seeing the Pasmers, "Well, Dan, it's all well enough, I suppose, but it seems too ridiculous."

"What's ridiculous about it, I should like to know?" he demanded.

"Oh, I don't know. Who'll look after you when you're married? Oh, I forgot Ma'am Pasmer!"

"I guess we shall be able to look after ourselves," said Dan; a little sulkily.

"Yes, if you'll be allowed to," insinuated his sister.

They spoke at the end of a talk in which he had fretted at the reticence of both his sister and his father concerning the Pasmers, whom they had just been to see. He was vexed with his father, because he felt that he had been influenced by Eunice, and had somehow gone back on him. He was vexed and he was grieved because his father had left them at the door of the hotel without saying anything in praise of Alice, beyond

William Dean Howells

the generalities that would not carry favour with Eunice; and he was depressed with a certain sense of Alice's father and mother, which seemed to have imparted itself to him from the others, and to be the Mavering opinion of them. He could no longer see Mrs. Pasmer harmless if trivial, and good-hearted if inveterately scheming; he could not see the dignity and refinement which he had believed in Mr. Pasmer; they had both suffered a sort of shrinkage or collapse, from which he could not rehabilitate them. But this would have been nothing if his sister's and his father's eyes, through which he seemed to have been looking, had not shown him Alice in a light in which she appeared strange and queer almost to eccentricity. He was hurt at this effect from their want of sympathy, his pride was touched, and he said to himself that he should not fish for Eunice's praise; but he found himself saying, without surprise, "I suppose you will do what you can to prejudice mother and Min."

"Isn't that a little previous?" asked Eunice. "Have I said anything against Miss Pasmer?"

"You haven't because you couldn't," said Dan, with foolish bitterness.

"Oh, I don't know about that. She's a human being, I suppose—at least that was the impression I got from her parentage."

"What have you got to say against her parents?" demanded Dan savagely.

"Oh, nothing. I didn't come down to Boston to denounce the Pasmer family."

"I suppose you didn't like their being in a flat; you'd have liked to find them in a house on Commonwealth Avenue or Beacon Street."

"I'll own I'm a snob," said Eunice, with maddening meekness.

"So's father."

"They are connected with the best families in the city, and they are in the best society. They do what they please, and they live where they like. They have been so long in Europe that they don't care for those silly distinctions. But what you say doesn't harm them. It's simply disgraceful to you; that's all," said Dan furiously.

"I'm glad it's no worse, Dan," said his sister, with a tranquil smile. "And if you'll stop prancing up and down the room, and take a seat, and behave yourself in a Christian manner, I'll talk with you; and if you don't, I won't. Do you suppose I'm going to be bullied into liking them?"

"You can like them or not, as you please," said Dan sullenly; but he sat down, and waited decently for his sister to speak. "But you can't abuse them—at least in my presence."

"I didn't know men lost their heads as well as their hearts," said Eunice. "Perhaps it's only an exchange, though, and it's Miss Pasmer's head." Dan started, but did not say anything, and Eunice smoothly continued: "No, I don't believe it is. She looked like a sensible girl, and she talked sensibly. I should think she had a very good head. She has good manners, and she's extremely pretty, and very graceful. I'm surprised she should be in love with such a simpleton."

"Oh, go on! Abuse me as much as you like," said Dan. He was at once soothed by her praise of Alice.

"No, it isn't necessary to go on; the case is a little too obvious. But I think she will do very well. I hope you're not marrying the whole family, though. I suppose that it's always a question of which shall be scooped up. They will want to scoop you up, and we shall want to scoop her up. I dare say Ma'am Pasmer has her little plan; what is it?"

Dan started at this touch on the quick, but he controlled

William Dean Howells

himself, and said, with dignity, "I have my own plans."

"Well, you know what mother's are," returned Eunice easily. "You seem so cheerful that I suppose yours are quite the same, and you're just keeping them for a surprise." She laughed provokingly, and Dan burst forth again—

"You seem to live to give people pain. You take a fiendish delight in torturing others. But if you think you can influence me in the slightest degree, you're very much mistaken."

"Well, well, there! It sha'n't be teased any more, so it sha'n't! It shall have its own way, it shall, and nobody shall say a word against its little girly's mother." Eunice rose from her chair, and patted Dan on the head as she passed to the adjoining room. He caught her hand, and flung it violently away; she shrieked with delight in his childish resentment, and left him sulking. She was gone two or three minutes, and when she came back it was in quite a different mood, as often happens with women in a little lapse of time.

"Dan, I think Miss Pasmer is a beautiful girl, and I know we shall all like her, if you don't set us against her by your arrogance. Of course we don't know anything about her yet, and you don't, really; but she seems a very lovable little thing, and if she's rather silent and undemonstrative, why, she'll be all the better for you: you've got demonstration enough for twenty. And I think the family are well enough. Mrs. Pasmer is thoroughly harmless; and Mr. Pasmer is a most dignified personage; his eyebrows alone are worth the price of admission." Dan could not help smiling. "All that there is about it is, you mustn't expect to drive people into raptures about them, and expect them to go grovelling round on their knees because you do."

"Oh, I know I'm an infernal idiot," said Dan, yielding to the mingled sarcasm and flattery. "It's because I'm so anxious; and you all seem so confoundedly provisional about it. Eunice, what do you suppose father really thinks?"

Eunice seemed tempted to a relapse into her teasing, but she did not yield. "Oh, father's all right—from your point of view. He's been ridiculous from the first; perhaps that's the reason he doesn't feel obliged to expatiate and expand a great deal at present."

"Do you think so?" cried Dan, instantly adopting her as an ally.

"Well, if I sad so, oughtn't it to be enough?"

"It depends upon what else you say. Look here, now, Eunice!" Dan said, with a laughing mixture of fun and earnest, "what are you going to say to mother? It's no use, being disagreeable, is it? Of course, I don't contend for ideal perfection anywhere, and I don't expect it. But there isn't anything experimental about this thing, and don't you think we had better all make the best of it?"

"That sounds very impartial."

"It is impartial. I'm a purely disinterested spectator."

"Oh, quite."

"And don't you suppose I understand Mr. and Mrs. Pasmer quite as well as you do? All I say is that Alice is simply the noblest girl that ever breathed, and—"

"Now you're talking sense, Dan!"

"Well, what are you going to say when you get home, Eunice? Come!"

"That we had better make the best of it."

"And what else?"

"That you're hopelessly infatuated; and that she will twist you round her finger."

"Well?"

"But that you've had your own way so much, it will do you good to have somebody else's a while."

"I guess you're pretty solid," said Dan, after thinking it over for a moment. "I don't believe you're going to make it hard for me, and I know you can make it just what you please. But I want you to be frank with mother. Of course I wish you felt about the whole affair just as I do, but if you're right on the main question, I don't care for the rest. I'd rather mother would know just how you feel about it," said Dan, with a sigh for the honesty which he felt to be not immediately attainable in his own case.

"Well, I'll see what can be done," Eunice finally assented.

Whatever her feelings were in regard to the matter, she must have satisfied herself that the situation was not to be changed by her disliking it, and she began to talk so sympathetically with Dan that she soon had the whole story of his love out of him. They laughed a good deal together at it, but it convinced her that he had not been hoodwinked into the engagement. It is always the belief of a young man's family, especially his mother and sisters, that unfair means have been used to win him, if the family of his betrothed are unknown to them; and it was a relief, if not exactly a comfort, for Eunice Mavering to find that Alice was as great a simpleton as Dan, and perhaps a sincerer simpleton.

XXXII

A week later, in fulfilment of the arrangement made by Mrs. Pasmer and Eunice Mavering, Alice and her mother returned the formal visit of Dan's people.

While Alice stood before the mirror in one of the sumptuously furnished rooms assigned them, arranging a ribbon for the effect upon Dan's mother after dinner, and regarding its relation to her serious beauty, Mrs. Pasmer came out of her chamber adjoining, and began to inspect the formal splendour of the place.

"What a perfect man's house!" she said, peering about. "You can see that everything has been done to order. They have their own taste; they're artistic enough for that—or the father is—and they've given orders to have things done so and so, and the New York upholsterer has come up and taken the measure of the rooms and done it. But it isn't like New York, and it isn't individual. The whole house is just like those girls' tailor-made costumes in character. They were made in New York, but they don't wear them with the New York style; there's no more atmosphere about them than if they were young men dressed up. There isn't a thing lacking in the house here; there's an awful completeness; but even the ornaments seem laid on, like the hot and cold water. I never saw a handsomer, more uninviting room than that drawing room. I suppose the etching will come some time after supper. What do you think of it all, Alice?"

William Dean Howells

"Oh, I don't know. They must be very rich," said the girl indifferently.

"You can't tell. Country people of a certain kind are apt to put everything on their backs and their walls and floors. Of course such a house here doesn't mean what it would in town." She examined the texture of the carpet more critically, and the curtains; she had no shame about a curiosity that made her daughter shrink.

"Don't, mamma!" pleaded the girl. "What if they should come?"

"They won't come," said Mrs. Pasmer; and her notice being called to Alice, she made her take off the ribbon. "You're better without it."

"I'm so nervous I don't know what I'm doing," said Alice, removing it, with a whimper.

"Well, I can't have you breaking down!" cried her mother warningly: she really wished to shake her, as a culmination of her own conflicting emotions. "Alice, stop this instant! Stop it, I say!"

"But if I don't like her?" whimpered Alice.

"You're not going to marry her. Now stop! Here, bathe your eyes; they're all red. Though I don't know that it matters. Yes, they'll expect you to have been crying," said Mrs. Pasmer, seeing the situation more and more clearly. "It's perfectly natural." But she took some cologne on a handkerchief, and recomposed Alice's countenance for her. "There, the colour becomes you, and I never saw your eyes look so bright."

There was a pathos in their brilliancy which of course betrayed her to the Mavering girls. It softened Eunice, and encouraged Minnie, who had been a little afraid of the Pasmers. They both kissed Alice with sisterly affection. Their father merely saw how handsome she looked, and Dan's heart seemed to melt in his breast with tenderness.

In recognition of the different habits of their guests, they had dinner instead of tea. The Portuguese cook had outdone himself, and course followed course in triumphal succession. Mrs. Pasmer praised it all with a sincerity that took away a little of the zest she felt in making flattering speeches.

Everything about the table was perfect, but in a man's fashion, like the rest of the house. It lacked the atmospheric charm, the otherwise indefinable grace, which a woman's taste gives. It was in fact Elbridge Mavering's taste which had characterised the whole; the daughters simply accepted and approved.

"Yes," said Eunice, "we haven't much else to do; so we eat. And Joe does his best to spoil us."

"Joe?"

"Joe's the cook. All Portuguese cooks are Joe."

"How very amusing!" said Mrs. Pasmer. "You must let me speak of your grapes. I never saw anything so—well!—except your roses."

"There you touched father in two tender spots. He cultivates both."

"Really? Alice, did you ever see anything like these roses?"

Alice looked away from Dan a moment, and blushed to find that she had been looking so long at him.

"Ah, I have," said Mavering gallantly.

"Does he often do it?" asked Mrs. Pasmer, in an obvious aside to Eunice.

Dan answered for him. "He never had such a chance before."

Between coffee, which they drank at table, and tea, which they were to take in Mrs. Mavering's room, they acted upon a suggestion from Eunice that her father should show Mrs. Pasmer his rose-house. At one end of the dining-room was a little apse of glass full of flowering plants growing out of the ground, and with a delicate fountain tinkling in their midst. Dan ran before the rest, and opened two glass doors in the further side of this half-bubble, and at the same time with a touch flashed up a succession of brilliant lights in some space beyond, from which there gushed in a wave of hothouse fragrance, warm, heavy, humid. It was a pretty little effect for guests new to the house, and was part of Elbridge Mavering's pleasure in this feature of his place. Mrs. Pasmer responded with generous sympathy, for if she really liked anything with her whole heart, it was an effect, and she traversed the half-bubble by its pebbled path, showering praises right and left with a fulness and accuracy that missed no detail, while Alice followed silently, her hand in Minnie Mavering's, and cold with suppressed excitement. The rose-house was divided by a wall, pierced with frequent doorways, over which the trees were trained and the roses hung; and on either side were ranks of rare and costly kinds, weighed down with bud and bloom. The air was thick with their breath and the pungent odours of the rich soil from which they grew, and the glass roof was misted with the mingled exhalations.

Mr. Mavering walked beside Alice, modestly explaining the difficulties of rose culture, and his method of dealing with the red spider. He had a stout knife in his hand, and he cropped long, heavy-laden stems of roses from the walls and the beds, casually giving her their different names, and laying them along his arm in a massive sheaf.

Mrs. Pasmer and Eunice had gone forward with Dan, and were waiting for them at the thither end of the rose-house.

"Alice! just imagine: the grapery is beyond this," cried the girl's mother.

"It's a cold grapery," said Mr. Mavering. "I hope you'll see it to-morrow."

"Oh, why not to-night?" shouted Dan.

"Because it's a cold grapery," said Eunice; "and after this rose-house, it's an Arctic grapery. You're crazy, Dan."

"Well, I want Alice to see it anyway," he persisted wilfully. "There's nothing like a cold grapery by starlight. I'll get some wraps." They all knew that he wished to be alone with her a moment, and the three women, consenting with their hearts, protested with their tongues, following him in his flight with their chorus, and greeting his return. He muffled her to the chin in a fur-lined overcoat, which he had laid hands on the first thing; and her mother, still protesting, helped to tie a scarf over her hair so as not to disarrange it. "Here," he pointed, "we can run through it, and it's worth seeing. Better come," he said to the others as he opened the door, and hurried Alice down the path under the keen sparkle of the crystal roof, blotched with the leaves and bunches of the vines. Coming out of the dense, sensuous, vaporous air of the rose-house into this clear, thin atmosphere, delicately penetrated with the fragrance, pure and cold, of the fruit, it was as if they had entered another world. His arm crept round her in the odorous obscurity.

"Look up! See the stars through the vines! But when she lifted her face he bent his upon it for a wild kiss.

"Don't! don't!" she murmured. "I want to think; I don't know what I'm doing."

"Neither do I. I feel as if I were a blessed ghost."

Perhaps it is only in these ecstasies of the senses that the soul ever reaches self-consciousness on earth; and it seems to be only the man-soul which finds itself even in this abandon. The woman-soul has always something else to think of.

"What shall we do," said the girl, "if we—Oh, I dread to meet your mother! Is she like either of your sisters?"

"No," he cried joyously; "she's like me. If you're not afraid of me, and you don't seem to be—"

"You're all I have—you're all I have in the world. Do you think she'll like me? Oh, do you love me, Dan?"

"You darling! you divine—" The rest was a mad embrace. "If you're not afraid of me, you won't mind mother. I wanted you here alone for just a last word, to tell you you needn't be afraid; to tell you to—But I needn't tell you how to act. You mustn't treat her as an invalid—you must treat her like any one else; that's what she likes. But you'll know what's best, Alice. Be yourself, and she'll like you well enough. I'm not afraid."

XXXIII

When she entered Mrs. Mavering's room Alice first saw the pictures, the bric-a-brac, the flowers, the dazzle of lights, and then the invalid propped among her pillows, and vividly expectant of her. She seemed all eager eyes to the girl, aware next of the strong resemblance to Dan in her features, and of the careful toilet the sick woman had made for her. To youth all forms of suffering are abhorrent, and Alice had to hide a repugnance at sight of this spectre of what had once been a pretty woman. Through the egotism with which so many years of flattering subjection in her little world had armed her, Mrs. Mavering probably did not feel the girl's shrinking, or, if she did, took it for the natural embarrassment which she would feel. She had satisfied herself that she was looking her best, and that her cap and the lace jacket she wore were very becoming, and softened her worst points; the hangings of her bed and the richly embroidered crimson silk coverlet were part of the coquetry of her costume, from which habit had taken all sense of ghastliness; she was proud of them, and she was not aware of the scent of drugs that insisted through the odour of the flowers.

She lifted herself on her elbow as Dan approached with Alice, and the girl felt as if an intense light had been thrown upon her from head to foot in the moment of searching scrutiny that followed. The invalid's set look broke into a smile, and she put out her hand, neither hot nor cold, but of a dry neutral, spiritual temperature, and pulled Alice down and kissed her.

William Dean Howells

"Why, child, your hand's like ice!" she exclaimed without preamble. "We used to say that came from a warm heart."

"I guess it comes from a cold grapery in this case, mother," said Dan, with his laugh. "I've just been running Alice through it. And perhaps a little excitement—"

"Excitement?" echoed his mother. "Cold grapery, I dare say, and very silly of you, Dan; but there's no occasion for excitement, as if we were strangers. Sit down in that chair, my dear. And, Dan, you go round to the other side of the bed; I want Alice all to myself. I saw your photograph a week ago, and I've thought about you for ages since, and wondered whether you would approve of your old friend."

"Oh yes," whispered the girl, suppressing a tremor; and Dan's eyes were suffused with grateful tears at his mother's graciousness.

Alice's reticence seemed to please the invalid. "I hope you'll like all your old friends here; you've begun with the worst among us, but perhaps you like him the best because he is the worst; I do."

"You may believe just half of that, Alice," cried Dan.

"Then believe the best half, or the half you like best," said Mrs. Mavering. "There must be something good in him if you like him. Have they welcomed you home, my dear?"

"We've all made a stagger at it," said Dan, while Alice was faltering over the words which were so slow to come.

"Don't try to answer my formal stupidities. You are welcome, and that's enough, and more than enough of speeches. Did you have a comfortable journey up?"

"Oh, very."

"Was it cold?"

"Not at all. The cars were very hot."

"Have you had any snow yet at Boston?"

"No, none at all yet."

"Now I feel that we're talking sense. I hope you found everything in your room? I can't look after things as I would like, and so I inquire."

"There's everything," said Alice. "We're very comfortable."

"I'm very glad. I had Dan look, he's my housekeeper; he understands me better than my girls; he's like me, more. That's what makes us so fond of each other; it's a kind of personal vanity. But he has his good points, Dan has. He's very amiable, and I was too, at his age—and till I came here. But I'm not going to tell you of his good points; I dare say you've found them out. I'll tell you about his bad ones. He says you're very serious. Are you?" She pressed the girl's hand, which she had kept in hers, and regarded her keenly.

Alice dropped her eyes at the odd question. "I don't know," she faltered. "Sometimes."

"Well, that's good. Dan's frivolous."

"Oh, sometimes—only sometimes!" he interposed.

"He's frivolous, and he's very light-minded; but he's none the worse for that."

"Oh, thank you," said Dan; and Alice, still puzzled, laughed provisionally.

"No; I want you to understand that. He's light-hearted too, and that's a great thing in this world. If you're serious you'll be apt to be heavyhearted, and then you'll find Dan of use. And I hope he'll know how, to turn your seriousness to account too, he needs something to keep him down—to keep him from blowing away. Yes, it's very well for people to be opposites. Only they must understand each other, If they do that, then they get along. Light-heartedness or heavy-heartedness comes to the same thing if they know how to use it for each other. You see, I've got to be a great philosopher lying here; nobody dares contradict me or interrupt me when I'm constructing my theories, and so I get them perfect."

"I wish I could hear them all," said Alice, with sincerity that made Mrs. Mavering laugh as light-heartedly as Dan himself, and that seemed to suggest the nest thing to her.

"You can for the asking, almost any time. Are you a very truthful person, my dear? Don't take the trouble to deny it if you are," she added, at Alice's stare. "You see, I'm not at all conventional and you needn't be. Come! tell the truth for once, at any rate. Are you habitually truthful?"

"Yes, I think I am," said Alice, still staring.

"Dan's not," said his mother quietly.

"Oh, see here, now, mother! Don't give me away!"

"He'll tell the truth in extremity, of course, and he'll tell it if it's pleasant, always; but if you don't expect much more of him you won't be disappointed; and you can make him of great use."

"You see where I got it, anyway, Alice," said Dan, laughing across the bed at her.

"Yes, you got it from me: I own it. A great part of my life was made up of making life pleasant to others by fibbing. I stopped it when I came here."

"Oh, not altogether, mother!" urged her son. "You mustn't be too hard on yourself."

She ignored his interruption: "You'll find Dan a great convenience with that agreeable habit of his. You can get him to make all your verbal excuses for you (he'll, do it beautifully), and dictate all the thousand and one little lying notes you'll have to write; he won't mind it in the least, and it will save you a great wear-and-tear of conscience."

"Go on, mother, go on," said Dan, with delighted eyes, that asked of Alice if it were not all perfectly charming.

"And you can come in with your habitual truthfulness where Dan wouldn't know what to do, poor fellow. You'll have the moral courage to come right to the point when he would like to shillyshally, and you can be frank while he's trying to think how to make y-e-s spell no."

"Any other little compliments, mother?" suggested Dan.

"No," said Mrs. Mavering; "that's all. I thought I'd better have it off my mind; I knew you'd never get it off yours, and Alice had better know the worst. It is the worst, my dear, and if I talked of him till doomsday I couldn't say any more harm of him. I needn't tell you how sweet he is; you know that, I'm sure; but you can't know yet how gentle and forbearing he is, how patient, how full of kindness to every living soul, how unselfish, how—"

She lost her voice. "Oh, come now, mother," Dan protested huskily.

Alice did not say anything; she bent over, without repugnance, and gathered the shadowy shape into her strong young arms, and kissed the wasted face whose unearthly coolness was like the leaf of a flower against her lips. "He never gave me a moment's trouble," said the mother, "and I'm sure he'll make you happy. How kind of you not to be afraid of me—"

"Afraid!" cried the girl, with passionate solemnity. "I shall never feel safe away from you!"

The door opened upon the sound of voices, and the others came in.

Mrs. Pasmer did not wait for an introduction, but with an affectation of impulse which she felt Mrs. Mavering would penetrate and respect, she went up to the bed and presented herself. Dan's mother smiled hospitably upon her, and they had some playful words about their children. Mrs. Pasmer neatly conveyed the regrets of her husband, who had hoped up to the last moment that the heavy cold he had taken would let him come with her; and the invalid made her guest sit down on the right hand of her bed, which seemed to be the place of honour, while her husband took Dan's place on the left, and admired his wife's skill in fence. At the end of her encounter with Mrs. Pasmer she called out with her strong voice, "Why don't you get your banjo, Molly, and play something?"

"A banjo? Oh, do!" cried Mrs. Pasmer. "It's so picturesque and interesting! I heard that young ladies had taken it up, and I should so like to hear it!" She had turned to Mrs. Mavering again, and she now beamed winningly upon her.

Alice regarded the girl with a puzzled frown as she brought her banjo in from another room and sat down with it. She relaxed the severity of her stare a little as Molly played one wild air after another, singing some of them with an evidence of training in her naive effectiveness. There were some Mexican songs which she had learned in a late visit to their country, and some Creole melodies caught up in a winter's sojourn to Louisiana. The elder sister accompanied her on the piano, not with the hard, resolute proficiency which one might have expected of Eunice Mavering, but with a sympathy which was perhaps the expression of her share of the family kindliness.

"Your children seem to have been everywhere," said Mrs. Pasmer, with a sigh of flattering envy. "Oh you're not going to stop!" she pleaded, turning from Mrs. Mavering to Molly.

"I think Dan had better do the rheumatic uncle now," said Eunice, from the piano.

"Oh yes! the rheumatic uncle—do," said Mrs. Pasmer. "We know the rheumatic uncle," she added, with a glance at Alice. Dan looked at her too, as if doubtful of her approval; and then he told in character a Yankee story which he had worked up from the talk of his friend the foreman. It made them all laugh.

Mrs. Pasmer was the gayest; she let herself go, and throughout the evening she flattered right and left, and said, in her good-night to Mrs. Mavering, that she had never imagined so delightful a time. "O Mrs. Mavering, I don't wonder your children love their home. It's a revelation."

XXXIV

"She's a cat, Dan," said his mother quietly, and not without liking, when he looked in for his goodnight kiss after the rest were gone; "a perfect tabby. But your Alice is sublime."

"O mother—"

"She's a little too sublime for me. But you're young, and you can stand it."

Dan laughed with delight. "Yes, I think I can, mother. All I ask is the chance."

"Oh, you're very much in love, both of you; there's no doubt about that. What I mean is that she's very high strung, very intense. She has ideals—any one can see that."

Dan took it all for praise. "Yes," he said eagerly, "that's what I told you. And that will be the best thing about it for me. I have no ideals."

"Well, you must find out what hers are, and live up to them."

"Oh, there won't be any trouble about that," said Dan buoyantly.

"You must help her to find them out too." He looked puzzled. "You mustn't expect the child to be too definite at first, nor to be always right, even when she's full of ideals. You must be very patient with her, Dan."

"Oh, I will, mother! You know that. How could I ever be impatient with Alice?"

"Very forbearing, and very kind, and indefatigably forgiving. Ask your father how to behave."

Dan promised to do so, with a laugh at the joke. It had never occurred to him that his father was particularly exemplary in these things, or that his mother idolised him for what seemed to Dan simply a matter-of-course endurance of her sick whims and freaks and moods. He broke forth into a vehement protest of his good intentions, to which his mother did not seem very attentive. After a while she asked—

"Is she always so silent, Dan?"

"Well, not with me, mother. Of course she was a little embarrassed; she didn't know exactly what to say, I suppose—"

"Oh, I rather liked that. At least she isn't a rattle-pate. And we shall get acquainted; we shall like each other. She will understand me when you bring her home here to live with us, and—"

"Yes," said Dan, rising rather hastily, and stooping over to his mother. "I'm not going to let you talk any more now, or we shall have to suffer for it to-morrow night."

He got gaily away before his mother could amplify a suggestion which spoiled a little of his pleasure in the praises— he thought they were unqualified and enthusiastic praises—she had been heaping upon Alice. He wished to go to bed with them all sweet and unalloyed in his thought, to sleep, to dream upon his perfect triumph.

Mrs. Pasmer was a long time in undressing, and in calming down after the demands which the different events of the evening had made upon her resources

"It has certainly been a very mixed evening, Alice," she said, as she took the pins out of her back hair and let it fall; and she continued to talk as she went back and forth between their rooms. "What do you think of banjo-playing for young ladies? Isn't it rather rowdy? Decidedly rowdy, I think. And Dan's Yankee story! I expected to see the old gentleman get up and perform some trick."

"I suppose they do it to amuse Mrs. Mavering," said Alice, with cold displeasure.

"Oh, it's quite right," tittered Mrs. Pasmer. "It would be as much as their lives are worth if they didn't You can see that she rules them with a rod of iron. What a will! I'm glad you're not going to come under her sway; I really think you couldn't be safe from her in the same hemisphere; it's well you're going abroad at once. They're a very self-concentrated family, don't you think—very self-satisfied? Of course that's the danger of living off by themselves as they do: they get to thinking there's nobody else in the world. You would simply be absorbed by them: it's a hair-breadth escape.

"How splendidly Dan contrasts with the others! Oh, he's delightful; he's a man of the world. Give me the world, after all! And he's so considerate of their rustic conceit! What a house! It's perfectly baronial—and ridiculous. In any other country it would mean something—society, entertainments, troops of guests; but here it doesn't mean anything but money. Not that money isn't a very good thing; I wish we had more of it. But now you see how very little it can do by itself. You looked very well, Alice, and behaved with great dignity; perhaps too much. You ought to enter a little more into the spirit of things, even if you don't respect them. That oldest girl isn't particularly pleased, I fancy, though it doesn't matter really."

Alice replied to her mother from time to time with absent

Yeses and Noes; she sat by the window looking out on the hillside lawn before the house; the moon had risen, and poured a flood of snowy light over it, in which the cold statues dimly shone, and the firs, in clumps and singly, blackened with an inky solidity. Beyond wandered the hills, their bare pasturage broken here and there by blotches of woodland.

After her mother had gone to bed she turned her light down and resumed her seat by the window, pressing her hot forehead against the pane, and losing all sense of the scene without in the whirl of her thoughts.

After this, evening of gay welcome in Dan's family, and those moments of tenderness with him, her heart was troubled. She now realised her engagement as something exterior to herself and her own family, and confronted for the first time its responsibilities, its ties, and its claims. It was not enough to be everything to Dan; she could not be that unless she were something to his family. She did not realise this vividly, but with the remoteness which all verities except those of sensation have for youth.

Her uneasiness was full of exultation, of triumph; she knew she had been admired by Dan's family, and she experienced the sweetness of having pleased them for his sake; his happy eyes shone before her; but she was touched in her self-love by what her mother had coarsely characterised in them. They had regarded her liking them as a matter of course; his mother had ignored her even in pretending to decry Dan to her. But again this was very remote, very momentary. It was no nearer, no more lasting on the surface of her happiness, than the flying whiffs of thin cloud that chased across the moon and lost themselves in the vast blue around it.

William Dean Howells

XXXV

People came to the first of Mrs. James Bellingham's receptions with the expectation of pleasure which the earlier receptions of the season awaken even in the oldest and wisest. But they tried to dissemble their eagerness in a fashionable tardiness. "We get later and later," said Mrs. Brinkley to John Munt, as she sat watching the slow gathering of the crowd. By half-past eleven it had not yet hidden Mrs. Bellingham, where she stood near the middle of the room, from the pleasant corner they had found after accidentally arriving together. Mr. Brinkley had not come; he said he might not be too old for receptions, but he was too good; in either case he preferred to stay at home. "We used to come at nine o'clock, and now we come at I'm getting into a quotation from Mother Goose, I think."

"I thought it was Browning," said Munt, with his witticism manner. Neither he nor Mrs. Brinkley was particularly glad to be together, but at Mrs. James Bellingham's it was well not to fling any companionship away till you were sure of something else. Besides, Mrs. Brinkley was indolent and good-natured, and Munt was active and good-natured, and they were well fitted to get on for ten or fifteen minutes. While they talked she kept an eye out for other acquaintance, and he stood alert to escape at the first chance. "How is it we are here so early—or rather you are?" she pursued irrelevantly.

"Oh, I don't know," said Munt, accepting the implication of his superior fashion with pleasure. "I never mind being among the first. It's rather interesting to see people come in—don't you think?"

"That depends a good deal on the people. I don't find a great variety in their smirks and smiles to Mrs. Bellingham; I seem to be doing them all myself. And there's a monotony about their apprehension and helplessness when they're turned adrift that's altogether too much like my own. No, Mr. Munt, I can't agree with you that it's interesting to see people come in. It's altogether too autobiographical. What else have you to suggest?"

"I'm afraid I'm at the end of my string," said Munt. "I suppose we shall see the Pasmers and young Mavering here to-night."

Mrs. Brinkley turned and looked sharply at him.

"You've heard of the engagement?" he asked.

"No, decidedly, I haven't. And after his flight from Campobello it's the last thing I expected to hear of. When did it come out?"

"Only within a few days. They've been keeping it rather quiet. Mrs. Pasmer told me herself."

Mrs. Brinkley gave herself a moment for reflection. "Well, if he can stand it, I suppose I can."

"That isn't exactly what people are saying to Mrs. Pasmer, Mrs. Brinkley," suggested Munt, with his humorous manner.

"I dare say they're trying to make her believe that her daughter is sacrificed. That's the way. But she knows better."

"There's no doubt but she's informed herself. She put me through my catechism about the Maverings the day of the picnic down there."

"Do you know them?"

"Bridge Mavering and I were at Harvard together."

"Tell me about them." Mrs. Brinkley listened to Munt's praises of his old friend with an attention superficially divided with the people to whom she bowed and smiled. The room was filling up. "Well," she said at the end, "he's a sweet young fellow. I hope he likes his Pasmers."

"I guess there's no doubt about his liking one of them—the principal one."

"Yes, if she is the principal one." There was an implication in everything she said that Dan Mavering had been hoodwinked by Mrs. Pasmer. Mature ladies always like to imply something of the sort in these cases. They like to ignore the prime agency of youth and love, and pretend that marriage is a game that parents play at with us, as if we were in an old comedy; it is a tradition. "Will he take her home to live?"

"No. I heard that they're all going abroad—for a year, or two at least."

"Ah! I thought so," cried Mrs. Brinkley. She looked up with whimsical pleasure in the uncertainty of an old gentleman who is staring hard at her through his glasses. "Well," she said with a pleasant sharpness, "do you make me out?'

"As nearly as my belief in your wisdom will allow," said the old gentleman, as distinctly as his long white moustache and an apparent absence of teeth behind it would let him. John Munt had eagerly abandoned the seat he was keeping at Mrs. Brinkley's side, and had launched himself into the thickening crowd. The old gentleman, who was lank and tall, folded himself down into it, He continued as tranquilly as if seated quite alone with Mrs. Brinkley, and not minding that his voice, with the senile crow in it, made itself heard by others. "I'm always surprised to find sensible people at these things of Jane's. They're most extraordinary things. Jane's idea of society is to turn a herd of human beings loose in her house, and see what will come of it. She has no more sense of hospitality or responsibility than the Elements or Divine Providence. You may come here and have a good time—if you can get it; she won't object; or you may die of solitude and inanition; she'd never know it. I don't know but it's rather sublime in her. It's like the indifference of fate; but it's rather rough on those who don't understand it. She likes to see her rooms filled with pretty dresses, but she has no social instincts and no social inspiration whatever. She lights and heats and feeds her guests, and then she leaves them to themselves. She's a kind woman— Jane is a very good-natured woman, and I really think she'd be grieved if she thought any one went away unhappy, but she does nothing to make them at home in her house—absolutely nothing."

"Perhaps she does all they deserve for them. I don't know that any one acquires merit by coming to an evening party; and it's impossible to be personally hospitable to everybody in such a crowd."

"Yes, I've sometimes taken that view of it. And yet if you ask a stranger to your house, you establish a tacit understanding with him that you won't forget him after you have him there. I like to go about and note the mystification of strangers who've come here with some notion of a little attention. It's delight-fully poignant; I suffer with them; it's a cheap luxury of woe; I follow them through all the turns and windings of their experience. Of course the theory is that, being turned loose here with the rest, they may speak to anybody; but the fact is, they can't. Sometimes I should like to hail some of these unfriended spirits, but I haven't the courage. I'm not individually bashful, but I have a thousand years of Anglo-Saxon civilisation behind me. There ought to be policemen, to show strangers about and be kind to them. I've just seen two pretty women cast away in a corner, and clinging to a small water-colour on the wall with a show of interest that would melt a heart of stone. Why do you come, Mrs. Brinkley? I should like to know. You're not obliged to."

"No," said Mrs. Brinkley, lowering her voice instinctively, as if to bring his down. "I suppose I come from force of habit I've been coming a long time, you know. Why do you come?"

"Because I can't sleep. If I could sleep, I should be at home in bed." A weariness came into his thin face and dim eyes that was pathetic, and passed into a whimsical sarcasm. "I'm not one of the great leisure class, you know, that voluntarily turns night into day. Do you know what I go about saying now?"

"Something amusing, I suppose."

"You'd better not be so sure of that. I've discovered a fact, or rather I've formulated an old one. I've always been troubled how to classify people here, there are so many exceptions; and I've ended by broadly generalising them as women and men."

Mrs. Brinkley was certainly amused at this. "It seems to me that there you've been anticipated by nature—not to mention art."

"Oh, not in my particular view. The women in America represent the aristocracy which exists everywhere else in both sexes. You are born to the patrician leisure; you have the accomplishments and the clothes and manners and ideals; and we men are a natural commonalty, born to business, to news-papers, to cigars, and horses. This natural female aristocracy of ours establishes the forms, usages, places, and times of society. The epicene aristocracies of other countries turn night into day in their social pleasures, and our noblesse sympathetically follows their example. You ladies, who can lie till noon next day, come to Jane's reception at eleven o'clock, and you drag along with you a herd of us brokers, bankers, merchants, lawyers, and doctors, who must be at our offices and counting-rooms before nine in the morning. The hours of us work-people are regulated by the wholesome industries of the great democracy which we're a part of; and the hours of our wives and daughters by the deleterious pleasures of the Old World aristocracy. That's the reason we're not all at home in bed."

"I thought you were not at home in bed because you couldn't sleep."

"I know it. And you've no idea how horrible a bed is that you can't sleep in." The old man's voice broke in a tremor. "Ah, it's a bed of torture! I spend many a wicked hour in mine, envying St. Lawrence his gridiron. But what do you think of my theory?"

"It's a very pretty theory. My only objection to it is that it's too flattering. You know I rather prefer to abuse my sex; and to be set up as a natural aristocracy—I don't know that I can quite agree to that, even to account satisfactorily for being at your sister-in-law's reception."

"You're too modest, Mrs. Brinkley."

"No, really. There ought to be some men among us—men without morrows. Now, why don't you and my husband set an example to your sex? Why don't you relax your severe sense of duty? Why need you insist upon being at your offices every morning at nine? Why don't you fling off these habits of lifelong industry, and be gracefully indolent in the interest of the higher civilisation?"

Bromfield Corey looked round at her with a smile of relish for her satire. Her husband was a notoriously lazy man, who had chosen to live restrictedly upon an inherited property rather than increase it by the smallest exertion.

"Do you think we could get Andy Pasmer to join us?"

"No, I can't encourage you with that idea. You must get on without Mr. Pasmer; he's going back to Europe with his son-in-law."

"Do you mean that their girl's married?"

"No-engaged. It's just out."

"Well, I must say Mrs. Pasmer has made use of her time." He too liked to imply that it was all an effect of her manoeuvring, and that the young people had nothing to do with it; this survival from European fiction dies hard. "Who is the young man?"

Mrs. Brinkley gave him an account of Dan Mavering as she had seen him at Campobello, and of his family as she just heard of them. "Mr. Munt was telling me about them as you came up."

"Why, was that John Munt?"

"Yes; didn't you know him?"

"No," said Corey sadly. "I don't know anybody nowadays. I seem to be going to pieces every way. I don't call sixty-nine such a very great age."

"Not at all!" cried Mrs. Brinkley. "I'm fifty-four myself, and Brinkley's sixty."

"But I feel a thousand years old. I don't see people, and when I do I don't know 'em. My head's in a cloud." He let it hang heavily; then he lifted it, and said: "He's a nice, comfortable fellow, Munt is. Why didn't he stop and talk a bit?"

"Well, Munt's modest, you know; and I suppose he thought he might be the third that makes company a crowd. Besides, nobody stops and talks a bit at these things. They're afraid of boring or being bored."

"Yes, they're all in as unnatural a mood as if they were posing for a photograph. I wonder who invented this sort of thing? Do you know," said the old man, "that I think it's rather worse with us than with any other people? We're a simple, sincere folk, domestic in our instincts, not gregarious or frivolous in any way; and when we're wrenched away from our firesides, and packed in our best clothes into Jane's gilded saloons, we feel vindictive; we feel wicked. When the Boston being abandons himself—or herself—to fashion, she suffers a depravation into something quite lurid. She has a bad conscience, and she hardens her heart with talk that's tremendously cynical. It's amusing," said Corey, staring round him purblindly at the groups and files of people surging and eddying past the corner where he sat with Mrs. Brinkley.

"No; it's shocking," said his companion. "At any rate, you mustn't say such things, even if you think them. I can't let you go too far, you know. These young people think it heavenly, here."

She took with him the tone that elderly people use with those older than themselves who have begun to break; there were authority and patronage in it. At the bottom of her heart she thought that Bromfield Corey should not have been allowed to come; but she determined to keep him safe and harmless as far as she could.

From time to time the crowd was a stationary mass in front of them; then it dissolved and flowed away, to gather anew; there were moments when the floor near them was quite vacant; then it was inundated again with silken trains. From another part of the house came the sound of music, and most of the young people who passed went two and two, as if they were partners in the dance, and had come out of the ball-room between dances. There was a good deal of nervous talk, politely subdued among them; but it was not the note of unearthly rapture which Mrs. Brinkley's conventional claim had implied; it was self-interested, eager, anxious; and was probably not different from the voice of good society anywhere.

XXXVI

"Why, there's Dan Mavering now!" said Mrs. Brinkley, rather to herself than to her companion. "And alone!"

Dan's face showed above most of the heads and shoulders about him; it was flushed, and looked troubled and excited. He caught sight of Mrs. Brinkley, and his eyes brightened joyfully. He slipped quickly through the crowd, and bowed over her hand, while he stammered out, without giving her a chance for reply till the end: "O Mrs. Brinkley, I'm so glad to see you! I'm going—I want to ask a great favour of you, Mrs. Brinkley. I want to bring—I want to introduce some friends of mine to you—some ladies, Mrs. Brinkley; very nice people I met last summer at Portland. Their father—General Wrayne —has been building some railroads down East, and they're very nice people; but they don't know any one—any ladies— and they've been looking at the pictures ever since they came. They're very good pictures; but it isn't an exhibition!" He broke down with a laugh.

"Why, of course, Mr. Mavering; I shall be delighted," said Mrs. Brinkley, with a hospitality rendered reckless by her sympathy with the young fellow. "By all means!"

"Oh; thanks!—thank you aver so much!" said Dan. "I'll bring them to you—they'll understand!" He slipped into the crowd again.

Corey made an offer of going. Mrs. Brinkley stopped him with her fan. "No—stay, Mr. Corey. Unless you wish to go. I fancy it's the people you were talking about, and you must help me through with them."

"I ask nothing better," said the old man, unresentful of Dan's having not even seemed to see him, in his generous preoccupation. "I should like to see how you'll get on, and perhaps I can be of use."

"Of course you can—the greatest."

"But why hasn't he introduced them to his Pasmers? What? Eh? Oh!" Corey made these utterances in response to a sharper pressure of Mrs. Brinkley's fan on his arm.

Dan was opening a way through the crowd before them for two ladies, whom he now introduced. "Mrs. Frobisher, Mrs. Brinkley; and Miss Wrayne."

Mrs. Brinkley cordially gave her hand to the ladies, and said, "May I introduce Mr. Corey? Mr. Mavering, let me introduce you to Mr. Corey." The old man rose and stood with the little group.

Dan's face shone with flattered pride and joyous triumph. He bubbled out some happy incoherencies about the honour and pleasure, while at the same time he beamed with tender gratitude upon Mrs. Brinkley, who was behaving with a gracious, humorous kindliness to the aliens cast upon her mercies. Mrs. Frobisher, after a half-hour of Boston society, was not that presence of easy gaiety which crossed Dan's path on the Portland pavement the morning of his arrival from Campobello; but she was still a handsome, effective woman, of whom you would have hesitated to say whether she was showy or distinguished. Perhaps she was a little of both, with an air of command bred of supremacy in frontier garrisons; her sister was like her in the way that a young girl may be like a young matron. They blossomed alike in the genial atmosphere of Mrs. Brinkley and of Mr. Corey. He began at once to make bantering speeches with them both. The friendliness of an old man and a stout elderly woman might not have been their ideal of success at an evening party, used as they were to the unstinted homage of young captains and lieutenants, but a brief experience of Mrs. Bellingham's hospitality must have taught them humility; and when a stout, elderly gentleman, whose baldness was still trying to be blond, joined the group, the spectacle was not without its points of resemblance to a social ovation. Perhaps it was a Boston social ovation.

"Hallo, Corey!" said this stout gentleman, whom Mrs. Brinkley at once introduced as Mr. Bellingham, and whose salutation Corey returned with "Hallo, Charles!" of equal intimacy.

Mr. Bellingham caught at the name of Frobisher. "Mrs. Major Dick Frobisher?"

"Mrs. Colonel now, but Dick always," said the lady, with immediate comradery. "Do you know my husband?"

"I should think so!" said Bellingham; and a talk of common interest and mutual reminiscence sprang up between them. Bellingham graphically depicted his meeting with Colonel Frobisher the last time he was out on the Plains, and Mrs. Frobisher and Miss Wrayne discovered to their great satisfaction that he was the brother of Mrs. Stephen Blake, of Omaba, who had come out to the fort once with her husband, and captured the garrison, as they said. Mrs. Frobisher accounted for her present separation from her husband, and said she had come on for a while to be with her father and sister, who both needed more looking after than the Indians. Her father had left the army, and was building railroads.

Miss Wrayne, when she was not appealed to for confirmation or recollection by her sister, was having a lively talk with Corey and Mrs. Brinkley; she seemed to enter into their humour; and no one paid much attention to Dan Mavering. He hung upon the outskirts of the little group; proffering unrequited sympathy and applause; and at last he murmured something about having to go back to some friends, and took himself off. Mrs. Frobisher and Miss Wrayne let him go with a certain shade—the lightest, and yet evident—of not wholly satisfied pique: women know how to accept a reparation on account, and without giving a receipt in full.

Mrs. Brinkley gave him her hand with an effect of compassionate intelligence and appreciation of the sacrifice he must have made in leaving Alice. "May I congratulate you?" she murmured.

"Oh yes, indeed; thank you, Mrs. Brinkley," he gushed tremulously; and he pressed her hand hard, and clung to it, as if he would like to take her with him.

Neither of the older men noticed his going. They were both taken in their elderly way with these two handsome young women, and they professed regret—Bellingham that his mother was not there, and Corey that neither his wife nor daughters had come, whom they might otherwise have introduced. They did not offer to share their acquaintance with any one else, but they made the most of it themselves, as if knowing a good thing when they had it. Their devotion to Mrs. Frobisher and her sister heightened the curiosity of such people as noticed it, but it would be wrong to say that it moved any in that self-limited company with a strong wish to know the ladies. The time comes to every man, no matter how great a power he may be in society, when the general social opinion retires him for senility, and this time had come for Bromfield Corey. He could no longer make or mar any success; and Charles Bellingham was so notoriously amiable, so deeply compromised by his inveterate habit of liking nearly every one, that his notice could not distinguish or advantage a newcomer.

He and Corey took the ladies down to supper. Mrs. Brinkley saw them there together, and a little later she saw old Corey wander off; forgetful of Miss Wrayne. She saw Dan Mavering,

William Dean Howells

but not the Pasmers, and then, when Corey forgot Miss Wrayne, she saw Dan, forlorn and bewildered looking, approach the girl, and offer her his arm for the return to the drawing-room; she took it with a bright, cold smile, making white rings of ironical deprecation around the pupils of her eyes.

"What is that poor boy doing, I wonder?" said Mrs. Brinkley to herself.

XXXVII

The next morning Dan Mavering knocked at Boardman's door before the reporter was up. This might have been any time before one o'clock, but it was really at half-past nine. Boardman wanted to know who was there, and when Mavering had said it was he, Boardman seemed to ponder the fact awhile before Mavering heard him getting out of bed and coming barefooted to the door. He unlocked it, and got back into bed; then he called out, "Come in," and Mavering pushed the door open impatiently. But he stood blank and silent, looking helplessly at his friend. A strong glare of winter light came in through the naked sash—for Boardman apparently not only did not close his window-blinds, but did not pull down his curtains, when he went to bed—and shone upon his gay, shrewd face where he lay, showing his pop-corn teeth in a smile at Mavering.

"Prefer to stand?" he asked by and by, after Mavering had remained standing in silence, with no signs of proposing to sit down or speak. Mavering glanced at the only chair in the room: Boardman's clothes dripped and dangled over it. "Throw 'em on the bed," he said, following Mavering's glance.

"I'll take the bed myself," said Mavering; and he sat down on the side of it, and was again suggestively silent.

Boardman moved his head on the pillow, as he watched Mavering's face, with the agreeable sense of personal security which we all feel in viewing trouble from the outside: "You seem balled up about something."

Mavering sighed heavily. "Balled up? It's no word for it. Boardman, I'm done for. Yesterday I was the happiest fellow in the world, and now—Yes, it's all over with me, and it's my own fault, as usual. Look; at that!" He jerked Boardman a note which he had been holding fast in his band, and got up and went to look himself at the wide range of chimney-pots and slated roofs which Boardman's dormer-window commanded.

"Want me to read it?" Boardman asked; and Mavering nodded without glancing round. It dispersed through the air of Boardman's room, as he unfolded it, a thin, elect perfume, like a feminine presence, refined and strict; and Boardman involuntarily passed his hand over his rumpled hair, as if to make himself a little more personable before reading the letter.

"DEAR MR. MAVERING,—I enclose the ring you gave me the other day, and I release you from the promise you gave with it. I am convinced that you wronged yourself in offering either without your whole heart, and I care too much for your happiness to let you persist in your sacrifice.

"In begging that you will not uselessly attempt to see me, but that you will consider this note final, I know you will do me the justice not to attribute an ungenerous motive to me. I shall rejoice to hear of any good that may befall you; and I shall try not to envy any one through whom it comes.—Yours sincerely,"

"ALICE PASMER.

"P.S.—I say nothing of circumstances or of persons; I feel that any comment of mine upon them would be idle."

Mavering looked up at the sound Boardman made in refolding the letter. Boardman grinned, with sparkling eyes. "Pretty neat," he said.

"Pretty infernally neat," roared Mavering.

"Do you suppose she means business?"

"Of course she means business. Why shouldn't she?"

"I don't know. Why should she?"

"Well, I'll tell you, Boardman. I suppose I shall have to tell you if I'm going to get any good out of you; but it's a dose." He came away from the window, and swept Boardman's clothes off the chair preparatory to taking it.

Boardman lifted his head nervously from the pillow.

"Oh; I'll put them on the bed, if you're so punctilious!" cried Mavering.

"I don't mind the clothes," said Boardman. "I thought I heard my watch knock on the floor in my vest pocket. Just take it out, will you, and see if you've stopped it?"

"Oh, confound your old Waterbury! All the world's stopped; why shouldn't your watch stop too?" Mavering tugged it out of the pocket, and then shoved it back disdainfully. "You couldn't stop that thing with anything short of a sledge-hammer; it's rattling away like a mowing-machine. You know those Portland women—those ladies I spent the day with when you were down there at the regatta—the day I came from Campobello—Mrs. Frobisher and her sister?" He agglutinated one query to another till he saw a light of intelligence dawn in Boardman's eye. "Well, they're at the bottom of it, I suppose. I was introduced to them on Class Day, and I ought to have shown them some attention there; but the moment I saw Alice—Miss Pasmer—I forgot all about 'em. But they didn't seem to have noticed it much, and I made it all right with 'em that day at Portland; and they came up in the fall, and I made an appointment with them to drive out to Cambridge and show them the place. They were to take me up at the Art Museum; but that was the day I met Miss Pasmer, and I—I forgot about those women again."

Boardman was one of those who seldom laugh; but his grin expressed all the malicious enjoyment he felt. He said nothing in the impressive silence which Mavering let follow at this point.

"Oh, you think it was funny?" cried Mavering. "I thought it was funny too; but Alice herself opened my eyes to what I'd done, and I always intended to make it all right with them when I got the chance. I supposed she wished me too."

Boardman grinned afresh.

"She told me I must; though she seemed to dislike my having been with them the day after she'd thrown me over. But if"— Mavering interrupted himself to say, as the grin widened on Boardman's face—"if you think it was any case of vulgar jealousy, you're very much mistaken, Boardman. She isn't capable of it, and she was so magnanimous about it that I made up my mind to do all I could to retrieve myself. I felt that it was my duty to her. Well, last night at Mrs. Jim Bellingham's reception—"

A look of professional interest replaced the derision in Boardman's eyes. "Any particular occasion for the reception? Given in honour of anybody?"

"I'll contribute to your society notes some other time, Boardman," said Mavering haughtily. "I m speaking to a friend, not an interviewer. Well, whom should I see after the first waltz—I'd been dancing with Alice, and we were taking a turn through the drawing-room, and she hanging on my arm, and I knew everybody saw how it was, and I was feeling well— whom should I see but these women. They were in a corner by themselves, looking at a picture, and trying to look as if they were doing it voluntarily. But I could see at a glance that they didn't know anybody; and I knew they had better be in the heart of the Sahara without acquaintances than where they were; and when they bowed forlornly across the room to me, my heart was in my mouth, I felt so sorry for them; and I told Alice who they were; and I supposed she'd want to rush right over to them with me—"

"And did she rush?" asked Boardman, filling up a pause which Mavering made in wiping his face.

"How infernally hot you have it in here!" He went to the window and threw it up; and then did not sit down again, but continued to walk back and forth as he talked. "She didn't seem to know who they were at first, and when I made her understand she hung back, and said, 'Those showy things?' and I must say I think she was wrong; they were dressed as quietly as nine-tenths of the people there; only they are rather large, handsome women. I said I thought we ought to go and speak to them, they seemed stranded there; but she didn't seem to see it; and, when I persisted, she said, 'Well, you go if you think best; but take me to mamma.' And I supposed it was all right; and I told Mrs. Pasmer I'd be back in a minute, and then I went off to those women. And after I'd talked with them a while I saw Mrs. Brinkley sitting with old Bromfield Corey in another corner, and I got them across and introduced them; after I'd explained to Mrs. Brinkley who they were; and they began to have a good time, and I—didn't."

"Just so," said Boardman.

"I thought I hadn't been gone any while at all from Alice; but the weather had changed by the time I had got back. Alice was pretty serious, and she was engaged two or three dances deep; and I could see her looking over the fellows' shoulders, as she went round and round, pretty pale. I hung about till she was free; but then she couldn't dance with me; she said her head ached, and she made her mother take her home before supper; and I mooned round like my own ghost a while, and then I went home. And as if that wasn't enough, I could see by the looks of those other women—old Corey forgot Miss Wrayne

William Dean Howells

in the supper-room, and I had to take her back—that I hadn't made it right with them, even; they were as hard and smooth as glass. I'd ruined myself, and ruined myself for nothing."

Mavering flung Boardman's chair over, and seated himself on its rungs.

"I went to bed, and waited for the next thing to happen. I found my thunderbolt waiting for me when I woke up. I didn't know what it was going to be, but when I felt a ring through the envelope of that note I knew what it was. I mind-read that note before I opened it."

"Give it to the Society for Psychical Research," suggested Boardman. "Been to breakfast?"

"Breakfast!" echoed Mavering. "Well, now, Boardman, what use do you suppose I've got for breakfast under the circumstances?"

"Well, not very much; but your story's made me pretty hungry. Would you mind turning your back, or going out and sitting on the top step of the stairs' landing, or something, while I get up and dress?"

"Oh, I can go, if you want to get rid of me," said Mavering, with unresentful sadness. "But I hoped you might have something to suggest, Boardy.'"

"Well, I've suggested two things, and you don't like either. Why not go round and ask to see the old lady?"

"Mrs. Pasmer?"

"Yes."

"Well, I thought of that. But I didn't like to mention it, for fear you'd sit on it. When would you go?"

"Well, about as quick as I could get there. It's early for a call, but it's a peculiar occasion, and it'll show your interest in the thing. You can't very well let it cool on your hands, unless you mean to accept the situation."

"What do you mean?" demanded Mavering, getting up and standing over Boardman. "Do you think I could accept the situation, as you call it, and live?"

"You did once," said Boardman. "You couldn't, unless you could fix it up with Mrs. Frobisher's sister."

Mavering blushed. "It was a different thing altogether then. I could have broken off then, but I tell you it would kill me now. I've got in too deep. My whole life's set on that girl. You can't understand, Boardman, because you've never been there; but I couldn't give her up."

"All right. Better go and see the old lady without loss of time; or the old man, if you prefer."

Mavering sat down on the edge of the bed again. "Look here, Boardman, what do you mean?"

"By what?"

"By being so confoundedly heartless. Did you suppose that I wanted to pay those women any attention last night from an interested motive?"

"Seems to have been Miss Pasmer's impression."

"Well, you're mistaken. She had no such impression. She would have too much self-respect, too much pride—magnanimity. She would know that after such a girl as she is I couldn't think of any other woman; the thing is simply impossible."

"That's the theory."

William Dean Howells

"Theory? It's the practice!"

"Certain exceptions."

"There's no exception in my case. No, sir! I tell you this thing is for all time—for eternity. It makes me or it mars me, once for all. She may listen to me or she may not listen, but as long as she lives there's no other woman alive for me."

"Better go and tell her so. You're wasting your arguments on me."

"Why?"

"Because I'm convinced already. Because people always marry their first and only loves. Because people never marry twice for love. Because I've never seen you hit before, and I know you never could be again. Now go and convince Miss Pasmer. She'll believe you, because she'll know that she can never care for any one but you, and you naturally can't care for anybody but her. It's a perfectly clear case. All you've got to do is to set it before her."

"If I were you, I wouldn't try to work that cynical racket, Boardman," said Mavering. He rose, but he sighed drearily, and regarded Boardman's grin with lack-lustre absence. But he went away without saying anything more; and walked mechanically toward the Cavendish. As he rang at the door of Mrs. Pasmer's apartments he recalled another early visit he had paid there; he thought how joyful and exuberant he was then, and how crushed and desperate now. He was not without youthful satisfaction in the disparity of his different moods; it seemed to stamp him as a man of large and varied experience.

XXXVIII

Mrs. Pasmer was genuinely surprised to see Mavering, and he pursued his advantage—if it was an advantage—by coming directly to the point. He took it for granted that she knew all about the matter, and he threw himself upon her mercy without delay.

"Mrs. Pasmer, you must help me about this business with Alice," he broke out at once. "I don't know what to make of it; but I know I can explain it. Of course," he added, smiling ruefully, "the two statements don't hang together; but what I mean is that if I can find out what the trouble is, I can make it all right, because there's nothing wrong about it; don't you see?"

Mrs. Pasmer tried to keep the mystification out of her eye; but she could not even succeed in seeming to do so, which she would have liked almost as well.

"Don't you know what I mean?" asked Dan.

Mrs. Pasmer chanced it. "That Alice was a little out of sorts last night?" she queried leadingly.

"Yes," said Mavering fervently. "And about her—her writing to me."

"Writing to you?" Mrs. Pasmer was going to ask, when Dan gave her the letter.

William Dean Howells

"I don't know whether I ought to show it, but I must. I must have your help, and I can't, unless you understand the case."

Mrs. Pasmer had begun to read the note. It explained what the girl herself had refused to give any satisfactory reason for—her early retirement from the reception, her mysterious disappearance into her own room on reaching home, and her resolute silence on the way. Mrs. Pasmer had known that there must be some trouble with Dan, and she had suspected that Alice was vexed with him on account of those women; but it was beyond her cheerful imagination that she should go to such lengths in her resentment. She could conceive of her wishing to punish him, to retaliate her suffering on him; but to renounce him for it was another thing; and she did not attribute to her daughter any other motive than she would have felt herself. It was always this way with Mrs. Pasmer: she followed her daughter accurately up to a certain point; beyond that she did not believe the girl knew herself what she meant; and perhaps she was not altogether wrong. Girlhood is often a turmoil of wild impulses, ignorant exaltations, mistaken ideals, which really represent no intelligent purpose, and come from disordered nerves, ill-advised reading, and the erroneous perspective of inexperience. Mrs. Pasmer felt this, and she was tempted to break into a laugh over Alice's heroics; but she preferred to keep a serious countenance, partly because she did not feel the least seriously. She was instantly resolved not to let this letter accomplish anything more than Dan's temporary abasement, and she would have preferred to shorten this to the briefest moment possible. She liked him, and she was convinced that Alice could never do better, if half so well. She would now have preferred to treat him with familiar confidence, to tell him that she had no idea of Alice's writing him that nonsensical letter, and he was not to pay the least attention to it; for of course it meant nothing; but another principle of her complex nature came into play, and she silently folded the note and returned it to Dan, trembling before her.

"Well?" he quavered.

"Well," returned Mrs. Pasmer judicially, while she enjoyed his tremor, whose needlessness inwardly amused her—"well, of course, Alice was—"

"Annoyed, I know. And it was all my fault—or my misfortune. But I assure you, Mrs. Pasmer, that I thought I was doing something that would please her—in the highest and noblest way. Now don't you know I did?"

Mrs. Pasmer again wished to laugh, but in the face of Dan's tragedy she had to forbear. She contented herself with saying: "Of course. But perhaps it wasn't the best time for pleasing her just in that way."

"It was then or never. I can see now—why, I could see all the time—just how it might look; but I supposed Alice wouldn't care for that, and if I hadn't tried to make some reparation then to Mrs. Frobisher and her sister, I never could. Don't you see?"

"Yes, certainly. But—"

"And Alice herself told me to go and look after them," interposed Mavering. He suppressed, a little uncandidly, the fact of her first reluctance.

"But you know it was the first time you had been out together?"

"Yes."

"And naturally she would wish to have you a good deal to herself, or at least not seeming to run after other people."

"Yes, yes; I know that."

"And no one ever likes to be taken at their word in a thing like that."

"I ought to have thought of that, but I didn't. I wish I had gone to you first, Mrs. Pasmer. Somehow it seems to me as if I were very young and inexperienced; I didn't use to feel so. I wish you were always on hand to advise me, Mrs. Pasmer." Dan hung his head, and his face, usually so gay, was blotted with gloom.

"Will you take my advice now?" asked Mrs. Pasmer.

"Indeed I will!" cried the young fellow, lifting his head. "What is it?"

"See Alice about this."

Dan jumped to his feet, and the sunshine broke out over his face again. "Mrs. Pasmer, I promised to take your advice, and I'll do it. I will see her. But how? Where? Let me have your advice on that point too."

They began to laugh together, and Dan was at once inexpressibly happy. Those two light natures thoroughly comprehended each other.

Mrs. Pasmer had proposed his seeing Alice with due seriousness, but now she had a longing to let herself go; she felt all the pleasure that other people felt in doing Dan Mavering a pleasure, and something more, because he was so perfectly intelligible to her. She let herself go.

"You might stay to breakfast."

"Mrs. Pasmer, I will—I will do that too. I m awfully hungry, and I put myself in your hands."

"Let me see," said Mrs. Pasmer thoughtfully, "how it can be contrived."

"Yes;" said Mavering, ready for a panic. "How? She wouldn't stand a surprise?"

"No; I had thought of that."

"No behind-a-screen or next-room business?"

"No," said Mrs. Pasmer, with a light sigh. "Alice is peculiar. I'm afraid she wouldn't like it."

"Isn't there any little ruse she would like?"

"I can't think of any. Perhaps I'd better go and tell her you're here and wish to see her."

"Do you think you'd better?" asked Dan doubtfully. "Perhaps she won't come."

"She will come," said Mrs. Pasmer confidently.

She did not say that she thought Alice would be curious to know why he had come, and that she was too just to condemn him unheard.

But she was right about the main point. Alice came, and Dan could see with his own weary eyes that she had not slept either.

She stopped just inside the portiere, and waited for him to speak. But he could not, though a smile from his sense of the absurdity of their seriousness hovered about his lips. His first impulse was to rush upon her and catch her in his arms, and perhaps this might have been well, but the moment for it passed, and then it became impossible.

"Well?" she said at last, lifting her head, and looking at him with impassioned solemnity. "You wished to see me? I hoped you wouldn't. It would have spared me something. But perhaps I had no right to your forbearance."

"Alice, how can you say such things to me?" asked the young fellow, deeply hurt.

She responded to his tone. "I'm sorry if it wounds you. But I only mean what I say."

"You've a right to my forbearance, and not only that, but to my—my life; to everything that I am," cried Dan, in a quiver of tenderness at the sight of her and the sound of her voice. "Alice, why did you write me that letter?—why did you send me back my ring?"

"Because," she said, looking him seriously in the face—"because I wished you to be free, to be happy."

"Well, you've gone the wrong way about it. I can never be free from you; I never can be happy without you."

"I did it for your good, then, which ought to be above your happiness. Don't think I acted hastily. I thought it over all night long. I didn't sleep—"

"Neither did I," interposed Dan.

"And I saw that I had no claim to you; that you never could be truly happy with me—"

"I'll take the chances," he interrupted. "Alice, you don't suppose I cared for those women any more than the ground under your feet, do you? I don't suppose I should ever have given them a second thought if you hadn't seemed to feel so badly about my neglecting them; and I thought you'd be pleased to have me try to make it up to them if I could."

"I know your motive was good—the noblest. Don't think that I did you injustice, or that I was vexed because you went away with them."

"You sent me."

"Yes; and now I give you up to them altogether. It was a mistake, a crime, for me to think we could be anything to each other when our love began with a wrong to some one else."

"With a wrong to some one else?"

"You neglected them on Class Day after you saw me."

"Why, of course I did. How could I help it?"

A flush of pleasure came into the girl's pale face; but she banished it, and continued gravely, "Then at Portland you were with them all day."

"You'd given me up—you'd thrown me over, Alice," he pleaded.

"I know that; I don't blame you. But you made them believe that you were very much interested in them."

"I don't know what I did. I was perfectly desperate."

"Yes; it was my fault. And then, when they came to meet you at the Museum, I had made you forget them; I'd made you wound them and insult them again. No. I've thought it all out, and we never could be happy. Don't think that I do it from any resentful motive."

"Alice? how could I think that?—Of you!"

"I have tried—prayed—to be purified from that, and I believe that I have been."

"You never had a selfish thought."

"And I have come to see that you were perfectly right in what you did last night. At first I was wounded."

"Oh, did I wound you, Alice?" he grieved.

"But afterward I could see that you belonged to them, and not me, and—and I give you up to them. Yes, freely, fully."

Alice stood there, beautiful, pathetic, austere; and Dan had halted in the spot to which he had advanced, when her eye forbade him to approach nearer. He did not mean to joke, and it was in despair that he cried out: "But which, Alice? There are two of them."

"Two?" she repeated vaguely.

"Yes; Mrs. Frobisher and Miss Wrayne. You can't give me up to both of them."

"Both?" she repeated again. She could not condescend to specify; it would be ridiculous, and as it was, she felt her dignity hopelessly shaken. The tears came into her eyes.

"Yes. And neither of them wants me—they haven't got any use for me. Mrs. Frobisher is married already, and Miss Wrayne took the trouble last night to let me feel that, so far as she was concerned, I hadn't made it all right, and couldn't. I thought I had rather a cold parting with you, Alice, but it was quite tropical to what you left me to." A faint smile, mingled with a blush of relenting, stole into her face, and he hurried on. "I don't suppose I tried very hard to thaw her out. I wasn't much interested. If you must give me up, you must give me up to some one else, for they don't want me, and I don't want them." Alice's head dropped lover, and he could come nearer now without her seeming to know it. "But why need you give me up? There's really no occasion for it, I assure you."

"I wished," she explained, "to show you that I loved you for something above yourself and myself—far above either—"

She stopped and dropped the hand which she had raised to fend him off; and he profited by the little pause she made to take her in his arms without seeming to do so. "Well," he said, "I don't believe I was formed to be loved on a very high plane. But I'm not too proud to be loved for my own sake; and I don't think there's anything above you, Alice."

"Oh yes, there is! I don't deserve to be happy, and that's the reason why I'm not allowed to be happy in any noble way. I can't bear to give you up; you know I can't; but you ought to give me up—indeed you ought. I have ideals, but I can't live up to them. You ought to go. You ought to leave me." She accented each little sentence by vividly pressing herself to his heart, and he had the wisdom or the instinct to treat their reconciliation as nothing settled, but merely provisional in its nature.

"Well, we'll see about that. I don't want to go till after breakfast, anyway; your mother says I may stay, and I'm awfully hungry. If I see anything particularly base in you, perhaps I sha'n't come back to lunch."

Dan would have liked to turn it alt off into a joke, now that the worst was apparently over; but Alice freed herself from him, and held him off with her hand set against his breast. "Does mamma know about it?" she demanded sternly.

"Well, she knows there's been some misunderstanding," said Dan, with a laugh that was anxious, in view of the clouds possibly gathering again.

"How much?"

"Well, I can't say exactly." He would not say that he did not know, but he felt that he could truly say that he could not say.

She dropped her hand, and consented to be deceived. Dan caught her again to his breast; but he had an odd, vague sense of doing it carefully, of using a little of the caution with which one seizes the stem of a rose between the thorns.

"I can bear to be ridiculous with you," she whispered, with an implication which he understood.

"You haven't been ridiculous, dearest," he said; and his tension gave way in a convulsive laugh, which partially expressed his feeling of restored security, and partly his amusement in realising how the situation would have pleased Mrs. Pasmer if she could have known it.

Mrs. Pasmer was seated behind her coffee biggin at the breakfast-table when he came into the room with Alice, and she lifted an eye from its glass bulb long enough to catch his flying glance of exultation and admonition. Then, while she regarded the chemical struggle in the bulb, with the rapt eye of a magician reading fate in his crystal ball, she questioned herself how much she should know, and how much she should ignore. It was a great moment for Mrs. Pasmer, full of delicious choice. "Do you understand this process, Mr. Mavering?" she said, glancing up at him warily for farther instruction.

"I've seen it done," said Dan, "but I never knew how it was managed. I always thought it was going to blow up; but it seemed to me that if you were good and true and very meek, and had a conscience void of offence, it wouldn't."

"Yes, that's what it seems to depend upon," said Mrs. Pasmer, keeping her eye on the bulb. She dodged suddenly forward, and put out the spirit-lamp. "Now have your coffee!" she cried, with a great air of relief. "You must need it by this time," she said with a low cynical laugh—"both of you!"

"Did you always make coffee with a biggin in France, Mrs. Pasmer?" asked Dan; and he laughed out the last burden that lurked in his heart.

Mrs. Pasmer joined him. "No, Mr. Mavering. In France you don't need a biggin. I set mine up when we went to England."

Alice looked darkly from one of these light spirits to the other, and then they all shrieked together.

They went on talking volubly from that, and they talked as far away from what they were thinking about as possible. They talked of Europe, and Mrs. Pasmer said where they would live and what they would do when they all got back there together. Dan abetted her, and said that they must cross in June. Mrs. Pasmer said that she thought June was a good month. He asked if it were not the month of the marriages too, and she answered that he must ask Alice about that. Alice blushed and laughed her sweet reluctant laugh, and said she did not know; she had never been married.

It was silly, but it was delicious; it made them really one family. Deep in his consciousness a compunction pierced and teased Dan. But he said to himself that it was all a joke about their European plans, or else his people would consent to it if he really wished it.

XXXIX

A period of entire harmony and tenderness followed the episode which seemed to threaten the lovers with the loss of each other. Mavering forbore to make Alice feel that in attempting a sacrifice which consulted only his good and ignored his happiness, and then failing in it so promptly, she had played rather a silly part. After one or two tentative jokes in that direction he found the ground unsafe, and with the instinct which served him in place of more premeditated piety he withdrew, and was able to treat the affair with something like religious awe. He was obliged, in fact, to steady Alice's own faith in it, and to keep her from falling under dangerous self-condemnation in that and other excesses of uninstructed self-devotion. This brought no fatigue to his robust affection, whatever it might have done to a heart more tried in such exercises. Love acquaints youth with many things in character and temperament which are none the less interesting because it never explains them; and Dan was of such a make that its revelations of Alice were charming to him because they were novel. He had thought her a person of such serene and flawless wisdom that it was rather a relief to find her subject to gusts of imprudence, to unexpected passions and resentments, to foibles and errors, like other people. Her power of cold reticence; which she could employ at will, was something that fascinated him almost as much as that habit of impulsive concession which seemed to came neither from her will nor her reason. He was a person himself who was so eager to give other people pleasure that he quivered with impatience to see them happy through his words or acts; he could not bear to think that any one to whom he was speaking was not perfectly comfortable in regard to him; and it was for this reason perhaps that he admired a girl who could prescribe herself a line of social conduct, and follow it out regardless of individual pangs—who could act from ideals and principles, and not from emotions and sympathies. He knew that she had the emotions and sympathies, for there were times when she lavished them on him; and that she could seem without them was another proof of that depth of nature which he liked to imagine had first attracted him to her. Dan Mavering had never been able to snub any one in his life; it gave him a great respect for Alice that it seemed not to cost her an effort or a regret, and it charmed him to think that her severity was part of the unconscious sham which imposed her upon the world for a person of inflexible design and invariable constancy to it. He was not long in seeing that she shared this illusion, if it was an illusion, and that perhaps the only person besides himself who was in the joke was her mother. Mrs. Pasmer and he grew more and more into each other's confidence in talking Alice over, and he admired the intrepidity of this lady, who was not afraid of her daughter even in the girl's most topping moments of self-abasement. For his own part, these moods of hers never failed to cause him confusion and anxiety. They commonly intimated themselves parenthetically in the midst of some blissful talk they were having, and overcast his clear sky with retrospective ideals of conduct or presentimental plans for contingencies that might never occur. He found himself suddenly under condemnation for not having reproved her at a given time when she forced him to admit she had seemed unkind or cold to others; she made him promise that even at the risk of alienating her affections he would make up for her deficiencies of behaviour in such matters whenever he noticed them. She now praised him for what he had done for Mrs. Frobisher and her sister at Mrs. Bellingham's reception; she said it was generous, heroic. But Mavering rested satisfied with his achievement in that instance, and did not attempt anything else of the kind. He did not reason from cause to effect in regard to it: a man's love is such that while it lasts he cannot project its object far enough from him to judge it reasonable or

William Dean Howells

unreasonable; but Dan's instincts had been disciplined and his perceptions sharpened by that experience. Besides, in bidding him take this impartial and even admonitory course toward her, she stipulated that they should maintain to the world a perfect harmony of conduct which should be an outward image of the union of their lives. She said that anything less than a continued self-sacrifice of one to the other was not worthy of the name of love, and that she should not be happy unless he required this of her. She said that they ought each to find out what was the most distasteful thing which they could mutually require, and then do it; she asked him to try to think what she most hated, and let her do that for him; as for her, she only asked to ask nothing of him.

Mavering could not worship enough this nobility of soul in her, and he celebrated it to Boardman with the passionate need of imparting his rapture which a lover feel. Boardman acquiesced in silence, with a glance of reserved sarcasm, or contented himself with laconic satire of his friend's general condition, and avoided any comment that might specifically apply to the points Dan made. Alice allowed him to have this confidant, and did not demand of him a report of all he said to Boardman. A main fact of their love, she said, must be their utter faith in each other. She had her own confidante, and the disparity of years between her and Miss Cotton counted for nothing in the friendship which their exchange of trust and sympathy cemented. Miss Cotton, in the freshness of her sympathy and the ideality of her inexperience, was in fact younger than Alice, at whose feet, in the things of soul and character, she loved to sit. She never said to her what she believed: that a girl of her exemplary principles, a nature conscious of such noble ideals, so superior to other girls, who in her place would be given up to the happiness of the moment, and indifferent to the sense of duty to herself and to others, was sacrificed to a person of Mavering's gay, bright nature and trivial conception of life. She did not deny his sweetness; that was perhaps the one saving thing about him; and she confessed that he simply adored Alice; that counted for everything, and it was everything in his favour that he could appreciate such a girl. She hoped, she prayed, that Alice might never realise how little depth he had; that she might go through life and never suspect it. If she did so, then they might be happy together to the end, or at least Alice might never know she was unhappy.

Miss Cotton never said these things in so many words; it is doubtful if she ever said them in any form of words; with her sensitive anxiety not to do injustice to any one, she took Dan's part against those who viewed the engagement as she allowed it to appear only to her secret heart. She defended him the more eagerly because she felt that it was for Alice's sake, and that everything must be done to keep her from knowing how people looked at the affair, even to changing people's minds. She said to all who spoke to her of it that of course Alice was superior to him, but he was devoted to her, and he would grow into an equality with her. He was naturally very refined, she said, and, if he was not a very serious person, he was amiable beyond anything. She alleged many little incidents of their acquaintance at Campobello in proof of her theory that he had an instinctive appreciation of Alice, and she was sure that no one could value her nobleness of character more than he. She had seen them a good deal together since their engagement, and it was beautiful to see his manner with her. They were opposites, but she counted a good deal upon that very difference in their temperaments to draw them to each other.

It was an easy matter to see Dan and Alice together. Their engagement came out in the usual way: it had been announced to a few of their nearest friends, and intelligence of it soon spread from their own set through society generally; it had been published in the Sunday papers while it was still in the tender condition of a rumour, and had been denied by some of their acquaintance and believed by all.

The Pasmer cousinship had been just in the performance of the duties of blood toward Alice since the return of her family from Europe, and now did what was proper in the circumstances. All who were connected with her called upon her and congratulated her; they knew Dan, the younger of them, much better than they knew her; and though he had shrunk from the nebulous bulk of social potentiality which every young man is to that much smaller nucleus to which definite betrothal reduces him, they could be perfectly sincere in calling him the sweetest fellow that ever was, and too lovely to live.

In such a matter Mr. Pasmer was naturally nothing; he could not be less than he was at other times, but he was not more; and it was Mrs. Pasmer who shared fully with her daughter the momentary interest which the engagement gave Alice with all her kindred. They believed, of course, that they recognised in it an effect of her skill in managing; they agreed to suppose that she had got Mavering for Alice, and to ignore the beauty and passion of youth as factors in the case. The closest of the kindred, with the romantic delicacy of Americans in such things, approached the question of Dan's position and prospects, and heard with satisfaction the good accounts which Mrs. Pasmer was able to give of his father's prosperity. There had always been more or less apprehension among them of a time when a family subscription would be necessary for Bob Pasmer, and in the relief which the new situation gave them some of them tried to remember having known Dan's father in College, but it finally came to their guessing that they must have heard John Munt speak of him.

Mrs. Pasmer had a supreme control in the affair. She believed with the rest—so deeply is this delusion seated—that she had made the match; but knowing herself to have used no dishonest magic in the process, she was able to enjoy it with a clean conscience. She grew fonder of Dan; they understood each other; she was his refuge from Alice's ideals, and helped him laugh off his perplexity with them. They were none the less sincere because they were not in the least frank with each other. She let Dan beat about the bush to his heart's content, and waited for him at the point which she knew he was coming to, with an unconsciousness which he knew was factitious; neither of them got tired of this, or failed freshly to admire the other's strategy.

William Dean Howells

XL

It cannot be pretended that Alice was quite pleased with the way her friends took her engagement, or rather the way in which they spoke of Dan. It seemed to her that she alone, or she chiefly, ought to feel that sweetness and loveliness of which every one told her, as if she could not have known it. If he was sweet and lovely to every one, how was he different to her except in degree? Ought he not to be different in kind? She put the case to Miss Cotton, whom it puzzled, while she assured Alice that he was different in kind to her, though he might not seem so; the very fact that he was different in degree proved that he was different in kind. This logic sufficed for the moment of its expression, but it did not prevent Alice from putting the case to Dan himself. At one of those little times when she sat beside him alone and rearranged his necktie, or played with his watch chain, or passed a critical hand over his cowlick, she asked him if he did not think they ought to have an ideal in their engagement. "What ideal?" he asked. He thought it was all solid ideal through and through. "Oh," she said, "be more and more to each other." He said he did not see how that could be; if there was anything more of him, she was welcome to it, but he rather thought she had it all. She explained that she meant being less to others; and he asked her to explain that.

"Well, when we're anywhere together, don't you think we ought to show how different we are to each other from what we are to any one else."

Dan laughed. "I'm afraid we do, Alice; I always supposed one ought to hide that little preference as much as possible. You don't want me to be dangling after you every moment?"

"No-o-o. But not—dangle after others."

Dan sighed a little—a little impatiently. "Do I dangle after others?"

"Of course not. But show that we're thoroughly united in all our tastes and feelings, and—like and dislike the same persons."

"I don't think that will be difficult," said Dan.

She was silent a moment, and then she said; "You don't like to have me bring up such things?"

"Oh yes, I do. I wish to be and do just what you wish."

"But I can see, I can understand, that you would sooner pass the time without talking of them. You like to be perfectly happy, and not to have any cares when—when you're with me this way?"

"Well, yes, I suppose I do," said Dan, laughing again. "I suppose I rather do like to keep pleasure and duty apart. But there's nothing you can wish, Alice, that isn't a pleasure to me."

"I'm very different," said the girl. "I can't be at peace unless I know that I have a right to be so. But now, after this, I'm going to do your way. If it's your way, it'll be the right way— for me." She looked sublimely resolved, with a grand lift of the eyes, and Dan caught her to him in a rapture, breaking into laughter.

"Oh, don't! Mine's a bad way—the worst kind of a way," he cried.

William Dean Howells

"It makes everybody like you, and mine makes nobody like me."

"It makes me like you, and that's quite enough. I don't want other people to like you!"

"Yes, that's what I mean!" cried Alice; and now she flung herself on his neck, and the tears came. "Do you suppose it can be very pleasant to have everybody talking of you as if everybody loved you as much—as much as I do?" She clutched him tighter and sobbed.

"O Alice! Alice! Alice! Nobody could ever be what you are to me!" He soothed and comforted her with endearing words and touches; but before he could have believed her half consoled she pulled away from him, and asked, with shining eyes, "Do you think Mr. Boardman is a good influence in your life?"

"Boardman!" cried Mavering, in astonishment. "Why, I thought you liked Boardman?"

"I do; and I respect him very much. But that isn't the question. Don't you think we ought to ask ourselves how others influence us?"

"Well, I don't see much of Boardy nowadays; but I like to drop down and touch earth in Boardy once in a while—I'm in the air so much. Board has more common-sense, more solid chunk-wisdom, than anybody I know. He's kept me from making a fool of myself more times—"

"Wasn't he with you that day with—with those women in Portland?"

Dan winced a little, and then laughed. "No, he wasn't. That was the trouble. Boardman was off on the press boat. I thought I told you. But if you object to Boardman—"

"I don't. You mustn't think I object to people when I ask you about them. All that I wished was that you should think yourself what sort of influence he was. I think he's a very good influence."

"He's a splendid fellow, Boardman is, Alice!" cried Dan. "You ought to have seen how he fought his way through college on such a little money, and never skulked or felt mean. He wasn't appreciated for it; the men don't notice these things much; but he didn't want to have it noticed; always acted as if it was neither here nor there; and now I guess he sends out home whatever he has left after keeping soul and body together every week."

He spoke, perhaps, with too great an effect of relief. Alice listened, as it seemed, to his tone rather than his words, and said absently—

"Yes, that's grand. But I don't want you to act as if you were afraid of me in such things."

"Afraid?" Dan echoed.

"I don't mean actually afraid, but as if you thought I couldn't be reasonable; as if you supposed I didn't expect you to make mistakes or to be imperfect."

"Yes, I know you're very reasonable, and you're more patient with me than I deserve; I know all that, and it's only my wish to come up to your standard, I suppose, that gives me that apprehensive appearance."

"That was what vexed me with you there at Campobello, when you—asked me—"

"Yes, I know."

"You ought to have understood me better. You ought to know now that I don't wish you to do anything on my account, but because it's something we owe to others."

"Oh, excuse me! I'd much rather do it for you," cried Dan; but Alice looked so grave, so hurt, that he hastened on: "How in the world does it concern others whether we are devoted or not, whether we're harmonious and two-souls-with-but-a-single-thought, and all that?" He could not help being light about it.

"How?" Alice repeated. "Won't it give them an idea of what—what—of how much—how truly—if we care for each other—how people ought to care? We don't do it for ourselves. That would be selfish and disgusting. We do it because it's something that we owe to the idea of being engaged—of having devoted our lives to each other, and would show—would teach—"

"Oh yes! I know what you mean," said Dan, and he gave way in a sputtering laugh. "But they wouldn't understand. They'd only think we were spoons on each other; and if they noticed that I cooled off toward people I'd liked, and warmed up toward those you liked, they'd say you made me."

"Should you care?" asked Alice sublimely, withdrawing a little from his arm.

"Oh no! only on your account," he answered, checking his laugh.

"You needn't on my account," she returned. "If we sacrifice some little preferences to each other, isn't that right? I shall be glad to sacrifice all of mine to you. Isn't our—marriage to be full of such sacrifices? I expect to give up everything to you." She looked at him with a sad severity.

He began to laugh again. "Oh no, Alice Don't do that! I couldn't stand it. I want some little chance at the renunciations myself."

She withdrew still further from his side, and said, with a cold anger, "It's that detestable Mrs. Brinkley."

"Mrs. Brinkley!" shouted Dan.

"Yes; with her pessimism. I have heard her talk. She influences you. Nothing is sacred to her. It was she who took up with those army women that night."

"Well, Alice, I must say you can give things as ugly names as the next one. I haven't seen Mrs. Brinkley the whole winter, except in your company. But she has more sense than all the other women I know."

"Oh, thank you!"

"You know I don't mean you," he pushed on. "And she isn't a pessimist. She's very kindhearted, and that night she was very polite and good to those army women, as you call them, when you had refused to say a word or do anything for them."

"I knew it had been rankling in your mind all along," said the girl "I expected it to coma out sooner or later. And you talk about renunciation! You never forget nor forgive the slightest thing. But I don't ask your forgiveness."

"Alice!"

"No. You are as hard as iron. You have that pleasant outside manner that makes people think you're very gentle and yielding, but all the time you're like adamant. I would rather die than ask your forgiveness for anything, and you'd rather let me than give it."

"Well, then, I ask your forgiveness, Alice, and I'm sure you won't let me die without it."

They regarded each other a moment. Then the tenderness gushed up in their hearts, a passionate tide, and swept them into each other's arms.

"O Dan," she cried, "how sweet you are! how good! how

lovely! Oh, how wonderful it is! I wanted to hate you, but I couldn't. I couldn't do anything but love you. Yes, now I understand what love is, and how it can do everything, and last for ever."

XLI

Mavering came to lunch the next day, and had a word with Mrs. Pasmer before Alice came in. Mr. Pasmer usually lunched at the club.

"We don't see much of Mrs. Saintsbury nowadays," he suggested.

"No; it's a great way to Cambridge," said Mrs. Pasmer, stifling, in a little sigh of apparent regret for the separation, the curiosity she felt as to Dan's motive in mentioning Mrs. Saintsbury. She was very patient with him when he went on.

"Yes, it is a great way. And a strange thing about it is that when you're living here it's a good deal further from Boston to Cambridge than it is from Cambridge to Boston."

"Yes," said Mrs. Pasmer; "every one notices that."

Dan sat absently silent for a time before he said, "Yes, I guess I must go out and see Mrs. Saintsbury."

"Yes, you ought. She's very fond of you. You and Alice ought both to go."

"Does Mrs. Saintsbury like me?" asked Dan. "Well, she's awfully nice. Don't you think she's awfully fond of formulating people?"

"Oh, everybody in Cambridge does that. They don't gossip; they merely accumulate materials for the formulation of character."

"And they get there just the same!" cried Dan. "Mrs. Saintsbury used to think she had got me down pretty fine," he suggested.

"Yes!" said Mrs. Pasmer, with an indifference which they both knew she did not feel.

"Yes. She used to accuse me of preferring to tack, even in a fair wind."

He looked inquiringly at Mrs. Pasmer; and she said, "How ridiculous!"

"Yes, it was. Well, I suppose I am rather circuitous about some things."

"Oh, not at all!"

"And I suppose I'm rather a trial to Alice in that way."

He looked at Mrs. Pasmer again, and she said: "I don't believe you are, in the least. You can't tell what is trying to a girl."

"No," said Dan pensively, "I can't." Mrs. Pasmer tried to render the interest in her face less vivid. "I can't tell where she's going to bring up. Talk about tacking!"

"Do you mean the abstract girl; or Alice?"

"Oh, the abstract girl," said Dan, and they laughed together. "You think Alice is very straightforward, don't you?"

"Very," said Mrs. Pasmer, looking down with a smile—"for a girl."

"Yes, that's what I mean. And don't you think the most circuitous kind of fellow would be pretty direct compared with the straight-forwardest kind of girl?"

There was a rueful defeat and bewilderment in Dan's face that made Mrs. Pasmer laugh. "What has she been doing now?" she asked.

"Mrs. Pasmer," said Dan, "you and I are the only frank and open people I know. Well, she began to talk last night about influence—the influence of other people on us; and she killed off nearly all the people I like before I knew what she was up to, and she finished with Mrs. Brinkley. I'm glad she didn't happen to think of you, Mrs. Pasmer, or I shouldn't be associating with you at the present moment." This idea seemed to give Mrs. Pasmer inexpressible pleasure. Dan went on: "Do you quite see the connection between our being entirely devoted to each other and my dropping Mrs. Brinkley?"

"I don't know," said Mrs. Pasmer. "Alice doesn't like satirical people."

"Well, of course not. But Mrs. Brinkley is such an admirer of hers."

"I dare say she tells you so."

"Oh, but she is!"

"I don't deny it," said Mrs. Pasmer. "But if Alice feels some-thing inimical—antipatico—in her atmosphere, it's no use talking."

"Oh no, it's no use talking, and I don't know that I want to talk." After a pause, Mavering asked, "Mrs. Pasmer, don't you think that where two people are going to be entirely devoted to each other, and self-sacrificing to each other, they ought to divide, and one do all the devotion, and the other all the self-sacrifice?"

Mrs. Pasmer was amused by the droll look in Dan's eyes. "I think they ought to be willing to share evenly," she said.

"Yes; that's what I say—share and share alike. I'm not selfish about those little things." He blew off a long sighing breath. "Mrs. Pasmer, don't you think we ought to have an ideal of conduct?"

Mrs. Pasmer abandoned herself to laughter. "O Dan! Dan! You will be the death of me."

"We will die together, then, Mrs. Pasmer. Alice will kill me." He regarded her with a sad sympathy in his eye as she laughed and laughed with delicious intelligence of the case. The intelligence was perfect, from their point of view; but whether it fathomed the girl's whole intention or aspiration is another matter. Perhaps this was not very clear to herself. At any rate, Mavering did not go any more to see Mrs. Brinkley, whose house he had liked to drop into. Alice went several times, to show, she said, that she had no feeling in the matter; and Mrs. Brinkley, when she met Dan, forbore to embarrass him with questions or reproaches; she only praised Alice to him.

There were not many other influences that Alice cut him off from; she even exposed him to some influences that might have been thought deleterious. She made him go and call alone upon certain young ladies whom she specified, and she praised several others to him, though she did not praise them for the same things that he did. One of them was a girl to whom Alice had taken a great fancy, such as often buds into a romantic passion between women; she was very gentle and mild, and she had none of that strength of will which she admired in Alice. One night there was a sleighing party to a hotel in the suburbs, where they had dancing and then supper. After the supper they danced "Little Sally Waters" for a finale, instead of the Virginia Reel, and Alice would not go on the floor with Dan; she said she disliked that dance; but she told him to dance with Miss Langham. It became a gale of fun, and in the height of it Dan slipped and fell with his partner. They laughed it off, with the rest, but after a while the girl began to cry; she had received a painful bruise. All the way home, while the others laughed and sang and chattered, Dan was troubled about this poor girl; his anxiety became a joke with the whole sleighful of people.

When he parted with Alice at her door, he said, "I'm afraid I hurt Miss Langham; I feel awfully about it."

"Yes; there's no doubt of that. Good night!"

She left him to go off to his lodging, hot and tingling with indignation at her injustice. But kindlier thoughts came to him before he slept, and he fell asleep with a smile of tenderness for her on his lips. He could see how he was wrong to go out with any one else when Alice said she disliked the dance; he ought not to have taken advantage of her generosity in appointing him a partner; it was trying for her to see him make that ludicrous tumble, of course; and perhaps he had overdone the attentive sympathy on the way home. It flattered him that she could not help showing her jealousy—that is flattering, at first; and Dan was able to go and confess all but this to Alice. She received his submission magnanimously, and said that she was glad it had happened, because his saying this showed that now they understood each other perfectly. Then she fixed her eyes on his, and said, "I've just been round to see Lilly, and she's as well as ever; it was only a nervous shock."

Whether Mavering was really indifferent to Miss Langham's condition, or whether the education of his perceptions had gone so far that he consciously ignored her, he answered, "That was splendid of you, Alice."

"No," she said; "it's you that are splendid; and you always are. Oh, I wonder if I can ever be worthy of you!"

Their mutual forgiveness was very sweet to them, and they went on praising each other. Alice suddenly broke away from this weakening exchange of worship, and said, with that air of coming to business which he lad learned to recognise and dread a little, "Dan, don't you think I ought to write to your mother?"

"Write to my mother?"

"Why, you have written to her. You wrote as soon as you got back, and she answered you."

"Yes; but write regularly?—Show that I think of her all the time?" When I really think I'm going to take you from her, I seem so cruel and heartless!"

"Oh, I don't look at it in that light, Alice."

"Don't joke! And when I think that we're going away to leave her, for several years, perhaps, as soon as we're married, I can't make it seem right. I know how she depends upon your being near her, and seeing her every now and then; and to go off to Europe for years, perhaps—Of course you can be of use to your father there; but do you think it's right toward your mother? I want you to think."

Dan thought, but his thinking was mainly to the effect that he did not know what she was driving at. Had she got any inkling of that plan of his mother's for them to come and stay a year or two at the Falls after their marriage? He always expected to be able to reconcile that plan with the Pasmer plan of going at once; to his optimism the two were not really incompatible; but he did not wish them prematurely confronted in Alice's mind. Was this her way of letting him know that she knew what his mother wished, and that she was willing to make the sacrifice? Or was it just some vague longing to please him by a show of affection toward his family, an unmeditated impulse of reparation? He had an impulse himself to be frank with Alice, to take her at her word, and to allow that he did not like the notion of going abroad. This was Dan's notion of being frank; he could still reserve the fact that he had given his mother a tacit promise to bring Alice home to live, but he postponed even this. He said: "Oh, I guess that'll be all right,

Alice. At any rate, there's no need to think about it yet awhile. That can be arranged."

"Yes," said Alice; "but don't you think I'd better get into the habit of writing regularly to your mother now, so that there needn't be any break when we go abroad?" He could see now that she had no idea of giving that plan up, and he was glad that he had not said anything. "I think," she continued, "that I shall write to her once a week, and give her a full account of our life from day to day; it'll be more like a diary; and then, when we get over there, I can keep it up without any effort, and she won't feel so much that you've gone."

She seemed to refer the plan to him, and he said it was capital. In fact, he did like the notion of a diary; that sort of historical view would involve less danger of precipitating a discussion of the two schemes of life for the future. "It's awfully kind of you, Alice, to propose such a thing, and you mustn't make it a burden. Any sort of little sketchy record will do; mother can read between the lines, you know."

"It won't be a burden," said the girl tenderly. "I shall seem to be doing it for your mother, but I know I shall be doing it for you. I do everything for you. Do you think it's right?"

"Oh; it must be," said Dan, laughing. "It's so pleasant."

"Oh," said the girl gloomily; "that's what makes me doubt it."

XLII

Eunice Mavering acknowledged Alice's first letter. She said that her mother read it aloud to them all, and had been delighted with the good account she gave of Dan, and fascinated with all the story of their daily doings and sayings. She wished Eunice to tell Alice how fully she appreciated her thoughtfulness of a sick old woman, and that she was going to write herself and thank her. But Eunice added that Alice must not be surprised if her mother was not very prompt in this, and she sent messages from all the family, affectionate for Alice, and polite for her father and mother.

Alice showed Dan the letter, and he seemed to find nothing noticeable in it. "She says your mother will write later," Alice suggested.

"Yes. You ought to feel very much complimented by that. Mother's autographs are pretty uncommon," he said, smiling.

"Why, doesn't she write? Can't she? Does it tire her?" asked Alice.

"Oh yes, she can write, but she hates to. She gets Eunice or Minnie to write usually."

"Dan," cried Alice intensely, "why didn't you tell me?"

"Why, I thought you knew it," he explained easily. "She likes to read, and likes to talk, but it bores her to write. I don't suppose I get more than two or three pencil scratches from her in the course of a year. She makes the girls write. But you needn't mind her not writing. You may be sure she's glad of your letters."

"It makes me seem very presumptuous to be writing to her when there's no chance of her answering," Alice grieved. "It's as if I had passed over your sisters' heads. I ought to have written to them."

"Oh, well, you can do that now," said Dan soothingly.

"No. No, I can't do it now. It would be ridiculous." She was silent, and presently she asked, "Is there anything else about your mother that I ought to know?" She looked at him with a sort of impending discipline in her eyes which he had learned to dread; it meant such a long course of things, such a very great variety of atonement and expiation for him, that he could not bring himself to confront it steadily.

His heart gave a feeble leap; he would have gladly told her all that was in it, and he meant to do so at the right time, but this did not seem the moment. "I can't say that there is," he answered coldly.

In that need of consecrating her happiness which Alice felt, she went a great deal to church in those days. Sometimes she felt the need almost of defence against her happiness, and a vague apprehension mixed with it. Could it be right to let it claim her whole being, as it seemed to do? Than was the question which she once asked Dan, and it made him laugh, and catch her to him in a rapture that served for the time, and then left her to more morbid doubts. Evidently he could not follow her in them; he could not even imagine them; and while he was with her they seemed to have no verity or value. But she talked them over very hypothetically and impersonally with Miss Cotton, in whose sympathy they resumed all their import, and gained something more. In the idealisation which the girl underwent in this atmosphere all her thoughts and purposes

William Dean Howells

had a significance which she would not of herself, perhaps, have attached to them. They discussed them and analysed them with a satisfaction in the result which could not be represented without an effect of caricature. They measured Alice's romance together, and evolved from it a sublimation of responsibility, of duty, of devotion, which Alice found it impossible to submit to Dan when he came with his simple-hearted, single-minded purpose of getting Mrs. Pasmer out of the room, and sitting down with his arm around Alice's waist. When he had accomplished this it seemed sufficient in itself, and she had to think, to struggle to recall things beyond it, above it. He could not be made to see at such times how their lives could be more in unison than they were. When she proposed doing something for him which he knew was disagreeable to her, he would not let her; and when she hinted at anything she wished him to do for her because she knew it was disagreeable to him, he consented so promptly, so joyously, that she perceived he could not have given the least thought to it.

She felt every day that they were alien in their tastes and aims; their pleasures were not the same, and though it was sweet, though it was charming, to have him give up so willingly all his preferences, she felt, without knowing that the time must come when this could not be so, that it was all wrong.

"But these very differences, these antagonisms, if you wish to call them so," suggested Miss Cotton, in talking Alice's misgivings over with her, "aren't they just what will draw you together more and more? Isn't it what attracted you to each other? The very fact that you are such perfect counterparts—"

"Yes," the girl assented, "that's what we're taught to believe." She meant by the novels, to which we all trust our instruction in such matters, and her doubt doubly rankled after she had put it to silence.

She kept on writing to Dan's mother, though more and more perfunctorily; and now Eunice and now Minnie Mavering acknowledged her letters. She knew that they must think she was silly, but having entered by Dan's connivance upon her folly, she was too proud to abandon it.

At last, after she had ceased to expect it, came a letter from his mother, not a brief note, but a letter which the invalid had evidently tasked herself to make long and full, in recognition of Alice's kindness in writing to her so much. The girl opened it, and, after a verifying glance at the signature, began to read it with a thrill of tender triumph, and the fond prevision of the greater pleasure of reading it again with Dan.

But after reading it once through, she did not wait for him before reading it again and again. She did this with bewilderment, intershot with flashes of conviction, and then doubts of this conviction. When she could misunderstand no longer, she rose quietly and folded the letter, and put it carefully back into its envelope and into her writing desk, where she sat down and wrote, in her clearest and firmest hand, this note to Mavering—

"I wish to see you immediately.

"ALICE PASMER."

XLIII

Dan had learned, with a lover's keenness, to read Alice's moods in the most colourless wording of her notes. She was rather apt to write him notes, taking back or reaffirming the effect of something that had just passed between them. Her note were tempered to varying degrees of heat and cold, so fine that no one else would have felt the difference, but sensible to him in their subtlest intention.

Perhaps a mere witness of the fact would have been alarmed by a note which began without an address, except that on the envelope, and ended its peremptory brevity with the writer's name signed in full. Dan read calamity in it, and he had all the more trouble to pull himself together to meet it because he had parted with unusual tenderness from Alice the night before, after an evening in which it seemed to him that their ideals had been completely reconciled.

The note came, as her notes were apt to come, while Dan was at breakfast, which he was rather luxurious about for so young a man, and he felt formlessly glad afterward that he had drunk his first cup of coffee before he opened it, for it chilled the second cup, and seemed to take all character out of the omelet.

He obeyed it, wondering what the doom menaced in it might be, but knowing that it was doom, and leaving his breakfast half-finished, with a dull sense of the tragedy of doing so.

He would have liked to ask for Mrs. Pasmer first, and interpose a moment of her cheerful unreality between himself and his interview with Alice, but he decided that he had better not do this, and they met at once, with the width of the room between them. Her look was one that made it impassable to the simple impulse he usually had to take her in his arms and kiss her. But as she stood holding out a letter to him, with the apparent intention that he should come and take it, he traversed the intervening space and took it.

"Why, it's from mother!" he said joyously, with a glance at the handwriting.

"Will you please explain it?" said Alice, and Dan began to read it.

It began with a good many excuses for not having written before, and went on with a pretty expression of interest in Alice's letters and gratitude for them; Mrs. Mavering assured the girl that she could not imagine what a pleasure they had been to her. She promised herself that they should be great friends, and she said that she looked forward eagerly to the time, now drawing near, when Dan should bring her home to them. She said she knew Alice would find it dull at the Falls except for him, but they would all do their best, and she would find the place very different from what she had seen it in the winter. Alice could make believe that she was there just for the summer, and Mrs. Mavering hoped that before the summer was gone she would be so sorry for a sick old woman that she would not even wish to go with it. This part of the letter, which gave Dan away so hopelessly, as he felt, was phrased so touchingly, that he looked up from it with moist eyes to the hard cold judgment in the eyes of Alice.

"Will you please explain it?" she repeated.

He tried to temporise. "Explain what?"

Alice was prompt to say, "Had you promised your mother to

take me home to live?"

Dan did not answer.

"You promised my mother to go abroad. What else have you promised?" He continued silent, and she added, "You are a faithless man." They were the words of Romola, in the romance, to Tito; she had often admired them; and they seemed to her equally the measure of Dan's offence.

"Alice—"

"Here are your letters and remembrances, Mr. Mavering." Dan mechanically received the packet she had been holding behind her; with a perverse freak of intelligence he observed that, though much larger now, it was tied up with the same ribbon which had fastened it when Alice returned his letters and gifts before. "Good-bye. I wish you every happiness consistent with your nature."

She bowed coldly, and was about to leave him, as she had planned; but she had not arranged that he should be standing in front of the door, and he was there, with no apparent intention of moving.

"Will you allow me to pass?" she was forced to ask, however, haughtily.

"No!" he retorted, with a violence that surprised him. "I will not let you pass till you have listened to me—till you tell me why you treat me so. I won't stand it—I've had enough of this kind of thing."

It surprised Alice too a little, and after a moment's hesitation she said, "I will listen to you," so much more gently than she had spoken before that Dan relaxed his imperative tone, and began to laugh. "But," she added, and her face clouded again, "it will be of no use. My mind is made up this time. Why should we talk?"

"Why, because mine isn't," said Dan. "What is the matter, Alice? Do you think I would force you, or even ask you, to go home with me to live unless you were entirely willing? It could only be a temporary arrangement anyway."

"That isn't the question," she retorted. "The question is whether you've promised your mother one thing and me another."

"Well, I don't know about promising," said Dan, laughing a little more uneasily, but still laughing. "As nearly as I can remember, I wasn't consulted about the matter. Your mother proposed one thing, and my mother proposed another."

"And you agreed to both. That is quite enough—quite characteristic!"

Dan flushed, and stopped laughing. "I don't know what you mean by characteristic. The thing didn't have to be decided at once, and I didn't suppose it would be difficult for either side to give way, if it was judged best. I was sure my mother wouldn't insist."

"It seems very easy for your family to make sacrifices that are not likely to be required of them."

"You mustn't criticise my mother!" cried Dan.

"I have not criticised her. You insinuate that we would be too selfish to give up, if it were for the best."

"I do nothing of the kind, and unless you are determined to quarrel with me you wouldn't say so."

"I don't wish a quarrel; none is necessary," said Alice coldly.

"You accuse me of being treacherous—"

"I didn't say treacherous!"

"Faithless, then. It's a mere quibble about words. I want you to take that back."

"I can't take it back; it's the truth. Aren't you faithless, if you let us go on thinking that you're going to Europe, and let your mother think that we're coming home to live after we're married?"

"No! I'm simply leaving the question open!"

"Yes," said the girl—sadly, "you like to leave questions open. That's your way."

"Well, I suppose I do till it's necessary to decide them. It saves the needless effusion of talk," said Dan, with a laugh; and then, as people do in a quarrel, he went back to his angry mood, and said "Besides, I supposed you would be glad of the chance to make some sacrifice for me. You're always asking for it."

"Thank you, Mr. Mavering," said Alice, "for reminding me of it; nothing is sacred to you, it seems. I can't say that you have ever sought any opportunities of self-sacrifice."

"I wasn't allowed time to do so; they were always presented."

"Thank you again, Mr. Mavering. All this is quite a revelation. I'm glad to know how you really felt about things that you seemed so eager for."

"Alice, you know that I would do anything for you!" cried Dan, rueing his precipitate words.

"Yes; that's what you've repeatedly told me. I used to believe it."

"And I always believed what you said. You said at the picnic that day that you thought I would like to live at Ponkwasset Falls if my business was there—"

"That is not the point!"

"And now you quarrel with me because my mother wishes me to do so."

Alice merely said: "I don't know why I stand here allowing you to intimidate me in my father's house. I demand that you shall stand aside and let me pass."

"I'll not oblige you to leave the room," said Dan. "I will go. But if I go, you will understand that I don't come back."

"I hope that," said the girl.

"Very well. Good morning, Miss Pasmer."

She inclined her head slightly in acknowledgment of his bow, and he whirled out of the room and down the dim narrow passageway into the arms of Mrs. Pasmer, who had resisted as long as she could her curiosity to know what the angry voices of himself and Alice meant.

"O Mr. Mavering, is it you?" she buzzed; and she flung aside one pretence for another in adding, "Couldn't Alice make you stay to breakfast?"

Dan felt a rush of tenderness in his heart at the sound of the kind, humbugging little voice. "No, thank you, Mrs. Pasmer, I couldn't stay, thank you. I—I thank you very much. I—good-bye, Mrs. Pasmer." He wrung her hand, and found his way out of the apartment door, leaving her to clear up the mystery of his flight and his broken words as she could.

"Alice," she said, as she entered the room, where the girl had remained, "what have you been doing now?"

"Oh, nothing," she said, with a remnant of her scorn for Dan qualifying her tone and manner to her mother. "I've dismissed Mr. Mavering."

"Then you want him to come to lunch?" asked her mother. "I should advise him to refuse."

"I don't think he'd accept," said Alice. Then, as Mrs. Pasmer stood in the door, preventing her egress, as Dan had done before, she asked meekly "Will you let me pass, mamma? My head aches."

Mrs. Pasmer, whose easy triumphs in so many difficult circumstances kept her nearly always in good temper, let herself go, at these words, in vexation very uncommon with her. "Indeed I shall not!" she retorted. "And you will please sit down here and tell me what you mean by dismissing Mr. Mavering. I'm tired of your whims and caprices."

"I can't talk," began the girl stubbornly.

"Yes, I think you can," said her mother. "At any rate, I can. Now what is it all?"

"Perhaps this letter, will explain," said Alice, continuing to dignify her enforced submission with a tone of unabated hauteur; and she gave her mother Mrs. Mavering's letter, which Dan had mechanically restored to her.

Mrs. Pasmer read it, not only without indignation, but apparently without displeasure. But, she understood perfectly what the trouble was, when she looked up and asked, cheerfully, "Well?"

"Well!" repeated Alice, with a frown of astonishment. "Don't you see that he's promised us one thing and her another, and that he's false to both?"

"I don't know," said Mrs. Pasmer, recovering her good-humour in view of a situation that she felt herself able to cope with. "Of course he has to temporise, to manage a little. She's an invalid, and of course she's very exacting. He has to humour her. How do you know he has promised her? He hasn't promised us."

"Hasn't promised us?" Alice gasped.

"No. He's simply fallen in with what we've said. It's because he's so sweet and yielding, and can't bear to refuse. I can understand it perfectly."

"Then if he hasn't promised us, he's deceived us all the more shamefully, for he's made us think he had."

"He hasn't me," said Mrs. Pasmer, smiling at the stormy virtue in her daughter's face. "And what if you should go home awhile with him—for the summer, say? It couldn't last longer, much; and it wouldn't hurt us to wait. I suppose he hoped for something of that kind."

"Oh, it isn't that," groaned the girl, in a kind of bewilderment. "I could have gone there with him joyfully, and lived all my days, if he'd only been frank with me."

"Oh no, you couldn't," said her mother, with cosy security. "When it comes to it, you don't like giving up any more than other people. It's very hard for you to give up; he sees that—he knows it, and he doesn't really like to ask any sort of sacrifice from you. He's afraid of you."

"Don't I know that?" demanded Alice desolately: "I've known it from the first, and I've felt it all the time. It's all a mistake, and has been. We never could understand each other. We're too different."

"That needn't prevent you understanding him. It needn't prevent you from seeing how really kind and good he is—how faithful and constant he is."

"Oh, you say that—you praise him—because you like him."

"Of course I do. And can't you?"

"No. The least grain of deceit—of temporising, you call it—spoils everything. It's over," said the girl, rising, with a sigh, from the chair she had dropped into. "We're best apart; we could only have been wretched and wicked together."

"What did you say to him, Alice?" asked her mother, unshaken by her rhetoric.

"I told him he was a faithless person."

"Then you were a cruel girl," cried Mrs. Pasmer, with sudden indignation; "and if you were not my daughter I could be glad he had escaped you. I don't know where you got all those silly, romantic notions of yours about these things. You certainly didn't get them from me," she continued, with undeniable truth, "and I don't believe you get them from your Church, It's just as Miss Anderson said: your Church makes allowance for human nature, but you make none."

"I shouldn't go to Julia Anderson for instruction in such matters," said the girl, with cold resentment.

"I wish you would go to her for a little commonsense—or somebody," said Mrs. Pasmer. "Do you know what talk this will make?"

"I don't care for the talk. It would be worse than talk to marry a man whom I couldn't trust—who wanted to please me so much that he had to deceive me, and was too much afraid of me to tell me the truth."

"You headstrong girl!" said her mother impartially, admiring at the same time the girl's haughty beauty.

There was an argument in reserve in Mrs. Pasmer's mind which perhaps none but an American mother would have hesitated to urge; but it is so wholly our tradition to treat the important business of marriage as a romantic episode that even she could not bring herself to insist that her daughter should not throw away a chance so advantageous from every worldly point of view. She could only ask, "If you break this engagement, what do you expect to do?"

"The engagement is broken. I shall go into a sisterhood."

"You will do nothing of the kind, with my consent," said Mrs. Pasmer. "I will have no such nonsense. Don't flatter yourself that I will. Even if I approved of such a thing, I should think it wicked to let you do it. You're always fancying yourself doing something very devoted, but I've never seen you ready to give up your own will, or your own comfort even, in the slightest degree. And Dan Mavering, if he were twice as temporising and circuitous"—the word came to her from her talk with him—"would be twice too good for you. I'm going to breakfast."

XLIV

The difficulty in life is to bring experience to the level of expectation, to match our real emotions in view of any great occasion with the ideal emotions which we have taught ourselves that we ought to feel. This is all the truer when the occasion is tragical: we surprise ourselves in a helplessness to which the great event, death, ruin, lost love, reveals itself slowly, and at first wears the aspect of an unbroken continuance of what has been, or at most of another incident in the habitual sequence.

Dan Mavering came out into the bright winter morning knowing that his engagement was broken, but feeling it so little that he could not believe it. He failed to realise it, to seize it for a fact, and he could not let it remain that dumb and formless wretchedness, without proportion or dimensions, which it now seemed to be, weighing his life down. To verify it, to begin to outlive it, he must instantly impart it, he must tell it, he must see it with others' eyes. This was the necessity of his youth and of his sympathy, which included himself as well as the rest of the race in its activity. He had the usual environment of a young man who has money. He belonged to clubs, and he had a large acquaintance among men of his own age, who lived a life of greater leisure; or were more absorbed in business, but whom he met constantly in society. For one reason or another, or for no other reason than that he was Dan Mavering and liked every one, he liked them all. He thought himself great friends with them; he dined and lunched with them; and they knew the Pasmers, and all about his engagement. But he did not go to any of them now, with the need he felt to impart his calamity, to get the support of come other's credence and opinion of it. He went to a friend whom, in the way of his world, he met very seldom, but whom he always found, as he said, just where he had left him.

Boardman never made any sign of suspecting that he was put on and off, according to Dan's necessity or desire for comfort or congratulation; but it was part of their joke that Dan's coming to him always meant something decisive in his experiences. The reporter was at his late breakfast, which his landlady furnished him in his room, though, as Mrs. Mash said, she never gave meals, but a cup of coffee and an egg or two, yes.

"Well?" he said, without looking up.

"Well, I'm done for!" cried Dan.

"Again?" asked Boardman.

"Again! The other time was nothing, Boardman—I knew it wasn't anything; but this—this is final."

"Go on," said Boardman, looking about for his individual salt-cellar, which he found under the edge of his plate; and Mavering laid the whole case before him. As he made no comment on it for a while, Dan was obliged to ask him what he thought of it. "Well," he said, with the smile that showed the evenness of his pretty teeth, "there's a kind of wild justice in it." He admitted this, with the object of meeting Dan's views in an opinion.

"So you think I'm a faithless man too, do you?" demanded Mavering stormily.

"Not from your point of view," said Boardman, who kept on quietly eating and drinking.

Mavering was too amiable not to feel Boardman's innocence of offence in his unperturbed behaviour. "There was no faithlessness about it, and you know it," he went on, half laughing, half crying, in his excitement, and making Boardman the avenue of an appeal really addressed to Alice. "I was ready to do what either side decided."

"Or both," suggested Boardman.

"Yes, or both," said Dan, boldly accepting the suggestion. "It wouldn't have cost me a pang to give up if I'd been in the place of either."

"I guess that's what she could never understand," Boardman mused aloud.

"And I could never understand how any one could fail to see that that was what I intended—expected: that it would all come out right of itself—naturally." Dan was still addressing Alice in this belated reasoning. "But to be accused of bad faith—of trying to deceive any one—"

"Pretty rough," said Boardman.

"Rough? It's more than I can stand!"

"Well, you don't seem to be asked to stand it," said Boardman, and Mavering laughed forlornly with him at his joke, and then walked away and looked out of Boardman's dormer-window on the roofs below, with their dirty, smoke-stained February snow. He pulled out his handkerchief, and wiped his face with it. When he turned round, Boardman looked keenly at him, and asked, with an air of caution, "And so it's all up?"

"Yes, it's all up," said Dan hoarsely.

"No danger of a relapse?"

"What do you mean?"

"No danger of having my sympathy handed over later to Miss Pasmer for examination?"

"I guess you can speak up freely, Boardman," said Dan, "if that's what you mean. Miss Pasmer and I are quits."

"Well, then, I'm glad of it. She wasn't the one for you. She isn't fit for you."

"What's the reason she isn't?" cried Dan. "She's the most beautiful and noble girl in the world, and the most conscientious, and the best—if she is unjust to me."

"No doubt of that. I'm not attacking her, and I'm not defending you."

"What are you doing then?"

"Simply saying that I don't believe you two would ever understand each other. You haven't got the same point of view, and you couldn't make it go. Both out of a scrape."

"I don't know what you mean by a scrape," said Dan, resenting the word more than the idea. Boardman tacitly refused to modify or withdraw it, and Dan said, after a sulky silence, in which he began to dramatise a meeting with his family: "I'm going home; I can't stand it here. What's the reason you can't come with me, Boardman?"

"Do you mean to your rooms?"

"No; to the Falls."

"Thanks. Guess not."

"Why not?"

"Don't care about being a fifth wheel."

William Dean Howells

"Oh, pshaw, now, Boardman! Look here, you must go. I want you to go. I—I want your support. That's it. I'm all broken up, and I couldn't stand that three hours' pull alone. They'll be glad to see you—all of them. Don't you suppose they'll be glad to see you? They're always glad; and they'll understand."

"I don't believe you want me to go yourself. You just think you do."

"No. I really do want you, Boardman. I want to talk it over with you. I do want you. I'm not fooling."

"Don't think I could get away." Yet he seemed to be pleased with the notion of the Falls; it made him smile.

"Well, see," said Mavering disconsolately. "I'm going round to my rooms now, and I'll be there till two o'clock; train's at 2.30." He went towards the door, where he faced about. "And you don't think it would be of any use?"

"Any use—what?"

"Trying to—to—to make it up."

"How should I know?"

"No, no; of course you couldn't," said Dan, miserably downcast. All the resentment which Alice's injustice had roused in him had died out; he was suffering as helplessly and hopelessly as a child. "Well," he sighed, as he swung out of the door.

Boardman found him seated at his writing-desk in his smoking-jacket when he came to him, rather early, and on the desk were laid out the properties of the little play which had come to a tragic close. There were some small bits of jewellery, among the rest a ring of hers which Alice had been letting him wear; a lock of her hair which he had kept, for the greater convenience of kissing, in the original parcel, tied with crimson ribbon; a succession of flowers which she had worn, more and more dry and brown with age; one of her gloves, which he had found and kept from the day they first met in Cambridge; a bunch of withered bluebells tied with sweet-grass, whose odour filled the room, from the picnic at Campobello; scraps of paper with her writing on them, and cards; several photographs of her, and piles of notes and letters.

"Look here," said Dan, knowing it was Boardman without turning round, "what am I to do about these things?"

Boardman respectfully examined them over his shoulder. "Don't know what the usual ceremony is," he said, he ventured to add, referring to the heaps of letters, "Seems to have been rather epistolary, doesn't she?"

"Oh, don't talk of her as if she were dead!" cried Dan. "I've been feeling as if she were." All at once he dropped his head among these witnesses of his loss, and sobbed.

Boardman appeared shocked, and yet somewhat amused; he made a soft low sibilation between his teeth.

Dan lifted his head. "Boardman, if you ever give me away!"

"Oh, I don't suppose it's very hilarious," said Boardman, with vague kindness. "Packed yet?" he asked, getting away from the subject as something he did not feel himself fitted to deal with consecutively.

"I'm only going to take a bag," said Mavering, going to get some clothes down from a closet where his words had a sepulchral reverberation.

"Can't I help?" asked Boardman, keeping away from the sad memorials of Dan's love strewn about on the desk, and yet not able to keep his eyes off them across the room.

"Well, I don't know," said Dan. He came out with his armful of coats and trousers, and threw them on the bed. "Are

William Dean Howells

you going?"

"If I could believe you wanted me to.'

"Good!" cried Mavering, and the fact seemed to brighten him immediately. "If you want to, stuff these things in, while I'm doing up these other things." He nodded his head side-wise toward the desk.

"All right," said Boardman.

His burst of grief must have relieved Dan greatly. He set about gathering up the relics on the desk, and getting a suitable piece of paper to wrap them in. He rejected several pieces as inappropriate.

"I don't know what kind of paper to do these things up in," he said at last.

"Any special kind of paper required?" Boardman asked, pausing in the act of folding a pair of pantaloons so as not to break the fall over the boot.

"I didn't know there was, but there seems to be," said Dan.

"Silver paper seems to be rather more for cake and that sort of thing," suggested Boardman. "Kind of mourning too, isn't it—silver?"

"I don't know," said Dan. "But I haven't got any silver paper."

"Newspaper wouldn't do?"

"Well, hardly, Boardman," said Dan, with sarcasm.

"Well," said Boardman, "I should have supposed that nothing could be simpler than to send back a lot of love-letters; but the question of paper seems insuperable. Manila paper wouldn't do either. And then comes string. What kind of string are you going to tie it up with?"

"Well, we won't start that question till we get to it," answered Dan, looking about. "If I could find some kind of a box—"

"Haven't you got a collar box? Be the very thing!" Boardman had gone back to the coats and trousers, abandoning Dan to the subtler difficulties in which he was involved.

"They've all got labels," said Mavering, getting down one marked "The Tennyson" and another lettered "The Clarion," and looking at them with cold rejection.

"Don't see how you're going to send these things back at all, then. Have to keep them, I guess." Boardman finished his task, and came back to Dan.

"I guess I've got it now," said Mavering, lifting the lid of his desk, and taking out a large stiff envelope, in which a set of photographic views had come.

"Seems to have been made for it," Boardman exulted, watching the envelope, as it filled up, expand into a kind of shapely packet. Dan put the things silently in, and sealed the parcel with his ring. Then he turned it over to address it, but the writing of Alice's name for this purpose seemed too much for him, in spite of Boardman's humorous support throughout.

"Oh, I can't do it," he said, falling back in his chair.

"Let me," said his friend, cheerfully ignoring his despair. He philosophised the whole transaction, as he addressed the package, rang for a messenger, and sent it away, telling him to call a cab for ten minutes past two.

"Mighty good thing in life that we move by steps. Now on the stage, or in a novel, you'd have got those things together and addressed 'em, and despatched 'em, in just the right kind of paper, with just the right kind of string round it, at a dash; and then you'd have had time to go up and lean your head against something and soliloquise, or else think unutterable things. But here you see how a merciful Providence blocks your way all along. You've had to fight through all sort of sordid little details to the grand tragic result of getting off Miss Pasmer's letters, and when you reach it you don't mind it a bit."

"Don't I?" demanded Dan, in as hollow a voice as he could. "You'd joke at a funeral, Boardman."

"I've seen some pretty cheerful funerals," said Boardman. "And it's this principle of steps, of degrees, of having to do this little thing, and that little thing, that keeps funerals from killing the survivors. I suppose this is worse than a funeral—look at it in the right light. You mourn as one without hope, don't you? Live through it too, I suppose."

He made Dan help get the rest of his things into his bag, and with one little artifice and another prevented him from stagnating in despair. He dissented from the idea of waiting over another day to see if Alice would not relent when she got her letters back, and send for Dan to come and see her.

"Relent a good deal more when she finds you've gone out of town, if she sends for you," he argued; and he got Dan into the cab and off to the station, carefully making him an active partner in the whole undertaking, even to checking his own bag.

Before he bought his own ticket he appealed once more to Dan.

"Look here! I feel like a fool going off with you on this expedition. Be honest for once, now, Mavering, and tell me you've thought better of it, and don't want me to go!"

"Yes—yes, I do. Oh yes, you've got to go. I I do want you. I— you make me see things in just the right light, don't you know.

That idea of yours about little steps—it's braced me all up. Yes—"

"You're such an infernal humbug," said Boardman, "I can't tell whether you want me or not. But I'm in for it now, and I'll go." Then he bought his ticket.

William Dean Howells

XLV

Boardman put himself in charge of Mavering, and took him into the smoking car. It was impossible to indulge a poetic gloom there without becoming unpleasantly conspicuous in the smoking and euchre and profanity. Some of the men were silent and dull, but no one was apparently very unhappy, and perhaps if Dan had dealt in absolute sincerity with himself, even he would not have found himself wholly so. He did not feel as he had felt when Alice rejected him. Then he was wounded to the quick through his vanity, and now; in spite of all, in spite of the involuntary tender swaying of his heart toward her through the mere force of habit, in spite of some remote compunctions for his want of candour with her, he was supported by a sense of her injustice, her hardness. Related with this was an obscure sense of escape, of liberation, which, however he might silence and disown it, was still there. He could not help being aware that he had long relinquished tastes customs, purposes, ideals, to gain a peace that seemed more and more fleeting and uncertain, and that he had submitted to others which, now that the moment of giving pleasure by his submission was past, he recognised as disagreeable. He felt a sort of guilt in his enlargement; he knew, by all that he had, ever heard or read of people in his position, that he ought to be altogether miserable; and yet this consciousness of relief persisted. He told himself that a very tragical thing had befallen him; that this broken engagement was the ruin of his life and the end of his youth, and that he must live on an old and joyless man, wise with the knowledge that comes to decrepitude and despair; he imagined a certain look for himself, a gait, a name, that would express this; but all the same he was aware of having got out of something. Was it a bondage, a scrape, as Boardman called it? He thought he must be a very light, shallow, and frivolous nature not to be utterly broken up by his disaster.

"I don't know what I'm going home for," he said hoarsely to Boardman.

"Kind of a rest, I suppose," suggested his friend.

"Yes, I guess that's it," said Dan. "I'm tired."

It seemed to him that this was rather fine; it was a fatigue of the soul that he was to rest from. He remembered the apostrophic close of a novel in which the heroine dies after much emotional suffering. "Quiet, quiet heart!" he repeated to himself. Yes, he too had died to hope, to love, to happiness.

As they drew near their journey's end he said, "I don't know how I'm going to break it to them."

"Oh, probably break itself," said Boardman. "These things usually do."

"Yes, of course," Dan assented.

"Know from your looks that something's up. Or you might let me go ahead a little and prepare them."

Dan laughed. "It was awfully good of you to come, Boardman. I don't know what I should have done without you."

"Nothing I like more than these little trips. Brightens you up to sere the misery of others; makes you feel that you're on peculiarly good terms with Providence. Haven't enjoyed myself so much since that day in Portland." Boardman's eyes twinkled.

"Yes," said Dan, with a deep sigh, "it's a pity it hadn't ended there."

"Oh, I don't know. You won't have to go through with it again. Something that had to come, wasn't it? Never been satisfied if you hadn't tried it. Kind of aching void before, and now you've got enough."

"Yes, I've got enough," said Dan, "if that's all."

When they got out of the train at Ponkwasset Falls, and the conductor and the brakeman, who knew Dan as his father's son, and treated him with the distinction due a representative of an interest valued by the road, had bidden him a respectfully intimate good-night, and he began to climb the hill to his father's house, he recurred to the difficulty before him in breaking the news to his family. "I wish I could have it over in a flash. I wish I'd thought to telegraph it to them."

"Wouldn't have done," said Boardman. "It would have given 'em time to formulate questions and conjectures, and now the astonishment will take their breath away till you can get your second wind, and then—you'll be all right."

"You think so?" asked Dan submissively.

"Know so. You see, if you could have had it over in a flash, it would have knocked you flat. But now you've taken all the little steps, and you've got a lot more to take, and you're all braced up. See? You're like rock, now—adamant." Dan laughed in forlorn perception of Boardman's affectionate irony. "Little steps are the thing. You'll have to go in now and meet your family, and pass the time of day with each one, and talk about the weather, and account for my being along, and ask how they all are; and by the time you've had dinner, and got settled with your legs out in front of the fire, you'll be just in the mood for it. Enjoy telling them all about it."

"Don't, Boardman," pleaded Dan. "Boardy, I believe if I could get in and up to my room without anybody's seeing me, I'd let you tell them. There don't seem to be anybody about, and I think we could manage it."

"It wouldn't work," said Boardman. "Got to do it yourself."

"Well, then, wait a minute," said Dan desperately; and Boardman knew that he was to stay outside while Dan reconnoitred the interior. Dan opened one door after another till he stood within the hot brilliantly lighted hall. Eunice Mavering was coming down the stairs, hooded and wrapped for a walk on the long verandahs before supper.

"Dan!" she cried.

"It's all up, Eunice," he said at once, as if she had asked him about it. "My engagement's off."

"Oh, I'm so glad!" She descended upon him with outstretched arms, but stopped herself before she reached him. "It's a hoax. What do you mean? Do you really mean it, Dan?"

"I guess I mean it. But don't—Hold on! Where's Minnie?"

Eunice turned, and ran back upstairs. "Minnie! Min!" she called on her way. "Dan's engagement's off."

"I don't believe it!" answered Minnie's voice joyously, from within some room. It was followed by her presence, with successive inquiries. "How do you know? Did you get a letter? When did it happen? Oh, isn't it too good?"

Minnie was also dressed for the verandah promenade, which they always took when the snow was too deep. She caught sight of her brother as she came down. "Why, Dan's here! Dan, I've been thinking about you all day." She kissed him, which Eunice was now reminded to do too.

"Yes, it's true, Minnie," said Dan gravely. "I came up to tell you. It don't seem to distress you much."

"Dan!" said his sister reproachfully. "You know I didn't mean to say anything I only felt so glad to have you back again."

"I understand, Minnie—I don't blame you. It's all right. How's mother? Father up from the works yet? I'm going to my room."

"Indeed you're not!" cried Eunice, with elder sisterly authority. "You shall tell us about it first."

"Oh no! Let him go, Eunice!" pleaded Minnie, "Poor Dan! And I don't think we ought to go to walk when—"

Dan's eyes dimmed, and his voice weakened a little at her sympathy. "Yes, go. I'm tired—that's all. There isn't anything to tell you, hardly. Miss Pasmer—"

"Why, he's pale!" cried Minnie. "Eunice!"

"Oh, it's just the heat in here." Dan really felt a little sick and faint with it, but he was not sorry to seem affected by the day's strain upon his nerves.

The girls began to take off their wraps. "Don't. I'll go with you. Boardman's out there."

"Boardman! What nonsense!" exclaimed Eunice.

"He'll like to hear your opinion of it," Dan began; but his sister pulled the doors open, and ran out to see if he really meant that too.

Whether Boardman had heard her, or had discreetly withdrawn out of earshot at the first sound of voices, she could not tell, but she found him some distance away from the snow-box on the piazza. "Dan's just managed to tell us you were here," she said, giving him her hand. "I'm glad to see you. Do come in."

"Come along as a sort of Job's comforter," Boardman explained, as he followed her in; and he had the silly look that the man who feels himself superfluous must wear.

"Then you know about it?" said Eunice, while Minnie Mavering and he were shaking hands.

"Yes, Boardman knows; he can tell you about it," said Dan, from the hall chair he had dropped into. He rose and made his way to the stairs, with the effect of leaving the whole thing to them.

His sisters ran after him, and got him upstairs and into his room, with Boardman's semi-satirical connivance, and Eunice put up the window, while Minnie went to get some cologne to wet his forehead. Their efforts were so successful that he revived sufficiently to drive them out of his room, and make them go and show Boardman to his.

"You know the way, Mr. Boardman," said Eunice, going before him, while Minnie followed timorously, but curious for what he should say. She lingered on the threshold, while her sister went in and pulled the electric apparatus which lighted the gas-burners. "I suppose Dan didn't break it?" she said, turning sharply upon him.

"No; and I don't think he was to blame," said Boardman, inferring her reserved anxiety.

"Oh, I'm quite sure of that," said Eunice, rejecting what she had asked for. "You'll find everything, Mr. Boardman. It was kind of you to come with Dan. Supper's at seven."

"How severe you were with him!" murmured Minnie, following her away.

"Severe with Dan?"

"No—with Mr. Boardman."

"What nonsense! I had to be. I couldn't let him defend Dan to me. Couple of silly boys!"

After a moment Minnie said, "I don't think he's silly."

"Who?"

"Mr. Boardman."

"Well, Dan is, then, to bring him at such a time. But I suppose he felt that he couldn't get here without him. What a boy! Think of such a child being engaged! I hope we shan't hear any more of such nonsense for one while again—at least till Dan's got his growth."

They went down into the library, where, in their excitement, they sat down with most of their outdoor things on.

Minnie had the soft contrary-mindedness of gentle natures. "I should like to know how you would have had Dan bear it," she said rebelliously.

"How? Like a man. Or like a woman. How do you suppose Miss Pasmer's bearing it? Do you suppose she's got some friend to help her?"

"If she's broken it, she doesn't need any one," urged Minnie.

"Well," said Eunice, with her high scorn of Dan unabated, "I never could have liked that girl, but I certainly begin to respect her. I think I could have got on with her—now that it's no use. I declare," she broke off, "we're sitting here sweltering to death! What are we keeping our things on for?" She began to tear hers violently off and to fling them on chairs, scolding, and laughing at the same time with Minnie, at their absent-mindedness.

A heavy step sounded on the verandah without.

"There's father!" she cried vividly, jumping to her feet and running to the door, while Minnie, in a nervous bewilderment, ran off upstairs to her room. Eunice flung the door open. "Well, father, we've got Dan back again." And at a look of quiet question in his eye she hurried on: "His engagement's broken, and he's come up here to tell us, and brought Mr. Boardman along to help."

"Where is he?" asked the father, with his ruminant quiet, pulling off first one sleeve of his overcoat, and pausing for Eunice's answer before he pulled off the other.

XLVI

"He's up in his room, resting from the effort." She laughed nervously, and her father made no comment. He took off his articles, and then went creaking upstairs to Dan's room. But at the door he paused, with his hand on the knob, and turned away to his own room without entering.

Dan must have heard him; in a few minutes he came to him.

"Well, Dan," said his father, shaking hands.

"I suppose Eunice has told you? Well, I want to tell you why it happened."

There was something in his father that always steadied Dan and kept him to the point. He now put the whole case fairly and squarely, and his candour and openness seemed to him to react and characterise his conduct throughout. He did not realise that this was not so till his father said at the close, with mild justice, "You were to blame for letting the thing run on so at loose ends."

"Yes, of course," said Dan, seeing that he was. "But there was no intention of deceiving any one of bad faith—"

"Of course not."

"I thought it could be easily arranged whenever it came to the point."

"If you'd been older, you wouldn't have thought that. You had women to deal with on both sides. But if it's all over, I'm not sorry. I always admired Miss Pasmer, but I've been more and more afraid you were not suited to each other. Your mother doesn't know you're here?"

"No, sir, I suppose not. Do you think it will distress her?"

"How did your sisters take it?"

Dan gave a rueful laugh. "It seemed to be rather a popular move with them."

"I will see your mother first," said the father.

He left them when they went into the library after supper, and a little later Dan and Eunice left Boardman in charge of Minnie there.

He looked after their unannounced withdrawal in comic consciousness. "It's no use pretending that I'm not a pretty large plurality here," he said to Minnie.

"Oh, I'm so glad you came!" she cried, with a kindness which was as real as if it had been more sincere.

"Do you think mother will feel it much?" asked Dan anxiously, as he went upstairs with Eunice.

"Well, she'll hate to lose a correspondent—such a regular one," said Eunice, and the affair being so far beyond any other comment, she laughed the rest of the way to their mother's room.

The whole family had in some degree that foible which affects people who lead isolated lives; they come to think that they are the only people who have their virtues; they exaggerate these, and they conceive a kindness even for the qualities which are not their virtues. Mrs. Mavering's life was secluded again from the family seclusion, and their peculiarities were intensified in her. Besides, she had some very marked peculiarities of her own, and these were also intensified by the solitude to which she was necessarily left so much. She meditated a great deal upon the character of her children, and she liked to analyse and censure it both in her own mind and openly in their presence. She was very trenchant and definite in these estimates of them; she liked to ticket them, and then ticket them anew. She explored their ancestral history on both sides for the origin of their traits, and there were times when she reduced them in formula to mere congeries of inherited characteristics. If Eunice was self-willed and despotic, she was just like her grandmother Mavering; if Minnie was all sentiment and gentle stubbornness, it was because two aunts of hers, one on either side, were exactly so; if Dan loved pleasure and beauty, and was sinuous and uncertain in so many ways, and yet was so kind and faithful and good, as well as shilly-shallying and undecided, it was because her mother, and her mother's father, had these qualities in the same combination.

When she took her children to pieces before their faces, she was sharp and admonitory enough with them. She warned them to what their characters would bring them to if they did not look out; but perhaps because she beheld them so hopelessly the present effect of the accumulated tendencies of the family past, she was tender and forgiving to their actions. The mother came in there, and superseded the student of heredity: she found excuse for them in the perversity of circumstance, in the peculiar hardship of the case, in the malignant misbehaviour of others.

As Dan entered, with the precedence his father and sister yielded him as the principal actor in the scene which must follow, she lifted herself vigorously in bed, and propped herself on the elbow of one arm while she stretched the other towards him.

"I'm glad of it, Dan!" she called, at the moment he opened the door, and as he came toward her she continued, with the amazing velocity of utterance peculiar to nervous sufferers of her sex: "I know all about it, and I don't blame you a bit! And I don't blame her! Poor helpless young things! But it's a perfect mercy it's all over; it's the greatest deliverance I ever heard of! You'd have been eaten up alive. I saw it, and I knew it from the very first moment, and I've lived in fear and trembling for you. You could have got on well enough if you'd been left to yourselves, but that you couldn't have been nor hope to be as long as you breathed, from the meddling and the machinations and the malice of that unscrupulous and unconscionable old Cat!"

By the time Mrs. Mavering had hissed out the last word she had her arm round her boy's neck and was clutching him, safe and sound after his peril, to her breast; and between her kissing and crying she repeated her accusals and denunciations with violent volubility.

Dan could not have replied to them in that effusion of gratitude and tenderness he felt for his mother's partisanship; and when she went on in almost the very terms of his self-defence, and told him that he had done as he had because it was easy for him to yield, and he could not imagine a Cat who would put her daughter up to entrapping him into a promise that she knew must break his mother's heart, he found her so right on the main point that he could not help some question of Mrs. Pasmer in his soul. Could she really have been at the bottom of it all? She was very sly, and she might be very false, and it was certainly she who had first proposed their going abroad together. It looked as if it might be as his mother said, and at any rate it was no time to dispute her, and he did not say a word in behalf of Mrs. Pasmer, whom she continued to rend in a thousand pieces and scatter to the winds till she had to stop breathless.

"Yes! it's quite as I expected! She did everything she could to trap you into it. She fairly flung that poor girl at you. She laid her plans so that you couldn't say no—she understood your character from the start!—and then, when it came out by accident, and she saw that she had older heads to deal with, and you were not going to be quite at her mercy, she dropped the mask in an instant, and made Alice break with you. Oh, I could see through her from the beginning! And the next time, Dan, I advise you, as you never suspect anybody yourself, to consult with somebody who doesn't take people for what they seem, and not to let yourself be flattered out of your sensor, even if you see your father is."

Mrs. Mavering dropped back on her pillow, and her husband smiled patiently at their daughter.

Dan saw his patient smile and understood it; and the injustice which his father bore made him finally unwilling to let another remain under it. Hard as it was to oppose his mother in anything when she was praising him so sweetly and comforting him in the moment of his need, he pulled himself together to protest: "No, no, mother! I don't think Mrs. Pasmer was to blame; I don't believe she had anything to do with it. She's always stood my friend—"

"Oh, I've no doubt she's made you think so, Dan," said his mother, with unabated fondness for him; "and you think so because you're so simple and good, and never suspect evil of any one. It's this hideous optimism that's killing everything—"

A certain note in the invalid's falling voice seemed to warn her hearers of an impending change that could do no one good. Eunice rose hastily and interrupted: "Mother, Mr. Boardman's here. He came up with Dan. May Minnie come in with him?"

Mrs. Mavering shot a glance of inquiry at Dan, and then let a swift inspection range over all the details of the room, and finally concentrate itself on the silk and lace of her bed, over which she passed a smoothing hand. "Mr. Boardman?" she cried, with instantly recovered amiability. "Of course she may!"

XLVII

In Boston the rumour of Dan's broken engagement was followed promptly by a denial of it; both the rumour and the denial were apparently authoritative; but it gives the effect of a little greater sagacity to distrust rumours of all kinds, and most people went to bed, after the teas and dinners and receptions and clubs at which the fact was first debated, in the self-persuasion that it was not so. The next day they found the rumour still persistent; the denial was still in the air too, but it seemed weaker; at the end of the third day it had become a question as to which broke the engagement, and why; by the end of a week it was known that Alice had broken the engagement, but the reason could not be ascertained.

This was not for want of asking, more or less direct. Pasmer, of course, went and came at his club with perfect immunity. Men are quite as curious as women, but they set business bounds to their curiosity, and do not dream of passing these. With women who have no business of their own, and can not quell themselves with the reflection that this thing or that is not their affair, there is no question so intimate that they will not put it to some other woman; perhaps it is not so intimate, or perhaps it will not seem so; at any rate, they chance it. Mrs. Pasmer was given every opportunity to explain the facts to the ladies whom she met, and if she was much afflicted by Alice's behaviour, she had a measure of consolation in using her skill to baffle the research of her acquaintance. After each encounter of the kind she had the pleasure of reflecting that absolutely nothing more than she meant had become known. The case

William Dean Howells

never became fully known through her; it was the girl herself who told it to Miss Cotton in one of those moments of confidence which are necessary to burdened minds; and it is doubtful if more than two or three people ever clearly understood it; most preferred one or other of several mistaken versions which society finally settled down to.

The paroxysm of self-doubt, almost self-accusal, in which Alice came to Miss Cotton, moved the latter to the deepest sympathy, and left her with misgivings which became an intolerable anguish to her conscience. The child was so afflicted at what she had done, not because she wished to be reconciled with her lover, but because she was afraid she had been unjust, been cruelly impatient and peremptory with him; she seemed to Miss Cotton so absolutely alone and friendless with her great trouble, she was so helpless, so hopeless, she was so anxious to do right, and so fearful she had done wrong, that Miss Cotton would not have been Miss Cotton if she had not taken her in her arms and assured her that in everything she had done she had been sublimely and nobly right, a lesson to all her sex in such matters for ever. She told her that she had always admired her, but that now she idolised her; that she felt like going down on her knees and simply worshipping her.

"Oh, don't say that, Miss Cotton!" pleaded Alice, pulling away from her embrace, but still clinging to her with her tremulous, cold little hands. "I can't bear it! I'm wicked and hard you don't know how bad I am; and I'm afraid of being weak, of doing more harm yet. Oh, I wronged him cruelly in ever letting him get engaged to me! But now what you've said will support me. If you think I've done right—It must seem strange to you that I should come to you with my trouble instead of my mother; but I've been to her, and—and we think alike on so few subjects, don't you know—'

"Yes, yes; I know, dear!" said Miss Cotton, in the tender folly of her heart, with the satisfaction which every woman feels in being more sufficient to another in trouble than her natural comforters.

"And I wanted to know how you saw it; and now, if you feel as you say, I can never doubt myself again."

She tempested out of Miss Cotton's house, all tearful under the veil she had pulled down, and as she shut the door of her coupe, Miss Cotton's heart jumped into her throat with an impulse to run after her, to recall her, to recant, to modify everything.

From that moment Miss Cotton's trouble began, and it became a torment that mounted and gave her no peace till she imparted it. She said to herself that she should suffer to the utmost in this matter, and if she spoke to any one, it must not be to same one who had agreed with her about Alice, but to some hard, skeptical nature, some one who would look at it from a totally different point of view, and would punish her for her error, if she had committed an error, in supporting and consoling Alice. All the time she was thinking of Mrs. Brinkley; Mrs. Brinkley had come into her mind at once; but it was only after repeated struggles that she could get the strength to go to her.

Mrs. Brinkley, sacredly pledged to secrecy, listened with a sufficiently dismaying air to the story which Miss Cotton told her in the extremity of her fear and doubt.

"Well," she said at the end, "have you written to Mr. Mavering?"

"Written to Mr. Mavering?" gasped Miss Cotton.

"Yes—to tell him she wants him back."

"Wants him back?" Miss Cotton echoed again.

"That's what she came to you for."

"Oh, Mrs. Brinkley!" moaned Miss Cotton, and she stared at her in mute reproach.

Mrs. Brinkley laughed. "I don't say she knew that she came for that; but there's no doubt that she did; and she went away bitterly disappointed with your consolation and support. She didn't want anything of the kind—you may comfort yourself with that reflection, Miss Cotton."

"Mrs. Brinkley," said Miss Cotton, with a severity which ought to have been extremely effective from so mild a person, "do you mean to accuse that poor child of dissimulation—of deceit—in such—a—a—"

"No!" shouted Mrs. Brinkley; "she didn't know what she was doing any more than you did; and she went home perfectly heart-broken; and I hope she'll stay so, for the good of all parties concerned."

Miss Cotton was so bewildered by Mrs. Brinkley's interpretation of Alice's latent motives that she let the truculent hostility of her aspiration pass unheeded. She looked helplessly about, and seemed faint, so that Mrs. Brinkley, without appearing to notice her state, interposed the question of a little sherry. When it had been brought, and Miss Cotton had sipped the glass that trembled in one hand while her emotion shattered a biscuit with the other, Mrs. Brinkley went on: "I'm glad the engagement is broken, and I hope it will never be mended. If what you tell me of her reason for breaking it is true—"

"Oh, I feel so guilty for telling you! I'd no right to! Please never speak of it!" pleaded Miss Cotton.

"Then I feel more than ever that it was all a mistake, and that to help it on again would be a—crime."

Miss Cotton gave a small jump at the word, as if she had already committed the crime: she had longed to do it.

"Yes; I mean to say that they are better parted than plighted. If matches are made in heaven, I believe some of them are unmade there too. They're not adapted to each other; there's too great a disparity."

"You mean," began Miss Cotton, from her prepossession of Alice's superiority, "that she's altogether his inferior, intellectually and morally."

"Oh, I can't admit that!" cried Miss Cotton, glad to have Mrs. Brinkley go too far, and plucking up courage from her excess.

"Intellectually and morally," repeated Mrs. Brinkley, with the mounting conviction which ladies seem to get from mere persistence. "I saw that girl at Campobello; I watched her."

"I never felt that you did her justice!" cried Miss Cotton, with the valour of a hen-sparrow. "There was an antipathy."

"There certainly wasn't a sympathy, I'm happy to say," retorted Mrs. Brinkley. "I know her, and I know her family, root and branch. The Pasmers are the dullest and most selfish people in the world."

"Oh, I don't think that's her character," said Miss Cotton, ruffling her feathers defensively.

"Neither do I. She has no fixed character. No girl has. Nobody has. We all have twenty different characters—more characters than gowns—and we put them on and take them off just as often for different occasions. I know you think each person is permanently this or that; but my experience is that half the time they're the other thing."

"Then why," said Miss Cotton, winking hard, as some weak people do when they thick they are making a point, "do you say that Alice is dull and selfish?"

"I don't—not always, or not simply so. That's the character of the Pasmer blood, but it's crossed with twenty different currents in her; and from some body that the Pasmer dulness and selfishness must have driven mad she got a crazy streak of piety; and that's got mixed up in her again with a nonsensical ideal of duty; and everything she does she not only thinks is right, but she thinks it's religious, and she thinks it's unselfish."

"If you'd seen her, if you'd heard her, this morning," said Miss Cotton, "you wouldn't say that, Mrs. Brinkley."

Mrs. Brinkley refused this with an impatient gesture. "It isn't what she is now, or seems to be, or thinks she is. It's what she's going to finally harden into—what's going to be her prevailing character. Now Dan Mavering has just the faults that will make such a girl think her own defects are virtues, because they're so different. I tell you Alice Pasmer has neither the head nor the heart to appreciate the goodness, the loveliness, of a fellow like Dan Mavering."

"I think she feels his sweetness fully," urged Miss Cotton. "But she couldn't endure his uncertainty. With her the truth is first of all things."

"Then she's a little goose. If she had the sense to know it, she would know that he might delay and temporise and beat about the bush, but he would be true when it was necessary. I haven't the least doubt in the world but that poor fellow was going on in perfect security, because he felt that it would be so easy for him to give up, and supposed it would be just as easy for her. I don't suppose he had a misgiving, and it must have come upon him like a thunder-clap."

"Don't you think," timidly suggested Miss Cotton, "that truth is the first essential in marriage?"

"Of course it is. And if this girl was worthy of Dan Mavering, if she were capable of loving him or anybody else unselfishly, she would have felt his truth even if she couldn't have seen it. I believe this minute that that manoeuvring, humbugging mother of hers is a better woman, a kinder woman, than she is."

"Alice says her mother took his part," said Miss Cotton, with a sigh. "She took your view of it."

"She's a sensible woman. But I hope she won't be able to get him into her toils again," continued Mrs. Brinkley, recurring to the conventional estimate of Mrs. Pasmer.

"I can't help feeling—believing—that they'll come together somehow still," murmured Miss Cotton. It seemed to her that she had all along wished this; and she tried to remember if what she had said to comfort Alice might be construed as adverse to a reconciliation.

"I hope they won't, then," said Mrs. Brinkley, "for they couldn't help being unhappy together, with their temperaments. There's one thing, Miss Cotton, that's more essential in marriage than Miss Pasmer's instantaneous honesty, and that's patience."

"Patience with wrong?" demanded Miss Cotton.

"Yes, even with wrong; but I meant patience with each other. Marriage is a perpetual pardon, concession, surrender; it's an everlasting giving up; that's the divine thing about it; and that's just what Miss Passer could never conceive of, because she is self-righteous and conceited and unyielding. She would make him miserable."

Miss Cotton rose in a bewilderment which did not permit her to go at once. There was something in her mind which she wished to urge, but she could not make it out, though she fingered in vague generalities. When she got a block away from the house it suddenly came to her. Love! If they loved each other, would not all be well with them? She would have liked to run back and put that question to Mrs. Brinkley; but just then she met Brinkley lumbering heavily homeward; she heard his hard breathing from the exertion of bowing to her as he passed.

His wife met him in the hall, and went up to kiss him. He smelt abominably of tobacco smoke.

"Hullo!" said her husband. "What are you after?"

"Nothing," said his wife, enjoying his joke "Come in here; I want to tell you how I have just sat upon Miss Cotton."

XLVIII

The relations between Dan and his father had always been kindly and trustful; they now became, in a degree that touched and flattered the young fellow, confidential. With the rest of the family there soon ceased to be any reference to his engagement; his sisters were glad, each in her way, to have him back again; and, whatever they may have said between themselves, they said nothing to him about Alice. His mother appeared to have finished with the matter the first night; she had her theory, and she did it justice; and when Mrs. Mavering had once done a thing justice, she did not bring it up again unless somebody disputed it. But nobody had defended Mrs. Pasmer after Dan's feeble protest in her behalf; Mrs. Mavering's theory was accepted with obedience if not conviction; the whole affair dropped, except between Dan and his father.

Dan was certainly not so gay as he used to be; he was glad to find that he was not so gay. There had been a sort of mercy in the suddenness of the shock; it benumbed him, and the real stress and pain came during the long weeks that followed, when nothing occurred to vary the situation in any manner; he did not hear a word about Alice from Boston, nor any rumour of her people.

At first he had intended to go back with Boardman and face it out; but there seemed no use in this, and when it came to the point he found it impossible. Boardman went back alone, and he put Dan's things together in his rooms at Boston and sent them to him, so that Dan remained at home.

He set about helping his father at the business with unaffected docility. He tried not to pose, and he did his best to bear his loss and humiliation with manly fortitude. But his whole life had not set so strongly in one direction that it could be sharply turned aside now, and not in moments of forgetfulness press against the barriers almost to bursting. Now and then, when he came to himself from the wonted tendency, and remembered that Alice and he, who had been all in all to each other, were now nothing, the pain was so sharp, so astonishing, that he could not keep down a groan, which he then tried to turn off with a cough, or a snatch of song, or a whistle, looking wildly round to see if any one had noticed.

Once this happened when his father and he were walking silently home from the works, and his father said, without touching him or showing his sympathy except in his tone of humorously frank recognition, "Does it still hurt a little occasionally, Dan?"

"Yes, sir, it hurts," said the son; and he turned his face aside, and whistled through his teeth.

"Well, it's a trial, I suppose," said his father, with his gentle, soft half-lisp. "But there are greater trials."

"How, greater?" asked Dan, with sad incredulity. "I've lost all that made life worth living; and it's all my own fault, too."

"Yes," said his father; "I think she was a good girl."

"Good!" cried Dan; the word seemed to choke him.

"Still, I doubt if it's all your fault." Dan looked round at him. He added, "And I think it's perhaps for the best as it is."

Dan halted, and then said, "Oh, I suppose so," with dreary resignation, as they walked on.

"Let us go round by the paddock," said his father, "and see if Pat's put the horses up yet. You can hardly remember your mother, before she became an invalid, I suppose," he added, as Dan mechanically turned aside with him from the path that led to the house into that leading to the barn.

"No; I was such a little fellow," said Dan.

"Women give up a great deal when they marry," said the elder. "It's not strange that they exaggerate the sacrifice, and expect more in return than it's in the nature of men to give them. I should have been sorry to have you marry a woman of an exacting disposition."

"I'm afraid she was exacting," said Dan. "But she never asked more than was right."

"And it's difficult to do all that's right," suggested the elder.

"I'm sure you always have, father," said the son.

The father did not respond. "I wish you could remember your mother when she was well," he said. Presently he added, "I think it isn't best for a woman to be too much in love with her husband."

Dan took this to himself, and he laughed harshly. "She's been able to dissemble her love at last."

His father went on, "Women keep the romantic feeling longer than men; it dies out of us very soon—perhaps too soon."

"You think I couldn't have come to time?" asked Dan. "Well, as it's turned out, I won't have to."

"No man can be all a woman wishes him to be," said his father. "It's better for the disappointment to come before it's too late."

"I was to blame," said Dan stoutly. "She was all right."

"You were to blame in the particular instance," his father answered. "But in general the fault was in her—or her temperament. As long as the romance lasted she might have deluded herself, and believed you were all she imagined you; but romance can't last, even with women. I don like your faults, and I don't want you to excuse them to yourself. I don't like your chancing things, and leaving them to come out all right of themselves; but I've always tried to make you children see all your qualities in their true proportion and relation."

"Yes; I know that, sir," said Dan.

"Perhaps," continued his father, as they swung easily along, shoulder to shoulder, "I may have gone too far in that direction because I was afraid that you might take your mother too seriously in the other—that you might not understand that she judged you from her nerves and not her convictions. It's part of her malady, of her suffering, that her inherited Puritanism clouds her judgment, and makes her see all faults as of one size and equally damning. I wish you to know that she was not always so, but was once able to distinguish differences in error, and to realise that evil is of ill-will."

"Yes; I know that," said Dan. "She is now—when she feels well."

"Harm comes from many things, but evil is of the heart. I wouldn't have you condemn yourself too severely for harm that you didn't intend—that's remorse—that's insanity; and I wouldn't have you fall under the condemnation of another's invalid judgment."

"Thank you, father," said Dan.

They had come up to the paddock behind the barn, and they laid their arms on the fence while they looked over at the horses, which were still there. The beasts, in their rough winter coats, some bedaubed with frozen clots of the mud in which they had been rolling earlier in the afternoon, stood motionless in the thin, keen breeze that crept over the hillside from the March sunset, and blew their manes and tails out toward Dan and his father. Dan's pony sent him a gleam of recognition from under his frowsy bangs, but did not stir.

"Bunch looks like a caterpillar," he said, recalling the time when his father had given him the pony; he was a boy then, and the pony was as much to him, it went through his mind, as Alice had ever been. Was it all a jest, an irony? he asked himself.

"He's getting pretty old," said his father. "Let's see: you were only twelve."

"Ten," said Dan. "We've had him thirteen years."

Some of the horses pricked up their ears at the sound of their voices. One of them bit another's neck; the victim threw up his heels and squealed.

Pat called from the stable, "Heigh, you divils!"

"I think he'd better take them in," said Dan's father; and he continued, as if it were all the same subject, "I hope you'll have seen something more of the world before you fall in love the next time."

"Thank you; there won't be any next time. But do you consider the world such a school of morals; then? I supposed it was a very bad place."

"We seem to have been all born into it," said the father. He lifted his arms from the fence, and Dan mechanically followed him into the stable. A warm, homely smell of hay and of horses filled the place; a lantern glimmered, a faint blot, in the loft where Pat was pitching some hay forward to the edge of the boards; the naphtha gas weakly flared from the jets beside

William Dean Howells

the harness-room, whence a smell of leather issued and mingled with the other smell. The simple, earthy wholesomeness of the place appealed to Dan and comforted him. The hay began to tumble from the loft with a pleasant rustling sound.

His father called up to Pat, "I think you'd better take the horses in now."

"Yes, sir: I've got the box-stalls ready for 'em."

Dan remembered how he and Eunice used to get into the box-stall with his pony, and play at circus with it; he stood up on the pony, and his sister was the ring-master. The picture of his careless childhood reflected a deeper pathos upon his troubled present, and he sighed again.

His father said, as they moved on through the barn: "Some of the best people I've ever known were what were called worldly people. They are apt to be sincere, and they have none of the spiritual pride, the conceit of self-righteousness, which often comes to people who are shut up by conscience or circumstance to the study of their own motives and actions."

"I don't think she was one of that kind," said Dan.

"Oh, I don't know that she was. But the chances of happiness, of goodness, would be greater with a less self-centred person—for you."

"Ah, Yes! For me!" said Dan bitterly. "Because I hadn't it in me to be frank with her. With a man like me, a woman had better be a little scampish, too! Father, I could get over the loss; she might have died, and I could have got over that; but I can't get over being to blame."

"I don't think I'd indulge in any remorse," said his father. "There's nothing so useless, so depraving, as that. If you see you're wrong, it's for your warning, not for your destruction."

Dan was not really feeling very remorseful; he had never felt that he was much to blame; but he had an intellectual perception of the case, and he thought that he ought to feel remorseful; it was this persuasion that he took for an emotion. He continued to look very disconsolate.

"Come," said his father, touching his arm, "I don't want you to brood upon these things. It can do no manner of good. I want you to go to New York next week and look after that Lafflin process. If it's what he thinks—if he can really cast his brass patterns without air-holes—it will revolutionise our business. I want to get hold of him."

The Portuguese cook was standing in the basement door which they passed at the back of the house. He saluted father and son with a glittering smile.

"Hello, Joe!" said Dan.

"Ah, Joe!" said his father; he touched his hat to the cook, who snatched his cap off.

"What a brick you are, father!" thought Dan. His heart leaped at the notion of getting away from Ponkwasset; he perceived how it had been irking him to stay. "If you think I could manage it with Lafflin—"

"Oh, I think you could. He's another slippery chap."

Dan laughed for pleasure and pain at his father's joke.

XLIX

In New York Dan found that Lafflin had gone to Washington
to look up something in connection with his patent. In his
eagerness to get away from home, Dan had supposed that his
father meant to make a holiday for him, and he learned with a
little surprise that he was quite in earnest about getting hold of
the invention he wrote home of Lafflin's absence; and he got a
telegram in reply ordering him to follow on to Washington.

The sun was shining warm on the asphalt when he stepped out
of the Pennsylvania Depot with his bag in his hand, and put it
into the hansom that drove up for him. The sky overhead was
of an intense blue that made him remember the Boston sky as
pale and grey; when the hansom tilted out into the Avenue he
had a joyous glimpse of the White House; of the Capitol
swimming like a balloon in the cloudless air. A keen March
breeze swept the dust before him, and through its veil the
classic Treasury Building showed like one edifice standing
perfect amid ruin represented by the jag-tooth irregularities of
the business architecture along the wide street.

He had never been in Washington before, and he had a
confused sense of having got back to Rome, which he remembered from his boyish visit. Throughout his stay he seemed to
be coming up against the facade of the Temple of Neptune;
but it was the Patent Office, or the Treasury Building, or the
White House, and under the gay Southern sky this reversion to
the sensations of a happier time began at once, and made itself
a lasting relief. He felt a lift in his spirits from the first. They

gave him a room at Wormley's, where the chairs comported themselves as self-respectfully upon two or three legs as they would have done at Boston upon four; the cooking was excellent, and a mercenary welcome glittered from all the kind black faces around him. After the quiet of Ponkwasset and the rush of New York, the lazy ease of the hotel pleased him; the clack of boots over its pavements, the clouds of tobacco smoke, the Southern and Western accents, the spectacle of people unexpectedly encountering and recognising each other in the office and the dining-room, all helped to restore him to a hopefuller mood. Without asking his heart too curiously why, he found it lighter; he felt that he was still young.

In the weather he had struck a cold wave, and the wind was bitter in the streets, but they were full of sun; he found the grass green in sheltered places, and in one of the Circles he plucked a blossomed spray from an adventurous forceythia. This happened when he was walking from Wormley's to the Arlington by a roundabout way of his own involuntary invention, and he had the flowers in his button-hole when Lafflin was pointed out to him in the reading room there, and he introduced himself. Lafflin had put his hat far back on his head, and was intensely chewing a toothpick, with an air of rapture from everything about him. He seemed a very simple soul to Dan's inexperience of men, and the young fellow had no difficulty in committing him to a fair conditional arrangement. He was going to stay some days in Washington, and he promised other interviews, so that Dan thought it best to stay too. He used a sheet of the Arlington letter-paper in writing his father of what he had done; and then, as Lafflin had left him, he posted his letter at the clerk's desk, and wandered out through a corridor different from that which he had come in by. It led by the door of the ladies parlour, and at the sound of women's voices Dan halted. For no other reason than that such voices always irresistibly allured him, he went in, putting on an air of having come to look for some one. There were two or three groups of ladies receiving friends in different parts of the room. At the window a girl's figure silhouetted itself against the keen light, and as he advanced

William Dean Howells

into the room, peering about, it turned with a certain vividness that seemed familiar. This young lady, whoever she was, had the advantage of Dan in seeing him with the light on his face, and he was still in the dark about her, when she advanced swiftly upon him, holding out her hand.

"You don't seem to know your old friends, Mr. Mavering," and the manly tones left him no doubt.

He felt a rush of gladness, and he clasped her hand and clung to it as if he were not going to let it go again, bubbling out incoherencies of pleasure at meeting her. "Why, Miss Anderson! You here? What a piece of luck! Of course I couldn't see you against the window—make you out! But something looked familiar—and the way you turned! And when you started toward me! I'm awfully glad! When—where are you—that is—"

Miss Anderson kept laughing with him, and bubbled back that she was very glad too, and she was staying with her aunt in that hotel, and they had been there a month, and didn't he think Washington was charming? But it was too bad he had just got there with that blizzard. The weather had been perfectly divine till the day before yesterday.

He took the spray of forceythia out of his buttonhole. "I can believe it. I found this in one, of the squares, and I think it belongs to you." He. offered it with a bow and a laugh, and she took it in the same humour.

"What is the language of forceythia?" she asked.

"It has none—only expressive silence, you know."

A middle-aged lady came in, and Miss Anderson said, "My aunt, Mr. Mavering."

"Mr. Mavering will hardly remember me," said the lady, giving him her hand. He protested that he should indeed, but she had really made but a vague impression upon him at Campobello. He knew that she was there with Miss Anderson; he had been polite to her as he was to all women; but he had not noticed her much, and in his heart he had a slight for her, as compared with the Boston people he was more naturally thrown with; he certainly had not remembered that she was a little hard of hearing.

Miss Van Hook was in a steel-grey effect of dress, and, she had carried this up into her hair, of which she worn two short vertical curls on each temple.

She did not sit down, and Dan perceived that the ladies were going out. In her tailor-made suit of close-fitting serge and her Paris bonnet, carried like a crest on her pretty little head, Miss Anderson was charming. She had a short veil that came across the base of her lively nose, and left her mouth and chin to make the most of themselves, unprejudiced by its irregularity.

Dan felt it a hardship to part with them, but he prepared to take himself off. Miss Anderson asked him how long he was to be in Washington, and said he must come to see them; they meant to stay two weeks yet, and then they were going to Old Point Comfort; they had their rooms engaged.

He walked down to their carriage with the ladies and put them into it, and Miss Anderson still kept him talking there.

Her aunt said: "Why shouldn't you come with us, Mr. Mavering? We're going to Mrs. Secretary Miller's reception."

Dan gave himself a glance. "I don't know—if you want me?"

"We want you," said Miss Anderson. "Very well, then, I'll go."

He got in, and they began rolling over that smooth Washington asphalt which makes talk in a carriage as easy as in a drawing-room. Dan kept saying to himself, "Now she's going to bring up Campobello;" but Miss Anderson never recurred to their former meeting, and except for the sense of old acquaintance which was manifest in her treatment of him he might have thought that they had never met before. She talked of Washington and its informal delights; and of those plans which her aunt had made, like every one who spends a month in Washington, to spend all the remaining winters of her life there.

It seemed to Dan that Miss Anderson was avoiding Campobello on his account; he knew from what Alice had told him that there had been much surmise about their affair after he had left the island, and he suspected that Miss Anderson thought the subject was painful to him. He wished to reassure her. He asked at the first break in the talk about Washington, "How are the Trevors?"

"Oh, quite well," she said, promptly availing herself of the opening. "Have you seen any of our Campobello friends lately in Boston?"

"No; I've been at home for the last month—in the country." He scanned her face to see if she knew anything of his engagement. But she seemed honestly ignorant of everything since Campobello; she was not just the kind of New York girl who would visit in Boston, or have friends living there; probably she had never heard of his engagement. Somehow this seemed to simplify matters for Dan. She did not ask specifically after the Pasmers; but that might have been because of the sort of break in her friendship with Alice after that night at the Trevors'; she did not ask specifically after Mrs. Brinkley or any of the others.

At Mrs. Secretary Miller's door there was a rapid arrival and departure of carriages, of coupes, of hansoms, and of herdics, all managed by a man in plain livery, who opened and shut the doors, and sent the drivers off without the intervention of a policeman; it is the genius of Washington, which distinguishes it from every other capital, from every other city, to make no show of formality, of any manner of constraint anywhere.

People were swarming in and out; coming and going on foot as well as by carriage. The blandest of coloured uncles received their cards in the hall and put them into a vast tray heaped up with pasteboard, smiling affectionately upon them as if they had done him a favour.

"Don't you like them?" asked Dan of Miss Anderson; he meant the Southern negroes.

"I adoye them," she responded, with equal fervour. "You must study some new types here for next summer," she added.

Dan laughed and winced too. "Yes!" Then he said solemnly, "I am not going to Campobello next summer."

They felt into a stream of people tending toward an archway between the drawing-rooms, where Mrs. Secretary Miller stood with two lady friends who were helping her receive. They smiled wearily but kindly upon the crowd, for whom the Secretary's wife had a look of impartial hospitality. She could not have known more than one in fifty; and she met them all with this look at first, breaking into incredulous recognition when she found a friend. "Don't go away yet," she said cordially, to Miss Van Hook and her niece, and she held their hands for a moment with a gentle look of relief and appeal which included Dan. "Let me introduce you to Mrs. Tolliver and to Miss Dixon."

These ladies said that it was not necessary in regard to Miss Anderson and Miss Van Hook; and as the crowd pushed them on, Dan felt that they had been received with distinction.

The crowd expressed the national variety of rich and poor, plain and fashionable, urbane and rustic; they elbowed and shouldered each other upon a perfect equality in a place where all were as free to come as to the White House, and they jostled quaint groups of almond-eyed legations in the yellows and purples of the East, who looked dreamily on as if puzzled past all surmise by the scene. Certain young gentlemen with the unmistakable air of being European or South American attaches found their way about on their little feet, which the stalwart boots of the republican masses must have imperilled; and smiled with a faint diplomatic superiority, not visibly admitted, but all the same indisputable. Several of these seemed to know Miss Anderson, and took her presentation of Mavering with exaggerated effusion.

"I want to introduce you to my cousin over yonder," she said, getting rid of a minute Brazilian under-secretary, and putting her hand on Dan's arm to direct him: "Mrs. Justice Averill."

Miss Van Hook, keeping her look of severe vigilance, really followed her energetic niece, who took the lead, as a young lady must whenever she and her chaperon meet on equal terms.

Mrs. Justice Averill, who was from the far West somewhere, received Dan with the ease of the far East, and was talking London and Paris to him before the end of the third minute. It gave Dan a sense of liberation, of expansion; he filled his lungs with the cosmopolitan air in a sort of intoxication; without formulating it, he felt, with the astonishment which must always attend the Bostonian's perception of the fact, that there is a great social life in America outside of Boston. At Campobello he had thought Miss Anderson a very jolly girl, bright, and up to all sorts of things; but in the presence of the portable Boston there he could not help regarding her with a sort of tolerance which he now blushed for; he thought he had been a great ass. She seemed to know all sorts of nice people, and she strove with generous hospitality to make him have a good time. She said it was Cabinet Day, and that all the secretaries' wives were receiving, and she told him he had better make the rounds with them. He assented very willingly, and at six o'clock he was already so much in the spirit of this free and simple society, so much opener and therefore so much wiser than any other, that he professed a profound disappointment with the two or three Cabinet ladies whose failure to receive brought his pleasure to a premature close.

"But I suppose you're going to Mrs. Whittington's to-night!" Miss Anderson said to him, as they drove up to Wormley's, where she set him down. Miss Van Hook had long ceased to say anything; Dan thought her a perfect duenna. "You know you can go late there," she added.

"No, I can't go at all," said Dan. "I don't know them."

"They're New England people," urged Miss Anderson; as if to make him try to think that he was asked to Mrs. Whittington's.

"I don't know more than half the population of New England," said Dan, with apparent levity, but real forlornness.

"If you'd like to go—if you're sure you've no other engagement—"

"Oh, I'm certain of that?"

"—we would come for you."

"Do!"

"At half-past ten, then."

Miss Anderson explained to her aunt, who cordially confirmed her invitation, and they both shook hands with him upon it, and he backed out of the carriage with a grin of happiness on his face; it remained there while he wrote out the order for his dinner, which they require at Wormley's in holograph. The waiter reflected his smile with ethnical warm-heartedness. For a moment Dan tried to think what it was he had forgotten; he thought it was some other dish; then he remembered that it was his broken heart. He tried to subdue himself; but there was something in the air of the place, the climate, perhaps, or a pleasant sense of its facile social life, that kept him buoyant in spite of himself. He went out after dinner, and saw part of a poor play, and returned in time to dress for his appointment with Miss Anderson. Her aunt was with her, of course; she seemed to Dan more indefatigable than she was by day. He could not think her superfluous; and she was very good-natured. She made little remarks full of conventional wisdom, and appealed to his judgment on several points as they drove along. When they came to a street lamp where she could see him, he nodded and said yes, or no, respectfully. Between times he talked with Miss Anderson, who lectured him upon Washington society, and prepared him for the difference he was to find between Mrs. Whittington's evening of invited guests and the Cabinet ladies' afternoon of volunteer guests.

"Volunteer guests is good," he laughed. "Do you mean that anybody can go?"

"Anybody that is able to be about. This is Cabinet Day. There's a Supreme Court Day and a Senators' Day, and a Representatives' Day. Do you mean to say you weren't going to call upon your Senator?"

"I didn't know I had any."

"Neither did I till I came here. But you've got two; everybody's got two. And the President's wife receives three times a week, and the President has two or three days. They say the public days at the White House are great fun. I've been to some of the invited, or semi-invited or official evenings."

He could not see that difference from the great public receptions which Miss Anderson had promised him at Mrs. Whittington's, though he pretended afterward that he had done so. The people were more uniformly well dressed, there were not so many of them, and the hostess was sure of knowing her acquaintances at first glance; but there was the same ease, the same unconstraint, the same absence of provincial anxiety which makes a Washington a lighter and friendlier London. There were rather more sallow attachés; in their low-cut white waistcoats, with small brass buttons, they moved more consciously about, and looked weightier personages than several foreign ministers who were present.

Dan was soon lost from the side of Miss Anderson, who more and more seemed to him important socially. She seemed, in her present leadership; to know more of life, than he; to be maturer. But she did not abuse her superiority; she kept an effect of her last summer's friendliness for him throughout. Several times, finding herself near him; she introduced him to people.

Guests kept arriving till midnight. Among the latest, when Dan had lost himself far from Boston in talk with a young lady from Richmond, who spoke with a slur of her vowels that fascinated him, came Mr. and Mrs. Brinkley. He felt himself grow pale and inattentive to his pretty Virginian. That accent of Mrs. Brinkley's recalled him to his history. He hoped that she would not see him; but in another moment he was greeting her with a warmth which Bostonians seldom show in meeting at Boston.

"When did you come to Washington?" she asked, trying to keep her consciousness out of her eyes, which she let dwell kindly upon him.

"Day before yesterday—no, yesterday. It seems a month, I've seen and done so much," he said, with his laugh. "Miss Anderson's been showing me the whole of Washington society. Have you been here long?"

"Since morning," said Mrs. Brinkley. And she added, "Miss Anderson?"

"Yes—Campobello, don't you know?"

"Oh yes. Is she here to-night?"

"I came with her and her aunt."

"Oh yes."

"How is all Boston?" asked Dan boldly.

"I don't know; I'm just going down to Old Point Comfort to ask. Every other house on the Back Bay has been abandoned for the Hygeia." Mrs. Brinkley stopped, and then she asked. "Are you just up from there?"

"No; but I don't know but I shall go."

"Hello, Mavering!" said Mr. Brinkley, coming up and taking his hand into his fat grasp. "On your way to Fortress Monroe? Better come with us. Why; Munt!"

He turned to greet this other Bostonian, who had hardly expressed his joy at meeting with his fellow-townsmen when the hostess rustled softly up, and said, with the irony more or less friendly, which everybody uses in speaking of Boston, or recognising the intellectual pre-eminence of its people, "I'm not going to let you keep this feast of reason all to your selves. I want you to leaven the whole lump," and she began to disperse them, and to introduce them about right and left.

Dan tried to find his Virginian again, but she was gone. He found Miss Anderson; she was with her aunt. "Shall we be tearing you away?" she asked.

"Oh no. I'm quite ready to go."

His nerves were in a tremble. Those Boston faces and voices had brought it all back again; it seemed as if he had met Alice. He was silent and incoherent as they drove home, but Miss Anderson apparently did not want to talk much, and apparently did not notice his reticence.

He fell asleep with the pang in his heart which had been there so often.

When Dan came down to breakfast he found the Brinkleys at a pleasant place by one of the windows, and after they had exchanged a pleased surprise with him that they should all happen to be in the same hotel, they asked him to sit at their table.

There was a bright sun shining, and the ache was gone out of Dan's heart. He began to chatter gaily with Mrs. Brinkley about Washington.

"Oh, better come on to Fortress Monroe," said her husband. "Better come on with us."

"No, I can't just yet," said Dan. "I've got some business here that will keep me for awhile. Perhaps I may run down there a little later."

"Miss Anderson seems to have a good deal of business in Washington too," observed Brinkley, with some hazy notion of saying a pleasant rallying thing to the young man. He wondered at the glare his wife gave him. With those panned oysters before him he had forgotten all about Dan's love affair with Miss Pasmer.

Mrs. Brinkley hastened to make the mention of Miss Anderson as impersonal as possible.

"It was so nice to meet her again. She is such an honest, wholesome creature, and so bright and full of sense. She always made me think of the broad daylight. I always liked that girl."

"Yes; isn't she jolly?" said Dan joyously. "She seems to know everybody here. It's a great piece of luck for me. They're going to take a house in Washington next winter."

"Yes; I know that stage," said Mrs. Brinkley. "Her aunt's an amusingly New-York respectability. I don't think you'd find just such Miss Mitford curls as hers in all Boston."

"Yes, they are like the portraits, aren't they?" said Dan; delighted. "She's very nice, don't you think?"

"Very. But Miss Anderson is more than that. I was disposed to be critical of her at Campobello for a while, but she wore extremely well. All at once you found yourself admiring her uncommon common-sense.

"Yes. That's just it," cried Dan. "She is so sensible!"

"I think she's very pretty," said Mrs. Brinkley.

"Well, her nose," suggested Dan. "It seems a little capricious."

"It's a trifle bizarre, I suppose. But what beautiful eyes! And her figure! I declare that girl's carriage is something superb."

"Yes, she has a magnificent walk."

"Walks with her carriage," mused Brinkley aloud.

His wife did not regard him. "I don't know what Miss Anderson's principles are, but her practices are perfect. I never knew her do an unkind or shabby thing. She seems very good and very wise. And that deep voice of hers has such a charm. It's so restful. You feel as if you could repose upon it for a thousand years. Well! You will get down before we leave?"

"Yes, I will," said Dan. "I'm here after a man who's after a patent, and as soon as I can finish up my business with him I believe I will run down to Fortress Monroe.'

"This eleven-o'clock train will get you there at six," said Brinkley. "Better telegraph for your rooms."

"Or, let us know," said Mrs. Brinkley, "and we'll secure them for you."

"Oh, thank you," said Dan.

He went away, feeling that Mrs. Brinkley was the pleasantest woman he ever met. He knew that she had talked Miss

Anderson so fully in order to take away the implication of her husband's joke, and he admired her tact. He thought of this as he loitered along the street from Wormley's to the Arlington, where he was going to find Miss Anderson, by an appointment of the night before, and take a walk with her; and thinking of tact made him think of Mrs. Pasmer. Mrs. Pasmer was full of tact; and how kind she had always been to him! She had really been like a mother to him; he was sure she had understood him; he believed she had defended him; with a futility of which he felt the pathos, he made her defend him now to Alice. Alice was very hard and cold, as when he saw her last; her mother's words fell upon her as upon a stone; even Mrs. Pasmer's tears, which Dan made her shed, had no effect upon the haughty girl. Not that he cared now.

The blizzard of the previous days had whirled away; the sunshine lay still, with a warm glisten and sparkle, on the asphalt which seemed to bask in it, and which it softened to the foot. He loitered by the gate of the little park or plantation where the statue of General Jackson is riding a cock-horse to Banbury Cross, and looked over at the French-Italian classicism of the White House architecture with a pensive joy at finding pleasure in it, and then he went on to the Arlington.

Miss Anderson was waiting for him in the parlour, and they went a long walk up the avenues and across half the alphabet in the streets, and through the pretty squares and circles, where the statues were sometimes beautiful and always picturesque; and the sparrows made a vernal chirping in the naked trees and on the green grass. In two or three they sat down on the iron benches and rested.

They talked and talked—about the people they knew, and of whom they found that they thought surprisingly alike, and about themselves, whom they found surprisingly alike in a great many things, and then surprisingly unlike. Dan brought forward some points of identity which he, and Alice had found in themselves; it was just the same with Miss Anderson. She found herself rather warm with the seal-skin sacque she had put on; she let him carry it on his arm while they walked, and then lay it over her shoulders when they sat down. He felt a pang of self-reproach, as if he had been inconstant to Alice. This was an old habit of feeling, formed during the months of their engagement, when, at her inspiration, he was always bringing himself to book about something. He replied to her bitterly, in the colloquy which began to hold itself in his mind, and told her that she had no claim upon him now; that if his thoughts wandered from her it was her fault, not his; that she herself had set them free. But in fact he was like all young men, with a thousand, potentialities of loving. There was no aspect of beauty that did not tenderly move him; he could not help a soft thrill at the sight of any pretty shape, the sound of any piquant voice; and Alice had merely been the synthesis of all that was most charming to this fancy. This is a truth which it is the convention of the poets and the novelists to deny; but it is also true that she might have remained the sum of all that was loveliest if she would; or if she could.

It was chiefly because she would not or could not that his glance recognised the charm of Miss Anderson's back hair, both in its straying gossamer and in the loose mass in which it was caught up under her hat, when he laid her sacque on her shoulders. They met that afternoon at a Senator's, and in the house of a distinguished citizen, to whose wife Dan had been presented at Mrs. Whittington's, and who had somehow got his address, and sent him a card for her evening. They encountered here with a jocose old friendliness, and a profession of being tired of always meeting Miss Anderson and Mr. Mavering. He brought her salad and ice, and they made an appointment for another walk in the morning, if it was fine.

He carried her some flowers. A succession of fine days followed, and they walked every morning. Sometimes Dan was late, and explained that it was his patent-right man had kept him. She was interested in the patent-right man, whom Dan began to find not quite so simple as at first, but she was not exacting with him about his want of punctuality; she was very easy-going; she was not always ready herself. When he began to beat about the bush, to talk insincerities, and to lose himself in intentionless plausibilities, she waited with serene patience for him to have done, and met him on their habitual ground of frankness and reality as if he had not left it. He got to telling her all his steps with his patent-right man, who seemed to be growing mote and more slippery, and who presently developed a demand for funds. Then she gave him some very shrewd, practical advice, and told him to go right into the hotel office and telegraph to his father while she was putting on her bonnet.

"Yes," he said, "that's what I thought of doing." But he admired her for advising him; he said to himself that Miss Anderson was the kind of girl his father would admire. She was good, and she was of the world too; that was what his father meant. He imagined himself arriving home and saying, "Well father, you know that despatch I sent you, about Lafflin's wanting money?" and telling him about Miss Anderson. Then he fancied her acquainted with his sisters and visiting them, and his father more and more fond of her, and perhaps in declining health, and eager to see his son settled in life; and he pictured himself telling her that he had done with love for ever, but if she could accept respect, fidelity, gratitude, he was ready to devote his life to her. She refused him, but they always remained good friends and comrades; she married another, perhaps Boardman, while Dan was writing out his telegram, and he broke into whispered maledictions on his folly, which attracted the notice of the operator.

One morning when he sent up his name to Miss Anderson, whom he did not find in the hotel parlour, the servant came back with word that Miss Van Hook would like to have him come up to their rooms. But it was Miss Anderson who met him at the door.

"It seemed rather formal to send you word that Miss Van Hook was indisposed, and Miss Anderson would be unable to walk this morning, and I thought perhaps you'd rather come up and get my regrets in person. And I wanted you to see our view."

She led the way to the window for it, but they did not look at it, though they sat down there apparently for the purpose. Dan put his hat beside his chair, and observed some inattentive civilities in inquiring after Miss Van Hook's health, and in hearing that it was merely a bad headache, one of a sort in which her niece hated to leave her to serve herself with the wet compresses which Miss Van Hook always bore on her forehead for it.

"One thing: it's decided us to be off for Fortress Monroe at last. We shall go by the boat to-morrow, if my aunt's better."

"To-morrow?" said Dan. "What's to become of me when you're gone?"

"Oh, we shall not take the whole population with us," suggested Miss Anderson.

"I wish you would take me. I told Mrs. Brinkley I would come while she was there, but I'm afraid I can't get off. Lafflin is developing into all sorts of strange propositions."

"I think you'd better look out for that man," said Miss Anderson.

"Oh, I do nothing without consulting my father. But I shall miss you."

"Thank you," said the girl gravely.

"I don't mean in a business capacity only."

They both laughed, and Dan looked about the room, which he found was a private hotel parlour, softened to a more domestic effect by the signs of its prolonged occupation by two refined women. On a table stood a leather photograph envelope with three cabinet pictures in it. Along the top lay a spray of withered forceythia. Dan's wandering eyes rested on it. Miss Anderson went and softly closed the door opening into the next room.

"I was afraid our talking might disturb my aunt," she said, and on her way back to him she picked up the photograph case and brought it to the light. "These are my father and mother. We live at Yonkers; but I'm with my aunt a good deal of the time in town—even when I'm at home." She laughed at her own contradictory statement, and put the case back without explaining the third figure—a figure in uniform. Dan conjectured a military brother, or from her indifference perhaps a militia brother, and then forgot about him. But the partial Yonkers residence accounted for traits of unconventionality in Miss Anderson which he had not been able to reconcile with the notion of an exclusively New York breeding. He felt the relief, the sympathy, the certainty of intelligence which every person whose life has been partly spent in the country feels at finding that a suspected cockney has also had the outlook into nature and simplicity.

On the Yonkers basis they became more intimate, more personal, and Dan told her about Ponkwasset Falls and his mother and sisters; he told her about his father, and she said she should like to see his father; she thought he must be like her father.

All at once, and for no reason that he could think of afterward, except, perhaps, the desire to see the case with her eyes, he began to tell her of his affair with Alice, and how and why it was broken off; he told the whole truth in regard to that, and did not spare himself.

She listened without once speaking, but without apparent surprise at the confidence, though she may have felt surprised. At times she looked as if her thoughts were away from what he was saying.

He ended with, "I'm sure I don't know why I've told you all

this. But I wanted you to know about me. The worst."

Miss Anderson said, looking down, "I always thought she was a very conscientious giyl." Then after a pause, in which she seemed to be overcoming an embarrassment in being obliged to speak of another in such a conviction, "I think she was very moybid. She was like ever so many New England giyls that I've met. They seem to want some excuse for suffering; and they must suffer even if it's through somebody else. I don't know; they're romantic, New England giyls are; they have too many ideals."

Dan felt a balm in this; he too had noticed a superfluity of ideals in Alice, he had borne the burden of realising some of them; they all seemed to relate in objectionable degree to his perfectionation. So he said gloomily, "She was very good. And I was to blame."

"Oh yes!" said Miss Anderson, catching her breath in a queer way; "she seyved you right."

She rose abruptly, as if she heard her aunt speak, and Dan perceived that he had been making a long call.

He went away dazed and dissatisfied; he knew now that he ought not to have told Miss Anderson about his affair, unless he meant more by his confidence than he really did—unless he meant to follow it up.

He took leave of her, and asked her to make his adieux to her aunt; but the next day he came down to the boat to see them off. It seemed to him that their interview had ended too hastily; he felt sore and restless over it; he hoped that something more conclusive might happen. But at the boat Miss Anderson and her aunt were inseparable. Miss Van Hook said she hoped they should soon see him at the Hygeia, and he replied that he was not sure that he should be able to come after all.

Miss Anderson called something after him as he turned from them to go ashore. He ran back eagerly to know what it was. "Better lookout for that Mr. Lafflin of yours," she repeated.

"Oh! oh yes," he said, indefinitely disappointed. "I shall keep a sharp eye on him." He was disappointed, but he could not have said what he had hoped or expected her to say. He was humbled before himself for having told Miss Anderson about his affair with Alice, and had wished she would say something that he might scramble back to his self-esteem upon. He had told her all that partly from mere weakness, from his longing for the sympathy which he was always so ready to give, and partly from the willingness to pose before her as a broken heart, to dazzle her by the irony and persiflage with which he could treat such a tragical matter; but he could not feel that he had succeeded. The sum of her comment had been that Alice had served him right. He did not know whether she really believed that or merely said it to punish him for some reason; but he could never let it be the last word. He tingled as he turned to wave his handkerchief to her on the boat, with the suspicion that she was laughing at him; and he could not console himself with any hero of a novel who had got himself into just such a box. There were always circumstances, incidents, mitigations, that kept the hero still a hero, and ennobled the box into an unjust prison cell.

L

On the long sunny piazza of the Hygeia Mrs. Brinkley and Miss Van Hook sat and talked in a community of interest which they had not discovered during the summer before at Campobello, and with an equality of hearing which the sound of the waves washing almost at their feet established between them. In this pleasant noise Miss Van Hook heard as well as any one, and Mrs. Brinkley gradually realised that it was the trouble of having to lift her voice that had kept her from cultivating a very agreeable acquaintance before. The ladies sat in a secluded corner, wearing light wraps that they had often found comfortable at Campobello in August, and from time to time attested to each other their astonishment that they needed no more at Old Point in early April.

They did this not only as a just tribute to the amiable climate, but as a relief from the topic which had been absorbing them, and to which they constantly returned.

"No," said Mrs. Brinkley, with a sort of finality, "I think it is the best thing that could possibly have happened to him. He is bearing it in a very manly way, but I fancy he has felt it deeply, poor fellow. He's never been in Boston since, and I don't believe he'd come here if he'd any idea how many Boston people there were in the hotel—we swarm! It would be very painful to him."

"Yes," said Miss Van Hook, "young people seem to feel those things."

"Of course he's going to get over it. That's what young people do too. At his age he can't help being caught with every pretty face and every pretty figure, even in the midst of his woe, and it's only a question of time till he seizes some pretty hand and gets drawn out of it altogether."

"I think that would be the case with my niece, too," said Miss Van Hook, "if she wasn't kept in it by a sense of loyalty. I don't believe she really dares much for Lieutenant Willing any more; but he sees no society where he's stationed, of course, and his constancy is a—a rebuke and a—a—an incentive to her. They were engaged a long time ago just after he left West Point—and we've always been in hopes that he would be removed to some post where he could meet other ladies and become interested in some one else. But he never has, and so the affair remains. It's most undesirable they should marry, and in the meantime she won't break it off, and it's spoiling her chances in life."

"It is too bad," sighed Mrs. Brinkley, "but of course you can do nothing. I see that."

"No, we can do nothing. We have tried everything. I used to think it was because she was so dull there at Yonkers with her family, and brooded upon the one idea all the time, that she could not get over it; and at first it did seem when she came to me that she would get over it. She is very fond of gaiety—of young men's society, and she's had plenty of little flirtations that didn't mean anything, and never amounted to anything. Every now and then a letter would come from the wilds where he was stationed, and spoil it all. She seemed to feel a sort of chivalrous obligation because he was so far off and helpless and lonely."

"Yes, I understand," said Mrs. Brinkley. "What a pity she couldn't be made to feel that that didn't deepen the obligation at all."

"I've tried to make her," said Miss Van Hook, "and I've been everywhere with her. One winter we were up the Nile, and another in Nice, and last winter we were in Rome. She met young men everywhere, and had offers upon offers; but it was of no use. She remained just the same, and till she met Mr. Mavering in Washington I don't believe—"

Miss Van Hook stopped, and Mrs. Brinkley said, "And yet she always seemed to me particularly practical and level-headed—as the men say."

"So she is. But she is really very romantic about some things; and when it comes to a matter of that kind, girls are about all alike, don't you think?"

"Oh yes," said Mrs. Brinkley hopelessly, and both ladies looked out over the water, where the waves came rolling in one after another to waste themselves on the shore as futilely as if they had been lives.

In the evening Miss Anderson got two letters from the clerk, at the hour when the ladies all flocked to his desk with the eagerness for letters which is so engaging in them. One she pulled open and glanced at with a sort of impassioned indifference; the other she read in one intense moment, and then ran it into her pocket, and with her hand still on it hurried vividly flushing to her room, and read and read it again with constantly mounting emotion.

"WORMLEY's HOTEL, Washington, April 7, 188-.

"DEAR MISS ANDERSON,—I have been acting on your parting advice to look out for that Mr. Lafflin of mine, and I have discovered that he is an unmitigated scamp. Consequently there is nothing more to keep me in Washington, and I should now like your advice about coming to Fortress Monroe. Do you find it malarial? On the boat your aunt asked me to come, but you said nothing about it, and I was left to suppose that you did not think it would agree with me. Do you still think so? or what do you think? I know you think it was uncalled for and in extremely bad taste for me to tell you what I did the other day; and I have thought so too. There is only one thing that could justify it—that is, I think it might justify it—if you thought so. But I do not feel sure that you would like to know it, or, if you knew it, would like it. I've been rather slow coming to the conclusion myself, and perhaps it's only the beginning of the end; and not the conclusion—if there is such a difference. But the question now is whether I may come and tell you what I think it is—justify myself, or make things worse than they are now. I don't know that they can be worse, but I think I should like to try. I think your presence would inspire me.

"Washington is a wilderness since Miss—Van Hook left. It is not a howling wilderness simply because it has not enough left in it to howl; but it has all the other merits of a wilderness.

"Yours sincerely,

"D. F. MAVERING."

 After a second perusal of this note, Miss Anderson recurred to the other letter which she had neglected for it, and read it with eyes from which the tears slowly fell upon it. Then she sat a long time at her table with both letters before her, and did not move, except to take her handkerchief out of her pocket and dry her eyes, from which the tears began at once to drip again. At last she started forward, and caught pen and paper toward her, biting her lip and frowning as if to keep herself firm, and she said to the central figure in the photograph case which stood at the back of the table, "I will, I will! You are a man, anyway."

She sat down, and by a series of impulses she wrote a letter, with which she gave herself no pause till she put it in the clerk's hands, to whom she ran downstairs with it, kicking her skirt into wild whirls as she ran, and catching her foot in it and stumbling.

"Will it go—go to-night?" she demanded tragically.

"Just in time," said the clerk, without looking up, and apparently not thinking that her tone betrayed any unusual amount of emotion in a lady posting a letter; he was used to intensity on such occasions.

The letter ran—

"DEAR MR. MAVERING,—We shall now be here so short a time that I do not think it advisable for you to come.

"Your letter was rather enigmatical, and I do not know whether I understood it exactly. I suppose you told me what you did for good reasons of your own, and I did not think much about it. I believe the question of taste did not come up in my mind.

"My aunt joins me in kindest regards.

"Yours very sincerely,

"JULIA V. H. ANDERSON.

"P.S.—I think that I ought to return your letter. I know that you would not object to my keeping it, but it does not seem right. I wish to ask your congratulations. I have been engaged for several years to Lieutenant Willing, of the Army. He has been transferred from his post in Montana to Fort Hamilton at New York, and we are to be married in June."

The next morning Mrs. Brinkley came up from breakfast in a sort of duplex excitement, which she tried to impart to her husband; he stood with his back toward the door, bending forward to the glass for a more accurate view of his face, from which he had scraped half the lather in shaving.

She had two cards in her hand: "Miss Van Hook and Miss Anderson have gone. They went this morning. I found their P.

P. C.'s by my plate."

Mr. Brinkley made an inarticulate noise for comment, and assumed the contemptuous sneer which some men find convenient for shaving the lower lip.

"And guess who's come, of all people in the world?"

"I don't know," said Brinkley, seizing his chance to speak.

"The Pasmers!—Alice and her mother! Isn't it awful?"

Mr. Brinkley had entered upon a very difficult spot at the corner of his left jaw. He finished it before he said, "I don't see anything awful about it, so long as Pasmer hasn't come too."

"But Dan Mavering! He's in Washington, and he may come down here any day. Just think how shocking that would be!"

"Isn't that rather a theory?" asked Mr. Brinkley, finding such opportunities for conversation as he could. "I dare say Mrs. Pasmer would be very glad to see him."

"I've no doubt she would," said Mrs. Brinkley. "But it's the worst thing that could happen—for him. And I feel like writing him not to come—telegraphing him."

"You know how the man made a fortune in Chicago," said her husband, drying his razor tenderly on a towel before beginning to strop it. "I advise you to let the whole thing alone. It doesn't concern us in any way whatever."

"Then," said Mrs. Brinkley, "there ought to be a committee to take it in hand and warn him."

"I dare say you could make one up among the ladies. But don't be the first to move in the matter."

"I really believe," said his wife, with her mind taken off the point by the attractiveness of a surmise which had just occurred to her, "that Mrs. Pasmer would be capable of following him down if she knew he was in Washington."

"Yes, if she know. But she probably doesn't. '

"Yes," said Mrs. Brinkley disappointedly. "I think the sudden departure of the Van Hooks must have had something to do with Dan Mavering."

"Seems a very influential young man," said her husband. "He attracts and repels people right and left. Did you speak to the Pasmers?"

"No; you'd better, when you go down. They've just come into the dining-room. The girl looks like death."

"Well, I'll talk to her about Mavering. That'll cheer her up."

Mrs. Brinkley looked at him for an instant as if she really thought him capable of it. Then she joined him in his laugh.

Mrs. Brinkley had theorised Alice Pasmer as simply and primitively selfish, like the rest of the Pasmers in whom the family traits prevailed.

When Mavering stopped coming to her house after his engagement she justly suspected that it was because Alice had forbidden him, and she had rejoiced at the broken engagement as an escape for Dan; she had frankly said so, and she had received him back into full favour at the first moment in Washington. She liked Miss Anderson, and she had hoped, with the interest which women feel in every such affair, that her flirtation with him might become serious. But now this had apparently not happened. Julia Anderson was gone with mystifying precipitation, and Alice Pasmer had come with an unexpectedness which had the aspect of fatality.

Mrs. Brinkley felt bound, of course, since there was no open enmity between them, to meet the Pasmers on the neutral ground of the Hygeia with conventional amiability. She was really touched by the absent wanness of the girls look, and by the later-coming recognition which shaped her mouth into a pathetic snide. Alice did not look like death quite, as Mrs. Brinkley had told her husband, with the necessity her sex has for putting its superlatives before its positives; but she was pale and thin, and she moved with a languid step when they all met at night after Mrs. Brinkley had kept out of the Pasmers' way during the day.

"She has been ill all the latter part of the winter," said Mrs. Pasmer to Mrs. Brinkley that night in the corner of the spreading hotel parlours, where they found themselves. Mrs. Pasmer did not look well herself; she spoke with her eyes fixed anxiously on the door Alice had just passed out of. "She is going to bed, but I know I shall find her awake whenever I go."

"Perhaps," suggested Mrs. Brinkley, "this soft, heavy sea air will put her to sleep." She tried to speak drily and indifferently, but she could not; she was, in fact, very much interested by the situation, and she was touched, in spite of her distaste for them both, by the evident unhappiness of mother and daughter. She knew what it came from, and she said to herself that they deserved it; but this did not altogether fortify her against their pathos. "I can hardly keep awake myself," she added gruffly.

"I hope it may help her," said Mrs. Pasmer; "the doctor strongly urged our coming."

"Mr. Pasmer isn't with you," said Mrs. Brinkley, feeling that it was decent to say something about him.

"No; he was detained." Mrs. Pasmer did not explain the cause of his detention, and the two ladies slowly waved their fans a moment in silence. "Are there many Boston People in the house?" Mrs. Pasmer asked.

"It's full of them," cried Mrs. Brinkley.

"I had scarcely noticed," sighed Mrs. Pasmer; and Mrs. Brinkley knew that this was not true. "Alice takes up all my thoughts," she added; and this might be true enough. She leaned a little forward and asked, in a low, entreating voice over her fan, "Mrs. Brinkley, have you seen Mr. Mavering lately?"

Mrs. Brinkley considered this a little too bold, a little too brazen. Had they actually come South in pursuit of him? It was shameless, and she let Mrs. Pasmer know something of her feeling in the shortness with which she answered, "I saw him in Washington the other day—for a moment." She shortened the time she had spent in Dan's company so as to cut Mrs. Pasmer off from as much comfort as possible, and she stared at her in open astonishment.

Mrs. Pasmer dropped her eyes and fingered the edge of her fan with a submissiveness that seemed to Mrs. Brinkley the perfection of duplicity; she wanted to shake her. "I knew," sighed Mrs. Pasmer, "that you had always been such a friend of his."

It is the last straw which breaks the camel's back; Mrs. Brinkley felt her moral vertebrae give way; she almost heard them crack; but if there was really a detonation, the drowned the noise with a harsh laugh. "Oh, he had other friends in Washington. I met him everywhere with Miss Anderson." This statement conflicted with the theory of her single instant with Dan, but she felt that in such a cause, in the cause of giving pain to a woman like Mrs. Pasmer, the deflection from exact truth was justifiable. She hurried on: "I rather expected he might run down here, but now that they're gone, I don't suppose he'll come. You remember Miss Anderson's aunt, Miss Van Hook?"

"Oh yes," said Mrs. Pasmer.

"She was here with her."

"Miss Van Hook was such a New York type—of a certain kind," said Mrs. Pasmer. She rose, with a smile at once so conventional, so heroic, and so pitiful that Mrs. Brinkley felt the remorse of a generous victor.

She went to her room, hardening her heart, and she burst in with a flood of voluble exasperation that threatened all the neighbouring rooms with overflow.

"Well," she cried, "they have shown their hands completely. They have come here to hound Dan Mavering down, and get him into their toils again. Why, the woman actually said as much! But I fancy I have given her a fit of insomnia that will enable her to share her daughter's vigils. Really such impudence I never heard of!"

"Do you want everybody in the corridor to hear of it?" asked Brinkley, from behind a newspaper.

"I know one thing," continued Mrs. Brinkley, dropping her voice a couple of octaves. "They will never get him here if I can help it. He won't come, anyway, now Miss Anderson is gone; but I'll make assurance doubly sure by writing him not to come; I'll tell him they've gone; and than we are going too."

"You had better remember the man in Chicago," said her husband.

"Well, this is my business—or I'll make it my business!" cried Mrs. Brinkley. She went on talking rapidly, rising with great excitement in her voice at times, and then remembering to speak lower; and her husband apparently read on through most of her talk, though now and then he made some comment that seemed of almost inspired aptness.

"The way they both made up to me was disgusting. But I know the girl is just a tool in her mother's hands. Her mother seemed actually passive in comparison. For skilful wheedling I could fall down and worship that woman; I really admire her. As long as the girl was with us she kept herself in the background and put the girl at me. It was simply a masterpiece."

"How do you know she put her at you?" asked Brinkley.

"How? By the way she seemed not to do it! And because from what I know of that stupid Pasmer pride it would be perfectly impossible for any one who was a Pasmer to take her deprecatory manner toward me of herself. You ought to have seen it! It was simply perfect."

"Perhaps," said Brinkley, with a remote dreaminess, "she was truly sorry."

"Truly stuff! No, indeed; she hates me as much as ever—more!"

"Well, then, may be she's doing it because she hates you—doing it for her soul's good—sort of penance, sort of atonement to Mavering."

Mrs. Brinkley turned round from her dressing-table to see what her husband meant, but the newspaper hid him. We all know that our own natures are mixed and contradictory, but we each attribute to others a logical consistency which we never find in any one out of the novels. Alice Pasmer was cold and reticent, and Mrs. Brinkley, who had lived half a century in a world full of paradoxes, could not imagine her subject to gusts of passionate frankness; she knew the girl to be proud and distant, and she could not conceive of an abject humility and longing for sympathy in her heart. If Alice felt, when she saw Mrs. Brinkley, that she had a providential opportunity to punish herself for her injustice to Dan, the fact could not be established upon Mrs. Brinkley's theory of her. If the ascetic impulse is the most purely selfish impulse in human nature, Mrs. Brinkley might not have been mistaken in suspecting her of an ignoble motive, though it might have had for the girl the last sublimity of self-sacrifice. The woman who disliked her and pitied her knew that she had no arts, and rather than adopt so simple a theory of her behaviour as her husband had advanced she held all the more strenuously to her own theory that Alice was practising her mother's arts. This was inevitable, partly from the sense of Mrs. Pasmer's artfulness which everybody had, and partly from the allegiance which we pay— and women especially like to pay—to the tradition of the playwrights and the novelists, that social results of all kinds are the work of deep, and more or less darkling, design on the part of other women—such other women as Mrs. Pasmer.

Mrs. Brinkley continued to talk, but the god spoke no more from behind the newspaper; and afterward Mrs. Brinkley lay a long time awake; hardening her heart. But she was haunted to the verge of her dreams by that girl's sick look, by her languid walk, and by the effect which she had seen her own words take upon Mrs. Pasmer—an effect so admirably disowned, so perfectly obvious. Before she could get to sleep she was obliged to make a compromise with her heart, in pursuance of which, when she found Mrs. Pasmer at breakfast alone in the morning, she went up to her, and said, holding her hand a moment, "I hope your daughter slept well last night."

"No," said Mrs. Pasmer, slipping her hand away, "I can't say that she did." There was probably no resentment expressed in the way she withdrew her hand, but the other thought there was.

"I wish I could do something for her," she cried.

"Oh, thank you," said Mrs. Pasmer. "It's very good of you." And Mrs. Brinkley fancied she smiled rather bitterly.

Mrs. Brinkley went out upon the seaward verandah of the hotel with this bitterness of Mrs. Pasmer's smile in her thoughts; and it disposed her to feel more keenly the quality of Miss Pasmer's smile. She found the girl standing there at a remote point of that long stretch of planking, and looking out over the water; she held with both hands across her breast the soft chuddah shawl which the wind caught and fluttered away from her waist. She was alone, said as Mrs. Brinkley's compunctions goaded her nearer, she fancied that the saw Alice master a primary dislike in her face, and put on a look of pathetic propitiation. She did not come forward to meet Mrs. Brinkley, who liked better her waiting to be approached; but she smiled gratefully when Mrs. Brinkley put out her hand, and she took it with a very cold one.

"You must find it chilly here," said the elder woman.

"I had better be out in the air all I could, the doctor said," answered Alice.

"Well, then, come with me round the corner; there's a sort of recess there, and you won't be blown to pierces," said Mrs. Brinkley, with authority. They sat down together in the recess, and she added: "I used to sit here with Miss Van Hook; she could hear better in the noise the waves made. I hope it isn't too much for you."

"Oh no," said Alice. "Mamma said you told her they were here." Mrs. Brinkley reassured herself from this; Miss Van Hook's name had rather slipped out; but of course Mrs. Pasmer had not repeated what she had said about Dan in this connection. "I wish I could have seen Julia," Alice went on. "It would have been quite like Campobello again."

"Oh, quite," said Mrs. Brinkley, with a short breath, and not knowing whither this tended. Alice did not leave her in doubt.

"I should like to have seen her, and begged her for the way I treated her the last part of the time there. I feel as if I could make my whole life a reparation," she added passionately.

Mrs. Brinkley believed that this was the mere frenzy of sentimentality, the exaltation of a selfish asceticism; but at the break in the girl's voice and the aversion of her face she could not help a thrill of motherly tenderness for her. She wanted to tell her she was an unconscious humbug, bent now as always on her own advantage, and really indifferent to others she also wanted to comfort her, and tell her that she exaggerated, and was not to blame. She did neither, but when Alice turned her face back she seemed encouraged by Mrs. Brinkley's look to go on: "I didn't appreciate her then; she was very generous and high-minded—too high-minded for me to understand, even. But we don't seem to know how good others are till we wrong them."

"Yes, that is very true," said Mrs. Brinkley. She knew that Alice was obviously referring to the breach between herself and Miss Anderson following the night of the Trevor theatricals, and the dislike for her that she had shown with a frankness some of the ladies had thought brutal. Mrs. Brinkley also believed that her words had a tacit meaning, and she would have liked to have the hardness to say she had seen an unnamed victim of Alice doing his best to console the other she had specified. But she merely said drily, "Yes, perhaps that's the reason why we're allowed to injure people."

"It must be," said Alice simply. "Did Miss Anderson ever speak of me?"

"No; I can't remember that she ever did." Mrs. Brinkley did not feel bound to say that she and Miss Van Hook had discussed her at large, and agreed perfectly about her.

"I should like to see her; I should like to write to her."

Mrs. Brinkley felt that she ought not to suffer this intimate tendency in the talk:

"You must find a great many other acquaintances in the hotel, Miss Pasmer."

"Some of the Frankland girds are here, and the two

Bellinghams. I have hardly spoken to them yet. Do you think that where you have even been in the right, if you have been harsh, if you have been hasty, if you haven't made allowances, you ought to offer some atonement?"

"Really, I can't say," said Mrs. Brinkley, with a smile of distaste. "I'm afraid your question isn't quite in my line of thinking; it's more in Miss Cotton's way. You'd better ask her some time."

"No," said Alice sadly; "she would flatter me."

"Ah! I always supposed she was very conscientious."

"She's conscientious, but she likes me too well."

"Oh!" commented Mrs. Brinkley to herself, "then you know I don't like you, and you'll use me in one way, if you can't in another. Very well!" But she found the girl's trust touching somehow, though the sentimentality of her appeal seemed as tawdry as ever.

"I knew you would be just," added Alice wistfully.

"Oh, I don't know about atonements!" said Mrs. Brinkley, with an effect of carelessness. "It seems to me that we usually make them for our own sake."

"I have thought of that," said Alice, with a look of expectation.

"And we usually astonish other people when we offer them."

"Either they don't like it, or else they don't feel so much injured as we had supposed."

"Oh, but there's no question—"

"If Miss Anderson—"

"Miss Anderson? Oh—oh yes!"

"If Miss Anderson for example," pursued Mrs. Brinkley, "felt aggrieved with you. But really I've no right to enter into your affairs, Miss Pasmer."

"Oh Yes, yes!—do! I asked you to," the girl implored.

"I doubt if it will help matters for her to know that you regret anything; and if she shouldn't happen to have thought that you were unjust to her, it would make her uncomfortable for nothing."

"Do you think so?" asked the girl, with a disappointment that betrayed itself in her voice and eyes.

"I never feel I myself competent to advise," said Mrs. Brinkley. "I can criticise—anybody can—and I do, pretty freely; but advice is a more serious matter. Each of us must act from herself—from what she thinks is right."

"Yes, I see. Thank you so much, Mrs. Brinkley."

"After all, we have a right to do ourselves good, even when we pretend that it's good to others, if we don't do them any harm."

"Yes, I see." Alice looked away, and then seemed about to speak again; but one of Mrs. Brinkley's acquaintance came up, and the girl rose with a frightened air and went away.

"Alice's talk with you this morning did her so much good!" said Mrs. Pasmer, later. "She has always felt so badly about Miss Anderson!"

Mrs. Brinkley saw that Mrs. Pasmer wished to confine the meaning of their talk to Miss Anderson, and she assented, with a penetration of which she saw that Mrs. Pasmer was gratefully aware.

She grew more tolerant of both the Pasmers as the danger of greater intimacy from them, which seemed to threaten at first seemed to pass away. She had not responded to their advances, but there was no reason why she should not be civil to them; there had never been any open quarrel with them. She often found herself in talk with them, and was amused to note that she was the only Bostonian whom they did not keep aloof from.

It could not be said that she came to like either of them better. She still suspected Mrs. Pasmer of design, though she developed none beyond manoeuvring Alice out of the way of people whom she wished to avoid; and she still found the girl, as she always thought her, as egotist, whose best impulses toward others had a final aim in herself. She thought her very crude in her ideas—cruder than she had seemed at Campobello, where she had perhaps been softened by her affinition with the gentler and kindlier nature of Dan Mavering. Mrs. Brinkley was never tired of saying that he had made the most fortunate escape in the world, and though Brinkley owned he was tired of hearing it, she continued to say it with a great variety of speculation. She recognised that in most girls of Alice's age many traits are in solution, waiting their precipitation into character by the chemical contact which time and chances must bring, and that it was not fair to judge her by the present ferment of hereditary tendencies; but she rejoiced all the same that it was not Dan Mavering's character which was to give fixity to hers. The more she saw of the girl the more she was convinced that two such people could only make each other unhappy; from day to day, almost from hour to hour, she resolved to write to Mavering and tell him not to come.

She was sure that the Pasmers wished to have the affair on again, and part of her fascination with a girl whom she neither liked nor approved was her belief that Alice's health had broken under the strain of her regrets and her despair. She did not get better from the change of air; she grew more listless and languid, and more dependent upon Mrs. Brinkley's chary sympathy. The older woman asked herself again and again what made the girl cling to her? Was she going to ask her finally to intercede with Dan? or was it really a despairing atonement to him, the most disagreeable sacrifice she could offer, as Mr. Brinkley had stupidly suggested? She believed that Alice's selfishness and morbid sentiment were equal to either.

Brinkley generally took the girl's part against his wife, and in a heavy jocose way tried to cheer her up. He did little things for her; fetched and carried chairs and cushions and rugs, and gave his attentions the air of pleasantries. One of his offices was to get the ladies' letters for them in the evening, and one night he came in beaming with a letter for each of them where they sat together in the parlour. He distributed them into their laps.

"Hello! I've made a mistake," he said, putting down his head to take back the letter he had dropped in Miss Pasmer's lap. "I've given you my wife's letter."

The girl glanced at it, gave a moaning kind of cry, and fell beak in her chair, hiding her face in her hands.

Mrs. Brinkley, possessed herself of the other letter, and, though past the age when ladies wish to kill their husbands for their stupidity, she gave Brinkley a look of massacre which mystified even more than it murdered his innocence. He had to learn later from his wife's more elicit fury what the women had all known instantly.

He showed his usefulness in gathering Alice up and getting her to her mother's room.

"Oh, Mrs. Brinkley," implored Mrs. Pasmer, following her to the door, "is Mr. Mavering coming here?"

"I don't know—I can't say—I haven't read the letter yet."

"Oh, do let me know when you've read it, won't you? I don't know what we shall do."

Mrs. Brinkley read the letter in her own room. "You go down," she said to her husband, with unabated ferocity; "and telegraph Dan Mavering at Wormley's not to came. Say we're going away at once."

Then she sent Mrs. Pasmer a slip of paper on which she had written, "Not coming."

It has been the experience of every one to have some alien concern come into his life and torment him with more anxiety than any affair of his own. This is, perhaps, a hint from the infinite sympathy which feels for us all that none of us can hope to free himself from the troubles of others, that we are each bound to each by ties which, for the most part, we cannot perceive, but which, at the moment their stress comes, we cannot break.

Mrs. Brinkley lay awake and raged impotently against her complicity with the unhappiness of that distasteful girl and her more than distasteful mother. In her revolt against it she renounced the interest she had felt in that silly boy, and his ridiculous love business, so really unimportant to her whatever turn it took. She asked herself what it mattered to her whether those children marred their lives one way or another way. There was a lurid moment before she slept when she wished Brinkley to go down and recall her telegram; but he refused to be a fool at so much inconvenience to himself.

Mrs. Brinkley came to breakfast feeling so much more haggard than she found either of the Pasmers looking, that she was able to throw off her lingering remorse for having told Mavering not to come. She had the advantage also of doubt as to her precise motive in having done so; she had either done so because she had judged it best for him not to see Miss Pasmer again, or else she had done so to relieve the girl from the pain of an encounter which her mother evidently dreaded for her. If one motive seemed at moments outrageously meddling and presumptuous, the other was so nobly good and kind that it more than counterbalanced it in Mrs. Brinkley's mind, who knew very well in spite of her doubt that she had, acted from a mixture of both. With this conviction, it was both a comfort and a pang to find by the register of the hotel, which she furtively consulted, that Dan had not arrived by the morning boat, as she groundlessly feared and hoped he might have done.

In any case, however, and at the end of all the ends, she had that girl on her hands more than ever; and believing as she did that Dan and Alice had only to meet in order to be reconciled, she felt that the girl whom she had balked of her prey was her innocent victim. What right had she to interfere? Was he not her natural prey? If he liked being a prey, who was lawfully to forbid him? He was not perfect; he would know how to take care of himself probably; in marriage things equalised themselves. She looked at the girl's thin cheeks and lack-lustre eyes, and pitied and hated her with that strange mixture of feeling which our victims aspire in us.

She walked out on the verandah with the Pasmers after breakfast, and chatted a while about indifferent things; and Alice made an effort to ignore the event of the night before with a pathos which wrung Mrs. Brinkley's heart, and with a gay resolution which ought to have been a great pleasure to such a veteran dissembler as her mother. She said she had never found the air so delicious; she really believed it would begin to do her good now; but it was a little fresh just there, and with her eyes she invited her mother to come with her round the corner into that sheltered recess, and invited Mrs. Brinkley not to come.

It was that effect of resentment which is lighter even than a touch, the waft of the arrow's feather; but it could wound a guilty heart, and Mrs. Brinkley sat down where she was, realising with a pang that the time when she might have been everything to this unhappy girl had just passed for ever, and henceforth she could be nothing. She remained musing sadly upon the contradictions she had felt in the girl's character, the confusion of good and evil, the potentialities of misery and harm, the potentialities of bliss and good; and she felt less and less satisfied with herself. She had really presumed to interfere with Fate; perhaps she had interfered with Providence. She would have given anything to recall her act; and then with a flash she realised that it was quite possible to recall it. She could telegraph Mavering to come; and she rose, humbly and gratefully, as if from an answered prayer, to go and do so.

She was not at all a young woman, and many things had come and gone in her life that ought to have fortified her against surprise; but she wanted to scream like a little frightened girl as Dan Mavering stepped out of the parlour door toward her. The habit of not screaming, however, prevailed, and she made a tolerably successful effort to treat him with decent compo-sure. She gave him a rigid hand. "Where in the world did you come from? Did you get my telegram?"

"No. Did you get my letter?"

"Yes."

"Well, I took a notion to come right on after I wrote, and I started on the same train with it. But they said it was no use trying to get into the Hygeia, and I stopped last night at the little hotel in Hampton. I've just walked over, and Mr. Brinkley told me you were out here somewhere. That's the whole story, I believe." He gave his nervous laugh, but it seemed to Mrs. Brinkley that it had not much joy in it.

"Hush!" she said involuntarily, receding to her chair and sinking back into it again. He looked surprised. "You know the Van Hooks are gone?"

He laughed harshly. "I should think they were dead from your manner, Mrs. Brinkley. But I didn't come to see the Van Hooks. What made you think I did?"

He gave her a look which she found so dishonest, so really insincere, that she resolved to abandon him to Providence as soon as she could. "Oh, I didn't know but there had been some little understanding at Washington."

"Perhaps on their part. They were people who seemed to take a good many things for granted, but they could hardly expect to control other people's movements."

He looked sharply at Mrs. Brinkley, as if to question how much she knew; but she had now measured him, and she said, "Oh! then the visit's to me?"

"Entirely," cried Dan. The old sweetness came into his laughing eyes again, and went to Mrs. Brinkley's heart. She wished him to be happy, somehow; she would have done anything for him; she wished she knew what to do. Ought she to tell him the Pasmers were there? Ought she to make up some excuse and get him away before he met them? She felt herself getting more and more bewildered and helpless. Those women might come round that corner any moment and then she know the first sight of Alice's face would do or undo everything with Dan. Did she wish them reconciled? Did she wish them for ever parted? She no longer knew what she wished; she only knew that she had no right to wish anything. She continued to talk on with Dan, who grew more and more at ease, and did most of the talking, while Mrs. Brinkley's whole being narrowed itself to the question. Would the Pasmers come back that way, or would they go round the further corner, and get into the hotel by another door?

The suspense seemed interminable; they must have already gone that other way. Suddenly she heard the pushing back of chairs in that recess. She could not bear it. She jumped to her feet.

"Just wait a moment, Mr. Mavering! I'll join you again. Mr. Brinkley is expecting—I must—"

* * * * * * * * *

William Dean Howells

One morning of the following June Mrs. Brinkley sat well forward in the beautiful church where Dan and Alice were to be married. The lovely day became a still lovelier day within, enriched by the dyes of the stained windows through which it streamed; the still place was dim yet bright with it; the figures painted on the walls had a soft distinctness; a body of light seemed to irradiate from the depths of the dome like lamplight.

There was a subdued murmur of voices among the people in the pews: they were in a sacred edifice without being exactly at church, and they might talk; now and then a muffled, nervous laugh escaped. A delicate scent of flowers from the masses in the chancel mixed with the light and the prevailing silence. There was a soft, continuous rustle of drapery as the ladies advanced up the thickly carpeted aisles on the arms of the young ushers and compressed themselves into place in the pews.

Two or three people whom she did not know were put into the pew with Mrs. Brinkley, but she kept her seat next the aisle; presently an usher brought up a lady who sat down beside her, and then for a moment or two seemed to sink and rise, as if on the springs of an intense excitement.

It was Miss Cotton, who, while this process of quiescing lasted, appeared not to know Mrs. Brinkley. When she became aware of her, all was lost again. "Mrs. Brinkley!" she cried, as well as one can cry in whisper. "Is it possible?"

"I have my doubts," Mrs. Brinkley whispered back. "But we'll suppose the case."

"Oh, it's all too good to be true! How I envy you being the means of bringing them together, Mrs. Brinkley!"

"Means?"

"Yes—they owe it all to you; you needn't try to deny it; he's told every one!"

"I was sure she hadn't," said Mrs. Brinkley, remembering how Alice had marked an increasing ignorance of any part she might have had in the affair from the first moment of her reconciliation with Dan; she had the effect of feeling that she had sacrificed enough to Mrs. Brinkley; and Mrs. Brinkley had been restored to all the original strength of her conviction that she was a solemn little unconscious egotist, and Dan was as unselfish and good as he was unequal to her exactions.

"Oh no?" said Miss Cotton. "She couldn't!" implying that Alice would be too delicate to speak of it.

"Do you see any of his family here?" asked Mrs. Brinkley.

"Yes; over there—up front." Miss Cotton motioned, with her eyes toward a pew in which Mrs. Brinkley distinguished an elderly gentleman's down-misted bald head and the back of a young lady's bonnet. "His father and sister; the other's a bridemaid; mother bed-ridden and couldn't come."

"They might have brought her in an-arm-chair," suggested Mrs. Brinkley ironically, "on such an occasion. But perhaps they don't take much interest in such a patched-up affair."

"Oh yes, they do!" exclaimed Miss Cotton. "They idolise Alice."

"And Mrs. Pasmer and Mister, too?"

"I don't suppose that so much matters."

"They know how to acquiesce, I've no doubt."

"Oh yes! You've heard? The young people are going abroad first with her family for a year, and then they come back to live with his—where the Works are."

"Poor fellow!" said Mrs. Brinkley.

"Why, Mrs. Brinkley, do you still feel that way?" asked Miss Cotton, with a certain distress. "It seems to me that if ever two young people had the promise of happiness, they have. Just see what their love has done for them already!"

"And you still think that in these cases love can do everything?"

Miss Cotton was about to reply, when she observed that the people about her had stopped talking. The bridegroom, with his best man, in whom his few acquaintances there recognised Boardman with some surprise, came over the chancel from one side.

Miss Cotton bent close to Mrs. Brinkley and whispered rapidly: "Alice found out Mr. Mavering wished it, and insisted on his having him. It was a great concession, but she's perfectly magnanimous. Poor fellow! how he does look!"

Alice, on her father's arm, with her bridemaids, of whom the first was Minnie Mavering, mounted the chancel steps, where Mr. Pasmer remained standing till he advanced to give away the bride. He behaved with great dignity, but seemed deeply affected; the ladies in the front pews said they could see his face twitch; but he never looked handsomer.

The five clergymen came from the back of the chancel in their white surplices. The ceremony proceeded to the end.

The young couple drove at once to the station, where they were to take the train for New York, and wait there a day or two for Mrs. and Mr. Pasmer before they all sailed.

As they drove along, Alice held Dan's wrist in the cold clutch of her trembling little ungloved hand, on which her wedding ring shone. "O dearest! let us be good!" she said. "I will try my best. I will try not to be exacting and unreasonable, and I know I can. I won't even make any conditions, if you will always be frank and open with me, and tell me everything."

He leaned over and kissed her behind the drawn curtains. "I will, Alice! I will indeed! I won't keep anything from you after this."

He resolved to tell her all about Julia Anderson at the right moment, when Alice was in the mood, and as soon as he thoroughly understood what he had really meant himself.

If he had been different she would not have asked him to be frank and open; if she had been different, he might have been frank and open. This was the beginning of their married life.

ABOUT THE AUTHOR

 **William Dean Howells** (March 1, 1837 – May 11, 1920) was an American realist author and literary critic.

Born in Martins Ferry, Ohio, originally Martinsville, to William Cooper and Mary Dean Howells, Howells was the second of eight children. His father was a newspaper editor and printer, and the father moved frequently around Ohio. Howells began to help his father with typesetting and printing work at an early age. In 1852, his father arranged to have one of Howells' poems published in the Ohio State Journal without telling him.

He wrote his first novel, The Wedding Journey, in 1872, but his literary reputation took off with the realist novel, A Modern Instance, published in 1882, which described the decay of a marriage. His 1885 novel The Rise of Silas Lapham is perhaps his best known, describing the rise and fall of an American entrepreneur in the paint business. His social views were also strongly reflected in the novels Annie Kilburn (1888) and A Hazard of New Fortunes (1890). He was particularly outraged by the trials resulting from the Haymarket Riot.

In 1904, he was one of the first seven chosen for membership in the American Academy of Arts and Letters, of which he became president.

Choose from Thousands of 1stWorldLibrary Classics By

A. M. Barnard
Ada Leverson
Adolphus William Ward
Aesop
Agatha Christie
Alexander Aaronsohn
Alexander Kielland
Alexandre Dumas
Alfred Gatty
Alfred Ollivant
Alice Duer Miller
Alice Turner Curtis
Alice Dunbar
Allen Chapman
Alleyne Ireland
Ambrose Bierce
Amelia E. Barr
Amory H. Bradford
Andrew Lang
Andrew McFarland Davis
Andy Adams
Angela Brazil
Anna Alice Chapin
Anna Sewell
Annie Besant
Annie Hamilton Donnell
Annie Payson Call
Annie Roe Carr
Annonaymous
Anton Chekhov
Archibald Lee Fletcher
Arnold Bennett
Arthur C. Benson
Arthur Conan Doyle
Arthur M. Winfield
Arthur Ransome
Arthur Schnitzler
Arthur Train
Atticus
B.H. Baden-Powell
B. M. Bower
B. C. Chatterjee
Baroness Emmuska Orczy
Baroness Orczy
Basil King
Bayard Taylor
Ben Macomber
Bertha Muzzy Bower
Bjornstjerne Bjornson

Booth Tarkington
Boyd Cable
Bram Stoker
C. Collodi
C. E. Orr
C. M. Ingleby
Carolyn Wells
Catherine Parr Traill
Charles A. Eastman
Charles Amory Beach
Charles Dickens
Charles Dudley Warner
Charles Farrar Browne
Charles Ives
Charles Kingsley
Charles Klein
Charles Hanson Towne
Charles Lathrop Pack
Charles Romyn Dake
Charles Whibley
Charles Willing Beale
Charlotte M. Braeme
Charlotte M. Yonge
Charlotte Perkins Stetson
Clair W. Hayes
Clarence Day Jr.
Clarence E. Mulford
Clemence Housman
Confucius
Coningsby Dawson
Cornelis DeWitt Wilcox
Cyril Burleigh
D. H. Lawrence
Daniel Defoe
David Garnett
Dinah Craik
Don Carlos Janes
Donald Keyhoe
Dorothy Kilner
Dougan Clark
Douglas Fairbanks
E. Nesbit
E. P. Roe
E. Phillips Oppenheim
E. S. Brooks
Earl Barnes
Edgar Rice Burroughs
Edith Van Dyne
Edith Wharton

Edward Everett Hale
Edward J. O'Biren
Edward S. Ellis
Edwin L. Arnold
Eleanor Atkins
Eleanor Hallowell Abbott
Eliot Gregory
Elizabeth Gaskell
Elizabeth McCracken
Elizabeth Von Arnim
Ellem Key
Emerson Hough
Emilie F. Carlen
Emily Bronte
Emily Dickinson
Enid Bagnold
Enilor Macartney Lane
Erasmus W. Jones
Ernie Howard Pie
Ethel May Dell
Ethel Turner
Ethel Watts Mumford
Eugene Sue
Eugenie Foa
Eugene Wood
Eustace Hale Ball
Evelyn Everett-green
Everard Cotes
F. H. Cheley
F. J. Cross
F. Marion Crawford
Fannie E. Newberry
Federick Austin Ogg
Ferdinand Ossendowski
Fergus Hume
Florence A. Kilpatrick
Fremont B. Deering
Francis Bacon
Francis Darwin
Frances Hodgson Burnett
Frances Parkinson Keyes
Frank Gee Patchin
Frank Harris
Frank Jewett Mather
Frank L. Packard
Frank V. Webster
Frederic Stewart Isham
Frederick Trevor Hill
Frederick Winslow Taylor

Friedrich Kerst
Friedrich Nietzsche
Fyodor Dostoyevsky
G.A. Henty
G.K. Chesterton
Gabrielle E. Jackson
Garrett P. Serviss
Gaston Leroux
George A. Warren
George Ade
Geroge Bernard Shaw
George Cary Eggleston
George Durston
George Ebers
George Eliot
George Gissing
George MacDonald
George Meredith
George Orwell
George Sylvester Viereck
George Tucker
George W. Cable
George Wharton James
Gertrude Atherton
Gordon Casserly
Grace E. King
Grace Gallatin
Grace Greenwood
Grant Allen
Guillermo A. Sherwell
Gulielma Zollinger
Gustav Flaubert
H. A. Cody
H. B. Irving
H.C. Bailey
H. G. Wells
H. H. Munro
H. Irving Hancock
H. R. Naylor
H. Rider Haggard
H. W. C. Davis
Haldeman Julius
Hall Caine
Hamilton Wright Mabie
Hans Christian Andersen
Harold Avery
Harold McGrath
Harriet Beecher Stowe
Harry Castlemon
Harry Coghill
Harry Houidini

Hayden Carruth
Helent Hunt Jackson
Helen Nicolay
Hendrik Conscience
Hendy David Thoreau
Henri Barbusse
Henrik Ibsen
Henry Adams
Henry Ford
Henry Frost
Henry James
Henry Jones Ford
Henry Seton Merriman
Henry W Longfellow
Herbert A. Giles
Herbert Carter
Herbert N. Casson
Herman Hesse
Hildegard G. Frey
Homer
Honore De Balzac
Horace B. Day
Horace Walpole
Horatio Alger Jr.
Howard Pyle
Howard R. Garis
Hugh Lofting
Hugh Walpole
Humphry Ward
Ian Maclaren
Inez Haynes Gillmore
Irving Bacheller
Isabel Cecilia Williams
Isabel Hornibrook
Israel Abrahams
Ivan Turgenev
J.G.Austin
J. Henri Fabre
J. M. Barrie
J. M. Walsh
J. Macdonald Oxley
J. R. Miller
J. S. Fletcher
J. S. Knowles
J. Storer Clouston
J. W. Duffield
Jack London
Jacob Abbott
James Allen
James Andrews
James Baldwin

James Branch Cabell
James DeMille
James Joyce
James Lane Allen
James Lane Allen
James Oliver Curwood
James Oppenheim
James Otis
James R. Driscoll
Jane Abbott
Jane Austen
Jane L. Stewart
Janet Aldridge
Jens Peter Jacobsen
Jerome K. Jerome
Jessie Graham Flower
John Buchan
John Burroughs
John Cournos
John F. Kennedy
John Gay
John Glasworthy
John Habberton
John Joy Bell
John Kendrick Bangs
John Milton
John Philip Sousa
John Taintor Foote
Jonas Lauritz Idemil Lie
Jonathan Swift .
Joseph A. Altsheler
Joseph Carey
Joseph Conrad
Joseph E. Badger Jr
Joseph Hergesheimer
Joseph Jacobs
Jules Vernes
Julian Hawthrone
Julie A Lippmann
Justin Huntly McCarthy
Kakuzo Okakura
Karle Wilson Baker
Kate Chopin
Kenneth Grahame
Kenneth McGaffey
Kate Langley Bosher
Kate Langley Bosher
Katherine Cecil Thurston
Katherine Stokes
L. A. Abbot
L. T. Meade

L. Frank Baum
Latta Griswold
Laura Dent Crane
Laura Lee Hope
Laurence Housman
Lawrence Beasley
Leo Tolstoy
Leonid Andreyev
Lewis Carroll
Lewis Sperry Chafer
Lilian Bell
Lloyd Osbourne
Louis Hughes
Louis Joseph Vance
Louis Tracy
Louisa May Alcott
Lucy Fitch Perkins
Lucy Maud Montgomery
Luther Benson
Lydia Miller Middleton
Lyndon Orr
M. Corvus
M. H. Adams
Margaret E. Sangster
Margret Howth
Margaret Vandercook
Margaret W. Hungerford
Margret Penrose
Maria Edgeworth
Maria Thompson Daviess
Mariano Azuela
Marion Polk Angellotti
Mark Overton
Mark Twain
Mary Austin
Mary Catherine Crowley
Mary Cole
Mary Hastings Bradley
Mary Roberts Rinehart
Mary Rowlandson
M. Wollstonecraft Shelley
Maud Lindsay
Max Beerbohm
Myra Kelly
Nathaniel Hawthrone
Nicolo Machiavelli
O. F. Walton
Oscar Wilde

Owen Johnson
P.G. Wodehouse
Paul and Mabel Thorne
Paul G. Tomlinson
Paul Severing
Percy Brebner
Percy Keese Fitzhugh
Peter B. Kyne
Plato
Quincy Allen
R. Derby Holmes
R. L. Stevenson
R. S. Ball
Rabindranath Tagore
Rahul Alvares
Ralph Bonehill
Ralph Henry Barbour
Ralph Victor
Ralph Waldo Emmerson
Rene Descartes
Ray Cummings
Rex Beach
Rex E. Beach
Richard Harding Davis
Richard Jefferies
Richard Le Gallienne
Robert Barr
Robert Frost
Robert Gordon Anderson
Robert L. Drake
Robert Lansing
Robert Lynd
Robert Michael Ballantyne
Robert W. Chambers
Rosa Nouchette Carey
Rudyard Kipling
Saint Augustine
Samuel B. Allison
Samuel Hopkins Adams
Sarah Bernhardt
Sarah C. Hallowell
Selma Lagerlof
Sherwood Anderson
Sigmund Freud
Standish O'Grady
Stanley Weyman
Stella Benson
Stella M. Francis

Stephen Crane
Stewart Edward White
Stijn Streuvels
Swami Abhedananda
Swami Parmananda
T. S. Ackland
T. S. Arthur
The Princess Der Ling
Thomas A. Janvier
Thomas A Kempis
Thomas Anderton
Thomas Bailey Aldrich
Thomas Bulfinch
Thomas De Quincey
Thomas Dixon
Thomas H. Huxley
Thomas Hardy
Thomas More
Thornton W. Burgess
U. S. Grant
Upton Sinclair
Valentine Williams
Various Authors
Vaughan Kester
Victor Appleton
Victor G. Durham
Victoria Cross
Virginia Woolf
Wadsworth Camp
Walter Camp
Walter Scott
Washington Irving
Wilbur Lawton
Wilkie Collins
Willa Cather
Willard F. Baker
William Dean Howells
William le Queux
W. Makepeace Thackeray
William W. Walter
William Shakespeare
Winston Churchill
Yei Theodora Ozaki
Yogi Ramacharaka
Young E. Allison
Zane Grey